DEFENDERS OF GRIFFON'S PEAK

THE HEROES OF DAE'RUN
VOLUME 2

CURTISS ROBINSON

Published by Beau Coup Publishing
http://beaucoupllc.com
Technical Assistance by Added Touches
http://addedtouches.com
Illustrations by Worasak Suwannarach

DEDICATION

Much has happened since the release of my first book in 2009 (Protectors of the Vale). I ended my association with AEG and EB (who failed to do much more than gladly take advantage of an inexperienced author and produce marginal results across the board). I ended my association with my original artist (who was unable to see my vision.) In retrospect, I have grown and learned some hard lessons. However, it is among adversity that the most brilliant blossoms bloom! Given the above, I wanted to personally dedicate this book to those who have truly gone the distance!

First and foremost, I must mention my dear wife Vicki. She gave great latitude in the use of family time and finances while sharing her own vision of the characters and storyline. She has done so with love in her heart, and sincere hope for success. Being an Army wife is tough enough, but she also manages to endure my endless pursuit of writing, martial arts, and gaming, while taking the time to be a wonderful mother to our four children. For your endless support, you have my eternal gratitude (to match the eternal love you have had all along). God bless you for being steadfast and resolute.

DEDICATION CONT'D

To my editor and dear friend, Darya Crockett, you have earned the honor of being the single-most dedicated professional associated with this work. Your tireless efforts have contributed immeasurably to the overall quality and content of this book. Of all the lessons learned, finding the right editor is perhaps the most valuable and the only thing more valuable is being friends with you. Thank you.

To my artist, Worasak Suwannarach (from Thailand), I wanted to say thanks for raising the bar on artwork. You have amazing skill and work ethic but more importantly, you took my vision, created a sketch, added color, and brought my characters to life. Great job!

Most of all I must thank God, who blessed me with every good thing in my life!

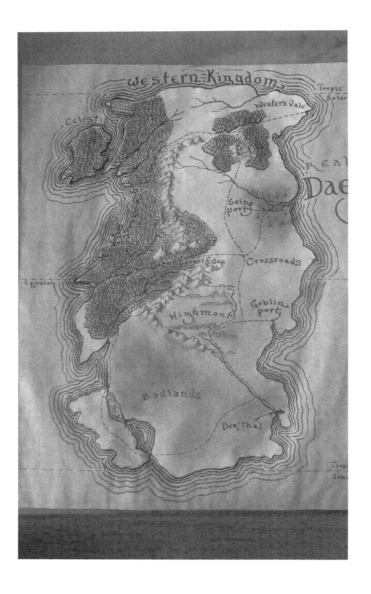

CONTENTS

PROLOGUE

Far above the deep, dark trees of Broadpine Forest, the six great towers of Griffon's Peak seem to thrust up into the heavens, piercing the clouds like enormous war-pikes of legendary titans. As one draws near, the landscape becomes a massive stone fortress built among the Blackridge Mountains. It bears white granite walls and a long, winding ramp leading down to a gargantuan drawbridge. Moving even closer, the true magnificence of the mighty human city becomes apparent. A company of knights mounted on proud warhorses could easily ride in columns of four out of the city, down the stone ramp, and across the drawbridge charging into any force foolish enough to attack by frontal assault. The wall supporting the drawbridge is lined with fearsome parapets engineered with dozens of ballistae capable of firing ten-foot-long, jagged harpoons. These walls bear an archer's landing long enough to employ a full company of archers abreast and wide enough for three rows of the long-bowmen to rain deadly missile fire down on approaching raiders. Most impressive of all are the ever-vigilant griffons that represent the city's namesake. These noble half-eagle, half-lion guardians reside among the highest reaches of the mountaintops and stone parapets. With powerful snapping beaks and leonine paws lined with razor-like claws, these airborne beasts patrol the city and its outskirts with unmatched ferocity.

Within the defensive perimeter, Griffon's Peak is a bustling city of fine merchant shops, wealthy townhouses, professional academies, and government offices representing the king's supreme authority. The city's great guild houses, mage towers, and troop barracks are equally impressive from a military perspective but just as every gem has its brilliant sparkle, there are always flaws found deep within, some unseen by the naked eye.

The shining gem that is Griffon's Peak has a vile series of underground dwellings as its chief flaw. Far beneath the well-manicured homes and neatly kempt streets, a labyrinth of twisting, turning tunnels run the length and breadth of the fair upper-city. Here, the poor and downtrodden are found scraping for food or begging for coin where goodly folk and wealthy aristocrats do not venture. It is a place of disorder, disease, and malcontent seldom discussed in civil conversation and too often ignored by the men and women in power. As such, it is a haven for those who seek to remain beyond the sight and reach of the law. In particular, it is the home and headquarters for a villainous band of cut throats known as The Legion.

Members of The Legion are tied into the city's operations as mercenaries and assassins serving anyone with a contract and the coin required to do business. One such contract called for the murder of Sergeant Vlaadimir de Valle, a human soldier in the Dae'run Alliance Army. The soldier revealed information that led to the indictment and capture of a wealthy merchant. He was accused of selling mystic relics to the Bloodcrest Forces, a powerful and wicked conglomeration of orcs and trolls backed by undead and tauren allies. The merchant was severely punished under the laws of the king resulting in banishment and forfeiture of all property. Infuriated, he called on The Legion to slay the soldier and his family.

Vlaadimir was returning to his home having spent the day training new recruits, when the assassins came. The first of more than a dozen killers emerged from the shadows like phantoms both silent and deadly, but the canny sergeant was not caught unaware. Good soldiers are always prepared. As the initial attack came in from behind, Vlaadimir drew and thrust his fine military blade to the rear in one motion. The assassin fell dead, still clutching the dagger meant to take Vlaadimir's life. He took up a defensive stance and slowly peered from left to right, fully aware of the approaching death squad.

The second assassin came into full view. He held twin *katars*, a pair of ancient weapons resembling short swords fashioned into punching blades. Vlaadimir saluted the killer with his shining sword, signifying an honorable battle and a true lack of fear. The dual-bladed foe came in with blinding speed thrusting his left blade high, then low with his right, and continuing the attack by slashing with the left, not unlike a boxer's jab-cross-hook punch combination. All three attacks were parried precisely and with such force that the reverberations numbed the villain's hands. Having lost the initiative, the assassin found the soldier's counter attack faster and stronger than he had anticipated. The heavier blade bashed repeatedly into the assassin's lighter blades, leaving an opening after several overhead blows. The last thing the assassin saw was a flash of steel as his head left his shoulders.

Five more murderers came with melee weapons and five others leveled crossbows at the soldier. Seeing his imminent demise, the soldier rushed in to finish the battle with valor and courage. Two bolts from the five crossbows buried themselves deep in his flesh. Three missed by a hairs breadth. Blood poured from his wounds but Vlaadimir cut another assassin down, leaving four to encircle him. The crossbowmen were working feverishly to re-cock their weapons while the others prepared to deliver the killing blow. Dizziness came from having lost too much blood, making Vlaadimir stumble forward and drop to one knee. Like wolves sensing the kill, the four sword-wielding attackers dashed forward. The soldier batted their attacks away recklessly and lashed out one last time, but fell short. He looked up and saw the crossbowmen leveling their cruel weapons in his direction. This time, all five bolts blasted through his armor with agonizing pain. The stalwart warrior fell dead and was quickly hacked to pieces.

The Legion sped to Vlaadimir's home to continue their killing spree, slaying his wife, oldest son, and two daughters; however, one escaped. The soldier's newborn son, Vlaad, named in honor of his father, was carried away by his aged grandmother to the steppes of the Blackridge Mountains, where they hid for some fifteen years.

During his self-imposed exile, Vlaad was raised by his grandmother and mentored by the traders, bards, and priests that passed through the small village of Bladeshire at the edge of the mountain steppes. He was quick to learn the art of reading and writing both in common and gnomish from his tutors. His mind was keen and curious, enabling him to master mathematics of both trade and engineering. His grandmother, who he loving called O'ma, had been the center of this education, always reminding him that duty was second only to justice. In her mind, it was Vlaad's purpose in life to become a cunning warrior so he might one day find and defeat the men who had killed his parents and three older siblings. It was a lesson taught daily and one that shaped the nature of the young boy. He was destined to live by the sword.

At age fifteen, Vlaad began learning the trade of blacksmithing. He found that the ring of steel on steel, as he hammered away, was an extension of his own heartbeat. As the blood rushed rhythmically through his body, the hammer would fall in sync. As his heart pumped hard with adrenaline his hammer fell faster and harder.

By the time he turned sixteen, he was no longer a boy apprentice; he had become a stout journeyman of the craft with powerful arms, broad shoulders, and a thick back. His mastery of metal working, mathematics, and engineering opened an entirely new world of arms and armor crafting. It was providence that he should learn to master the wares he created.

By age seventeen, he was crafting fine suits of mail, swords, spear points, and arrowheads for sale at the local market. In exchange for many of his best items, soldiers, warriors, and mercenaries traded countless hours of personal training in the martial arts. Vlaad quickly became a fine swordsman and was accomplished in the spear, mace, and ax as well, but simply cutting another man down held little appeal for the youth. His sharp mind and deeply embedded values called for something more.

One day, just after his eighteenth year, a stranger passed through the small village of Bladeshire. He had been adventuring in the wilds for some time and had need of extensive repairs to his armor. After several recommendations from more than a few of the local shopkeepers, given Vlaad's growing reputation as a master armor smith, the stranger sought him out.

Vlaad was hammering away, as usual, when the smithy's doorway became filled with a giant of a man. Vlaad stopped his work and turned to the visitor, noticing that the towering warrior stood nearly a foot taller than he.

"Hello friend and welcome to my shop. How may I be of service?" Vlaad asked pleasantly.

In a strange dialect that was a combination of unusually rolling consonants and dulled vowels the huge warrior said, "Vell met young mon, I ahm Andar Razamun of ze 'interlandz and I ahm in need of repairz from many battlez. Can zhou 'elp me?"

Vlaad was a little confused by the foreign accent. He thought the man said that his name was Andar and that he was from the Hinterlands. He just couldn't be sure, but curiosity compelled him to smile and nod in response.

Andar said, "Bery vell. I can pay zhou now two gol' coinz to make ze repairz. Do ve haf a dealz?"

The young smith wiped his palms off on his leather apron and extended his well-calloused hand to the warrior and said, "I will work on your armor, but you need only pay if you are satisfied with my services. I would like to hear about your adventures as a down payment if you would honor me with a few stories."

Andar looked piercingly at the youth as if measuring him up. The young man stood barely six feet tall and was strong, but not unusually so. He had thick, dark eyebrows and a full goatee but had shaved his head completely bald like the elite guard of Griffon's Peak. It wasn't his physical appearance that caught Andar's attention. He saw strength and discipline in the blacksmith's deep brown eyes and sensed both honor and integrity within him like the knights of ancient legend. He asked, "Are zhou so zertain zhat I vill pay vhen ze verk is done? I ahm a stran-ger 'ere and un-accustomed to such trust vrom utherz."

Vlaad smiled as he ciphered through the thick accent. He was pretty sure the warrior asked if he was certain that the big man would pay after the work was complete, since he was a stranger that others did not usually trust. He nodded and repeated a phrase his O'ma had often said throughout the years: "Everyone pays sooner or later. It is only a matter of time. This is the law of justice to which we are all bound."

The larger man thought for a moment and then laughed a deep and hearty laugh. He reached out and grasped the waiting hand Vlaad still held out to him. He shook it eagerly. Andar immediately noticed that although his hand dwarfed the blacksmith's, there was great strength in Vlaad's grip and the dark piercing eyes that he looked into were filled with fire and strength as well. This simple blacksmith was more than he appeared. He was ironically similar to the unshaped and untempered steel the blacksmith forged—ready to be formed into a keen and valuable blade. Andar Razamun was intrigued. He said, "I 'ave ze story for zhou but it iz not my own adventure. It is ze legend of ze Zhield Vorrior."

Vlaad sat down and listened intently as the foreigner recounted the tale of the shield warrior. It was an old tale that Andar explained was passed down from father to son among his people. Apparently, there was once a great sword master known as Vlorin. He was the tribal chief of his people and had been in dozens of battles but had never been defeated. He had fought invading every manner of evil men from neighboring clans, not to mention lesser races and wild beasts. His skill with a sword was said to be unparalleled and his reputation grew and grew until it began to attract the greatest fighters from all over the realm who wanted to test the warrior's skills. They wanted to earn the right to be known as the greatest swordsman in all the land by defeating him in single combat.

Vlorin fought every manner of weapons master for years and years, never tasting defeat until one day an elf came to claim the title from across the Great Sea. The elf was slender and agile compared to the powerful human from the Hinterlands. Certain that he would quickly dispatch the smaller elf, the hero of the Hinterlands came in quickly and powerfully only to be easily dodged by the elf who managed to nick the great warrior's leg as he passed. Enraged, Vlorin turned and charged in again, but the agile elf spun to the side and evaded the warrior's second series of attacks while scoring another minor hit. The elf took the initiative and came in slashing with such speed and precision that the human could barely see the flashing steel as the elf scored hit after hit. It was apparent that Vlorin had finally found his better, a truly superior swordsman, and would soon die at his hands.

Vlorin fought back swinging his blade in vain until finally, the elf backed away and asked for the human to admit defeat. Suffering from a score of cuts and puncture wounds, he conceded to the elf just before collapsing from blood loss. The elf never said a word. He simply shook the blood from his fine sword, sheathed it, and walked away. Some say that the elf was a god sent to punish the warrior for his arrogance. Others say the elf was a wandering *kensai,* an ancient word meaning sword saint, usually given to a wandering warrior who has dedicated his life to combat. Whatever the case, the lesson was a turning point in the life of Vlorin. He was convinced his ego had led to his downfall and so he vowed to live out his life with humility and in defense of others as payment for this vice. It was thought to be the origin of the proverb *that pride cometh before the fall.*

Some months later, after fully recovering from the near fatal defeat at the hands of the elven sword master, the warrior decided that if indeed it was his pride that had brought about his defeat, then he must focus on building skill with a shield—a tool of humility. He was convinced that protecting others in combat would be the best way to serve honorably. As the days became weeks and then months, the warrior learned that his focus on the shield had not only given him much-needed humility, but it greatly increased his overall skill on the battlefield. He was able to turn not only the attacks directed at him, but he could interdict the attacks meant to cut down his fellow warriors.

Not long after this revelation, the Hinterlands were invaded by a band of trolls and their hired mercenaries. The ensuing battle was bloody and both sides lost troops by the hundreds. On the second day of fighting, the trolls and men faced off across a deep valley. A troll messenger delivered a challenge to Vlorin's troops that called for the battle to be settled in single combat to avoid a prolonged and costly conflict. It was an ancient custom that still stands today. Not wanting to see any more of his brothers die, Vlorin humbly moved forward to accept the challenge. The champion of the trolls and mercenaries was an elf, but not just any elf. He was the sword master who had come so close to killing Vlorin not long ago. Vlorin knew their first encounter was a lesson in humility sent by the gods. Perhaps this second meeting was a test to see how well he had learned.

The elf stepped confidently forward and drew his perfectly balanced weapon that had tasted Vlorin's blood no more than two winter's before. Vlorin remembered the cruel blade well. He drew his own sword and retrieved a well-worn shield from the straps on his back. The elf laughed mockingly, thinking the shield was a display of weakness and a lack of confidence in the human's sword craft. Vlorin saw his former overconfidence and pride in the elf.

The two circled for a moment but this would be a different fight than the last time the two had met. The elf noticed the human's defensive posture with the shield held to the front and just below eye level. The sword he carried was in the high guard position above his shoulder. The warrior was relaxed with his weight distributed equally on both feet and centered over his hips. The elf moved in and slashed at the human with blinding speed to test the defensive stance. The sword rang out against the shield with no effect. The human barely moved having anticipated the blow. The elf came around to the human's weapon side and thrust forward like a viper then circled low for a leg cut. The warrior mirrored the attack with his shield, easily deflecting the thrust and parrying the low cut with minimal effort. The elf glared wickedly at Vlorin.

The trolls and humans watched with awe as the two continued the series of probing attacks met with defensive counters. Several strikes were issued by the elf and all were turned by the warrior who had not even attempted to swing his sword offensively up to this point.

The elf circled again and dodged left and then right trying to use footwork to get inside the human's impenetrable defenses. Just as the warrior adjusted to compensate for the feint, the elf saw his opening and thrust quickly for the human's torso. The reaction was instinctive but amazingly fast as Vlorin spun his back leg around to move offline from the strike and simultaneously guided the thrust harmlessly past. The elf was now committed forward, facing too far to the human's right to retract and dodge. Vlorin dove forward and shield-bashed the lighter and quicker elf. The resounding clang reverberated through the human's shield and the elf's helm. Staggering, the stunned elf tried to regain his balance and position, but Vlorin was already in motion. The human sliced downward with his blade, battering the elf's curved blade away from his grip. In desperation, the elf dove forward to recover his weapon. He recovered and set in his stance quickly but saw the grim human peering over his shield with his sword in the high guard position again. The elf's confidence melted away like snow in early spring.

The elf knew it was only a matter of time before the human crushed him with his mighty shield or disarmed him again leaving him defenseless. His speed and cunning were useless against the sheer simplicity of the warrior's defense. As if commanded by divine intervention, he removed his helmet and took a knee admitting defeat honorably. The shield warrior had won without ever shedding the blood of his enemy.

The humans cheered and the trolls gnashed their teeth and hissed evilly. Vlorin never moved an inch or responded in any way. The elf stood and with both hands he planted his fine weapon in the ground. He bowed to his rival, turned, and walked away. Vlorin cautiously sheathed his weapon and replaced the shield on his back. He walked up to the elven blade and removed it from the ground with one mighty pull. It hummed with magic and Vlorin knew immediately that its enchantment was powerful but there was something else. The blade seemed to speak to him, somehow imparting knowledge and experience of its own accord. He realized that this weapon, not the elf, had been the cause of his only defeat in combat. Likewise, it had been the catalyst for his greatest victory, the victory over himself.

Vlaad made note of the ironic tale. Just as he had expressed to Andar that everyone pays sooner or later, Vlorin had paid for his arrogance and overconfidence. The elf had paid for his as well. It was the law of justice to which are all bound. O'ma's wisdom paralleled the tale perfectly.

CHAPTER 1
MANHOOD

Vlaad began working the dents out of the sturdy plate armor after hearing the tale. It was obvious that this armor had seen more than a few battles, but Vlaad was glad to take up the challenge. He noticed immediately that the breastplate was curiously light in weight given the strength of the metal. As Vlaad slammed his hammer down again and again, the steel rang out evenly and precisely with his heartbeat. It was a musical masterpiece in perfect cadence that made Vlaad fall into a deep meditation of his work. He forgot his task for several hours and pictured the battle between the elf and the great warrior of the Hinterlands. It was as real as if he had actually been there. In his mind, the battlefield was a rocky, mountainous plateau covered in snow with gnarled trees covered in ice. He could almost feel the sting of the wind on his face and hear its howling as it blew through the wintry peaks. The resounding clang of his hammer blows finally brought him back to the smithy where he found that his work was complete. The fine armor was perfectly restored.

Vlaad stretched his tight muscles and walked to the entrance of his smithy, where he noticed for the first time that night had long since fallen. He had been working furiously many hours not even stopping for dinner. Smiling, he realized solace was often found in his work and that was a rare thing for most humans, particularly a young man not yet twenty winter's old.

Vlaad closed up his shop and walked to the small cottage where he and O'ma lived. Along the way he replayed the scene in the tale of the shield warrior. It just seemed to appeal to him as if he was destined to be more than a blacksmith and a swordsman. He opened the door and noticed that his grandmother had fallen asleep in her favorite chair waiting for him. He smiled, grabbed a warm blanket, and covered her up. His dinner was waiting for him on the small table in the rustic little dining alcove. Roasted game hen and potatoes had been lovingly prepared by O'ma with just the right seasoning. It was cold, but his hunger was great, making the meal simply delicious. Vlaad washed up and prepared to get some sleep, but his mind was still far too busy with the stranger and his wonderful morality tale. When sleep finally came, his dreams were of epic battles with justice being served by his every blow.

Morning came with the glimmer of sunshine peeking through the window and the crowing of the rooster. Vlaad jumped up, threw on his clothes, and moved into the common room where O'ma was already preparing breakfast. He took a moment to observe his dear grandmother. She kept her grey hair a ruddy brown with some secret concoction of tree bark and berries, but the grey was showing through. Her eyes were still filled with life and energy, but the endless wrinkles and slightly sagging folds of skin made her look venerable. Although O'ma moved slowly, her actions were always precise and well-coordinated. Her posture showed the effects of age as the years had slowly bent her once-proud frame, but Vlaad saw steady determination in her will to fight off old age for a while longer. He loved and admired her dearly. She was the only family he had ever known.

"Vlaad, you worked very late last night," O'ma began while she served him warm bread, freshly baked, with sweet butter and blackberry jam.

"O'ma, I met the most unusual man yesterday. His name is Andar. He is from the Hinterlands and he speaks with a foreign accent. He asked me to repair his armor for two gold coins!" he said excitedly.

"Well, I certainly hope you got the money before you began the work or you might find it hard to stand while he pulls your leg," she replied comically.

"I am sure he will pay. He told me a tale that followed the proverb about justice. It made me think he was an honorable man, a man to be trusted," Vlaad returned.

"Dear boy, I have taught you to be a good judge of character and to act with honor and integrity, but not all men are so lucky to have a good O'ma guiding them," his grandmother said with pride.

"I will be careful O'ma, but I truly believe Andar is an honorable man. Besides, what is the worst thing that can happen?" Vlaad asked with a smile.

"Well, you are the one who worked past dark and missed my good cooking for this Andar fellow.

If he pays you less than he promised, then I guess you will have learned a lesson more valuable than the coin you lost. I suppose that is the worst thing that can possibly happen," she replied with her hands on her hips and a loving grin on her face.

Vlaad nodded, scooped up more bread with jam, and headed out the door.

"Remember what your O'ma has taught you all your life—duty is second only to justice. Every step you take in life must be to fulfill your destiny, Vlaad!" she called as he continued down the road toward the merchant lane where his shop was located.

The sun had crested the Blackridge Mountains and the town of Bladeshire was already bustling with activity. A merchant caravan had arrived early and was downloading its goods and uploading local wares to be sold in far-off provinces. Vlaad dashed into his shop and secured a box of steel arrowheads for trade. The head merchant was a wild-looking dwarf with a long, black beard that stretched down his ample belly. He was known respectfully as Boss. He was barking orders to his team of dwarven workers when Vlaad opened the chest of arrowheads to show him.

"Eh Vlaad, wha' ye got fer me t'day?" Boss asked with a raised eyebrow.

The young blacksmith said, "The finest steel arrowheads Bladeshire has to offer."

"Heh," the dwarf scoffed, "Me kin be makin' better uns in Dragonforge."

This was a game Vlaad had learned to play every time the gruff dwarf came through Bladeshire. It was a ploy Boss used to undervalue all of Bladeshire's outgoing goods, while overvaluing all of Bladeshire's incoming goods to keep the most profit for him. Vlaad had learned to play the game well over the last few months and usually enjoyed the exchange when all was said and done.

Vlaad challenged the dwarf to his claim by saying, "I hear the dwarves of Dragonforge have run into a vein of bad iron and even poorer mithril. Let me see the arrowheads your dwarven smiths have crafted and then we can agree to a price."

The blustering dwarf jumped down from his wagon and stomped around cursing and spitting in response. Finally he said, "Ne'er have me kin mined bad iron or mithril. Ta even sa'gest such a thing be fightin' words!"

Vlaad simply packed up his box of fine wares and said, "Very well then, I will sell my goods to the merchants in Griffon's Peak. They appreciate my hard work and expert craftsmanship. They will likely pay a fair price for both."

The dwarf pulled hard at his beard, fumed some more, and stomped around like a madman. He finally replied as Vlaad was walking away, "Ye can'na sell ta dem in Grif'ins Peak. Ye'll upset da balance o' da 'ntire 'economy. Wit' da way day mark up prices and da way yer king throws his coin about, ye'll have da 'ntire human archer company shooting' wobbly arrows fer a gold each draw. No, I can'na let ye do it."

"I will gladly accept one silver coin for a dozen. I have a full gross here which comes to twelve silver," Vlaad said calmly.

The dwarf grabbed at his chest and leaned heavily on the wagon as if he were mortally wounded. He huffed and puffed as if trying to catch his breath and said, "Twelve silver? Yer killin' me boy. How'm I s'posed ta run a bus'ness wit' ye bleedin' me out like dis?"

Vlaad began packing up again when the dwarf, having miraculously recovered from his momentary state of agony, came forward and grabbed the chest. He said, "I'll give ye ten fer da lot o' it."

Vlaad smiled and said, "You know you will clear more than twice that, but I am a fair man and times are tough. I accept your offer."

The dwarf threw the chest into the wagon and paid Vlaad the ten silver pieces. When no one was looking, he slipped two more silver coins into the blacksmith's hand with a wink. Vlaad nodded back, knowing full well that it was all a show for the other merchants and in many ways to keep the respect among his dwarven workers. As Vlaad turned to walk away, the dwarf went back to barking orders at his kinsmen.

Andar walked up shortly after the haggling began and had witnessed the entire display. He smiled broadly as the young smith headed his way.

"I 'ave never zeen anyone deal with ze dwarf as zhou 'ave. I can zee zhou are an educated mon as vell as a one of skillz. Perhaps ve can arrange more business," the huge warrior stated more than he asked.

Vlaad nodded and escorted Andar to his perfectly repaired armor. It was mounted on an armor stand as if it were a holy relic to be worshipped. The shining silver breastplate, pauldrons, and bracers were freshly oiled and polished, giving off a radiant glow from the morning sun. The armored thigh plates, knee cops, and greaves were displayed similarly on lush velvet below. By the look on the warrior's face, Vlaad could tell that he was impressed beyond words. Incidentally, he thought back to his dear grandmother who had always said, "It is all in the presentation of the work you do that matters most." Of course she had been referring to cooking a fine meal, but Vlaad had used the lesson in his business as well.

Andar spoke with a great smile on his face, "As ve agreed." He drew out a hefty pouch that jingled with many coins. He opened the bag and Vlaad noticed that it was filled with gold. There was easily a king's ransom within. The burly patron withdrew two gold coins and paid Vlaad for his work.

"Thank you," Vlaad said as he accepted his payment. He was glad that he had been right about Andar. He was an honorable man as expected.

Andar spoke again, "Now zhat ve 'ave concluded ze business at hand, I 'ave a new deal for zhou. If zhou are villing, I vill take zhou as my hireling. Do zhou know zhis verd? It means I pay zhou to accompany me vherever I go. It meanz zhou leave zhis place for ze life of ze varrior. Vhat say zhou?"

Vlaad felt compelled to join the stranger for a life of adventuring, but he was uncertain what would become of his dear O'ma if he left. He knew she was capable of caring for herself, but she was growing old and had no one else to help her. He was truly torn.

Andar could see the struggle on Vlaad's face. He put his enormous hand on the younger man's shoulder and said, "Zhou have time. Conzider it and ve vill speak again on ze morrow."

Vlaad nodded and said, "Thank you for the generous offer. I will."

Andar walked to the inn where he was staying and Vlaad went to work in his shop. He took a sheet of his finest steel and started thinking about designing a shield. He had made shields before, but nothing that he thought was worthy of combat. He looked at the thin sheet metal and began to imagine something that would serve as both a defensive device as well as an offensive weapon. The story of the shield warrior had inspired him. After a long while, he decided to start with a simple heater shield. Traditional round shields were useful and easily maneuverable but not as durable as a heater. Kite shields and tower shields were much stronger but somewhat unwieldy. The heater shield was the best of both worlds.

The design formed in his mind and his body responded. With a metal scribe, he outlined the pattern and began cutting the sheet metal. When he was done, the alloy was perfectly measured to cover Vlaad's body from shoulder to mid-thigh. Satisfied with the dimensions, Vlaad took a metal auger and drilled holes for the straps and for a center spike. He trimmed the outer edges with reinforcing steel strips to prevent any chance of splitting. These were riveted on with nickel fasteners, although expensive, they were far more durable than copper or bronze. Next, he fashioned the center spike from a small spear point design and attached it to the body of the heater. He took smaller studs and attached them to the shield in a perfect circle around the center spike. His last step was to attach the leather straps and an arm brace. When it was complete, Vlaad slipped it on to test the weight. It seemed solid enough to take heavy blows from both edged and blunt weapons, but only combat would tell for certain. It was much heavier than he anticipated, but then again, he wasn't used to fighting with a shield at all. He thought it might work well once he got used to maneuvering it.

Vlaad grabbed a sword from the collection of blades he had in stock and took a few test swings to measure its weight and balance. He lifted the heater and crouched as he imagined the great warrior, Vlorin, from Andar's story. He raised the sword in the high guard position and peeked over the top of his new heater. He was imagining the lightning quick cuts and thrusts of the elven warrior. In his mind, the entire scene formed and played through as Andar had told it. The elf would slide in and spin around as Vlaad angled his shield and maneuvered his position to deflect the attacks. He waited until the precise moment when the elf overextended his final thrust and with coiled legs he sprang forward, stunning the attacker and then with one decisive blow, he disarmed his imaginary enemy.

Before he realized what was going on, Andar was behind him. The giant from the Hinterlands had come by to discuss the future with Vlaad but had remained unannounced while he watched Vlaad pantomime the battle with his new shield. As Vlaad was just about retire from his imaginary battle, Andar came forward making corrections on the stance and fighting position of the young warrior.

Andar adjusted his posture slightly forward and said, "Ze shield varrior leans into his enemy like zhis." He rotated the shield upward slightly and said, "Ze shield varrior keepz hiz elbow pointed downvard so ze veight of ze shield restz in ze shoulder, not ze forearmz." He pushed in on Vlaad's rear leg, forcing the knee to bend and the heel to rise slightly off of the ground. He said, "Ze shield varrior is coiled like ze serpent zo he can lunge forvard vhen his enemy makez hiz miztakez. Zhis is ze vay of Vlorin."

Vlaad noticed immediately how the slight

corrections had alleviated the weight of the shield on his arm, set his strength forward, and prepared him to move quickly. It was all so simple yet the details hadn't been apparent to him before Andar's instruction.

Vlaad asked, "Andar, can you teach me to fight as a shield warrior?"

Andar replied sternly, "No, zhis is impossible. Zhere vas only one shield varrior and his name vas Vlorin of ze 'interlandz."

Vlaad was perplexed. He asked with obvious confusion, "Are you not a shield warrior?"

The huge fighter smiled and said, "No. I am hiz descendant by blood but hiz vayz 'ave been lost for centuries. I am ze student of ze old vays so I can teach you some zhings. I am ze defenzodor. Zhis means de-fend-er in your dialect."

Vlaad was still unsure what the difference was between a true shield warrior and a defender, but he accepted the explanation and asked, "Can you teach me to fight as a defender?"

"Zhis I can do, but it meanz zhou serve as ze hireling as ve discuzzed earlier," he returned. "Are zhou now ready?"

Vlaad thought for a moment and replied, "I believe this is my destiny. I have considered it since we met and this is my calling. I must return to my home and make some arrangements, but I will serve as your hireling when I return."

Andar smiled broadly and said, "Zhis is good. I vill train zhou as a defenzodor and ve vill make great legendz togezher."

Vlaad hung the sword and shield on the wall and walked back home. The sun was already setting. He could smell the food his O'ma had prepared long before he walked in the small cottage.

It was the delicious aroma of rabbit stew. As he moved inside to the dining area, his grandmother was setting the table and bringing out the pot of stew.

"Be sure to wash your hands before you eat," she said.

Some things never seem to change, Vlaad thought silently. He was a successful blacksmith and businessman, yet to O'ma he would always be the little boy orphaned by The Legion. She would always mother over him. That much he was certain. Without argument, he went to the wash basin and poured some water to clean his hands. As he looked at his rough calloused hands, he realized that he was no longer the boy he once was no matter how often O'ma mothered over him. It was his time to live on the road. It was time to find his destiny. He finished washing and sat down at the table. O'ma served a large bowl of stew with some bread. He did not eat immediately and the old woman, who had cared for him all of his life, noticed the hesitation.

O'ma began casually while serving herself a portion of the stew, "I can see by the look on your face that something is troubling you. When I consider your age, my first instinct is that you have fallen in love, but since I have seen no girls around your shop and that is the only place you go other than home, I must assume it must be something else. I know you so well, Vlaad. I have watched you grow from a child into a handsome young man with great potential. I have to guess that your fate has come calling. Am I right?"

"Yes O'ma," Vlaad said without hesitation. He was amazed that somehow she just knew.

"Grandmothers tend to know these things. It is our nature to know. So tell me, what will you do?

Where will you go?" she asked.

"O'ma, I have agreed to work for the foreigner from the Hinterlands. He has promised to teach me the art of the shield. I already know so much about the sword but simply cutting a man down with a blade is a common skill. I wish to become something more…something honorable, something nobler. This is my chance to fulfill my destiny," he said.

"Vlaad, I am so proud of you. You are so much like your father who wanted to serve others. I also see your mother in you as well. You have her compassion for the innocent. Always remember that duty is second only to justice. You must find those responsible for the murder of your family. Will you promise me?" she pleaded.

"I will O'ma. I will find them one day and they will pay to satisfy justice," Vlaad vowed.

"Good, now tell me about your plans," she asked.

"Well, I am not sure where I am going or when I will return. I guess my future is uncertain at this point, but I will make you proud and I will return soon to see you," he replied.

"I see, and what of your shop?" she asked.

"You must sell the materials and items that I leave behind to Boss, the dwarven merchant. Use the money for food and supplies until I return," he said assuredly.

"Well, you will need a few things for your trip," O'ma began. "I know that you can make better armor and weapons that I could ever afford to buy, but I do have something that you cannot craft on your own," she said while walking over to a small alcove in her room. She withdrew a small coffer and brought it out in the open. She took a tiny key from a thin necklace around her neck and unlocked the small but sturdy lock. She opened the box and withdrew two small vials containing a dark liquid. She handed the potions to Vlaad and said, "These will heal you when you are gravely injured. Do not waste them on smaller wounds that you can bandage. These are meant to save your life."

Vlaad took the two tiny vials, inspected the innocuous bottles, wrapped them in a soft cloth, and deposited them in his pocket. He looked curiously at the box as his grandmother withdrew a simple band of gold that could have been a wedding ring. When he noticed the way his O'ma was staring at the ring, he realized that it was special indeed. She seemed hard pressed to part with it, but after a moment she said, "This ring has magical properties. I was saving it for the day when you took up the sword to fulfill your destiny. This trinket will sustain you in the coldest winter without shelter. It will protect you from fire to some degree and even shield you from the arcane attacks of wizards for a short while. Don't go walking in front of a dragon or meddling with warlocks to test its power though." She laughed a little at the expression on Vlaad's face and then continued, "This ring of protection belonged to your father. He said it was given to him by his father and he would have wanted you to have it."

"If it belonged to my father, then how did you obtain it? I thought he died as we fled Griffon's Peak," he asked.

"Your father sensed his end long before his death. He must have known that he was making powerful enemies when he reported the man who was later responsible for his murder," she said.

Vlaad was awestruck by this revelation.

O'ma continued when she saw the sad look of doubt painted on her grandson's face. "You must never question his motives. Yes, he knew he would be in danger, but his duty was to the king and justice was required. That is who your father was and I am proud to have known him, in spite of losing my only daughter when The Legion came for him."

Vlaad took the ring and slid it over his finger. It fit perfectly. He said, "I will be careful. Do not worry for me."

She hugged him tightly and kissed him on the cheek. Vlaad had to take a deep breath to keep from shedding tears. O'ma was unable to speak as tears fell down her aged cheeks. She smiled a bit and walked away. Vlaad gathered his pack and left for the smithy. Upon arriving, he selected a fine ring mail hauberk that he had crafted a few months ago. It was lighter than plate mail and sturdier than chain mail, which made it appropriate for a young warrior not yet accustomed to wearing armor. He selected steel bracers and greaves for his arms and legs. They were light but durable. His final addition was the sword and shield he had been using when Andar gave him his first lesson as a defender. The sword was a simple, straight design but the shield was as fine an item as he had ever crafted. He was very proud of its detailed workmanship and as a defender, the heater would be key to his survival.

Andar walked in shortly after and looked the young warrior over. He tightened the straps of the ring mail Vlaad wore and ran his massive hand over the outer edge of the heater shield. He nodded and said only one word, "Impressive." He turned and walked out the door. Vlaad followed carrying only his combat equipment and the pack on his back.

CHAPTER 2
THE LONG ROAD

The life of a defender is an ongoing search for those in need of protection but the talents of a defender are not always appropriate for every situation. Incidentally, Vlaad and Andar moved from town to town, methodically canvassing the area, but not necessarily patrolling for evil doers as the soldiers of Griffon's Peak would. The key to being a defender was building a network of informants who could direct their specialized skills to the greatest effect.

Perhaps the greatest resource in Andar's network was a bard, Don of Westrun, who had traveled the Eastern Kingdoms singing about epic battles, great tragedies, and famous heroes. Don was quite an extraordinary man being skilled in just about every trade in the land. It was common for wandering minstrels to pick up numerous skills in their travels, but Don was exceptional in his craft. He could play the guitar, sing, build any manner of dwelling from wood or stone, and he even dabbled in magic. He had also served as both teacher and priest from time to time when the need arose, but his greatest skill was moving information.

Some thought it was the comely appearance and lyrical voice of the bard that enabled him to extract information from men and women alike, but it was more than sharp attire and a handsome face that helped others open up to him. He was simply the most genuine, caring human in all the realms. More often than not he worked for little or no payment as he threw in a hand to help those in need. This made him the perfect liaison for the defenders who also seemed dedicated to helping others.

As Andar and Vlaad passed through Westrun, home of the famous bard, Don was found strumming a tune and singing for a small group of children at recess from their school work. The bard gave the warriors a charming nod and a wink as they approached; conveying that he was glad to see them and would be most interested to share some information when he was done with his song.

Vlaad had never met the bard before, but he heard his name often around Bladeshire. He noticed how his music almost magically entranced his audience. He was dressed in the breeches and tunic of a commoner with high, leather boots and a wide, matching belt, but as he strummed his instrument, he seemed noble, almost regal as a baron or count might be in their finest garb. The calm sea green eyes, patrician nose, and neatly trimmed salt and peppered mustache identified him as a local to these parts, but still he was somehow different than the villagers here.

Vlaad listened as the minstrel played his rolling tune and sang a morality tale about good and evil. In the song, Don explained that there was once a small turtle who loved to swim in his pond and bath in the warmth of the sun. He was a good-natured turtle with a generous disposition. One day a scorpion came to the edge of the pond where the turtle was swimming and asked the turtle to let him climb on his back to ride to the other side. The turtle knew the scorpion was wicked and said that if he let him climb on his back, the scorpion would sting him since that was the nature of scorpions. The scorpion said, "I know you are a good-natured turtle and want to help others. It is in your nature. Just help me across the water. I won't sting you because if I do, then I will surely drown in the water." The good-natured turtle agreed. Halfway across the water, the scorpion stung the turtle. As the turtle struggled against the poison, he asked the scorpion, "Why would you do such a thing? Now we will both die." The scorpion said, "You knew my nature before you agreed to help me, just as I knew yours. We cannot change who we are and we must do that which we were meant to do."

As the song ended, the bard leaned forward and said, "Listen to me my fine, young turtles. Be good natured, but beware of the scorpions who will always seek to do you harm. Wisdom comes from making good choices but you must learn the difference between good and evil. Now go back inside and heed the words of your schoolmaster who has been charged with teaching you these things."

Andar walked up to the bard, shook his hand with great enthusiasm, and said, "I vill never tire of zhat tale. It is good to zee you comrade."

Don returned the handshake and replied, "It has been far too long since we have shared a drink in fellowship. Can we sit for a while and share a tale or two?"

"Zertainly, but first allow me to introduce my nevest azzociate. Vlaad of ze Blackridge Steppez, zhis is Don, ze Bard of Vestrun," the massive fighter said in his thick accent.

Vlaad extended his hand and said, "Well met, Don of Westrun. I have heard of your travels. It is an honor to meet you."

The bard was impressed by the strength of the young warrior's grip, but more so by the precision and tone of his words. Vlaad's speech made him wonder what such an educated man was doing in the service of a rugged warrior like Andar when an easier life as a scribe or merchant would surely be an option. He quickly replied to Vlaad, "Well met indeed, my young friend. Tell me, how is it that you have come to be in the service of Andar?"

Vlaad's mind raced back to the morality tale Don had been singing just moments ago. He said, "Is it not obvious? It is in my nature, and we must do that which we were meant to do."

Andar made the connection and laughed a deep belly laugh. Don bowed with a smile and said, "So true, so true. Let us adjourn to a more private place where we can partake of a fine meal and share the details of our individual natures."

The threesome traveled down the main road through Westrun to a small tavern called The Smoking Boar, where the smell of smoked pork ribs lured passersby in like the siren's song of legend. The tavern was small but tidy. Nearly all of the tables were full, but three stools at the bar were empty and waiting for the companions. As they pulled up to the bar, a lovely woman came from the kitchen area to take their orders.

"Welcome to the Smoking Boar, I am Theila. What can I get for you fine gentlemen?" the young woman asked as she winked at Don, the Bard of Westrun.

Vlaad found himself staring intently at the beautiful serving maid. She had long, brown hair pulled back and secured with a small leather retainer and a large pin, but the shorter tendrils dangled uncooperatively along the sides of her angelic face. The high eyebrows and long lashes made him think that she was of noble birth. Her charming smile made her deep brown eyes seem young and innocent but she was older than Vlaad by at least a few years. She wore a low-cut blouse and a long skirt that revealed lovely curves in all the right places. As his gaze passed over her more feminine charms, he realized that he had already spent far too much time gawking and the barmaid had noticed. He quickly said, "The ribs please. I would like the smoked ribs."

Theila smiled and said, "We have a juicy *rack* of lamb as well or perhaps you might prefer the roasted *breast* of chicken."

It was obvious that the witty young woman was teasing the younger man having noticed his lingering eyes on her alluring curves, which made Vlaad blush and stammer a bit as he said, "Nnnoo, thank you. The ribs will do nicely."

Andar and Don were trying not to laugh, but both snickered and then as Theila walked away, they both fell into raucous laughter. Vlaad was embarrassed but he simply had never seen a more attractive woman in his life. He knew it would only make matters worse if he asked about her, but some things were well worth the price to be paid.

"Who is she?" he asked his fellow companions.

Andar stopped laughing, leaned back to let Vlaad have clear view of Don, who leaned a bit forward and said, "Theila is my daughter."

Suddenly, Vlaad realized that he had been wrong. The price was now far greater than he could have imagined as he was embarrassed by getting caught staring, and even worse, she was the daughter of the famous bard who he was supposed to be working with. He bowed his head in humiliation and the other two went back to their hearty laughing.

Andar and Don talked at length about adventuring and places they had been over the past several months. Vlaad listened intently; ever grateful that the conversation had migrated away from his humiliation. Theila brought their food and sat down for a moment to listen to her father discuss matters of business. The conversation moved into discussion of a few local threats.

"You know the *gnolls* are massing in the northern edge of Westrun near the cliffs? They might become emboldened enough to attack the city if their numbers continue to grow," Don said with a serious tone.

Vlaad knew that gnolls were nomadic humanoids similar to their smaller kobold cousins. They were vicious pack hunters that resembled a cross between a man and a hyena. Luckily, they were not very industrious and often had poor weapons and old scavenged armor so they rarely proved to be a serious threat, unless they came in great numbers.

Andar thought for a moment and said, "Perhapz ve can build a small team to check it out. Vlaad and I vill be ze melee varriors. Ve might need a mage and a good archer for ranged attackz."

Theila immediately jumped into the conversation saying, "Papa, I will come and you can watch over me. The four of us will be unstoppable."

The bard was already shaking his head before she had completed her request. "I do not think it is fitting for you to be with a bunch of adventuring types. What would your mother think? I am sure she would never approve."

She continued, "Mother has been gone for a decade now, may she rest in peace. I am a grown woman and a fair spell wielder. You need me and I hate working here for poor wages and even smaller tips. You must give me a chance."

Don knew his daughter well and saw much of her mother in her as she crossed her arms in defiance. He also knew that she was growing powerful in her arcane skills and could be a much-needed asset, but he feared for her safety as any father would. He sighed and looked at his massive friend beside him who only nodded in response. Finally he said, "You may come, but if things get dicey, you have to promise to be careful. Gnolls are not a race known for peace or remorse. They will kill a woman as quick as a man and never think twice about it."

Andar smiled and said, "Do not fear for ze girl. I vill azzign Vlaad to protect her."

Vlaad's face went beet red as everyone looked his way. He said in a shaky boyish tone, "I will see to it. None will harm her while I draw breath."

Theila smiled and said, "Fair enough."

Andar slapped the bard on the back and said, "See, ve 'ave nothing to vorry aboutz."

Don was unconvinced, but he knew Andar would never let harm come to any of them and he knew the argument was futile with Theila anyway, so he resigned himself to the agreement.

Theila wrapped her father in a loving hug and said, "When do we leave?"

Don said, "We will pack tonight and leave early tomorrow. We should not be gone long so pack lightly."

Andar, Vlaad, and Don continued to chat about problems throughout the Eastern Kingdoms until well past dark and into the late evening. Just before midnight, the trio adjourned to the nearby inn for some much-needed sleep, having agreed to rise at first light and begin the trek to the northern side of the province. The gnolls would be waiting.

Dawn broke at just after five, waking Vlaad with the first rays of the morning sun peeking through the eastern window. He climbed out of bed and stretched the soreness from his muscles. He had been unaccustomed to wearing armor but after several weeks of traveling and hours of endless daily training with Andar, he was slowly getting used to it. Vlaad got dressed, buckled his sword around his waist, threw on a padded vest, and then the ring mail armor. He slung his pack over his shoulders and secured his shield over it. He took the time to glance in the mirror on the wall and thought that he looked the part of an adventurer, but he still felt like a novice. So far his adventures had consisted of a lot of walking and no fighting. Of course, Andar had spent a few hours each day teaching him about tactics and shield techniques, but there was only one way to become a great defender. He had to defend something. He laughed at the ridiculousness of the thought as he imagined using his shield to stop the rain from falling or maybe to block the sun from shining. Heck, he could do that with an umbrella. He considered this over and over as he moved down the stairs and outside, smiling and shaking his head all the while.

Theila was waiting in front of the inn. She had her hair pinned up again, but she wore loose-fitting pants and a tunic that made her look somewhat less feminine than she had last night. He wondered if she had intentionally dressed this way to keep from distracting him or if it was meant to simply be more comfortable while she traveled. He decided it must be the latter. After all, Theila probably had better things to do than plan her wardrobe around Vlaad's gawking.

"Well, good morning Vlaad," Theila said, "did

you sleep well?"

Vlaad was immediately flushed with nervousness and barely managed to stammer, "I-I-um slept well. Thank you." He noticed that instead of looking directly at the lovely woman, he was staring at his boots. He felt so uneasy around her and simply could not imagine why. He had seen many women in his lifetime and several were probably as beautiful as Theila, but there was something about her that was different. He managed to gather his wits and a bit of courage, at least enough to look her in the eye when the Bard of Westrun joined them. It was a welcome distraction from his discomfort.

"Hail and good morn. The road awaits us, so let's find Andar and be on our way," Don said.

Andar was coming out of the inn just as the bard finished his statement. He said in his deep rolling dialect, "Vell met friends. Are ve ready to zet out on ze road?"

Vlaad walked up to the great warrior and said with obvious exaggeration, "We have been waiting all morning for you, great one."

Andar smiled and threw his thick arm around younger man's shoulder. He said, "I zee zhat zhou 'ave been vaiting, but not all morning. I vas vatching zhou and Theila vrom ze vindow only moments ago."

Vlaad flushed a deep crimson and the great warrior laughed mightily. Don was unsure what the joke was about and Theila smiled slightly as if she knew but would never tell. The foursome began the long walk to the edge of Westrun.

It was a cool morning and although still quite early, the town of Westrun was already busy with merchants and travelers. As the group passed beyond the border of the city limits, farmland stretched both far and wide. It was peaceful and pleasant for several miles with the smell of freshly turned soil and the sound of birds in the air.

By noon, the group had moved well beyond the edge of the city and was nearing the coast where they were certain to find the gnoll inhabitants. Andar walked calmly and easily in his heavy plate armor with the fabulous shield strapped across his back and a large, curved blade at his side. Vlaad was beginning to feel the weight of the ring mail cut into his shoulders again and the fine sword at his side was constantly rubbing his hip. He realized that he had much to learn and much growing to do before he was half the fighter his mentor was. He truly admired the sheer power and confidence Andar exuded.

Theila was walking comfortably beside her father. She seemed perfectly at ease on the road. Her lightweight clothing, lack of armor, and weapons made the trip easy for her. The bard wore leather armor and a common traveling cloak. His pack seemed light and oddly, he carried his guitar strapped to his back as if it would protect him in the same manner that a shield would protect a warrior. Needless to say, he was also very much at ease on the road.

"We should take a moment for lunch," Don said, "there is no telling when we will be afforded the opportunity to eat once we make contact with the gnolls."

"I am starving," Theila responded, "and a break would be welcome to my aching feet."

Andar only nodded and dropped his pack to the ground. Vlaad was so thankful that the others had suggested the break. He did not want to admit that he was more than ready to stop and rest, but his feet were aching as well as numerous other sore muscles. He quietly unpacked some dried fruit and smoked venison from his pack. As he ate and rested, he found himself looking at Theila. She was unaware of his gaze, which enabled him to take the time to study her features for a moment. Her wispy frame was never meant for heavy labor or long journeys, but would have made a fine build for a dancer or perhaps a diplomat in some noble court. Her face was lovely with the same tendrils of hair waving rebelliously across her eyes, no matter how she tried to keep them pinned up out of the way. Theila had long, thin fingers that were nicely manicured and better suited for playing music, painting, or sculpting great works of art than for work in the fields or out in the wilderness adventuring. He thought with certainty that she had no place here, but he was glad she had come.

Vlaad snapped out of his day dreaming when the hyena-like barking of gnolls announced the arrival of enemies. Andar stood quickly, mounted his great shield on his arm, and drew his fine, curved blade. He stood calmly and resolutely, ever the picture of confidence. Don jumped up and pulled his traveling cloak back revealing a wide, leather belt bearing dozens of finely crafted throwing knives around his torso. He had the look of grim determination in his eyes that was a blend of concern for the safety of the party and experience in combat. Theila moved behind her father and the northerner from the Hinterlands. She produce a thin wand and took a well-balanced fighting stance as if she had seen combat on several occasions. Vlaad did not remember drawing his own blade or setting his shield in position, but he found himself prepared and ready for the fight that was coming.

Don said, "They will come all at once, without fear or concern for tactics, but be wary. They are cunning pack runners not unlike wolves. Some will taunt and probe while others will strike from the blind side."

Andar looked at his pupil and nodded as if to imply that he knew Vlaad would use everything he had been taught so far. Vlaad responded with a sword salute and took up the stance of the defender to the right of his mentor. He had his knees bent slightly and his posture was forward as he had been taught. The shield was balanced comfortably on his arm with the weight supported by the shoulder not the forearm. He was ready.

The gnolls appeared from an outcropping of rocks a few long strides away. They wore mismatched pieces of armor scavenged from their previous victims. Most had clubs, but a few had swords which were likely acquired in the same manner as the armor. Each hyena-man stood about five feet tall but was densely muscled and weighed easily as much as Vlaad. They had sharp teeth and scraggly fur that was matted with dirt and gore. They were foul beasts indeed.

Andar took a few steps forward and braced for the coming attacks. Vlaad was only a step behind, and to his right with Theila and Don several steps to his rear. Five of the wretched humanoids came in and made probing attacks just as Don had predicted. Their clubs rang off of the shining shield Andar held, but none managed to break his defenses. Andar barely moved at all. He merely turned or angled his shield to intercept the blows and waited patiently. Vlaad held his position, knowing that sooner or later the gnolls would seek an easier target.

The five leading gnolls backed away and regrouped. Several more started circling around toward the more vulnerable humans in the rear. The bard was waiting when one angled past Andar. Don drew and slung one blade after another at the beast until it moved no more. Vlaad saw another trying to move to his right for a better position. It came in and hammered its crude weapon against his heater shield. Vlaad accepted the blows and held his position. He was about to move in for his first counter attack when several blasts of arcane magic whizzed past him and knocked the attacking gnoll to the ground. The magic seemed to wrack the beast with agony long after the energy of the attack had dissipated. Vlaad glanced back and saw Theila give an approving nod. She had put her wand to good use early and had proven her worth to him all at once.

The five gnolls who had initiated the battle were tiring of the futile attempts to hit Andar and came in with two on either side and one coming head on. Andar sprang forward with the speed of a cobra. His mighty shield struck the center-most gnoll and sent him flying backward to land unmoving on its back. This opened angles of attack to the remaining four. The defender spun about and parried the two who had been on his left with the flashing steel of his blade, while his shield blocked the other two. Vlaad took the opportunity to drive his fine steel into the side of one of the attackers. The beast howled and turned his attack on the younger defender. In agony and desperation, the gnoll came in furiously. It swung its club from right to left with a two-handed grip that Vlaad easily deflected with his shield using a slight shuffle of his feet to gain proper position. It attacked again from left to right this time and Vlaad let the swing fly by, overbalancing the enemy. As its club went low, Vlaad chopped down across the gnoll's wrists, nearly severing both hands. The creature dropped its weapon and ran off howling in agony.

As Andar continued to dodge and block, the pathetic gnolls simply could not find an angle to get past the ever-present shield defense. This occupied the remaining three and several of the flanking gnolls doubled back to attack the defender, instead of facing the bard's deadly barrage of throwing knives or the warlock's cruel wand. There were now six gnolls trying to overpower and out maneuver Andar, leaving Don, Theila, and Vlaad free to move into attack positions. Vlaad moved in and struck the rusty shoulder pauldron of the closest gnoll. It turned on him but was struck down by another series of arcane blasts from Theila's wand before Vlaad could swing his sword. The gnoll to the far left fell with three daggers protruding from its body. Don had dispatched it with deadly precision. The remaining four seemed uninterested in anything other than breaking the defenses of the great warrior. Andar moved with the grace of a cat and the power of a raging bull. He accepted dozens of attacks and only swung his sword to parry or disarm his opponents. It enraged his enemies such that they became careless in their frustration, allowing Theila and Don to easily fire at range and slay the gnolls without risk of being engaged themselves. Vlaad had never imagined such selfless dedication in combat as Andar showed. He had effectively directed the course of the battle without ever soiling his blade. This was the epitome of defense and teamwork. This was the nature of the defender. In no time, the remaining gnolls were dead or incapacitated. Vlaad thought to himself that he had been wise to follow Andar. This would be his life's work. He would be a defender until age or death claimed him.

At the conclusion of the battle, Don went about recovering and cleaning his blades from the slain gnolls while Andar inspected his great shield for damage. Theila tucked away her wand and brushed the dangling strands of brown hair from her face. Vlaad wiped his blade clean on one of the gnolls and replayed the battle in his mind. Hindsight had shown a near flawless melee.

"Vlaad, zhou fought ze enemy vell today. I zee zhat zhou vere uninjured. Zhis is good. Ze art of ze shield vill serve zhou vell, but zhou vill be hit sooner or later. Vhen you are hit, zhou must remain focused on ze fight. Pain and blood mean nozhing to ze defenzodor. Only ze next attack of ze enemy matterz. Zhou must never forget zhis," Andar said with pride as he taught yet another lesson to his pupil.

Vlaad considered the words. He thought it was impossible for Andar to be hit, but then he remembered the damaged plate mail he had repaired at their first meeting. The sturdy armor had been severely damaged and it had taken considerable effort to hammer it back into shape. He could only imagine what hellish battle could have scored so many hits on the near invulnerable warrior. He finally replied saying, "I will remember."

Don interrupted, "We fought well. The fortunes were with us. Next time, we might not be so lucky. I recommend that we devise a plan for the next battle. Theila and Vlaad will be the backup team while Andar holds the enemies at bay and I work from the distance. Any who break away from Andar will fall to Vlaad with Theila as his firepower."

Theila smiled as she noticed the slight reddening of Vlaad's face. She said, "It will be my honor to work closely with Vlaad. He is quite skilled with the sword and shield. I am sure our combined talents will prove more effective together than individually."

Andar smiled as well.

Vlaad smiled sheepishly and said, "I will do my part. None will break through."

Don said, "It is agreed then. We will fight as pairs and in depth, but still our small troupe has limitations. We must never allow the enemy to surround us or mass their forces beyond the number we fought today. Even the legendary Andar cannot hold an army off indefinitely."

Andar smiled again and said humbly, "Zhis is true. Even Vlorin ze first and greatest 'ad hiz limitz."

Vlaad caught the sad undertone and wondered how Vlorin had met his final days. It was a question for another day perhaps. The team went about gathering up their supplies and field packs for the continuation of the journey to the coast.

CHAPTER 3
THE COAST OF GNOLLS

The road from Westrun to the coast was a long and winding route that took the rest of the day to complete. As night was falling, the group set up a small camp overlooking the great cliffs of Westrun. Far below, the Great Sea stretched endlessly with white-capped waves crashing against the rocks far below. It was already becoming a cool night and the small fire would be little comfort come morning. Vlaad and Andar would be warm enough with their layers of padded clothing that kept the rigid armor from cutting into their flesh with every blow of their enemies, but the bard and his daughter had only their cloaks to fend off the chill of night.

Vlaad walked over to Theila and offered his cloak to the warlock as extra protection. He thought it was the honorable thing to do and without a word, he turned and moved back to his place near the fire. The female smiled and accepted the cloak without a word. She found the gesture both kind and chivalrous. Of course, the bard and the senior defender noticed the growing bond of friendship but said nothing.

Don drew his guitar from its soft leather case and adjusted the strings with the tuning gear at the headpiece. The gentle plucking of the strings was soothing. In a few moments, the bard was strumming the instrument gently. The chords were more than soothing; they were relaxing, like a warm bath or the massaging hands of a skilled masseuse. Vlaad had heard that the gift of the bard was to create enchanted tunes. Some tunes were simply the tales of heroes or of life and love, but other melodies could actually heal the body and mind like the one Don played now. Still other tunes could inspire warriors to fight valiantly and with great fervor. Vlaad had always believed these were fanciful tales perpetuated by bards to make money, but perhaps he had been wrong. His mind and body were feeling truly at ease with every mellow stroke of the strings. As Don began to sing along with the chords, something amazing happened. Vlaad felt the pain in his shoulders from wearing the heavy armor disappear. His throbbing feet were eased of their aching. Even his worries seemed to take flight and leave him pleasantly behind.

Vlaad lay back on the hard ground against his pack and looked at the stars. He wondered what the future would bring for him. Thoughts of glory and honor danced in his head. They were the musings of all warriors. He pictured himself leading great armies against the evil minions of the world. His enemies fell before his might, having failed to pierce his broad shield. He considered Theila as a likely ally in those daydreams. She was beside him blasting away with her wand and felling countless foes, but his thoughts left glory and honor soon after and became dreams of love and companionship as sleep took him.

The night passed quietly and uneventfully with each member of the team taking turns watching for possible enemy activity. Vlaad had the last watch and was awake when the sun rose from the east. He noticed Andar and Don stirring with the rising of the sun. He took the last few moments before the day's work began to watch Theila sleep. She was an angel, a being of pure goodness and grace. He realized that his admiration of the lovely, young woman was fast growing into something deeper. He wondered if she would ever feel the same for him.

Andar was the first to rise. He began the day with stretching and soon after he took his shield and sword in hand and walked through an imaginary battle that exercised his mind, body, and soul as one. The movements were fluid and yet powerful. He began with the stance of the defender and worked pivoting on his front foot to change the angles of his shield posture. His body always seemed to align with his footwork. Vlaad realized that given Andar's body dynamics and strength, he would be likely able to absorb the full impact of nearly any blow. Even the charge of a full-grown bull could be absorbed if the body was properly positioned and the shield was sturdy, but Andar would never have to absorb such an attack. His footwork and ability to angle the deflection of the blow would reduce the power of such an attack to an insignificant level.

Vlaad watched as the defender used his sword more as a second, smaller, parrying shield than a weapon to hack and slash at an enemy. As he turned and angled his body in sync with his shield, the sword came around with varying degrees of speed to deflect imaginary weapons, turning the thrusts of spears, the slashes of swords, and even the pounding of heavy, blunt weapons like the clubs used by the gnolls from the last fight. Vlaad found himself pantomiming the movements of his mentor. He could envision the incoming attacks as he moved his imaginary sword and shield like his teacher. He could almost feel the grip of the wrapped sword hilt in his hand as well as the weight of the steel heater shield on his arm. It was suddenly more than just a mock battle. It became a dance of focused battle meditation. His body and mind were united by the movements. He angled left and blocked then dodged right and parried with his sword. He shot forward and shield bashed an imaginary foe. Another came from behind and found his upraised shield waiting for the attack. He pivoted and danced away, falling back into the defensive stance unique to his style of fighting. More came in and all found his shield waiting or the parrying twists of his sword. When he finished his exercise, he was lathered in sweat and feeling quite exhilarated. He noticed that Don had been watching as he moved back to his neatly stacked equipment.

"You move well, young master. I have watched your mentor on many such mornings, but I thought he was unique in his morning ritual exercises. You have the same spirit. One day you will become as he is. You will be a great defender," Don said with admiration and respect.

Vlaad was humbled by the compliment. He stripped down to his under shorts and moved to rinse off in a nearby brook. The water was very shallow, but clear and cold. As he washed the sweat and dirt from his body, Andar walked over and threw a towel to him. He caught the cloth and nodded in gratitude.

"I vas told zhat zhou performed ze shield dance zhis morning," the northerner asked.

Vlaad responded, "I was watching you and it seemed fitting that I follow your movements. The shield dance is part of being a defender, is it not?"

"Indeed, my young friend, but zhou must not learn zhese thingz incorrectly. If zhou practice improperly, zhen zhou vill have to retrain ze movements one 'undred times for each mistake to correct each flaw. It must be more zhan mimicry. It must be pervection," he said with a serious tone and the thick accent of his homeland.

"I see," Vlaad replied. "Will you show me correctly so that I can master the moves?"

"But of course I vill," he said with pride and sincerity, "but not today. Ve 'ave many zhings to do first."

"Like what?" the younger man asked.

"Vell, I zhink zhou might vant to put on ze clothes before ze young voman vakes up. I do not zhink zhou vould be able to bear ze 'umiliation if zhe saw zhou naked," the great warrior teased.

"Right!" Vlaad responded, feeling suddenly very vulnerable and somewhat embarrassed.

Vlaad shook the dust out of his clothes and threw them back on. He was still wet and the cloth stuck to his body and hung oddly on his frame, but he moved back to the camp and spent an hour reviewing the shield dance with Andar.

Theila woke just as the defenders were completing the lesson. She moved over to her father who was cooking breakfast. She asked, "Father, what were the warriors doing so early this morning?"

Don said, "They were exercising. The shield dance is a series of fighting maneuvers that are used to hone their combat skills. It is in many ways a ritual of mediation as well as a physical application of techniques. In all of my travels, I have never seen warriors take their art as seriously as the defenders. They seem almost fanatical about perfecting their skills."

Theila thought that it was a little odd, but she accepted it as part of who the warriors were. She often practiced her own art after all. She preferred the privacy of a secluded chamber that enabled her to focus her summoning powers to the open plains or even the woodlands common to this area.

"Breakfast will be ready in a few minutes," Don said.

"I will wash up and return soon then," she replied.

As Theila moved toward the small brook to refresh herself, the three men discussed plans to scout along the cliffs for more gnolls. The warlock bent down at the brook and washed her hands. She splashed the cool, clear water on her face and decided to take the time to rinse her hair while she was there. She removed the pins and let the long, brown mass fall to her shoulders. As she leaned forward to wet her hair, she got the feeling that she was being watched. Her hand went immediately to the slender wand in her sleeve as she looked up. She saw a large band of gnolls creeping her way with considerable stealth. When they realized Theila had spotted their approach, the creatures moved into a sprint toward her.

Theila had time to yell, "Papa!" once before she started blasting the gnolls with her wand. She knew she was too far away to get help immediately, but she felt certain her skills would hold the enemy off long enough for backup to arrive. She had enough time to cast a quick spell that would both slow and weaken the slavering dog-men, but it would never be enough without the life-draining spells she had no time to cast.

The gnolls closed in quickly and drew their rusty blades and crude clubs. The closest enemy took several arcane bolts from her wand, but the others were upon her before it fell dead. The warlock knew she was in trouble and tried to dodge as the first club came down hard, clipping her shoulder and sending her to her knees. Her arm went numb, immediately causing her to drop the wand. Another club hit her squarely in the back as she tried to recover. The pain was excruciating as she fell to the ground out of breath. Theila rolled to the right and managed to avoid a killing blow meant to crush her skull. There were several of the beasts surrounding her now. She thought it was the end until something flew in among the gnolls taking many of them to the ground.

Theila crawled away as fast as she could, given the pain in her shoulder. She managed to roll out of harm's way as one gnoll reached for her. It was then that she saw her savior. Vlaad had launched himself among the throng of enemies with nothing more than his shield. He had no weapon and no armor, but fought valiantly nonetheless. She counted more than a dozen gnolls surrounding the young defender who was hard pressed to keep his shield moving fast enough to keep the villains at bay. She was hurt, but unwilling to give up. Though breathing was torture given the last clubbing she had taken, Theila managed to call upon the darker magic of her art. One gnoll grew pale and then seemed to age decades all at once. It was a powerful spell meant to slowly drain the life force of the victim, but Theila was desperate and pulled mightily on the beast's soul. It was all she could do without passing out, but one less gnoll gave Vlaad a fighting chance.

Two gnolls came in with swords slashing. Vlaad dodged the first and blocked the second but was in no position to avoid taking a solid hit from a club-wielding gnoll that came in from his right. The weapon caught him in the side of the head and sent him reeling into the path of another club which caught him in the ribs. He heard several of them crack with the blow. Darkness was clouding his vision but he willed it away. He dodged back and positioned himself between the band of assailants and Theila. Blood ran freely down his face and his ribs ached, making it hard to breathe. The gnolls tried to circle around him in order to make quick work of the warrior. They never saw Don and Andar charge in.

"Cover them!" Don yelled as he drew and released more than a dozen daggers in the blink of an eye. Several hit the two closest gnolls and a few drew the attention of the others.

Andar drove his shield into the back of the group and sent two flying forward. He spun about and caught one gnoll in the throat with the edge of his shield and one with his fine blade. Both fell to the ground and lay unmoving. He ducked low as a rusty sword passed overhead, narrowly missing his head. He thrust outward, kicking with all of his strength. His heavy boot caught the sword-wielding gnoll in the chest. Bones cracked and the beast flew back a dozen feet. Andar flew forward and planted his blade through its body and into the ground beneath.

Vlaad had to take a knee as his head swam with dizziness. He was laboring for breath and the pain was excruciating. He took a deep breath and steadied himself, remembering that a defender must put pain aside. His work was a matter of focus and pain was a deadly distraction. He willed it away and stood, shield in hand. Nothing would get past him. He would die first.

Theila was safe for the moment, but her right arm hung awkwardly at her side. It pained her greatly and the effects were written on her face clearly, but anger was there too. She murmured something in a demonic tongue that was indecipherable to Vlaad and then lifted her good arm, summoning flame from the abyss into her palm. One gnoll turned to attack Vlaad, but was consumed as Theila released the hell fire into its flesh. It screamed and writhed in agony. She turned the attack on another gnoll and it too fell to the ground screaming.

The remaining gnolls turned and fled the fearsome humans. Don let fly several throwing knives for good measure, taking one last gnoll down before turning to aid his daughter. Andar stood resolutely, covering the group just in case any of the enemies returned.

"Theila, are you all right?" Don said.

She replied, "I am alive, but hurt badly. I think my shoulder is broken."

"Vlaad, you are bleeding badly from the gash on your head," Theila said as she noticed the defender still standing almost statue-like in front of her.

"I am fine," he wheezed as blood frothed out of his mouth.

Andar walked up and said, "Zhou fought vell, but it is over now. Conzidering ze vounds zhou 'ave sustained, I think zhou should rest for ze time being."

Vlaad turned to Theila and said, "Forgive me for not coming sooner. I...I..." and then he collapsed.

Don quickly examined the young fighter. He said, "His ribs are broken and I think his lung is punctured. He will die if we do not get him to a healer soon. His head is pretty bad too."

Theila's eyes welled with tears. She said, "He saved me. He didn't even have a sword or his armor, but he fought anyway. We can't let him die."

Andar smiled a calm, knowing smile then said,

"Ze boy vill survive if ve can get him back to camp vithout killing 'im. Ze boy'z O'ma gave 'im ze potion of curing. It vill save 'im I think."

The massive warrior gently lifted his apprentice into his huge arms and started walking back to the camp. Theila was in pain as well but she ran ahead and tore his pack apart looking for the potion. She found two vials wrapped in cloth tucked away in a pouch on his sword belt. Using her teeth and one good arm, she pulled the stopper out of one. The concoction smelled awful, but she poured it into Vlaad's mouth and pinched his nose off to help him swallow. The dark liquid went down easily and almost immediately his breathing became less labored and the deep gash on his head closed up. The results were amazing.

Don looked at his daughter with awe. He said, "The vial had a powerful healing agent indeed. He might just make it. What about your own wounds? Perhaps you should also drink from the other vial."

Theila was suffering and needed healing badly, but her thoughts were dedicated to the young man cradled in her lap. She never took her eyes off the defender as his wounds continued to mend right before her eyes. Vlaad slowly opened his eyes and saw the lovely maiden looking down at him. It was the most beautiful thing he had ever seen. For once he did not blush. He just looked up and said the first thing that he thought, "Am I dead?"

Don and Andar laughed.

Theila said, "No, you are not dead though you were indeed close to death. You are very much alive thanks to the potion we found among your gear."

Vlaad sat up and looked around. He felt incredibly well given his near-death experience. He closed his eyes and said a silent prayer, "Thank heaven and my dear O'ma."

The huge northerner placed his hand on Vlaad's shoulder. His eyes seemed to say, "Well done, you have the heart of a defender and your skills are growing day by day," but no words were spoken.

Don clasped Vlaad's hand in both of his. He was clearly thankful to him for saving Theila's life at nearly the cost of his own, but he had no words to express his thanks. He just held the defender's hand and squeezed it warmly.

Theila winced as the throbbing of her wrecked shoulder reminded her that she also needed aid. Vlaad went immediately to his gear and retrieved the last potion. He uncorked it and handed it to the warlock. She smiled through the pain and said, "Thank you for saving my life and now for healing my wounds."

Vlaad motioned for her to drink. Theila took a long, deep draught from the vial. The taste was awful and the concoction was like slimy pond scum, but she swallowed hard and it went down. The pain began to subside as the torn muscle and tendons corrected themselves. The shoulder seemed to return to its normal configuration with incredible speed. In moments, Theila was working the arm back and forth to ensure it was limber and strong.

"I am healed. The healing power of the potion is unbelievable!" she said.

"From this point forward, we must avoid such grave injuries as there are no more healing draughts to save us," Vlaad reported humorously.

The others laughed at the irony since no one ever intended to get hurt, but in the adventuring business, such things were inevitable.

"Perhapz ve should return to Vestrun. Ve 'ave slain many gnolls and zhould report our progress to ze people so zhey vill know ze road is zafe for travel," Andar suggested.

"I agree," Don added. "We could pursue the gnolls, but they are not a brave race of humanoids and I suspect they are scattered across the countryside by now. Besides, I have new material for the start of an epic tale that I wish to put to music."

Vlaad and Theila seemed a bit disappointed. They felt responsible for the journey being cut short but they packed their gear without much fuss. The road had not been long but the experience had been harrowing. They were both ready for time to rest and reflect on the experience that had taught them both a valuable lesson. They were not seasoned warriors but they would be with more training. There would always be adventures, but only after they were ready.

CHAPTER 4
UNDERWORLD

Gorka had spent his early years struggling to overcome his half-orc heritage. His human mother had abandoned him in his father's orc village at birth and his orc father, a huge and fierce brute named Trog, had always treated him as a slave. He often beat him severely and tormented him for pleasure. It was the way of things for a half-breed. His orcish features were repulsive to humans he met. Their first thoughts would always be of his human mother being ravished by a foul orc and that he was the vile offspring of that beastly union. His smaller stature would make him appear inferior and weak to his stout, orcish kin. He was thus destined to be a loner, shunned by all.

Gorka had accepted this fate long ago. He had never sought out his mother who would never want him and he had slain his father after a particularly savage beating long ago. He thought back to that moment often, as a reminder of what he must always be prepared to do to survive. He was only twelve winters old when his massive father had come home to their mud hut dwelling after losing badly while gambling with the *bones.* He spent his wrath on the small half-orc boy, beating him with a stick until it broke and then with his fists until Gorka was certain that death would be his only escape from the cruelty of his father. As the small boy lay on the floor bleeding, Trog poured his remaining fury into a bottle of potent liquor called *troll's blood.* It was so named for its color as well as its tendency to make one who drank it more resilient to pain as if they had troll blood running through their veins. In this case, Trog drank himself into a stupor. Gorka cut his throat while he was sleeping. He still remembered in vivid detail how the great orc had gurgled for several moments, choking on his own blood before death took him. The warm liquid had covered his hands. Sometimes he could almost feel the sticky substance on his palms and smell its metallic scent in the air. It was the only pleasant memory he had of his parents.

Gorka was now well past his thirty-second winter having found his niche as an assassin working for The Legion below the streets of Griffon's Peak. It was one vocation where a half-orc fit in. Here he had advantages that he capitalized on throughout his life. Gorka had far greater strength and endurance than any human as a gift from his father's genes, not to mention incredible cunning and a complete lack of remorse. From his mother's side, he drew on far greater intellect than his father's kin were known for and superior agility than the heavier orcs could develop. These gifts enabled him to master his parent's languages, orcish and common, the latter being the trade language of humans. He had mastered the science of assassination, focusing particularly on stealth, poisons, daggers, and strangulation. He was a professional killer but none of these skills had benefited him more than his half-orc visage. Gorka had bristly black hair cropped short as a soldier might wear. His high, sloping forehead and deep-set eyes gave him a brooding and fearsome countenance. He had his mother's human flesh tones, sharp cheekbones, and thin lips, but a broad face from his father and two enlarged lower teeth protruded wickedly from his mouth, adding a feral look to the half-orc. In the dim light that assassins preferred, Gorka looked almost demonic.

It was irony that his greatest curse, his facial features, had set him on a lonely road of isolation while tempering his survival skills like dwarven steel. He would always strike fear in the hearts and minds of his prey. His employers would always feel confident that he would gladly kill for money with no second thoughts regarding morality or consequence. His orcish kin would underestimate him and his human kin would fear him. The evil that had spawned and left its mark on him had shaped his life into a machine built for killing perfection. Gorka never thought twice about embracing his true nature. He was born to it and bred for it.

The Legion had invited Gorka into their ranks when he was barely fifteen winters old. They would never accept him as an equal, but they used him for the most menial and vilest tasks that human assassins refused. He had slain beggars as favors to the wealthy merchants of Griffon's Peak, often with no financial gain, but he consistently acquired notoriety and infamy. He had slain thieves and even other assassins who had brought shame or treachery into the ranks of the guild, thus furthering his reputation. He had even slain a colony of plague bearers once. He mercilessly ended their suffering, every man, woman, and child; some say for their own good, but Gorka reveled in the hunt, never the mercy of the task.

These contracts hadn't made Gorka wealthy in the way the other assassins gained gold and silver for killing wealthy merchants, noblemen, or wizards. No, these contracts had been an investment in Gorka's name, which had later earned him respect as one of the most feared assassins in the realm. He became particularly infamous for his ability to disappear after the deed was done. This trademark gave the local authorities such difficulty they nicknamed him *The Shade*, a legendary evil spirit that was known for appearing long enough to drain the life from its victims and then simply vanishing.

Professionally, Gorka earned the first rank of *enforcer* after only two years of service and he progressed through the following ranks rapidly, gaining promotions every fifth year afterward. This was an achievement few others attained, partially because few assassins lived long enough to be promoted through the ranks and partially because others lacked the staying power to spend their entire life in the trade. Incidentally, Gorka was due his final promotion this year to the rank of *soul collector*. This was a rank second only to the *guild master*, but there was no pride in the promotion. The status was purely political. It was a way for the guild to haggle higher prices for the employment of their hit men. The half-orc assassin still accepted low-end contracts frequently, but now the guild also offered more high-end contracts than before. It was just good business.

Gorka always remained focused on the mark no matter how much he stood to gain. In his mind, the gain was never part of the equation since the price for failure was always the same. If he failed to execute his plan precisely, it would cost him the one thing he could not afford to lose—his life. Through the years he had seen filthy beggars fight savagely to avoid death while the merchants and higher priced targets usually begged for their life and never so much as raised a finger to defend themselves. This was why he never took any contract at face value. Each contract was the same to him. It was always a challenge and an opportunity. The challenge was a test of his skills of stealth, fighting, and intelligence gathering. The opportunity was to improve his reputation and release his endless hatred and vengeance on others.

Today was no different. The half-orc had work to do. Gorka moved quietly through the catacombs early this morning having been summoned by the guild master to accept a new contract. He passed a number of low-level enforcers tasked with guarding the entryway to the main office and though each killer made note of the passing legend, none dared to meet his gaze for fear of being slain on the spot. Many cowered and stayed clear of the assassin, but a few brave souls showed respect, bowing as if he was a king of their forsaken world. Gorka acknowledged none of them. They were no different than the beggars he had slain for free. He would kill them indiscriminately if they moved against him. None were safe in his presence. After all, they were nothing more than young fools hoping to find their own fortunes and fame and he was certain they had no idea what it meant to be a true killer.

As he walked deeper and deeper into the underground labyrinth, his mind scrolled through a variety of hits he had made in his career. He could see their faces fresh in his mind as if he had only just sent them to the abyss. He could hear their screams as they pleaded for their lives. He could feel their blood wash over his hands as he drove his blade into their bodies. He could smell their breath as they breathed their dying gasps in his face but most of all he could taste their fear. It was delicious, like a steak cooked rare and dripping with tantalizing juices. He licked his lips unconsciously and smiled evilly.

Gorka found himself at the guild master's door. He knocked three times loudly.

A voice from behind the steel-bound oak door said, "I have summoned The Shade and only he may enter."

Gorka responded in kind saying, "You cannot summon that which has no master."

The voice said, "Hmmm…then would The Shade join me long enough to discuss business?"

He replied, "I will."

The door swung open and dim light washed over the outer hallway. Gorka stepped through the portal and glanced around. There was nothing spectacular about the room that would lead him to believe this office belonged to the most powerful underworld boss in the region. He saw a simple desk, several torches mounted on the walls, and an old man writing on yellowed parchment.

"I am considering a difficult task for you, one that will determine your worthiness to become a soul collector for The Legion," the guild master said.

"If another promotion is the reason we are

meeting, then we are both wasting our time. You will always have work for me and I will always take my mark. This is the nature of our relationship," Gorka said dispassionately.

"You are ever the assassin of assassins. This is why I have promoted you before and why you will be promoted again, but your words ring of great truth. I will not waste your time with petty enticements for I know your heart, Gorka Darkstorm, but I will need you as my second in command when you return from this task," the older assassin declared.

Gorka was surprised at the announcement. He had always been a loner, which was not the purpose of a commander or his second. He nodded in quiet respect and said, "Let us play the cards we have before us instead of gambling with the future. Tell me of the mark."

The guild master was experienced enough to recognize resistance from his deadliest hit man, but he let the matter drop and conceded to discuss the contract. He handed the parchment to the half-orc and said, "There is one who is rumored to be nearly immortal."

"Nearly immortal is no different than mortal," he responded casually.

"True, but this mark was beyond the skills of several of my other employees and a fair number of mercenaries," the boss returned matter of factly.

"It is not my nature to boast, so just tell me the details and I will do the rest," Gorka responded.

"Always concerned with fact, this is a fine quality in a professional killer. Very well, I will refrain from spreading rumor and gossip. Your mark is a giant of a man, easily your size and strength. He is a warrior from the northlands known for his skill with arms and warfare. He will be easily recognized by his foreign accent and reputation," the guild master said.

Gorka read the contract thoroughly. He said, "The contract says the man is from the Hinterlands and answers to the name Andar Razamun."

"That is true; do you know this man?" the boss asked.

"I have heard of him. He is a defender, a shield master. He has never been beaten in single combat or in a hundred battles, even with overwhelming odds. This man carries the *Aegis Shield of Griffon's Peak*, a gift from the king. He is the King's Champion, though he serves abroad more so than among city folk," Gorka said with measured tones of respect.

"I see that you do subscribe to rumor and gossip, but I have never known you to fear another being. Is this man beyond your skill?" he asked sarcastically, knowing full well the answer.

The assassin cast the guild master an evil look. It was so terrible and cold that the guild master unconsciously reached for his hidden dagger. Gorka noticed the movement and smiled inwardly. He knew the guild master was a powerful man in command of The Legion, but Gorka commanded something the boss could never match. He was the master of fear and that was a power that no man or army could defeat. Gorka responded calmly, "There is a difference between respect for skill and fear of the man with the skill. I will meet my end one day by old age, treachery, or combat. Perhaps this man will be the one who brings about the end of The Shade, but I am he that others fear."

"So you accept the contract then?" the older man asked.

"Of course I will accept the contract. I would never turn from this challenge," he replied, thinking that his infamy would be great indeed with such a mark taken by his hand.

"Very well Gorka, Master of Shadows. Your mark was last traveling through Bladeshire heading toward Westrun. He was seen in the company of a young blacksmith named Vlaad. Will you set out immediately or would tomorrow morning work better for you?" the guild master asked, implying great urgency.

"I plan to leave tonight and I will return in less than a ten-day," the half-orc returned confidently as he took the contract and walked away.

The guild master shrugged off the insubordinate act of turning and leaving without being properly dismissed. He knew Gorka was beyond such illusions or politics.

***

Bladeshire had been quiet since Vlaad departed with the northerner. O'ma had managed to busy herself with a small garden and the daily chores required in her small cottage. She thought about her grandson often though she rarely worried for his safety. She knew his keen mind and well-trained sword arm would carry him through nearly any hardship. She smiled to herself, knowing that she had raised him well. He would do his duty. She was confident in that.

Night fell, bringing peace along with it. O'ma often spent the early evening listening to the sound of the crickets and watching the fire leap about in the stone hearth. Tonight was somehow different. She noticed the distinct absence of the insects. The silence was strange indeed, but she sat back in her chair and watched the fire dance before her eyes. She sensed that she was no longer alone.

"You might as well come out. I know you are in here," she said.

The shadows seemed to open up and yield the intruder at her command. A soft, but menacing voice said, "You are perceptive old one. Few can detect my presence and even fewer would simply invite me to appear. Do you know who I am?" the assassin asked as he moved in front of the old woman revealing his grim visage.

O'ma squinted in the dim firelight to fully take in the details of the murderer's face. She saw the deep-set eyes and jutting lower teeth that marked the intruder as an orc of some sort. She realized that he was probably a half-orc by his size and human traits. She shook her head to indicate that she did not know him.

Gorka stood motionless for another moment to let her piece together the details of his identity. He wanted this very perceptive woman to recognize him for his talents. It suited his purposes and tantalized his desire to taste her fear. He wanted her to panic, to gasp in terror, but she sat unmoving as if he was nothing more than a stone in the hearth or a part of the mantelpiece. He was intrigued at her self-control.

"I do not know you nor do I care to. I know what you are and that is all that matters," O'ma said with sincere calm in her voice.

"If you know what I am then perhaps you also know why I am here," Gorka said with an equally calm voice.

"You must be here to kill me as I have nothing to steal," she replied.

"How wrong you are. You have something very valuable that I require though it must be given. I cannot take it from you as a thief would pocket gold or jewels. I sense that you do not fear death. It is common for those long in years to learn that death takes us all sooner or later, but you have gone beyond understanding. You have accepted that soon death will come for you. What do you see when you look at me?" Gorka asked.

"I see that you are a wicked killer. I assume that you are one known as The Shade, but rumor and superstition have no place in my mind or heart, so do as you will," O'ma said defiantly.

"I have been known by many names, but you have guessed correctly. Some call me The Shade. Others call me the Master of Shadows; you may call me by my true name. I am Gorka Darkstorm," the assassin said with a bow. "Since you have shown such courage, I might spare your life in exchange for a few moments of your time. Would you speak with me?"

"I do not have a choice as I see it. I am an old woman with no weapons or means of defense. You are a trained killer with many weapons and the nature to use them. It seems obvious that you will have your way," she returned logically.

Gorka merely nodded at the obvious assessment. "I am looking for a man who is not from these parts. He is large in stature and speaks with a foreign accent. He carries a magnificent shield that shines like polished silver—a gift of the king that marks him as the Champion of Griffon's Peak. I was told that your grandson, Vlaad, was seen traveling with him," the assassin mentioned.

O'ma shifted uneasily in her chair. Her face went pale. She had no fear of death or pain, but she feared greatly for her dear grandson, particularly when it concerned The Legion.

"I see that you know something about this man, but fear for the boy makes you hesitate. I could swear an oath to do him no harm, but such promises are hollow given the nature of my business. What can I offer to you that would be worth the information I seek?" Gorka purred as he drank in the sweet taste of fear welling within the woman.

"There is no reward to tempt me or any promise that I can trust from you, Master of Shadows," she replied.

Gorka sensed more than fear; raw terror was building in the old woman. It lingered in the air like fine perfume leading him to sensual pleasures. He responded coldly, "There is one promise that you can trust, for you know my nature and my duty. I will promise to send you the remains of your grandson after I dismember him slowly and painfully if you do not tell me that which I have asked."

O'ma was shaken but still held her composure, at least outwardly. She was, however, unsure how to proceed. If she helped the half-orc, it could lead to Vlaad's death once Gorka found his target. If she said nothing, the killer would certainly seek vengeance for her defiance, making Vlaad's death a gruesome one. She was trapped.

The assassin said, "I can see the struggle in your eyes. You should know that I will find the man known as Andar Razamun and Vlaad with or without your help, but I am willing to spare the boy's life and yours if you aid me. Do not think of your assistance as betrayal; it is quite the opposite. Your assistance is a guarantee that Vlaad will not die by my hand. The alternative is also guaranteed."

O'ma gave in to the half-orc's demands. She said, "The northerner is my grandson's employer. He is a great adventurer who has taken Vlaad as an apprentice. They move around frequently, but I believe they have moved out of Bladeshire toward Westrun. Andar is a shield warrior of the Hinterlands and known for his expertise in combat."

Gorka smiled and said, "I knew most of that already so I know you speak the truth, but is that all you can reveal to me?"

"That is all that I know," she returned honestly.

"I believe you," Gorka said as he drew his deadly keen blade. "I will leave a message for my target and your grandson. If I fail to find them, I am certain they will come looking for me."

O'ma closed her eyes and waited for the end. She could feel Gorka move into position with the tip of his blade just under her chin. The point was razor sharp and it easily pierced her skin, but did not go beyond. She steeled her will and took a long, deep breath that she was sure to be her last. Moments came and went, but the blade did not move. O'ma opened one eye to see the evil half-orc leering at her, just inches away. She could smell his breath and feel it hot on her cheek. He smiled revealing the orcish tusks clearly. In spite of the self-control shown by the old woman, Gorka reveled in the power he had over her. She had no fear for her own life but the boy was her weakness. He drank in the feeling of power like a fine wine. It was delicious to him.

"I have changed my mind. Instead of leaving your corpse as my invitation to Andar and Vlaad, I have decided that you will live to see the fruits of my labor. If you have misled me, Vlaad will suffer the most painful death I can imagine. His body will feel the pain of one hundred deaths before I let him expire. I will send his remains to you so that you can live out your days knowing that his death was the most horrible I could imagine. If you have been honest with me, then you will see him alive again," he promised. "I know that you may think Vlaad is in danger if I am to kill his mentor, but you must believe his safety is tied to your honesty, now more so than the fate of the northlander. Your words may not guarantee his protection, but they could guarantee his death. Do you have anything to add now that you know in your heart I will certainly slay him to punish you?" the assassin asked calmly with those wickedly evil eyes staring right through her.

O'ma replied, "I have been truthful."

"Very well, but should you see them, be sure to let them know I stopped by to visit," he said confidently.

Without another word, Gorka backed out of the small room and moved into the night. O'ma watched him go. Once he was gone she released her breath. She had been unconsciously holding it to keep from panicking. She knew that he would have certainly killed her had she shown weakness. She was surprised that he did not kill her for sport or for simple cruelty, but she was thankful that he had not. She looked down at her withered hands and was thankful that their trembling had not given her away. She was not afraid for her own life, but her beloved grandson was now in great peril and that was more horrifying than a dozen assassins holding their weapons to her throat. She prayed that somehow the assassin would fail. All she could do was pray.

CHAPTER 5
A GLIMPSE OF THE PAST

Vlaad watched the sun rise from the east over the white-capped rolling waves of the Great Sea. He saw the early morning rays burn away the night, leaving red streaks across the sky reminding him of blood. As he thought of his mentor, the powerful warrior from the Hinterlands, his mind flashed back almost fifteen years to a time when he was a much younger man. He relived the last moments of Andar's life.

Andar, the famous defender, had been training him in the ways of the shield warrior. They had left Bladeshire, traveled around the outskirts of several towns, and had recently traveled to Westrun in search of adventure. It was in Westrun that he had met Theila and her father, Don the Bard. It was an exciting time in his life. The foursome had returned from battling a tribe of vicious gnolls. It had been a near fatal battle for Vlaad. He recalled the quiet journey back to the town inn where they stayed for several weeks to watch over the townsfolk, just in case the gnolls became emboldened and chose to attack.

Vlaad was sleeping soundly when a loud crash woke him from his slumber. The noise had come from Andar's room across the hall. Uncertain what the matter was, Vlaad moved across the hall and into his mentor's room. The window was broken out and no one remained inside. Vlaad ran to the shattered window and saw two dark figures circling in the alley below. The light was dim, but he was sure the larger was Andar. He held his gleaming shield and fine curved blade but was otherwise unarmored. The slightly smaller of the two was dressed in black leather and held a long dagger in his right hand.

At first, Vlaad thought a foolish burglar had broken into his mentor's room, but that notion made little sense as Andar would have surely killed a mere burglar. His mind racing, Vlaad managed to piece together the scenario before him. The two had struggled upstairs long enough for Andar to shield slam his assailant out of the window, which had explained the crash that woke Vlaad. Both had fallen to the ground below and were now engaged in deadly combat. Even that seemed unlikely given the northerner's great skill and strength, but somehow Vlaad assumed that was what must have happened so far.

Vlaad watched the two continue to circle for a moment and then the assailant moved in. He was a blur of motion as he moved in close, thrusting for Andar's heart, but the defender shifted his mighty shield to the right just far enough to deflect the strike. The second attack followed immediately as the smaller combatant flipped his weapon in his hand so that the point was now facing downward while his other hand pulled down on the top of the shield exposing Andar's face. The blade sliced in drawing a long, red line across his cheek, narrowly missing his left eye.

The defender growled, dropped low, and scooped the other man onto his shield and over his back, but the agile assailant managed to hand-spring over the defender and landed on his feet. It was then that the light revealed the attacker's dark profile. Vlaad saw the prominent orcish features and knew immediately that this was no mere burglar. The attacker was a professional assassin and he had been obviously well trained. It was the same nightmare that had taken his father. Vlaad remembered how his O'ma had described assassins working for The Legion and how they had slain his family.

Vlaad felt certain that his mentor would soon crush the assassin, but his own fears began to overwhelm him, given his past. He found himself vaulting through the window and landing near the two below.

Andar yelled to his apprentice, "Stay back, zhou cannot 'elp."

The assassin smiled. His yellowed tusks protruded demonically.

Andar moved between Vlaad and the assassin, taking up the defensive stance he was famous for. The shield was perfectly balanced and his sword was in the high guard position. As Vlaad looked on in astonishment, he noticed that Andar's back was shredded from broken glass. It was then that he realized the assassin must have thrown the defender through the window!

The killer came in with the speed of a viper. His blade moved from right to left then back to the right with two powerful slashes. Andar blocked both easily but was unable to counter the attack as the killer skipped back out of range. The assassin came in again with a heart line thrust and as the larger man blocked, the assassin pushed upward on his great shield revealing the lead leg of the defender. The dagger sliced across it with amazing speed. Andar shuffled backward and cut horizontally with his sword to regain his position but the assassin was already well out of range. Vlaad saw the deep crimson run down Andar's tree trunk-like leg, but the defender felt nothing. He was too deeply focused on the villain before him.

Vlaad knew he would never be able help without a sword or his shield, but he couldn't stand by and watch his friend and mentor fall to the dagger-wielding fiend. He summoned his courage and charged in empty handed.

Andar called out, "No Vlaad!"

But it was too late. The assassin shifted to meet Vlaad with the wicked dagger leading. The first cut should have ended his life but instead left a thin, red line across his throat. Vlaad staggered in disbelief. The weapon had moved so quickly that he had been unable to see it dart in and out. In that moment of hesitation, the assassin smashed him in the jaw with his left hand dropping him to the ground in a daze. The killer kicked out catching Vlaad in the ribs with more than enough force to take his wind and leave him lying helpless, though still quite aware of the unfolding events. Vlaad couldn't breathe much less move to escape.

Andar rushed in to save Vlaad. He slammed his shield into the villain's face sending him reeling backward. The curved blade of the northlander came in almost simultaneously, hitting the killer in the midsection but did not pierce the leather armor he wore. He shield-slammed him again but the assassin turned and angled inward, leaving Andar standing to his right and open for attack. The assassin snaked in with his left hand pinning the defender's sword arm close to his body. The dagger came down at the precise point where the defender's neck and shoulder meet. Andar managed to spin one last time with the mighty shield, but there was no strength in the attack. The curved blade followed, slashing outward, but had neither precision nor power behind it. The great warrior fell to his knees and then dropped face first into the dust. Blood poured out of the deep wound with the slowing beat of his heart.

The assassin bowed respectfully to the prostrate defender saying, "You fought with honor and courage Andar Razamun. Know that your death was delivered by Gorka Darkstorm, The Shade of Griffon's Peak. As for you, young warrior, tell your O'ma I kept my word. You'll not die by my hand...at least not this day."

Vlaad struggled to rise, to do something to save his friend and teacher. He managed to drag himself to his hands and knees as the assassin turned and disappeared into the shadows. He crawled to Andar and rolled him onto his back as the last light of life was quickly leaving his eyes.

"Andar, Andar," he said, "stay with me, don't die, please don't die."

The great warrior raised his blood-soaked hand and grasped Vlaad's shoulder. He whispered, "Zhou are now ze last defenzodor. Take ze Aegiz Zheild and ze elven blade of Vlorin. Zhey vill protect zhou."

Vlaad nodded and asked, "But what will I do with your sword and shield? I am no defender, I know so little."

"Zhou vill do zhour duty," he said faintly.

"I'm not ready, I have so much left to learn," Vlaad said tearfully.

"Ze sword...it vill teach zhou. It is ze soul of Vlorin. It holds ze soul of all ze defenzodor's who 'ave held it before me...and soon it vill 'ave mine."

Vlaad held his mentor in his arms as the great warrior's life ended. He held on long after a crowd had gathered with curiosity. Don and Theila were among those who rushed in and tried to comfort the young defender, but without success. He just kept playing the final fight over and over in his head while he embraced his dead master's limp form. Vlaad knew there was nothing he could have done differently to change the outcome. The assassin was too fast, too cunning. The young defender closed his eyes and vowed revenge. His duty would never end as long as the assassin lived and as long as The Legion conducted business. He would exact justice somehow. His father, mother, siblings, and now his friend had been killed by assassins.

Don spoke softly, "Let him go, son. Andar is gone, but you have your entire life left to live. You must move on. There is work to be done."

Theila was right there beside him as well. Her tear-streaked face was a mixture of sadness for Vlaad, grief for the loss of Andar, and anger. Vlaad saw the fires of hate in those beautiful eyes. She said, "We will find the culprit. If it takes forever, we will track down the one responsible." He knew she would be with him when the time for vengeance came. It was those dark eyes and the fire in them that promised more than words ever could. Seeing her allegiance renewed Vlaad's strength. He stood up, bowed to his former master, and collected the items bequeathed to him with Andar's dying breath.

The sword came alive when Vlaad held it. A voice in his head said, "Vlaad of the Steppes of the Blackridge Mountains, last of the line of shield warriors, you are appointed guardian of the Blade of Vlorin and inheritor of its knowledge. Seek our guidance in times of need and we will teach you."

Turning to Theila he said, "Your father is right, we have much work to do."

Theila nodded with sad approval. She and Vlaad stepped aside as Don covered the fallen warrior with his cloak. It had been the turning point in their lives. As he watched the death shroud cover his friend and noble master, he thought back to the duty his O'ma always spoke of. First, The Legion had orphaned him, now it had taken his dear friend and mentor. Closing his eyes, he vowed again to dedicate his life to the eradication of The Legion with Gorka Darkstorm's death as his ultimate goal. Nothing else would matter until his duty was done.

The night passed in mourning with Theila, Don, and Vlaad caring for Andar's body in preparation for the burial ceremony. A voice came into the warrior's mind again. It called his name. At first, Vlaad thought it was his imagination, but the urging was persistent though somewhat distant. He walked over to the Sword of Vlorin, placed his hand on the hilt, and the voice became clear.

"You are Vlaad of the Steppes from the Blackridge Mountains. I sense that you are born of the shorter-lived races so our time is limited, but your heart is strong and your mind is keen. We have much to do," the sword imparted magically.

Vlaad spoke aloud, "What is this? Who are you?"

Theila had been resting on the couch nearby. She opened her eyes, looked at him quizzically, and said, "What do you mean? You know who I am. Are you all right?"

Vlaad looked at her and said, "Not you Theila, I hear...something...a voice."

Theila took a look around and watched him for a moment, unsure what was transpiring.

"I am the spirit of battle, Vlaad. I am bound to the sword of Andar, once the sword of his father, and his grandfather, back to his ancient ancestor Vlorin and before him I belonged to the race of elven sword saints. Through me you will learn all that they knew," the sentient blade transmitted.

Vlaad thought to himself, concentrating on the voice in his head. He said, "I am willing to learn, but unsure how to proceed. What must I do?"

"You must trust your forebears. We will guide you," it said.

Vlaad looked at Theila and said, "The sword…it speaks to me."

Theila smiled and said, "Then you have been set to follow in Andar's footsteps. My father told me all about the intelligent blade of Vlorin. It is a great gift and a curse from what I have been told, for it imparts wisdom, but seeks control of its wielder. Embrace the knowledge, but remember that you are its master. Never forget that or it will consume you."

Don awoke having heard the conversation. He said, "You must be strong in spirit, unwavering in willpower, and disciplined in mind to master the Sword of Vlorin, but if you do, your skills will grow quickly and you will become all that Andar was and more."

Vlaad nodded. He looked at the sword and shield. The sword would teach him and the shield would protect him. Just as he was about to walk away to find some much-needed solace, a warm wind swirled around the body of Andar creating a small vortex. Vlaad watched in amazement as the vortex took on the outline of Andar's form. It swirled faster and glowed for a moment with eldritch energy just before it swept over Vlaad. The small tornado surrounded the young warrior blurring him out from the view of the surrounding people. Vlaad closed his eyes and held very still. He felt as if his body were on fire and then all of the sudden it was over.

Theila came forward saying, "Vlaad are you all right?"

The defender opened his eyes and said in an unusually deep voice, "I am fine, I think. I feel...different."

"You *are* different," the warlock said quickly, "you have changed."

"What do you mean changed?" he asked.

"You look like Andar...sort of," she replied.

The sword spoke, "You are imbued with the spirit of Andar, just as he was imbued with his father's spirit and his grandfather before him. It is a gift to help you adapt to your new responsibilities."

Vlaad willed his thoughts into the intelligent weapon, "In what way have I changed and how will these changes help me?"

The sword replied, "You have taken on a few physical traits of your former master to include some of his wisdom, some of his strength, and the capacity for combat premonition, that is, you can now learn to *see* the attacks of your enemies before they land and in some cases, before they are even thrown. It is called the gift of Vlorin, the first shield warrior."

Vlaad took a moment to look back before he left. Andar's body was gone and the death shroud was all that remained. The mighty warrior was now part of him.

***

Vlaad came back to the present with the rocking of the ship beneath his feet. He was thirty-two years old now with more than fifteen years of experience as a defender and professional adventurer. Since the death of Andar Razamun, he had taken on dozens of quests in search of Gorka Darkstorm, The Shade, his nemesis—none of which had successfully satisfied the need for justice. The infamous assassin had eluded him at every turn. He had lived up to his namesake being no more than a phantom, a specter, a shadow in the night. Vlaad had slain countless assassins working for The Legion, but the organization was likewise living up to its namesake as it had hundreds of operatives in its hierarchy. Sometimes it seemed futile, but Vlaad never lost hope. He never forgot the promise to his O'ma, who had long since passed from this world to the next, and he had never forgotten his vow to avenge Andar. He would spend his lifetime fighting evil if that was what it took and it would be a life well spent.

A voice from the crow's nest called down, "Bladerun Bay ahead."

The vessel's commander, Commodore Samuel Bailey replied, "Aye, drop sails. Set oars an' pull 'er in to port smoothly."

Vlaad was always impressed by the professional seamanship the crew of the *Crusader* showed. It was a testament to the leadership of the commander to have such fine sailors and officers. When Commodore Bailey walked up and placed his thick arm around Vlaad's shoulders, the defender mentioned his observations.

"Commodore, I have never seen such a fine crew or such precision in sailing. You and your men work like the gods themselves bred you for this purpose," Vlaad said with genuine appreciation.

"My good man, I appreciate your words and I will forward those regards to the crew. It is always good to hear that our services are recognized as exemplary," Samuel said in his husky deep voice, "but let's not speak of sailing. Instead, tell me of your quest to find that black-hearted devil, Darkstorm."

Vlaad thought for a minute and replied, "There is little to tell, my friend. I have searched every inch of our world and I seem to miss The Shade at every turn. My companion Theila and I chased him into the Raptor Highlands from Westrun nearly fifteen years ago, but found only a trail of dead bodies leading back to the Wetlands. We served with the local patrols for weeks hoping to catch him there, but he moved on to the Jaggedspine Valley to the far south. I spent a few years fighting pirates and every manner of wild animal imaginable, but he evaded us again. Several years fighting undead in UnDae'run led me to his hideout in the north, but he moved again and again. This last adventure was a long shot, but I had heard that he was working with the Bloodcrest Forces in Dek'Thal. I signed on to lead a small contingent of volunteers against the massing northern armies of Neggish Grimtusk, but my prey never appeared. Now I am heading back to rejoin Theila in Griffon's Peak. Perhaps she will be able to divine Gorka's location for me one day."

Commodore Bailey nodded in quiet regard. He was a wise and thoughtful officer with many resources but he had no leads to help with the defender's quest. He smiled and slapped the warrior on the back saying, "I am ever at your service, Vlaad. If I hear anything, you will be the first to know."

Vlaad turned and extended his hand in friendship, "Commodore, your loyalty is priceless to me. It is good seeing you again."

Samuel shook the gauntleted hand and said,

"Farewell, old chap. May the gods watch over you."

Vlaad replied, "The same to you."

The boatswain's mate was tying up to the docks as they parted company. Vlaad grabbed his pack and headed across the ramp and down the dock toward the port city of Blackmarsh. As he neared the end of the docks, he saw a familiar face that made his heart skip a beat. Theila had come to meet him.

"To what do I owe this unexpected visit?" the defender asked coyly.

Theila responded nonchalantly, "Who says I am here to meet you?"

Vlaad walked up to the warlock, wrapped his arms around her, and said, "It has been too long. I am so glad to see you."

Theila returned his affections with her own embrace and replied, "We are a team, aren't we? We should stick together."

"Of course you are right, but this trip was quite dangerous. Many good men and elves lost their lives, not to mention dwarves and gnomes. The orcs were fearsome and cruel beyond anything I have ever seen. They were well armed and armored too. It was a bloodbath that I am thankful you did not have to witness," he explained.

Theila knew Vlaad's protective nature was the real reason that she had been asked to remain behind. It was only the second time in a decade and a half that he had asked her not to fight beside him, but she understood. Theila knew that Vlaad loved her deeply. She loved him equally, but his duty and her respect for it had never allowed their feelings to blossom. She had remained more of a sister to him than anything, though she longed for a deeper, more intimate relationship. After all, what more could any woman want? Vlaad was dashing and charming. He was a fine protector and had made a small fortune adventuring. He lived by a code of morality that guaranteed his faithfulness and honor. Perhaps one day, they would marry and have children, but for now they were as close as two people could be, closer in many ways than married couples.

"Tell me about your latest adventure," Theila asked with the fire of anticipation dancing in her eyes.

"Well, we assembled a great army of elves, men, dwarves, and gnomes to fight the enemy. We moved from Port Archer to Forestedge where the orcs had captured the elven city. The enemy was entrenched and had a powerful allied force of trolls, tauren, and undead waiting for us. Their leader was a cunning and devious beast named Neggish Grimtusk, who led the battle against us. The knights of Griffon's Peak were slain in the initial charge save one, the paladin Landermihl, who was severely wounded when we recovered him. The dwarven infantry took heavy losses as well, but held against the enemy. They were led by a dwarven hunter called Gaedron. I spent most of the battle fighting beside two elves and a gnome on the southern edge of the city. The gnome was a warlock like you, though not nearly as powerful. The elves were siblings. The brother, a fine elf named Wavren, was a hunter armed with an incredible new weapon he called a blunderbuss and he commanded the largest bear I have ever seen as his ally. The sister, Rosabela by name, was a druidic shape shifter and healer. Together we fought dozens of undead summoned from the city's graveyard. The battle was long and savage, but we won when an elf spirit was summoned to fight Neggish Grimtusk in single combat. It was like the tale of Vlorin and the elven sword saint. The two champions fought so that others would be spared. Apparently, the summoned spirit was once the captain of the city guard. He had fallen in the first battle when Forestedge was invaded several days earlier," Vlaad surmised.

"But did you find your nemesis?" she asked hopefully.

"I did not, but I believe he is lurking in the orc-filled lands to the south. Being half-orc, I assume he may have thrown in with his orcish brethren over the past few years, but no one seemed to know anything about him," Vlaad replied with great frustration.

"What will we do now? It seems as though the trail has run cold," Theila mentioned.

"The trail has grown cold, but my fate seems intertwined with his. We will meet again, I am sure of that. In the meantime, I think we should return to Griffon's Peak. The Legion will always creep out from some dark hole and I want to be there when they do. Don't you?" he asked rhetorically, knowing that she would always be with him.

Theila thought it might be nice to settle down one day and raise a family, but at nearly thirty-four years, her time was running out for that dream. She always reminded herself that Vlaad had saved her life soon after they had first met and on numerous occasions since. He had always been there for her. She felt obligated to help him root out evil ever since Andar had died, but secretly she prayed that the road would end one day and their days of adventuring would be constrained to the bedroom. She giggled with that thought.

"What is so funny?" Vlaad asked curiously.

"Nothing," she replied.

"Come on now, I know you too well. What devilment are you planning?" he prodded.

"Honestly, I am planning no devilment. I just had an ironic thought that is all. It was entertaining. Perhaps you should learn to laugh more. It is said that laughter is good for the soul," she mentioned intending to change the subject.

"I laugh," he said, "I just tend to take life seriously most of the time. I suppose it is my nature. Do you think I am too serious?"

"I think that you have taken your duty very seriously, but that is an admirable quality. Perhaps a little more time spent enjoying life might be a pleasant change, but no, I do not think you are too serious," she replied.

"Very well, I will make time for more smiling," he said teasingly, "but first we must head to Griffon's Peak."

"It is late afternoon," Theila reminded him, "perhaps we should wait until morning to make the trip. We could spend the night here at Blackmarsh and you could practice smiling."

Vlaad laughed heartily. "As you wish, we can stay the night and set out at daybreak."

The two sat by the fire catching up on their time spent apart in the common room of the inn, which also served as the local tavern for weary travelers. There were few patrons drinking and chatting when they entered and far fewer by the time they felt the need for sleep. Hours had quickly passed and night had long since fallen. The conversation had included more details about the battle at Forestedge, The Legion, and of course, Gorka. It seemed he was always part of their conversation. Vlaad wondered what would become of them once the vile killer was gone. He looked away, off into the distance at the thought and Theila picked up on it immediately. She reached out and warmly grabbed his thickly calloused hand. The touch brought Vlaad back to the present.

"We must rest if we plan to rise early for the trip to the city. Perhaps we should continue this conversation on the road tomorrow," Vlaad stated.

"I am ready for a good night's sleep anyway," Theila returned with a yawn. "Sleep well."

"You too," he replied as she stood and left for her room. Vlaad never took his eyes off of her lovely form as she slowly climbed the stairs. Her gently swaying hips were as much of an invitation for Vlaad to join her as if she had simply come out and said the words, but Vlaad knew he could never commit to her as she needed, not while his adversary was alive and while The Legion remained in business. Duty was second only to justice and both demanded his full attention.

Theila paused once at the top of the stairs and glanced over her shoulder. She knew Vlaad was watching. He always watched. She knew he loved her, but she did not know if his ever-present gaze came more from the love of a protective brother or that of a man so deeply in love that he feared his touch would spoil the perfect beauty of the feeling. She hoped for the latter and her side-long glance showed it clearly. As she walked away, she smiled inwardly knowing that his heart was pounding in his chest from that simple but powerful glance.

Morning came quickly with the rising of the sun over the wetlands of Blackmarsh. Vlaad walked up to Theila's room after completing his morning exercises. His body was alive and tingling with energy having completed the shield dance just as

Andar had taught him so long ago. The sword of Vlorin had imparted many other exercise forms, particularly sword drills, but none had the revitalizing effect of the shield dance. As he drew near Theila's door, he overheard a strange guttural language coming from behind the door. It was the tongue of the abyss. Apparently, Theila was still engaged in her own rituals. He knew the door would be magically sealed so he did not bother knocking. He just listened.

Theila had summoned a protector demon called a *voidwalker*. Vlaad recognized its deep masculine voice which was unlike that of the higher pitched and shrill voice of the imp or the sultry feminine voice of the succubus that she had dominion over. The deep, guttural tones it emitted were indecipherable to the defender, but he knew by Theila's words that it was reporting information it had gathered regarding The Legion. This was not a protector demon's purpose, but a skillful warlock could compel her servants to do many secondary tasks. Truly, the demon was best known for its ability to keep foes at bay while Theila worked her most powerful spells. This made it a tremendous ally and deadly enemy for certain.

Vlaad could picture the thing in his mind. This particular demon was made of mostly smoke and ash, but it was as tough and fearsome as a bull rhino. It looked vaguely humanoid with two massive arms and a broad chest, but it had nothing more than billowing smoke below its waist and wicked, scythe-like claws at the ends of its wide hands. Its eyes were flame and its face was a mask of smoke. Vlaad was glad it watched over her in his absence but he despised the thing, as it was pure evil just as all creatures from the abyss were. Of course, it had to obey the warlock that summoned it, such is the nature of a summoned creature, but it was evil nonetheless. Incidentally, Vlaad found his sword and shield suddenly at the ready instead of remaining in their respective resting places at his side and on his back. He returned them and tried to relax.

The door opened suddenly and Theila's lovely face was barely inches from his own. She said, "You are up early. Did you think I was sleeping in this morning?"

"I...I came to see if you wanted breakfast," he quickly stammered, feeling slightly embarrassed for eavesdropping on her privacy.

"Vlaad, I have known you for too many years to fall for such fantasy," she accused with her tiny hands on her hips. "What were you doing out here?"

The great defender found himself looking at his boots. He whispered trying to avoid the question, "I'm hungry and I just wanted to know if you would join me for a bite."

She threw her head back and laughed an almost musical laugh. "Of course I will, but you should know that a warlock knows many things and spying on her could get you turned into something...unnatural."

Vlaad pictured himself as a huge toad. In his mind's eye the toad wore his clothing and carried his weapons and equipment. He smiled and then started laughing at the thought. Theila laughed a bit too as they adjourned for breakfast.

"Zaashik told me some interesting things this morning," Theila began, "you know, the big demon, the protector?"

"Yes, I am familiar with him," Vlaad said with

obvious dissatisfaction. "What did the beast tell you?"

The warlock knew Vlaad despised all things evil, but it still surprised her to hear his tone given the nature of their association and the value of the information it had previously imparted.

She said, "Zaashik has given us the next piece of the puzzle to bring down The Legion. Apparently, a new threat to the realm has surfaced and the assassins have plans to incorporate it into their own designs."

"Well, what is this new threat?" Vlaad asked with sincere curiosity.

Theila leaned forward and whispered, "Do you know the disease called *lycanthropy*?"

Vlaad shook his head having never heard of the illness or how it might be used by the assassin's guild.

Theila continued even more quietly as if he assassins were listening at that very moment. She said, "Lycanthrope is a disease carried by evil creatures called *lycans.* It is a sickness that turns anyone infected by it into a monstrous half-human, half-wolf abomination. Eons ago these creatures were called werewolves, but unlike them, these are more powerful. They are not limited by carnal desires to kill and devour sentient beings as a werewolf is. The lycans can shape-shift at will and control their beastly forms like druids of the elven race. Some say that lycans were once druids, having fallen from the ways of nature, having been consumed by their lust for power."

Vlaad had the look of deadly seriousness that he wore more often than not. In his mind, he could only imagine how powerful the assassin's guild would become with such terrible allies. He knew their pairing must never come to pass.

"What else do we know of these lycans? Do they have any weakness we might exploit? Where can we find them?" he asked too quickly for Theila to answer.

"Zaashik told me nothing more but perhaps the library of Griffon's Peak might have some answers. We can begin there," she said hopefully.

The sword of Vlorin interrupted the conversation with its telepathic intrusions. "Vlaad, the beasts you seek are known to us. In fact, having passed from warrior to warrior for thousands of years, there are few creatures or beings that are not."

Vlaad was always cautious when the sword spoke. He realized some years ago that the sentient weapon had a wealth of knowledge but it always gave information at a high price. At first, just after Andar had been slain by Gorka Darkstorm, Vlaad spoke with the blade daily. He had been so driven to master his skills as a defender that there was no price too high to pay. He had quickly gained mastery of the shield as a result. The sword had tempted him to go beyond studying the shield saying that mastery of the sword was just as important. It had even used the story of Vlorin's defeat at the hands of the last elven sword saint to convince him. Vlaad had almost turned away from the path of the defender as a result. It was then that he realized the sword had a malicious aspect fed by envy and hatred. It would never be satisfied as long as another item, in this case the defender's shield, was more important than it was. In addition, the sword longed to be in the hands of an elven sword saint, or any long-lived race that might truly benefit from its endless experience and wisdom but ever since the victory Vlorin had over the last sword saint, the sentient blade had been bound to a human line of successors. Unfortunately, humans were simply too short lived. It was monotonous training a new wielder every fifty years or less and the sword wanted to elevate its wielder to nearly god-like power. It thirsted for glory. It was a blade of conquest.

Vlaad paused a moment to listen to the sword. It said, "The lycans were, in fact, once elven druids, just as the woman said, but they have grown in numbers using the old ways of the werewolves. Many of the creatures now were once human like you. They sought power and gave up their humanity for it, gaining near immortality. The first and most powerful lycans are likely elves in some form or another, but the assassin's guild will most likely seek to join the human variant to gain longevity among other things."

Vlaad considered the information and replied, "Sword of Vlorin, I am no fool. I can sense your desire to find an ageless owner. You would have me seek this disease that I might become timeless just as your former elven masters were or perhaps you hope that I will fall in battle and one of the beasts already infected might claim you, but your desires will remain unfulfilled. I am Vlaad of the Steppes, son of Vlaadimir de Valle and the last defender, descended from the order of Vlorin, the shield warrior and student of Andar Razamun. I will not be swayed from my purpose. Duty is second only to justice and what you seek is folly."

The sword became silent and an overwhelming feeling of peace emanated from the blade. The spirit of Andar and every goodly man before him back to Vlorin himself seemed to swell with pride and satisfaction, giving Vlaad even more assurance that he was doing the right thing. Vlaad took a deep breath and sighed aloud.

Theila turned to look at him and said, "So are we off to Griffon's Peak?"

Vlaad nodded and walked with his companion to their horses. It was a five-day ride to the great city of men, and he had many things to consider in that time.

CHAPTER 6
THE CITY OF MEN

The royal library of Griffon's Peak was a magnificent edifice with every manner of book, scroll, parchment, and historical recording since the dawn of mankind thousands of years ago. The halls of the library were vast, spanning nearly twice the length and breadth of the royal palace. The library staff required more than four hundred workers to keep the colossal works organized, cataloged, and accounted for. This was equivalent to a battalion-sized element of infantrymen. Needless to say, Vlaad and Theila stood in awe as they entered. Fortunately, a scholarly looking librarian approached and offered to help.

"Welcome to the great library of Griffon's Peak. By your appearances I assume you have never been here before," the librarian stated more than asked.

Theila responded, "We have never been inside, though we are both from Griffon's Peak, well, the surrounding villages actually."

The scholar smiled and said, "My name is Pelion and I am in charge of the eastern bloc, but I am very familiar with the entire collection here. How may I help you?"

Vlaad spoke up, "Well met, Pelion. I am Vlaad of the Blackridge Steppes and my companion is Theila of Westrun. We are looking for ancient lore regarding creatures of the night. Theila's father is Don, the Bard of Westrun, and we are doing research for him. He is always seeking tales to tell and songs to write. Can you help us?"

Pelion put his hands on his hips and asked,

"Can you be more specific? I can take you to the eastern historical archives dedicated to the undead or I can take you to the opposite end of the library which consists of mythological beings and other fictitious musings."

Theila interjected, "We were thinking that a story about shape shifters might be fun to research. I heard a story once of a druid who fell from the path of nature and became a cursed creature that lived on human flesh. It was called a lycan I believe."

Pelion nodded and said, "That is actually in the elven section on the second floor of the northern wing. It is a good thing you were able to narrow your search or we would have been running around all day in this labyrinth of never-ending shelves. Please follow me."

Pelion escorted the companions to the proper place. There were well over one hundred volumes regarding elven druids. Apparently, their contributions to the library were extensive. The librarian pointed to a black, leather-bound tome on the third shelf. The title was scribed in elvish.

"We cannot read elvish. Do you have a translation in common tongue?" Vlaad asked.

Pelion frowned and said, "This book is all we have on the subject, but I assure you it covers the history of lycanthrope to include its progenitor, Lord Carnage, and the rise of the lycan pack of Celes'tia."

Theila asked, "May we borrow the book to have it translated?"

Pelion laughed a strange bird-like cackling. When he stopped he said, "Are you insane? I just said this is the only book we have on the subject and I doubt that you would find anyone who can read this variation of elvish anyway. It was written in ancient elvish by a druid of the grove some five hundred years ago."

"What good is a book that no one can read?" Vlaad asked. "And how did the library acquire it anyway? If it was written by a druid in ancient elvish, it was likely never meant for humans eyes."

Pelion glared at the warrior and clutched the book close to his chest. He said with great ire, "We had a translator who could read and write ancient elvish just a few months ago, but he has been gone for a while on business. Until he returns, I am afraid that you will simply have to research other topics for the Bard of Westrun."

Theila smiled and said, "Very well, thank you for your help. When should we return to speak with the translator?"

"Well, the translator is actually due back any day now. He usually comes by twice a year during his travels around the realm. You see, he is a Protector of the Vale and a Druid of the Grove from Celes'tia," the scholar said with pride in that he knew such a hero.

"He is a Protector of the Vale and a Druid of the Grove?" Vlaad asked rhetorically.

"That's right. I have met with him on every visit he has made to Griffon's Peak in the past twenty years. I would even say we are close associates, though to say I was his close friend might be an exaggeration. Incidentally, he is the author of this very book," Pelion remarked offhandedly.

Theila gave a puzzled look to Vlaad and asked, "You said the book was penned some five hundred years ago. Do you mean to say that the author of the book is over five hundred years old?"

"Young lady," the older scholar started, "some elves live well beyond one thousand years, and most would if not cut down by orcs or slain by other monstrous villains. In fact, the author of this particular volume, Da'Shar by name, is closer to fifteen hundred years old I believe."

Vlaad's mouth fell open.

"I know this elf. I have fought beside him against the orcs in Forestedge. He is indeed a powerful and wise druid, though I had no idea that he was among the oldest of the elves in the realm," Vlaad mentioned quickly.

"Sure you know Da'Shar. You, a brute from the mountains, know him you say? Well, I cannot fathom how that could ever be possible much less the remote chance that you fought with him in the Battle of Forestedge. I happen to be chronicling the life of Da'Shar. It is my life's work so I think that I would know if you had any association with him," the librarian remarked caustically.

Vlaad raised an eyebrow at the thin, balding man. He had never been called a brute before and being referred to as such by a snobbish bookworm made him want to reach out shake the man right out of his girly little robes. Theila interceded just in time.

"Vlaad, perhaps you are mistaken. Surely, this important scholar knows everything about this author, Da'Shar. Let's just go and perhaps he will be willing to help us when we return," she urged.

Vlaad got the underlying message. He realized that throttling the little man might make it difficult to ever access the book in the future. He swallowed his pride and bowed to the scholar.

"Perhaps I have made a mistake. Would you forgive me and please consider assisting us again in the future?" Vlaad asked with grace and humility.

Pelion nodded and managed a sarcastic smile. He spoke as the two were leaving, "There is one other who might be able to help you. A man came in a few days ago in search of this very tome. He was able to read it as if it were his native language. His name is Landermihl and he lives in the palace. He happens to be a famous paladin in service to the king, who actually fought alongside Da'Shar in the Battle of Forestedge, but you probably already know him too."

As the scholar laughed at Vlaad's expense the defender turned and waved goodbye. His last words to the man were, "I know Lord Landermihl well. He alone survived the initial charge at Forestedge and would have died had it not been for the intervention of his god and finest dwarven infantry in the realm, who pulled him out of the fray. When you see him, tell him Vlaad of the independent companies stopped by."

The scholar stopped laughing as the defender spun about, revealing the Aegis Shield of Griffon's Peak under his cloak, the very shield given to Andar Razamun by the king for protecting the city from invading barbarians twenty years ago. It was the symbol of the King's Champion, which meant he was in fact the single greatest warrior in the realm. It was during that moment of realization that Pelion wished he could take back his sarcasm. Indeed, Vlaad was no mere brute from the mountains, but was the renowned Cavalier of Bladeshire, Champion of the King of Griffon's Peak and a true hero of the Battle of Forestedge. Pelion weakly returned the black tome to its place and hoped he would be able to find the words and the courage to apologize when the hero returned for it. He felt sick

all of the sudden, particularly when he thought of
Vlaad reporting him to the king, or worse, coming
back to bash in his skull for being such an impudent
fool.

Vlaad moved through the royal courtyard in
search of Lord Landermihl without molestation.
Guards came to attention as he passed. Knights
saluted him as he met their gaze. Theila knew Vlaad
commanded great respect among the members of
the king's court, but she never considered her
companion, who was so humble and patient around
her, to be treated with such respect, perhaps even
considered a nobleman by some. Then again, they
rarely came to court, as their duties were in the field
hunting The Legion.

Truth be told, Vlaad was not a nobleman, but
he was perhaps the finest warrior in the realm and
his expertise gave him a measure of respect that
even counts, barons, and dukes often failed to
attain. More importantly, Vlaad's contributions had
been exemplary, having fought every manner of
evil in the land from orc to troll, ogre to giant,
wyvern to dragon, and everything in between.
Theila loved him for all that he was but more
importantly, for what he was not. He was neither a
braggart, nor a pompous fool. He was neither self-
absorbed nor callous to the plight of the needy. He
was a goodly man, plain and simple.

Landermihl was praying to his god when Vlaad
entered the holy temple of paladin's order. He and
Theila waited for some time before the great holy
warrior rose from his kneeling position. Unlike
Vlaad, Landermihl was a nobleman, born to the
same house of the king, but far enough removed
that he had no chance of inheriting the kingdom. He
had been accepted into the Order of Light at the age

of eighteen and had served honorably ever since, but one thing was common between the defender and the paladin; they both lived to fight evil. It was their life's quest.

As Landermihl turned away from the shrine to exit the chapel, he saw Vlaad and smiled broadly. His eyes quickly glanced Theila's way and at first he smiled at her beauty, but the smile faded as he felt the taint of demons in her aura. His hand went to the massive war hammer at his side, but only for a moment. He somehow knew that Vlaad would never associate with evil. The only possibility remaining was that Theila was a summoner. He had known many in his adventures and most were goodly folk with incredible power. It only took a single, whispered word to discern the truth. The incantation would always reveal an evil doer like a bonfire at midnight to a paladin. In Theila's case, there was no such aura when he cast the simple spell, but the woman had been saturated by the presence of demons, that much was certain.

"Hail and well met Vlaad, Champion of the King, Cavalier of Bladeshire, Defender of the Line of Vlorin," the paladin greeted formally.

"Hail to you Lord Landermihl, Paladin of Light, Justice-bringer, and Knight of Griffon's Peak," the defender replied as he embraced the holy warrior.

"I see that you travel in good company," Landermihl commented as he held Vlaad at arm's length and looked over to Theila.

"May I introduce, Theila of Westrun, daughter of Don the Bard, and Warlock of the Black Gate," he replied.

Theila bowed low to the paladin as she was of common birth and held no regal titles given by the king. Landermihl bowed in response, though not nearly so low, according to tradition.

"I am honored to meet you Theila of Westrun. I have never met your famous father, but I have heard of him and the stories he tells in every province where I have traveled. I daresay he is better known than our own beloved king in some parts," the paladin remarked with a smile.

"Sire, it is my honor to make your acquaintance," Theila returned formally.

Landermihl was impressed. He was often less formal particularly among commoners outside the royal court and so he paid little mind to indiscretions with customs and courtesies, but it pleased him greatly to see the old traditions honored. He felt immediately endeared to Theila, in spite of her being a conjurer of demon-kind.

"The pleasure is all mine," he returned with sincerity.

"Well now that we are all acquainted, I have a matter of business to discuss with you, if you have a moment to spare," Vlaad asked rhetorically.

The paladin nodded and ushered his guests to a small alcove holding a few chairs and a small table. It was an unassuming room, but private and comfortable enough. Vlaad began explaining his never-ending quest to dismantle The Legion. He mentioned the information Theila had gathered regarding the possible union of the lycan pack and the assassin's guild. Lastly, he mentioned the book written by Da'Shar that he had hoped would shed some light on their new adversaries.

Landermihl took in the situation and considered it for many moments before speaking. Finally he said, "First of all, let me preach for a moment about relying on ill-gotten information from demons of the abyss. I am sure you realize that any creature bound against its will has every intention of breaking those bonds and killing its master should the chance present itself. That being said, I would be cautious about trusting any such information as I am certain it has at least some misinformation mixed in to cause chaos. It is the nature of such creatures to be false."

Theila rolled her eyes and crossed her arms defiantly but remained silent.

Vlaad was nodding in agreement as he despised the foul things that Theila conducted business with daily.

Landermihl continued, "The information you have gathered is true and can be corroborated by my own information. It is why I recently sought out the very book that you were seeking."

Vlaad interrupted, "So you have read it then. Tell us about it."

The paladin nodded and returned to his discussion, "The book was a gift to me from Da'Shar a long time ago when rumors of the lycan of Celes'tia began to spread. Da'Shar had penned the book hundreds of years before when the first of his order fell from the ways of nature to follow the darker paths. He had hoped that understanding the nature of the evil beings and the disease, lycanthrope, would raise awareness and prevent the pack from being able to grow and return to civilized lands."

Theila interrupted, "So what do we know about these creatures? Are they truly immortal or ageless and powerful?"

The holy warrior shrugged and said, "We do not truly know the extent of their power. The were-creatures, mostly werewolves, are savage nightstalkers that feed on the flesh of sentient beings, preferably human-kind. Once a human is attacked by a were-creature, it will likely become infected by lycanthrope and will become a were-beast, thus increasing the size of the pack, but not always. The book says that not all are susceptible to the disease. Those who cannot be turned are often devoured."

Theila seemed satisfied but Vlaad prodded further. "Will they fall to blades, arrows, and other conventional weapons or must we use special items such as silvered weapons as the legends indicate?"

Landermihl shrugged again. "The tome discusses much about the history of the druids and the first lycan, but does not give those details. I can assure you of their prowess. A were-creature is not a true lycan. It is a servant of the pack leader. It has the strength of ten men and the speed of a jungle cat. It can regenerate if not slain outright, but can be killed though I cannot say by what means. The pack leader, on the other hand, is always a true lycan and a most fearsome beast. It can call for the destruction of any of its pack members to weed out the weak and the unworthy, so its servants are loyal to the death or perhaps because of their fear of death. The pack leader can assume three forms unlike its were-creature servants. In addition to the humanoid form, (be it human, elf, or otherwise) and the half-man, half-beast form (be it a werewolf or otherwise) that the were-creature servants can assume, the pack leader can fully turn into the beast it has bonded with, just as a druid can shape-shift into a bear or cat for example. This additional aspect enables the lycan master to commune with other beasts and call them to his aid. A true lycan has many evil allies to help him survive."

Vlaad was finally satisfied. He said, "I think we

have a good idea what we are up against, but perhaps it would be wise to call upon those who specialize in this area."

Theila agreed saying, "The author seems to be the subject matter expert. Since you both know him and Pelion said he was due to return to this area soon, I think it might be in our best interest to contact him."

Vlaad and Landermihl smiled at the presumptuous woman, but agreed. The discussion was over so they moved back out of the great cathedral to the courtyard. Upon reaching the front gate, Vlaad sent a guard to find a herald willing to travel to Celes'tia. Moments later, a thin man wearing the robes of a wizard came forward with the guard. The man was obviously a spell wielder. He wore his long, black hair pulled back into a ponytail and carried a variety of pouches that no doubt held various items, wands, and magical ingredients for spell casting. He was not an old man as most wizards seemed to be, but instead seemed to be youthful and vigorous unlike the wizards with normally weak constitutions.

"Hail, Vlaad and Landermihl, heroes of the Battle of Forestedge and to you my lovely maiden," the thin fellow called.

"Well met," Vlaad returned, "you seem to know me, but forgive me as I do not know your name."

The wizard bowed deeply and said, "I am Maejis, Wizard of the Northern Tower and Master of Frost. I was summoned to assist you by the king himself."

"The king knows we are here and that we need assistance?" Theila asked in astonishment.

Landermihl smiled and explained, "He is a

good king with many powerful advisors. I am certain he knows many things we cannot begin to fathom. In particular, I am sure he has taken quite an interest in the arrival of his champion, and you, a warlock, who have arrived unannounced in his court to speak with me, his spiritual advisor, and commander of the Knights of Griffon's Peak."

Theila's respect for the king grew immensely. She felt small surrounded by so many powerful allies, but this area was not her forte. She had never been a diplomat, politician, or great leader. That was beyond her interest or training. She was satisfied to tag along until her skills were required. She was certain that she would be able to contribute more on the road—much more.

Maejis smiled politely and began to explain how he might be of service. Apparently, he was a frost mage, being of the Northern Tower, but he was trained in many arcane arts to include teleportation. He explained that each kingdom had an enchanted portal that could be used by a skillful wizard to move quickly across great expanses of land or sea. Wizards did not have the power to transport an army or similar force, but he could easily transport a small group of four or five, given that he had certain rare and expensive reagents required to open the magic gateway. In this case, the king's wizard had everything he needed to open the portal.

Vlaad asked if he could bring Da'Shar here immediately, but Maejis said no. Apparently, he could only take a group to other places; in this case, he could take them to Celes'tia and then back once they found Da'Shar. He motioned to Theila and mentioned that summoning others (often against their will) to a location was the work of warlocks.

Theila blushed and indicated that she had not mastered that level of conjuration yet, but that she would soon be able to. In the meantime, they agreed to make the trip to Celes'tia.

Maejis looked somewhat comical with his robes, ponytail, and youthful visage, but when he began casting the spell of teleportation, everyone took an unconscious step back. His hands worked in small concentric circles as he murmured the incantation. He drew forth a rune stone carved with the arcane sigil for travel and threw it into the air. It hovered in midair for a moment and then a fiery portal opened up before them. Through it the adventurers could see Celes'tia. Theila was the first to move through, completely at ease. This magic was, after all, part of her specialty. Vlaad and Landermihl paused with obvious mistrust for such things, but when Maejis prompted them to move quickly or be left behind, they stepped through. Maejis followed last, closing the portal behind him.

Teleportation was not as easy as merely stepping through a doorway and arriving at the destination regardless of how the portal may have looked. As the heroes stepped through the gate, magic whisked them through both space and time at an alarming rate. To anyone watching from either side, it appeared to be an instantaneous transition, but nothing could be farther from the truth. The portal was actually a corridor more so than a doorway, and each of the travelers felt as if they had fallen off of a high cliff upon entering. The lack of gravity and incredible acceleration twisted their guts in knots and then suddenly they were on the other side. The tremendous deceleration resulted in a feeling of vertigo and left the warriors queasy, but not the spell casters. For some reason, Maejis and

Theila had no ill effects. Perhaps it had something to do with understanding the flow of magic and not resisting its ebb and flow. Whatever the underlying cause, Theila smirked as Landermihl and Vlaad both heaved and then vomited as they arrived in Celes'tia. Maejis walked forward, stood beside Theila, and joined in her smirking.

CHAPTER 7
COMPANIONS

Celes'tia was just as beautiful as ever. It was late autumn and the leaves were turning brown and shades of gold. To say it was spectacular would be an understatement. It was a wide-eyed experience that often left outsiders speechless and fully entranced. The foursome had appeared inside the elven mage tower, which held the portal stone, but all around them they saw the influence of elven magic and nature. They collected themselves and moved down the stairs into the hub of the city where the glorious vision of natural perfection had its dumbfounding effect. Theila was paralyzed with awe; Vlaad was equally stunned though he had been to Celes'tia before. Landermihl and Maejis paused, smiled, and breathed deeply, hoping to take in the beauty bodily.

As they moved through the temple grounds and toward the merchant bazaar, Theila noticed that every manner of goodly race was present. She saw gnomes and dwarves shuffling through their goods while humans and elves bartered their own wares. While she took in the spectacle of the fair city a voice called out to her companions.

"Vlaad, Landermihl, over here…it is me, Rosabela," a sultry female voice chimed like sweet elven music.

Vlaad turned just in time to find himself in a full embrace of the elf maiden. He returned the warm greeting, but felt odd with Theila so close by. He extracted himself from the hug and blushed deeply. Thankfully another elf helped ease the situation. Rosabela's brother, Wavren, came up and also embraced the defender and then the paladin.

"It is good to see you all and so soon. It has been too long since last we parted company," Wavren said. "What brings you to Celes'tia?"

Landermihl answered saying, "We seek Da'Shar. There is a problem we hope he can help us with. Do you know where we might find him?"

Rosabela replied quickly, "He is soon to set out for the Eastern Kingdom. If we are quick we might catch him at the docks. Is it urgent?"

Vlaad remained silent, thinking that it was best to let Landermihl handle business with the elves. He felt strangely uncomfortable with both Rosabela and Theila so close. He remembered how amazing Rosabela had been in the battle with the undead and he was afraid his admiration of the stunning she-elf would be noticed by Theila. In his heart, he knew that no one would ever compare to Theila. No one would be more beautiful than or as close as he was to her, but he was smart enough to realize that women could be territorial, possessive, and jealous…ironically just like men. He felt confident that it would be wise to simply avoid drawing attention to himself.

Landermihl answered Rosabela with a nod and set out immediately for the docks. It was a quick hike from Celes'tia to SurCel'est Village where the harbor was located, but upon arrival they found that they had missed Da'Shar by several minutes. He was on his way to Bladerun Bay, the human port to the Eastern Kingdom. Nothing could be done now but try to meet him there.

Wavren made a point to formalize previously delayed introductions.

He said, "I am sure that the mission you are on is an important one, but now is as good a time as any for greetings."

He moved toward Theila and extended his hand as humans tended to do in a first meeting. He was dressed in woodland garb covering the finest chain mail armor in the realm. He smiled a charming smile that seemed to make his emerald green eyes sparkle like dwarven-cut gemstones.

He said, "I am Wavren of Celes'tia, Protector of the Vale, and Hunter of Clan Ursa. This is my sister, Rosabela."

Theila was intrigued by his rugged appearance. He had his long, black hair twisted in braids with feathers and beads that gave him a feral almost wildly handsome look. He was slightly taller than Vlaad and well muscled, though nowhere as dense as her human companion. He wore a dagger and reverse edged ax on his hips and carried a most unusual weapon that could only be one of the dwarven-engineered kind known as a blunderbuss. She had heard about them from her father.

She replied, "I am Theila of Westrun, Warlock of the Black Gate, and lifelong companion of Vlaad. Well met."

Maejis yawned, not at all interested in such pleasantries, but he managed to say, "Well met all. I am Maejis, Wizard of the Northern Tower and advisor to the King of Griffon's Peak."

Vlaad felt most uncomfortable with Theila so enchanted by the elven hunter, but she had mentioned they were companions. That eased his mind a bit.

Rosabela nudged her brother to the side and eagerly grabbed Theila's hand. She said, "It is good to meet you, Theila. You must forgive me for seeming so overjoyed at seeing Vlaad and Landermihl and then failing to make introductions with you, but our last battle was quite challenging and I have great love and respect for these two."

The warlock smiled and tried in vain to brush the long, brown tendrils of hair that constantly dangled across her eyes. She said, "No apology needed. I have known Vlaad all of his adult life and he commands the love and respect of many, though he would never admit to such things. I am certain Landermihl is no different."

Wavren took the opportunity to ask about the problems in the city of men. When the human companions hesitated to answer, he suggested a place with more privacy might be more suitable. Everyone nodded and they moved to the inn. Once inside, the party of six sat around a large table in the corner and began discussing The Legion and suspicions about their future alliance with the lycanthropes.

Wavren sat resolutely with a scowl on his face. He had heard legends of were-beasts and the stories of their lycan masters, but it was Rosabela who was greatly distressed at the news. She cared little about the assassin's guild but her deep, green eyes flashed with hatred at the mention of the lycans. Being a druid, she abhorred any creature that defied the will of nature and for one of her order to break his druidic vows lusting for dark power required immediate attention and action soon after. These were by far the worst of all threats to her order and the balance they swore to maintain. Her mentor, Da'Shar, had taught her long ago that oftentimes the service to nature as a druid would threaten to consume her. Self-sacrifice and hardship were required daily and when a druid was no longer able to serve honorably, the remaining members of the fallen druid's order would be charged with his eradication. Not unlike a pack of wolves, when the group was strong the order would survive, conversely when one became weak the others would tear the weak link apart to maintain the integrity of the pack. It was one of the oldest laws of nature.

Maejis sat calmly beside Landermihl and watched the scene unfold. He was the epitome of patience and serenity having spent his entire life studying both elemental magic and that of the arcane. He understood how the lust for power could easily corrupt even a righteous man to become evil. It was a struggle all wizards and warlocks faced sooner or later, particularly as the decay of old age set in and death could be seen approaching. It was the chief reason so many spell wielders turned to *lichdom*. He often considered the tales of great mages preparing their bodies for the transformation into that of a mummified yet living corpse. Immortality was hard to resist even at the cost of spending eternity as a fetid, rotting zombie. He assumed living an immortal life as a were-creature would be only slightly different than that of a lich. In many ways, there were definite advantages, but he kept his thoughts private as few would understand.

As the companions concluded the meeting, the elves decided that they must join in the quest to prevent the assassin's guild from joining the lycan pack and seek to destroy the abomination that was the pack leader. The humans knew the lycans were a threat, but the assassin's guild had long been a thorn in the side of the King of Griffon's Peak and would become unstoppable if they made the lycans allies. The resulting party may have had varying motivations but in the end, they had the same mission.

Rosabela announced, "We must find Da'Shar. He has the wisdom and experience we need to fight these villains. We will be fighting blindly without his guidance."

Wavren agreed and added, "Da'Shar is a powerful ally. My own mentor, Gaedron of Dragonforge, would be a fine addition to the team as well. I will send word to him to meet us in Griffon's Peak."

Landermihl concluded the meeting saying, "We will have a fine team with two hunters, two druids, a wizard, a warlock, a defender, and a paladin. May our enemies tremble before our righteous fury."

Vlaad felt confident that the group would be a powerful one, but he wondered if they would prevail against the cunning and deadly assassin's guild combined with werewolves. It was a challenge he would gladly face, but his heart longed to bring his nemesis, Gorka Darkstorm, to justice.

Maejis cleared his throat and said, "Are we ready to move back to Griffon's Peak? If so, I am prepared to open the portal."

The others agreed and the wizard began his arcane invocations. Just as before, the mage murmured the words in some ancient tongue and moved his hands in an ever-widening circular pattern until the portal opened. On the other side stood the mage tower, but just as before, the gut-wrenching experience through space and time was not as simple as it looked. Upon arrival, Rosabela, Maejis, and Theila seemed unaffected by the mystic torment that had Vlaad, Landermihl, and now Wavren bent over heaving.

Vlaad wiped the long line of saliva from his mouth and mumbled something about taking the long way from now on. Landermihl said nothing, but tried to recover his dignity in silence. Wavren was shaking violently on all fours as he tried to recover from the vertigo and nausea. The spell casters made every effort not to stare or giggle at the mighty warrior types who had been all but incapacitated by the trip.

Maejis called to a young steward in the mage tower. When the boy came over, he whispered instructions to him and later explained that the adventurers would be staying in the royal inn close to the mage quarter of the city. Room and board were to be provided at the expense of the king and no luxury would be spared. Upon arrival at the inn, each of the companions was escorted to their room by an entourage of servants. Armor and weapons were taken by the royal armorers for polishing and sharpening. Personal gear and clothing was taken by the royal launderers for cleaning and pressing. The females were taken into the hot spring baths by young maidens for every manner of care from bathing to massaging to painting of fingernails and toenails. The males were escorted to adjacent steam rooms and then bathing pools for their own needs, though they were not nearly as pampered as the females. After nearly two hours of relaxing care, the heroes were rejoined in the common room of the royal palace to await an audience with the king, but other pressing matters demanded his attention and the meeting was delayed. It took nearly two days for the king to grant them an audience, but the group was well entertained during the wait.

Theila and Rosabela had become very familiar during their time in Griffon's Peak, having shared many stories beginning with the pampering session, which they were still chatting about days later as they were in awe of their treatment. Wavren, Vlaad, Landermihl, and Maejis had enjoyed the cultured respite, but were more interested in the coming meeting with the Sovereign of Griffon's Peak. They discussed politics and other problems throughout the realms.

Wavren, having been used to living in the outdoors with his bear companion, was feeling a bit out of place. He enjoyed a bath as much as any man or elf, but the extent of the treatment was beyond excessive in his opinion. He chalked it up to cultural differences between humans and elves and wondered what would be next? In Celes'tia, a great feast would be in order and then business would follow, but he doubted that these things would happen in the city of men.

"Tell me," Wavren began, "does the king treat all of his guests in this manner?"

Rosabela and Theila paused to hear the answer as did Vlaad and Landermihl. All eyes fell to Maejis who had coordinated the gathering for the king.

Maejis spoke softly saying, "The king is aware of the very real threat that we will soon be asked to investigate and ultimately destroy. He does not wish to undervalue the gathering of such formidable allies for this mission nor does he wish to seem less than hospitable to those who willingly put themselves in harm's way for the good of Griffon's Peak."

Landermihl nodded in agreement and added, "My friends, we will likely face the most cunning of enemies in the assassin's guild as well as the most vicious of enemies in the lycan pack. No doubt our good king wishes to be rid of such enemies that are pestilent in nature to his fine kingdom. I would expect that if he is taking time to meet with us personally, then he sees this mission as one of epic proportions. I am honored to serve in this capacity as I am certain you all are as well."

Once again, Theila felt small and out of place among the great heroes, but she smiled and remained silent knowing that her place was beside her eternal companion, Vlaad. She was comforted in knowing that as a team they were magnificent and inseparable. She wondered if the same could be said for Wavren and Rosabela or even Landermihl and Maejis. No, she was certain that no pair of heroes could compare to the connection she had with Vlaad nor could they match the power she and Vlaad brought to the group.

In response to Landermihl, Wavren spoke on behalf of the elves. He said, "Rosabela and I have fought in our homeland against many foes, but none such as these. We recognize that their growth in the Eastern Kingdom will likely spread into the Western Kingdom if left unchecked. It is likely that this group may have originated in the west and actually spread here in fact, so we are also honored to serve as representatives of the elven nation and as Protectors of the Vale among our human brothers."

As if on cue the outer doors opened and in stomped a rugged dwarf accompanied by a tall and fearsome elf. The dwarf was clad in animal skins covering magnificent dwarven chain mail armor. He carried twin glimmering blue axes on his hips and held a cunning weapon of dwarven engineering, some knew as a blunderbuss, but the word *gun* was more common to humans. The elf held only a staff but was clad in leather armor that had to be dragon skin of some sort by the way it undulated in a serpent-like fashion. It was likely just as impenetrable and unrestrictive as dragon's hide. In spite of the rarity of the armor he wore, the elf's headdress was even more intriguing. It was a protective helmet, face guard, and gorget made from the head of a beast. It gave the elf the feral appearance of a great black cat.

Rosabela jumped up and ran into the arms of the approaching elf. She said, "Da'Shar, I have missed you so. It is wonderful to see you here; did you know we were looking for you?"

Before the druid could answer the dwarf said, "Good news be travlin' fast 'round 'ere lass."

Da'Shar smiled as he held his student at arm's length looking deep into her emerald orbs. He said, "You are indeed a sight for these old eyes. I have missed you child. As Gaedron mentioned, good news travels fast. We were enroute to Griffon's Peak for business when we were magically invited to this meeting."

Wavren walked up to shake his mentor's hand, but the old hunter hauled him in like a big fish at the end of a short line and embraced him as a father. "It be a good thing ta see ya 'gain boyo." He paused for a moment and held Wavren at arm's length not unlike Da'Shar and Rosabela, but his look was not one of good tidings. He crinkled up his nose and said, "What in da name o' Moradin is dat smell lad? Ye been paradin' 'round wit' a bunch o' old women?"

The elven hunter said, "The smell is an amazing invention called soap. Although I spend a great deal of time in the wild, a good bath is not unwelcome from time to time."

The dwarf smiled and winked saying, "Well ye might be as fine a hunter as I ever did train, but ye canna deny being an elf no matter how ye try ta be dwarf-like."

Da'Shar whispered, "Thank goodness!" in Rosabela's ear, but everyone heard anyway, creating a round of laughter at the surly dwarf's expense. The dwarf ignored it all.

Vlaad and Landermihl came forward and greeted the newcomers. It was a grand reunion of heroes from the Battle of Forestedge, except for Theila who again felt somewhat left out and of course Jael'Kutter was not present. The warlock began to think that she might never forgive Vlaad for asking her to remain behind during the last adventure. She took a deep breath, stood up, and introduced herself to Da'Shar and Gaedron. Maejis followed her lead and before long introductions were complete and they were left again awaiting His Majesty, the king.

Perhaps twenty more minutes passed before the king's herald came through the massive double doors separating the common room from the corridor leading to the king's audience chamber.

The herald called in a powerful, tenor voice, "His Royal Majesty King Xorren Kael, Sovereign of Griffon's Peak and Regent of Dae'gon will see you now. Please follow me."

The companions stood up and filed in one behind the other. Maejis was first in line, being familiar with the etiquette expected by the human king. The others followed his lead and showed great respect as they proceeded down the corridor and into the audience chamber. Maejis moved to the far left and the others took up standing positions, each beside a high-backed chair, in a semi-circle from left to right in front of the great king. When all had taken their positions, the great double doors closed and Maejis took a knee. Like dominoes, each adventurer to his right followed suit. When all were kneeling, the great king stood and welcomed his guests.

"Welcome to Griffon's Peak and the hall of heroes," he began. "This fortress has long been the home to those who have lived their lives in defense of the good people of the Eastern Kingdom of Dae'gon just as each of you serve to protect the goodly races. You are here as my guests and you honor me with your courageous service. Please rise and sit comfortably. You are among friends here."

The party of heroes followed as Maejis stood and moved into the seat to his right. Each of the ten took note that King Xorren Kael was dressed in the traditional royal fashion of human kings having great finery and perfectly tailored attire. His long robe was a deep blue silken fabric trimmed in a pure white fur from the northlands, probably one of the great cats of that region. His tunic was black and billowy as were his pants, which were tucked into his shining black boots. A great golden belt encircled his waist, which was accompanied by matching golden bracers around his muscular forearms. A thick, single-banded, golden diadem rested on his prominent brow restraining his heavy auburn hair. He wore a mustache and neatly trimmed goatee that framed his broad human features. He fit the part of king perfectly.

"My advisors tell me that you seek both the assassin's guild and the lycan pack. Both have been troublesome to the region separately, but I am sure you can imagine the chaos they would cause if united in purpose," the king said in his melodic baritone voice.

Da'Shar and Gaedron looked at each other with confusion, having arrived late and finding themselves less than fully informed of the situation.

Da'Shar's normally stoic, angular features became somehow more sharp and serious at the mention of the lycan pack. It was no surprise that he was greatly disturbed by the news. He despised any abomination of nature but lycans were a perversion of druid magic on top of being evil creatures delighting in the destruction of anything good or beautiful. Gaedron crossed his burly arms over his barrel-like chest and scowled foully. He was no elf, but as a Protector of the Vale and a master hunter, his duty required him to seek out and destroy any such evil beings that could not be brought to justice. Needless to say, he was certain neither lycan nor assassin would surrender willingly. It was all the same to him anyway.

Vlaad stood up and immediately gained the full attention of the audience. He said, "Good King and my fellow heroes, I have spent the better part of my life tracking down The Legion of assassins. This organization is rooted deeply within the strata of Griffon's Peak and cannot be easily purged, much like the rotting flesh of leprosy. If we remove part by blade or fire, the host suffers greatly and often times the disease remains. It is a plague of society that can only be destroyed by seeking out the leadership which is its source of strength. If the leadership becomes intertwined with the lycans, they will become even more powerful individually, not to mention increasing their number as an organization. I pledge my honor and my life to bring about their end. Duty is second only to justice."

Theila smiled and said, "I am with Vlaad in this endeavor. The enemies of Vlaad are my enemies as well."

Rosabela stood as Vlaad returned to his seat. She was quite the opposite in appearance to the defender, being more a delicate butterfly by comparison, but she was no less imposing than the powerful, rugged warrior. She said, "I know little about the assassin's guild, but they seem to be a parallel threat with the lycans, who are no less infectious and no less difficult to remove. They are more of a literal disease than a figurative one. Their bite spreads a blood infection that not only turns the victim into a vicious beast, but it also compels the victim to join the lycan pack or die. None are safe as long as they roam freely."

Da'Shar nodded in agreement but remained silent, having nothing more to add and being very impressed by the commanding presence his student projected. He thought that she would make a fine mentor one day when his time was done. "I am well pleased with this one," he said to himself.

Wavren spoke next, "I am not familiar with these lycans or assassins but if they can be tracked and slain then I will serve alongside my sister and any who pursue these villains."

It was Gaedron's turn to nod and feel pride in the young elf who he had trained from the beginning. He had much to add unlike Da'Shar and said, "Aye lad, both lycan and assassin can be tracked an' slain but de trick is how. Few know de 'istory o' de lycan pack o' Celes'tia or dat me an' Da'Shar sought out an' killed da las' pack leader."

Da'Shar scowled even more than before, but he remained silent as the dwarf continued.

Gaedron continued, "Ya see, me an' long ears here (referring to Da'Shar), got called ta track down and bring a rogue druid to justice b'fore da druidic council. I'm fer gussin' dat was some four o' five hunnerd years ago. I was but a lad back den, likin' yerself boyo. Anyway, me an' Da'Shar spent nearly all winter lookin' fer da pack leader, who happened ta be one o' Da'Shar's former apprentices. He was an elf who had lost 'is way, jus' likin' the old tales go. When we finally caught up ta him, he had become obsessed wit' pow'r and was busy buildin' himself a lycan army. Da'Shar was thinkin' to lit'rally bring him back alive to face da druids. I had me own ideas not much wantin' ta fight more 'an a hunnerd wolf-men so I set ta stitchin' him up wit' quarrels from me crossbow, no blunderbuss back then," he said off handedly.

"Da'Shar was forced ta join in de fight as a result. He shape-shifted inta a bear an' went ta work. At any rate, de pack leader, who called himself Lord Carnage, was no match fer us. He took off an' finally evaded us by diving off'n a cliff. I fig'red him dead, but Da'Shar knew bett'r. When we finally caught up ta him, he had turned back inta 'is elf form an' lay dyin' on da riv'r banks below. I fig'red our work was done, but he said somethin' I'll ne'er ferget afore he passed on to de next world. He said de soul o' Lord Carnage was eternal."

Da'Shar was no longer scowling. He had a sad look on his face and was looking down as if the story was playing over and over in his mind. He didn't look up, but said, "It is true; Lord Carnage was the first of the lycans. He was once my apprentice and a fine druid of the grove, but he was also my younger brother, So'larian. He was my ultimate failure. I failed to prepare him as a druid, I failed to teach him as a mentor, and I was unable to bring him back alive as the druidic council ordered. My failures have cost many elves their lives and now the plague of my failures has taken the lives of humans as well."

The room was silent for a long while. Landermihl broke the silence saying, "You cannot be held responsible for another's choices, but as a master druid, your responsibility was to your student. I have read the book you wrote on the matter and I am certain you have fulfilled your duty. The pack leader is no elf. He is human and though he calls himself by the same name, he cannot be your brother, So'larian. We will unite against this one and end his evil just as you and Gaedron did before."

"No, there is more," Da'Shar interrupted. "The essence of a druid is an eternal thing once bound to nature. It is the source of druidic power and the reason why So'larian died so readily these many years ago. He transferred his life essence into another using the lycanthropic disease as a medium. He may wear the appearance of a human, but he has only become the proverbial wolf in sheep's clothing. I have known this day would come since that day he spoke his last words. It is why I penned the book you read and many others like it given to each of the goodly races. I must bring him back alive so that the druidic council can exorcise his spirit from the immortal shell he now wears or he will simply find another host to transfer his soul into and the cycle will begin anew."

Wavren, being astute in observations and more than a mere beast tracker, assembled the final picture and said, "This is the missing piece of the puzzle I have long been seeking. Da'Shar and Gaedron were once more than allies, they were close friends. Lord Carnage was the wedge that separated you so long ago and it has only been recently that these old wounds have been cleansed and mended. It is why Da'Shar seems so dissatisfied with the methods of hunters. It is why Gaedron, being a dwarf, was welcome as an elf among the Protectors of the Vale."

Rosabela interrupted saying, "Da'Shar prefers the windwraith form to that of the bear, Gaedron prefers the blunderbuss to a crossbow, and how could Lord Carnage survive the attacks of both Da'Shar and Gaedron? The story doesn't make sense."

Wavren jumped back into the conversation. He said, "I am willing to bet that Da'Shar was not simply using the bear form by coincidence back then. I noticed that Gaedron never once mentioned his *ally*, Ol' Blackmaw or any other summoned bear that is as much a part of him as his blunderbuss is now. Finally, I bet there is more to killing a lycan than shooting it with a crossbow."

Gaedron smiled broadly and said, "Aye boyo, ye be right. I been knowin' Da'Shar since a'fore I had a beard. We were more 'n good friends, we were brothers in spirit an' purpose. As adults, we were allies working as a team not unlike yerself an' yer own ally, Stonetalon. Ye might know dat I was trained by Daenek Torren to become the first Hunter o' Clan Ursa. I was da first hunter an' Da'Shar was me ally to fight as a cohort pair. A perfect blend of melee and ranged combat we were, but when we failed ta bring back So'larian or Lord Carnage as he calls 'imself, Da'Shar an' I went our separate ways. Da'Shar chose the path of the windwraith, relying on stealth and speed having lost me ranged firepow'r an' I became a beast tamer ta substitute the loss of his front line fighting power. When I found me first ally, Ol' Blackmaw's great-great-great-grand patriarch, I turned away from da elven ways and returned ta me own heritage. I crafted me first blunderbuss soon after. As fer killin' a true lycan, ye be right ag'in. It ain't so easy as I thought. Jus' shootin' it or hittin' it can hurt or slow 'em down, but endin' its life be another matter."

The king raised his finger indicating that he had something to add. He said, "I have information about fighting lycan-kind that may be useful. The werewolf type can be killed by sword, bow, or magic though they regenerate at an incredible rate and their sheer ferocity makes these methods costly. Few swordsmen can stand toe to toe long enough to strike a killing blow. Only the precise shot though the heart or head by a skillful archer will bring one down, which is nearly impossible given their speed and ability to dodge in combat. Finally, these beasts are resistant to all but the most powerful magic and few wizards are able to cast quick enough to avoid being disemboweled in the process. The pack leaders, or true lycans as you call them, are enigmatic. They prefer to send their minions into the fray and escape to live on and spread the disease so that the pack never dies. My reports indicate that they are stronger, faster, and more cunning than their lesser werewolf minions."

Maejis took the opportunity to add, "This is why we have all been summoned. Vlaad and Landermihl are trained and experienced in holding the enemy at bay. Vlaad does this as a shield specialist and Landermihl with his protective and healing spells. Gaedron and Wavren are by reputation, the greatest marksmen in the realm. Theila, Da'Shar, Rosabela, and I bring the abyssal, elemental, natural, and eldritch spell-casting skills to the fight."

King Xorren Kael continued, "Although the lycan threat has been the focus of the conversation, do not underestimate The Legion. This organization covets the lycan's power and in particular, their near immortality. They will use stealth, trickery, bribery, murder, and deceit to get it and neither fear nor death will slow their advance."

Theila stood up and asked the final question, "Where shall we begin?"

Maejis replied, "The assassins seek the lycans. We must find the lair of the lycan pack before they do. Given that The Legion is an organization based on information trafficking, they have a distinct advantage and a head start. There is a man who has lived his life passing information to the king though. He knows how to find the lair of the lycan pack and will guide you."

Theila asked, "Well, who is this informant?"

"Am I late," a very familiar tenor voice sang out.

Theila turned and saw her father entering the room under guard of a dozen swordsmen. She was overjoyed to see him and ran into his loving embrace.

Each of the other heroes knew of the famous tale spinner and traveling minstrel, but none knew he was employed by the king himself. Of all the titles to have, Secret Agent of the King of Griffon's Peak was the most unexpected, yet somehow it seemed to suddenly make perfect sense. Being a bard was the perfect cover and enabled the secret agent free access to nearly every city and town in the realm.

"Don, the Bard of Westrun, will be your guide," Maejis said as a matter of introduction.

Curtiss Robinson

CHAPTER 8
ALLIANCE

Deep within the high, roughhewn walls of Dek'Thal, city of orcs and hub of the Bloodcrest Forces, another meeting was taking place. Several cowled humans, under close watch of a dozen massive orc guards, sat around a long, rectangular table awaiting arrival of the newly promoted High Commander of the Bloodcrest Forces. They sat in silence, not trusting the orc soldiers with even the minutest details of their purpose for requesting an audience with their former guild master. Many shared the same thoughts, however. They wondered if Gorka Darkstorm had ever truly abdicated his position as the most powerful crime lord in the human underworld. This thought persisted as they considered how quickly he had climbed through the orcish ranks into his current position. It was particularly unusual given that he was a half-orc, not a full blood. There was always great enigma surrounding the cunning half-orc; some say it was his stock in trade.

After a short wait, High Commander Gorka Darkstorm simply entered the council chambers and sat down among the delegation of assassins from The Legion. There was no pomp and circumstance unlike the human world. There was no herald to announce his introduction. In fact, there were no personal bodyguards surrounding him at all times. He even waved away the orc soldiers who had been watching the small troupe of humans since their arrival in Dek'Thal. It was a testament to Gorka's

confidence and a throwback to his simple
upbringing. He was self-reliant. He wanted no help.
He needed no help. Each of the killers present was
prepared to pay well-deserved respect given he was
perhaps the deadliest assassin and now commander
of the most powerful group of all the Bloodcrest
Forces.

In perfect common dialect, the high
commander said, "Hail and well met to you all.
Welcome to Dek'Thal, home of orcs and
headquarters of the Bloodcrest Forces."

The delegation of humans noticed that he
commanded perfect inflection and enunciation of
the common trade language of humans. He was no
mindless brute. In fact, he appeared to be an
educated leader, something few orcs or half-orcs
could claim. In unison the six hooded assassins
stood and said, "Hail to The Shade, Blight of the
Living, Gorka Darkstorm, high commander of orcs,
and former guild master of The Legion."

It was tiresome for Gorka to hear title after
title, but some cultural aspects of the human nation
could not be avoided. He accepted the hollow praise
knowing that any one of these killers would gladly
plant their blade in his back if given the
opportunity. He smiled knowing that any such
attempt would fail at the cost of the attacker's life.
Gorka motioned for a servant to bring a variety of
succulent meats, thick bread, blocked cheese, and
deep, black ale.

"Please sit and partake of the good food and
powerful drink of my homeland," Gorka asked
pleasantly, but with such piercing eye contact that
each man felt compelled to eat and drink or be
immediately slain in spite of their training not to do
so. Rule number one for an assassin was never trust

food and drink that could so easily be poisoned by treacherous cohorts. Each man took a small portion of each item but none immediately ingested any.

Gorka smiled and said, "Some habits are hard to break I see. Consider this. If I wanted any of you dead, you would have been torn apart long before you made it into my fortress."

The men stared blankly not knowing what to say to the sheer audacity Gorka displayed. In a huff, Gorka rolled his eyes and leaned forward to prepare his own meal as a show of good faith. As he began eating, the humans slowly followed his lead. There was silence for many minutes. Each assassin was focused on his plate, but none ever truly lost sight of the half-orc in their peripheral vision. They all noticed that he never took his eyes off of them either.

Finally, Gorka broke the silence. He asked, "So what brings you to Dek'Thal? Are you looking to join the Bloodcrest Forces? We don't normally allow humans in the Orc Army, but we might have work for you in the infiltration department."

The assassin to Gorka's right stopped eating and replied, "Master Darkstorm, we have come with information for you. The Legion is planning to…expand and we thought it would be prudent to discuss this matter with you as a formal courtesy."

"I see," was the only reply given to include a complete vacancy of body language.

The contingent of assassins shifted nervously in their chairs. In most meetings with such powerful leaders, The Legion often threw a small bit of information out and waited for a telling response. Many times that response was met with some form of consent or acknowledgement. Sometimes it was met with hostility. The response, be it words, tone, or otherwise often set the stage for the rest of the discussion. Since Gorka had intentionally left a void, the other assassins were unsure how to proceed. The leader of the six assassins, a man called *Cutter* for obvious reasons, was particularly dumbfounded as to how he should continue. The lack of sound was maddening, but the assassins were disciplined. None gave any indication of breaking the silence until they knew how to respond without giving away more than they had been instructed to.

Gorka reveled in the game, but he decided to prompt the leader to continue more out of boredom and a lack of time required to fully engage the group than any real interest. He said, "I know that you are planning to form an alliance with the lycan pack near Shadowshire. Their leader would be a powerful ally or a deadly adversary. It is risky business. In fact, one of my lieutenants has already made contact with the one known as Lord Carnage with a similar proposal from the orcs. His body was torn apart and sent to me in pieces. I can only assume that he prefers to renegotiate before accepting my offer."

The humans went from a look of sheer shock that Gorka knew so much already, to one of sincere respect. None doubted that Gorka would have the alliance or the pack leader's head. Most telling of all was the nonchalant approach to the matter. Gorka was not personally offended that his lieutenant had been slain. Most likely, he had anticipated the move and had willingly sent the poor underling to his death. This was accepted as the way of things among orcs and sometimes in the assassin's guild.

Cutter nodded and tried to regain his

composure. He said, "If you have already sent an orc to bring this were-creature into your organization, and you knew that The Legion was doing the same, then I assume you approve of this move and will not stand against the expansion, especially since we are long-standing allies."

Gorka frowned and said, "No."

Cutter looked around at his fellow assassins and then back to Gorka. He wanted to ask what Gorka meant by simply saying no. Gorka could see the confusion building among the humans. He elected to wait for a few minutes to see if they were capable of figuring out the big picture. It was evident and simple in his mind, but the delegation of humans was unable to get past two obstacles that clouded their understanding. Their own preconceived notions about Gorka and foolish overconfidence in their own superiority were their weaknesses. It was tough for a human, particularly a human assassin of the dreaded guild known as The Legion, to concede that an orc or even worse, a half-orc, might be controlling the entire situation like some god-like puppet master pulling their strings. As each man discovered the truth on his own, Gorka smiled truly reveling in each of their expressions.

The six assassins came to know that the simple answer *no* did not indicate that Gorka disapproved of the alliance. Neither did it indicate that he stood against The Legion if they chose to expand. It meant that the humans were acting as he had directed through cunning manipulations. He had set up the entire ploy to have The Legion form an alliance with the lycans and ultimately do his bidding, since the orcs could not. Every detail down to the arrival of the delegation of assassins had been

Gorka's work. The final revelation was that Gorka was undoubtedly the power behind The Legion.

There remained one question. Each man wondered why. Why had the former guild master gone through such lengths? Gorka took the opportunity to explain the details as he read that very question on each man's face.

He said, "The lycans will not accept orcs into their pack. I do not care why they have discriminated in this manner. I simply require their alliance and that is where the humans of Griffon's Peak, specifically The Legion, come into play. Your race will bridge the gap that orcs could not. This will be for our purposes. I have set the pieces in place and so the game is now ready to be played. Your presence here was a test to validate the secrecy of my intricate plans. I believe your ignorance of my role proves that even the greatest source of intelligence gathering in the realm does not suspect my involvement. This gives us the advantage. The alliance between the assassin's guild and the lycans will be known, but the secret alliance with the Bloodcrest Forces will be hidden. We now control the element of surprise and thus, the greatest element of power on the battlefield."

Each man nodded in agreement.

Gorka averted his gaze downward as he spoke again, "Sadly, I must ensure that advantage is maintained. Surprise is a function of secrecy as every assassin is taught from day one. None of my orc soldiers know or even suspect my involvement with the humans or the lycans. It is why I dismissed the guards when you arrived. None can be trusted with this information."

Cutter noticed that a long, bladed dagger had suddenly appeared in the half-orc's thick hand. He noticed the cold presence of death in the eyes of the master assassin as Gorka slowly looked up. The other assassins drew weapons, but Cutter did not. He was paralyzed with fear and knew that resistance would be futile against the demon standing before him. His last thought was a silent hope that the end would be painless and quick as The Shade came forward driving his dagger at the perfect upward angle under his sternum to pierce his heart. Darkness came quickly. It was a painless death, an answer to his godless prayers.

The other assassins were ready and formed a circle around the half-orc. They prepared to fight to the last, and hoped that even if a thousand orcs came, they might at least kill the one responsible for their deaths.

Gorka spoke in a bone-chilling tone, "Each assassin of The Legion is given a capsule of pure arsenic to be used as a final preventative measure against betraying the secrets of the organization. It is a measure to prevent those secrets from falling into the hands of those who stand against us. You must see that I am still in command of The Legion. You must realize that your duty now requires your death. You will die in service of the assassin's guild. Take the poison now and avoid the pain, agony, and disgrace that await your disobedience to my orders."

Two of the assassins drew the deadly capsules from hidden pockets without hesitation and swallowed the poison without another thought. Perhaps they chose death over the fear of pain their guild master promised or perhaps they simply followed the ingrained training The Legion had driven deep into their mind. Whatever the case, the arsenic acted quickly. A few convulsions later, both were dead.

Gorka spoke again. He said in a chilling voice, "And then there were three. So be it, but just for sport, you should know that a cunning assassin might find a secret trap door on the west wall that leads to an underground corridor. The corridor ends near a swift river. It is the only possible escape should you survive, but that is an enticement beyond your reach and I am the door between you and that prize. Now then… you have hope, let's see what you do with it."

The remaining three assassins were seasoned fighters with dozens of confirmed kills under their proverbial belts. Each was trained to find vital areas with sword, dagger, and bow. They felt confident that any three assassins of The Legion would be more than enough to kill one old, half-breed, has-been assassin, but Gorka was the guild master, past and present. He was the High Commander of the Bloodcrest Forces, a leader of fearsome orc warriors. He was infamous beyond any other assassin in the history of Griffon's Peak. He was The Shade…death incarnate. This would be far from an easy mark.

Gorka moved forward to engage a sword and dagger-wielding assassin. The human was smaller than Gorka, but solid in build and sure-footed. He managed to get his sword up in time to deflect the initial slashing attack but The Shade moved like lightning, shifted sideways, and kicked the assassin in the ribs. He fell backward with a gasp. The fiery pain in his side and sudden inability to breathe was enough to convince him that several ribs were broken. The blood frothing in his mouth indicated that his lung had been pierced by one of the shattered bones. He would die slowly and in agony as promised. Gorka never gave him a second thought knowing he was no longer a threat.

The remaining two moved in unison to attack the half-orc. The assassin to the right slashed with a dagger in each hand, narrowly missing Gorka just as the assassin to the left threw two small darts, both obviously tipped with poison. In a spinning flash of movement, The Shade evaded the darts and slashed up and then down across the wrists of the dagger-wielding attacker. Both tendons and arteries were severed leaving him unable to hold a weapon and likely to die a slow and agonizing death as promised. He fell to the ground in shock as his life poured out of the deep wounds onto the floor.

The dart-throwing killer quickly peddled backward and unleashed volley after volley of poisoned missiles. Several missed as a result of Gorka's uncanny ability to dodge, but three found their mark. Two darts stuck in Gorka's fine leather armor. One penetrated both Gorka's defenses and armor protection just under his left arm. The insidious toxin hit the bloodstream immediately and Gorka broke into a cold sweat as his large, black pupils dilated. The half-orc gritted his teeth, pulled a small vial from his belt, tore out the stopper with his teeth, and guzzled the contents. Although still shaky, the master assassin regained his fighting stance and motioned for the last attacker to come on. The dart thrower had expended every missile he had and was forced to draw a spiked mace from his belt. It was an unconventional weapon for an assassin, but deadly nonetheless. He circled for a moment, hoping the poison would outlast the anti-toxin.

Gorka took a deep breath and said, "Half-orcs are blessed with one true advantage humans always forget. We have the constitution of a lion. Next, understand that I have forgotten more about the science of toxins than you ever learned. If you add these together you get one pissed off killer who can't be slain with a poisoned dart! Now come on and finish it, if you have the guts."

The remaining assassin paused long enough to consider the other five dead and dying men on the floor. He took another moment to reconsider taking the poison. It was a second too long. Gorka darted across the floor slashing and stabbing at every possible angle in the blink of an eye. The mace-wielding human could never hope to dodge or block the whirlwind of death that consumed him. Not every strike hit, but far too many did. When the terrifying violence ended, he was alive, though just barely. He was blind and pain shot from nearly every part of his body. He realized that the master assassin had severed three fingers from his right hand, the hand that had been holding the mace. He would never grasp a weapon again. The tendons in his left shoulder were cut cleanly. That arm would never move on its own again. Both hamstrings had been sliced leaving him immobile. Finally, both eyes had been gouged out with surgical precision, yet somehow he was alive though perfectly incapacitated. Fear welled up in him like a spring of putrid black venom as he sensed The Shade was standing over him.

The assassin cursed Gorka, "You filthy half-breed son of a whore. Finish me! Finish me!"

The master assassin sat down heavily beside him still suffering from the poison in his body. He drew the arsenic capsule from the assassin's hidden pocket and said, "Perhaps the poison would be welcome right about now."

The desperate and suffering human said, "Yes, yes, fine; give it to me."

The half-orc smiled and said, "I won't break my promise. Your death will be slow, agonizing, and filled with disgrace due to you, but I am not without mercy. You can have the arsenic, but I won't give it to you so easily."

The blind and crippled assassin sensed Gorka moving beside him and then heard the tik…tik…tik across the room that could only be the sound of his pill bouncing across the stone floor.

"Now crawl like a maggot through the blood of your brothers to find your death. It will be challenging given your lack of sight, savaged legs, and useless shoulder, but I left you one good arm. Don't worry; I will tell you when you are close, just like a game children play. Oh and if you cry out or curse me again, I'll cut out your tongue for good measure," Gorka promised evilly.

The three grievously wounded humans died painfully, slowly, and without honor. It had been a slaughter and aside from the poisoned dart that had failed to kill the master assassin, Gorka had dispatched them all effortlessly.

Curtiss Robinson

CHAPTER 9
PREDATORS AND PREY

Don the Bard woke early on the day following the king's meeting with all of the adventurers. He was curious about their background and motives and how they would fare against the savage lycans and the most powerful underworld organization in the realm. He was particularly worried about the elves and the dwarf. As he considered the many things he knew for fact, he found himself methodically reviewing each hero in his mind.

Don knew Maejis fairly well from serving the king for countless years, and of course he knew Landermihl similarly. Both were veterans of combat and fully understood how best to meet any threat. Vlaad might as well have been his son-in-law or nephew given his relationship with his daughter Theila, so he had few concerns about him. As a pair, Theila and Vlaad were a powerful force having both melee and spell-casting aspects. They would probably be the core participants of the group. The elves and that dwarf were unknown to him for the most part. Of course he had heard of Gaedron, Da'Shar, Rosabela, and Wavren from the Battle of Forestedge, but the details were always sketchy in such a grand melee.

Don found himself wandering the halls as he mentally evaluated these mysterious outlanders in his mental framework. The bard walked past the guest rooms and noticed that Vlaad was already awake and exercising. He was moving with grace and power through the prearranged fighting movements unique to defenders. It always amazed him to see the warrior move like his old friend

Andar. It was as if Andar had never died, but merely become Vlaad given their similarities.

Theila was also awake and exercising, though not physically. She was memorizing spells and exercising her summoning powers. Don could tell that his daughter had called on a vile imp from the abyss instead of her powerful protector demon or the sultry and seductive succubus. The imp's high-pitched voice had a nerve-wracking effect on Don, not to mention the acrid smell of burning brimstone that was unmistakable and ever present when the imp was about. In spite of the innate danger Theila faced summoning demons, he was certain that she was quite capable of controlling them. After all, he had seen her in action dozens of times. She was amazing and he was proud of her.

Further down the hall Don came to the side-by-side rooms of the two hunters. Both Wavren and Gaedron were already awake and gone, probably outside where they felt most at home. He stepped past their dormitories and came to the last two rooms occupied by the elven druids. Da'Shar was sitting cross-legged on his bunk studying an ancient tome that was undoubtedly related to his mortal enemies, the lycans. The druid looked up as Don approached.

"Good morn, Don of Westrun. How did you sleep?" the elf asked.

"Very well thank you. I was wondering if you would speak with me about your companions," the bard asked respectfully.

"For certain," he returned, "what is it that you wish to know?"

Don found himself at a loss for words, which was quite unusual for a bard. He paused not wanting to simply reveal that he was uncertain regarding the four westlanders.

Da'Shar was a perceptive elf and quickly discerned the nature of Don's concerns from his body language. He closed the book and gave a disarming smile.

"You are the father of the one called Theila I am told. I have to assume that you are concerned for her safety in the upcoming mission, which brings you here to investigate our…qualifications as adventurers," Da'Shar stated simply.

Don blushed slightly and said, "I suppose that is the crux of the matter, but I do not mean to offend. I guess I am trying to plan ahead for the coming battles."

The druid tilted his head to one side quizzically indicating that if there was more, then the bard should share all concerns.

When the bard offered nothing more, Da'Shar said, "We do not know you or the other humans very well, though I have witnessed both Vlaad and Landermihl in battle. Both are courageous and skilled, particularly for the shorter-lived races, but this does not ease my mind concerning the talents or motivations of the humans in this adventure, but I am thankful for your willingness to fight nonetheless. I suppose I have left much to faith. I intuitively know that we will all fight well."

Don said, "I see, but I am not one for faith. I prefer to know the facts concerning what assets we have and any shortcomings as well."

The elf nodded in consent and said, "I suppose you might be interested to know that I have served as a Protector of the Vale and Druid of the Grove for most of my countless years of life. I am a healer, shape shifter, and spell caster by profession, just as Rosabela, my student and spirit daughter is. I probably know more about lycans than any other being in the realm, which should give us an advantage when we fight them. I do not know much about this assassin's guild you refer to as The Legion. I have to assume that they are well trained and well-resourced making them a cunning and deadly adversary. I will rely on my human companions to serve as the subject matter experts in this area."

Don was impressed. The elf had given him enough information to decide that having Da'Shar on the team would be a great asset. He asked, "What can you tell me about the others?"

The elf said, "The hunters are powerful front line fighters with great beasts at their command. Both are expert marksmen and skilled trackers such that no enemy, lycan or assassin, will evade us for long. I have known the dwarf for centuries and although we often disagree on procedures, I am certain he would die before allowing harm to come to his companions. The elven hunter is Rosabela's brother. He is an honorable warrior. I have not known him long, but rest assured that he is reliable and courageous. His only fault is that he has adopted many of his dwarven mentor's habits making him far less elven than dwarven for my tastes."

Don smiled seeing only reflections of good feelings from Da'Shar. He said, "Da'Shar, your love of the hunters and your druidic pupil speak volumes to me. I will leave you to your studies and I thank you for your words of comfort."

The druid nodded and went back to reading as Don left the room. He moved to the next room where he saw Rosabela. She was sitting in the exact same position as her master. She was reading an elvish book that appeared to contain the science of alchemy.

Rosabela did not look up from the book, but simply said, "Do you require more facts than my mentor provided already?"

Don felt again somewhat awkward but managed to put on his most charming smile and say, "No, I think I have enough facts, but I wanted to wish you a good morning."

Rosabela continued to read and said, "Thank you, and good morning to you."

Don was unaccustomed to being excused and so quickly ignored. In his business he had to be a masterful conversationalist in order to gather information. His brilliant smile and charming demeanor usually did the trick to get things going, but this one was immune to his charisma. It intrigued him of course so he simply changed tactics and continued.

"I can see that you are engrossed in your study of potions so I will not bother you further, but if you find a few moments at some point, I would like to hear your thoughts on the lycans," the smooth bard remarked as he turned to leave the room.

The heavy book closed with a snap and the bard knew he had the elf-maid's attention. He paused and then turned as she began to speak.

Rosabela spoke in a low and firm voice, "The lycans are a perversion of nature as I am sure you know. They are consumed by the lust for power and have traded their souls and twisted their bodies for it. I am not surprised that it is the race of men who now serve the pack leader. The shorter-lived races often spend their few years in a futile pursuit of power only to die and be forgotten; however, these abominations now have near immortality.

Ironically, they serve as slaves to the pack leader who holds their lives in his hand. I can tell you this; if they had known that the costs of their beastly power and longevity were slavery and a never-ending hunger, they would not have so eagerly become werewolves."

"I see," the bard began, "but was it not an elf who was the first true lycan? I believe it was a druid of your order was it not?"

The lovely elven druid felt her blood boil for a moment. Her deep green eyes were bright with an inner fire that was both fury and discipline. Don wasn't sure if she was angry at him for placing blame on her druidic order or simply angry that she had to accept his words as the truth, but there could be no doubt that she was livid with rage.

The anger passed and Rosabela smiled a beguiling smile that could have easily enthralled Don had he been caught unaware, but he was a bard and an agent of the king. He could not so easily be charmed. Then she spoke.

"Don of Westrun, most famous of bards, and servant of the King of Griffon's Peak, you play a dangerous game. I can see that you are a man of cunning and great intellect. These are fine traits that I admire in a man. I understand that you seek to weigh and measure all of us so that you can pass on our strengths to your king. It is a noble thing that you do for your people. I find it...appealing...even...enticing," the she-elf purred as she shifted her weight to one side revealing a perfectly sculpted leg through a long slit in her beautiful elven dress and then, like a unicorn in the forest, the lovely enticement disappeared as she shifted her weight again.

Don was well past his fiftieth winter but still

felt desire and the urges of all men. He found himself captivated by the druid, which seemed odd yet perfectly natural. For a moment, he wanted nothing more than to rush over and embrace the lovely elf-maid. She was alluring and perhaps the most beautiful woman he had ever seen. As he considered these things, he realized that she had moved close to him and was barely inches away.

Rosabela slipped behind him and whispered in a sweet and promising voice, "You have great influence over others with brilliant words and crafty manipulations, but I am of nature and have an understanding of base desires at the most primitive, animalistic level."

Don nodded in total agreement as the seductive druid brushed her lips gently against his ear when she spoke. It sent a shiver down his spine. He turned to face her, hoping to pull her in close for a kiss, but found that she was gone. He spun around in confusion and found her sitting in the same place and in the same position as he had found her. She was holding the alchemy book just like before acting as if nothing had happened. For a moment, he thought he had imagined the whole thing, but how could that be?

Rosabela looked up for a moment as said, "That will be all. Now if you will excuse me, I must continue my studies."

Don stepped backward and turned to leave. He found Da'Shar standing right in front of him. The elf did not look happy.

"Excuse me please," Don said in a shaky voice as he tried to move past.

Da'Shar spoke sternly, "I feel compelled to advise you not to play mind games with a druid, particularly that one in there," he said pointing at

Rosabela. "She has a gift you see. Her will is indomitable and she has amazing powers of persuasion, but I guess now you know that first hand. One last thing…she is a shape shifter and if she wanted to, she could have taken the form of a powerful bear and torn you to pieces for simply invading her privacy."

The bard saw no jest in the eyes of Da'Shar. He glanced back at the lithe young elf and realized that he had learned a valuable lesson at the cost of his humility. Enigmatic druids are better left alone rather than being interrogated.

Don nodded and said, "My thanks for your advice and my sincere apologies for disturbing your student."

Da'Shar stepped aside and let the man pass without another word. As Don left, he moved into the room where Rosabela was innocently reading her book. He marveled at her peaceful demeanor and reveled in the knowledge that she was his student. One day, she would probably sit at the head of the druidic council.

Rosabela paused for a moment and said, "He deserved it."

Da'Shar replied in his fatherly tone, "Perhaps, but we need him. Let's try to work on a little more tolerance."

"Yes, Da'Shar, I am certain you're right," she said half-heartedly.

The elder druid walked out as Rosabela giggled mischievously. Da'Shar shook his head and smiled.

***

A light jingling sounded, which signaled breakfast was being served. Word spread quickly throughout the palace as foreign dignitaries, high-ranking officials, and local noblemen came to the feast hall to eat. Among the group were the eight heroes and Don the Bard. They sat across from each other ironically separated by the table in much the same way their two continents were separated by the Great Sea. Ever the diplomat, Don came in and sat beside the king.

The druids shared the belief that he had probably just briefed the regent on the latest discoveries. Rosabela smiled at the thought and Da'Shar spared a quick half-smile at his expense as well. Landermihl, Maejis, Vlaad, and Theila had no idea what the joke was, but protocol demanded that they remain silent in spite of wanting to ask.

When the king sat down at the head of the table, the morning feast began. As expected, the delicate elves ate mostly fruit and some nuts while the humans ate large slabs of bacon, eggs poached with a white sauce, fresh bread with creamy butter, and spicy sausage links. Gaedron ate more than a dozen of the thick sausage links and half again that amount in eggs. It was a shocking spectacle to the noblemen, but they said nothing.

After a few minutes, the king stood and said, "It is good to see everyone this morning. I must assume the food is acceptable and by your gracious nods it must be so. This is good, for no one should undertake missions of great importance on an empty stomach."

Many of the noblemen cheered saying, "Hear! Hear!" in unison.

The heroes wondered what mission the nobles were about to undertake.

King Xorren Kael spoke again, "As many of you know, we are besieged by treachery here in the kingdom of Griffon's Peak as well in this very city, your city. Monsters and villains walk about with courage in the light of day, knowing that few have the power to stop their evil from spreading or even dare to oppose them. Well, today is a first day of many days to come where wicked and foul beasts will find their wretched work at an end."

He paused long enough for the nobles to cheer again.

The king began introductions. "I have assembled the finest team of heroes the realms have to offer. From the west, far across the Great Sea, I am proud to welcome four Protectors of the Vale: Da'Shar and Rosabela of Celes'tia—two powerful shape shifters, spell wielders, and healers belonging to the ancient society of druids; Wavren of Celes'tia and Gaedron of Dragonforge are hunters, beast wardens, and the finest of marksmen in the land."

The four heroes stood, bowed slightly, and returned to their seats as the noblemen clapped and cheered with fervor.

King Kael spread his arms and patted the air to calm the clapping and cheering. He said, "And from the east I submit four gallant heroes who need little introduction. Vlaad of the Blackridge Steppes, Champion of Griffon's Peak, and warrior by trade accompanied by Theila of Westrun, mistress of the arcane, who are paired with Maejis and Landermihl, high councilors of Griffon's Peak and noblemen of Dae'gon."

There was more cheering and applause as the four humans stood and humbly bowed before the king.

"Last but not least," the king announced, "I give you Don of Westrun, Royal Bard of Griffon's Peak and traveling minstrel."

Don made a deep bow and smiled broadly. He was used to being in the spotlight and reveled in his notoriety. The group stood and cheered louder than ever. He was loved by all and respected as any nobleman's equal, which spoke volumes about his character.

As the cheering quieted, the king said, "This magnificent group will bring an end to chaos that spreads in this fair city and abroad. Know that your lands and your subjects will have little to fear after they purge the kingdom of the pestilence that infects Dae'gon. They will cut the head from the snake, so to speak, and The Legion will fall."

Again the nobles cheered but the heroes looked from one to another with much less enthusiasm. The king had indeed promised much for the adventurers to deliver. In truth, there would likely always be villainy and chaos about no matter how well their mission went. Although the heroes knew this to be true, none spoke up. In silence, they consented to do as the king promised.

After the morning meal concluded, the king and the nobles departed en masse while the heroes lingered to discuss how they would accomplish the king's lofty goals.

Gaedron began, "I ain't ne'er backed down from a fight afore an' I ain't 'bout ta start now, but da king might be finding' more'n a few disappointed nobles when we fall short o' his lofty ambitions. I don' think we can eradicate evil no matter how many o' da Legion's boys we cut down."

The elves nodded in agreement. The humans crossed their arms in defiance as if even discussing the matter was treason against the king, though none spoke immediately.

After a long pause with deafening silence, Don smiled his most diplomatic smile and began, "I think we can do many great things for the entire kingdom if we work together. The king believes that if we prevent The Legion from joining with the lycans, we will inevitably kill or capture both leaders and many of the senior members of both organizations, in essence, cutting the head off of the snake as he said to the nobles. I believe this to be our most likely outcome."

Da'Shar said, "My people have fought the lycans before. It is not impossible to kill the pack leader, but it is not as simple as mustering an army to fight orcs on some battlefield out in the open. These villains are cunning and secretive. From what I know of The Legion, they are also both cunning and secretive. I believe we will search far and wide without a single encounter for days and days and then, when the enemy chooses to reveal himself, we will be in for the fight of our lives."

Maejis responded directly to the druid, "If that is the hand that fate deals us, then we must prepare for it and see this campaign through to the end. The alternative is a criminal underworld with not only endless resources, but infinitely more powerful members. That threat to this city is one that will surely spread to all other cities in Doerun until our civilization is destroyed. We have no alternative. This is the only course regardless of the political promises the king has made to the noblemen."

Landermihl nodded in agreement. Wavren shrugged indifferently. Rosabela and Theila remained silent, but both had reservations painted on their faces. Vlaad starred off into the distance as if he had greater concerns to deal with.

Don addressed the group again, "So do we

press on? We must all be committed and unified if we are to survive. All doubts must be voiced now. Vlaad, please speak your thoughts and then let us hear from the others."

Vlaad had been fully immersed in the memories of his countless engagements with The Legion. He recalled numerous encounters, many of which never came to blows and those that had were always unconventional in nature, resulting in the escape of the assassin more often than not. He imagined a snake, as the king had referred to band of assassins, but this snake was nearly insubstantial. How many times had he closed his grip, certain that the enemy was in his grasp only to find an empty hand when he opened his clenched fist? He thought of his dead father, mother, brother, and sisters. He remembered the promise he had made to O'ma so many years ago that he would bring justice. He remembered the killing blow that took his master's life and the evil brute that delivered it. His entire life had been dedicated to stopping The Legion, yet somehow he felt doubtful that this mission would succeed.

Vlaad finally spoke after many moments of silent reflection, "I will commit to this fight though I fear the king has given us an unattainable goal. Even if we destroy The Legion and the lycan pack, there will be another villain or group of villains to fill the void they leave behind."

Don smiled and spoke saying, "Very well, we have Vlaad's support. Theila and Rosabela have abstained from voicing their concerns, but now is the last opportunity we have to do so. Please be forthcoming and share your thoughts."

Rosabela said, "I am committed to this fight as well, but it will be you who face the noblemen when their promise is unfulfilled. My concerns are for you when the time comes to face them in their disappointment."

Landermihl stood drawing the attention of everyone as he spoke, "I remember a story that I believe addresses this problem. If you will permit me a moment, I will share this tale."

All nodded in acquiescence.

The paladin began, "Mankind is divided into three distinct groups. The first are sheep who spend their day looking for grass to eat. When the grass is green they dine joyfully for a short time, but when it is gone, they complain that there is not enough green grass and must move to another field. This is all they are concerned with. The second are wolves who spend their day stalking the sheep. They know the sheep will wander about concerned only with eating grass, making them easy targets. The wolves rely on the foolishness of the sheep to score an easy meal. The third are guard dogs that spend the day watching over the sheep. They know the wolves are out there waiting to kill the sheep and as such, they must remain ever vigilant, often barking orders to the sheep to stay close."

The other adventurers were listening intently as Landermihl's ice blue eyes flashed brightly with sincerity. His deep baritone voice rang of truth as the story continued.

Landermihl paused for a moment and then continued, "The sheep often whine that the guard dog is too serious and that there are no wolves about more often than not. They take the vigilance of the guard dogs for granted. The wolves wait patiently for the sheep to become complacent, knowing that their foolishness will be their undoing. When the wolves finally attack, the sheep call to the guard dogs for help and try to escape, but the ones that wandered too far are quickly slain before the guard dog can do anything. The guard dog chases off the wolves and returns to the herd having saved all but one or two, yet upon their return, the sheep blame them for the loss of their dead brothers. The guard dog does not argue, but instead, he quietly returns to his post knowing the sheep will never be satisfied nor will they ever comprehend the nature of his duty. They will never accept that his unending vigil and constant barking, while annoying, has a purpose that saves lives."

The adventurers nodded solemnly knowing that the noblemen were obviously the sheep who might never be satisfied. They accepted that there will always be wolves about and as a guard dog, their duty is to protect the sheep until the end of their days. No other words were spoken or required. Grim faced and determined each hero rose from their seats ready to take up the challenge.

Curtiss Robinson

CHAPTER 10
THE ROAD TO BLADESHIRE

In spite of the hollow promises the king made to the noblemen, the heroes set about making preparations for the trip to Shadowshire where the lycan pack was rumored to live. Each adventurer checked and rechecked their personal gear to include the weapons, armor, and shields of the warriors as well as the wands, reagents, and spell books of the casters. In addition to the combat equipment, each member of the team carried a backpack with rations, water, a bedroll, and a variety of personal items. There would be many towns along the way for resupply, but it was best to be prepared.

The meeting time for departure was mid-afternoon allowing the heroes plenty of time to visit the merchants for last-minute items, but the king had been gracious and quite generous with his personal vendors and stores. Each warrior was given a fine charger with light barding (horse-fitted armor) to protect it should they encounter enemies along the road. The casters were given palominos, which were better suited for speed than combat. Of course Landermihl had his own steed, a powerful warhorse clad in heavy barding that shined brilliantly in the sunlight, but could stop a crossbow bolt from close range. There were two draft horses in tow carrying the additional food and water stores needed for the trip.

When the group finally met at the appointed hour, the city guard ushered them to the gate and down the massive ramp with cheering merchants and applauding citizens on both sides. The nobles had quickly spread the word of the mission that lay ahead of the nine. Don the Bard waved and smiled like a celebrity while the other humans merely nodded or saluted the crowd professionally. The four from the Western Kingdom were far more solemn. Rosabela was intently focused on the mission; Da'Shar was mentally reviewing what he knew about the previous lycan pack leader. Wavren was unaccustomed to all of the attention and felt strangely out of place while Gaedron was simply being himself—a grumpy, old dwarf.

The city guard and human onlookers were soon left behind as the mounted adventurers trotted through the Blackridge Mountains and approached the city of Bladeshire. It was at this point that the hunters and druids stopped and dismounted. The humans looked on curiously as Rosabela and Da'Shar tethered their mounts to the rear of the draft horses with Gaedron and Wavren following suit. The hunters whistled loudly and out of nowhere two massive bears came rolling in. Vlaad and Landermihl recognized the allies of the hunters but Maejis and Theila drew their wands defensively.

Don the Bard cleared his throat as a warning not to shoot at the bears and then said, "May I introduce the front-line fighters of our now complete team: Ol' Blackmaw, ally of Gaedron and Stonetalon, ally of Wavren."

As if on cue the bears stood up on their hind legs and roared mightily. Gaedron's bear was a great white beast with the tale-tell black mouth filled with wicked teeth, just as his namesake indicated. He stood ten feet tall and had massive paws ending in scythe-like, flesh-rending claws. Wavren's ally was just as tall but covered in a ruddy red-brown fur. Its great paws ended in grey-black claws that could likely gouge the mountainous stone they resembled in color, no doubt the source of his name.

Theila whispered to Vlaad, "I am glad they are on our side."

Vlaad nodded and replied, "Wait 'til you see them in combat. There is something comforting about having a couple of two thousand pound bears that cannot be reasoned with, have no remorse, and simply will not stop until dead or recalled by their masters."

Theila thought there was a lot warlocks had in common with the hunters given the nature of their allies, but where her demons were summoned and bound to her will, these beasts were willfully loyal, a characteristic that would make her profession significantly less dangerous if it were possible to summon a willing demon. She quickly dismissed the absurd notion. Her demons might be more treacherous, but they were infinitely more powerful and versatile. She smiled broadly at that realization and accepted the lack of love and loyalty as a small sacrifice.

Rosabela and Da'Shar paid little attention to the spectacle the bears presented. Instead, they drew on their own craft and shape shifted into very unusual beasts that resembled the lightning-quick predatory cats of the open plains, but seemed somewhat less…substantial. At first glance, the humans thought their eyes were simply unable to focus on the ethereal beasts but as they rubbed and blinked to better focus their sight, the image never improved.

Wavren noticed the shared looks of astonishment and explained, "The druidic travel form is not of this world. It is an otherworldly beast that is impossible to track, incredibly fast, and able to blend into the surrounding environment like the chameleon. Do not try to look directly at them, but just have faith they are about as they scout ahead and report back periodically."

Maejis watched the two semi-transparent cats dash off with great admiration. Such magic was beyond his capabilities, but understanding it wasn't. He made a mental note to study the two druids closely over the coming days and weeks. A mage draws his power from endless study and a full comprehension of how and why the elemental and the arcane forces work. Perhaps one day he might find the key to the same astral forces which govern the druidic travel form, but for now he was content to watch and learn.

Without another word, Gaedron and Wavren took off through the woods leaving the five humans to follow along the road with the spare horses and supplies. The road was a short distance from Griffon's Peak to Bladeshire and after less than an hour of riding, the group reunited at the edge of the human trade village. This was a good place to stop for a brief rest and the smell of roasting pheasant was being carried on the wind in their direction with mouth-watering and stomach-rumbling effects few could resist.

Don said with a wink, "I think we will need to gather some local information before we proceed. I'll be back in a short while."

Theila and Vlaad laughed at the poorly concealed excuse to stop and eat, but none argued the point.

Gaedron said, "Aye, and if'n da bard finds any trouble, I'll back 'im up. I an' Wavren will be at da bar."

Now it was Rosabela and Da'Shar who laughed at the even poorer disguised excuse to go inside and eat. Vlaad paid a stable boy to secure the mounts and was the last to enter the tavern. What he found inside was a warm and hospitable establishment that hadn't changed since he was a boy. The same serving maids, barkeep, and patrons that he had grown up around were all present. It was like a delightful homecoming to see so many familiar faces. He felt right at home.

As the heroes dined on roasted pheasant with red potatoes and fresh bread made from sweet grain, many of the patrons came to greet Vlaad. Most shook his hand and clapped him on the back, but some asked for tales of his life on the road. Vlaad was never one much for telling stories so he quickly deferred to Don, who was more than happy to entertain the growing crowd.

Don unslung his guitar and tuned it up with a small musical device called a *pitch pipe.* Once the strings were perfectly tuned and shortly after a few test chords, Don was ready. He began strumming a ballad to recount the life of Andar and the early days of Vlaad, the last defender. He sang about the evil men Vlaad and Theila had brought to justice and of course the one who was always just beyond their reach. Gorka was cast in a dark and wicked light using trickery to escape time after time, but Vlaad knew that it was more than simply tricks or luck. Gorka was the epitome of evil and a mastermind of villainy.

The song continued with the appointment of Vlaad as the Champion of Griffon's Peak and how his mastery of the shield made him the finest warrior in the realms. Vlaad thought this was quite an exaggeration as he had endless experience to draw on from his enchanted blade, the sword of Vlorin, which also happened to give him the advantage of combat precognition so that he often saw the incoming attack a split second before it was landed and sometimes even before it was launched. He also happened to be one of the finest blacksmiths in the realm enabling him to craft amazingly light yet durable armor and other essential items over the years to enhance his own ability to endure even the most powerful strikes of his enemies, but epic tales are never about blacksmiths and their skills.

Don strummed faster and faster, building increasing tempo with the Battle of Forestedge. He sang about the dozens of orcs, tauren, trolls, and undead that he single-handedly defeated, many of which fell dead from exhaustion being unable to penetrate his defenses. Vlaad almost laughed out loud thinking that was the most ridiculous thing he had ever heard. In truth, he had fought very little in the final battle compared to the heroic charge of Landermihl. Even Wavren, Gaedron, Da'Shar, and Rosabela played greater parts than he did, but this was his hometown and the truth was lost in the telling. As the song ended, many of the locals bought ale and mead for the heroes. Vlaad sat quietly and sipped cinnamon cider, feeling less than worthy of the gratitude the men showed him.

Landermihl came up to Vlaad, threw his arm around his shoulders and said, "Today is your day, defender. Tomorrow might be mine or someone else's. You should learn that heroism is the light that brightens the otherwise dreary lives of average men. Help these goodly folk to have hope and cheer. Do not let this opportunity pass you by as it is as much your duty to do this as it is to carry that sword and shield."

Vlaad looked into the deep azure pools that were the paladin's eyes and saw sincerity and honor. He stood up from his barstool and said, "For every hero praised by the masses there are countless who go unrecognized. Let us toast the finest heroes and heroines the realm has to offer."

Everyone stood up and raised their mugs.

Vlaad spoke with sincere appreciation saying, "Raise your glasses to Wavren, Rosabela, Da'Shar, and Gaedron. These are our brothers from the Western Kingdom, veterans of the Battle of Forestedge, Protectors of the Vale, and dear friends."

The crowd cheered in unison, "Hear! Hear! To the Protectors of the Vale."

Vlaad continued, "Raise your glasses to Landermihl, Maejis, Theila, and Don. These are our brothers from the Eastern Kingdom known as heroes in their own right, and noble veterans of Griffon's Peak!"

The crowd cheered again, "Hear! Hear! To the veterans of Griffon's Peak!"

Vlaad took a long draw from his cinnamon cider and sat down beside Theila.

She said, "I didn't know you were such a toastmaster."

"I'm not," he began, "but if I must suffer such praises then so should everyone else."

The warlock put her hand on Vlaad's and squeezed it gently. She loved that he was a humble man with honorable values. He was everything good to her and nothing could change that. Vlaad returned the affection with a tight squeeze of his own.

As evening progressed, the group of adventurers split into their own smaller cliques with Da'Shar and Rosabela sitting quietly in the corner discussing matters of nature while Gaedron and Wavren sat at the bar talking loudly like a pair of dwarves more so than a dwarf and an elf. Landermihl and Maejis discussed the king's business and politics while Vlaad and Theila sat closely in front of the crackling fire discussing not much at all, but enjoying the hissing and popping of the oak logs. Don the Bard mingled with everyone. He was truly in his element among others. He told tales and listened to rumors indiscriminately. None of them knew there was treachery afoot as they enjoyed their night in Bladeshire.

Chapter 11
Ambush

The Legion had been tracking the heroes since their arrival in Griffon's Peak with updates moving along intricate messenger channels almost hourly. The chief of operations for the assassin's guild, a sickly looking human known as The Plague to his victims or Master Plague to his underlings, had anticipated the move from Griffon's Peak to Bladeshire and predicted the next move on to Shadowshire. His informants had been so effective that he could have planned the first hit as early as the night before the group had left the city, but that would have been a suicide mission allowing little chance for success. The second opportunity was along the road from Griffon's Peak to Bladeshire, but again, there would have been little advantage for the assassins in the light of day and out in the open, particularly facing such powerful adversaries. No, The Plague preferred the natural element of the assassin…the dark of night.

Several assassins had already infiltrated the inn even before the heroes arrived in mid-afternoon. Two rogues posing as merchants from the Wetlands were stationed at the only inn Bladeshire had to offer weary travelers. Two more posed as town guards patrolling the streets. More than twenty others were steadily trafficking information through the small village with unbelievable efficiency. The band of killers had set up a base of operations in the back room of the local bakery. Many of the runners were disguised as patrons and passersby who constantly gave a series of hand signals, or passed written coded messages, or whispered code words from one to another. The network appeared perfectly normal to every onlooker. This was how The Legion conducted business and why they were so effective. They knew everything about the team from Griffon's Peak down to the number of drinks each hero consumed.

The Plague decided the best course of action would be to slip into the quarters of each hero, isolating them from the others and then simultaneously kill them while they slept. He was certain the first attempt would only have limited success given the nature of the targets, but his orders from the guild master were to weaken the group if total elimination was not possible. This was an attainable goal.

The master assassin had assigned a specific killer by his or her specialty to each hero. Knowing the nature of paladins and druids as healers, The Plague assigned cut throats instead of toxin experts to Landermihl, Da'Shar, and Rosabela. He appointed his *garrotters*, strangulation experts, to Maejis, Don, and Theila who lacked the physical strength to resist such attacks and would be less deadly at close range being primarily ranged combatants. Two poison specialists were ordered to take out the hunters, Gaedron and Wavren. Vlaad was the wild card. He was not particularly vulnerable to any form of attack. All assassination attacks rely on stealth to strike unseen, but even if an assassin was discovered, he could often finish the job if he still had the element of surprise. The problem with Vlaad was that as a defender, he could hold out indefinitely according to legend. Not wanting to take any chances, The Plague decided to slay Vlaad himself. It would be an excellent opportunity to strengthen his reputation; after all, infamy gained is worth more than gold to a hired killer.

Coordination was tricky but at exactly one hour before sunrise, the assassins planned to strike. That was when most people are in their deepest sleep and would allow time to escape before dawn. If all went well, the nine adventurers would awake in the abyss and The Legion would stand unopposed to complete their business with the lycans in Shadowshire.

Everything was in place shortly after the adventurers had eaten and retired for the evening. The quiet night invited the spirit of death to collect souls for the underworld like a farmer at harvest time.

***

Jael'Kutter came to Rosabela's dreams almost every night where his non-corporeal restrictions had little power over him and where their love could flourish with limitless imagination. He was the Spirit of Vengeance and the Elemental Protector of Forestedge. His sworn duty as an elf now carried over into eternity following his death and resurrection by mystic forces. Rosabela had been granted the ability to summon his corporeal form with the life stone of Celestial's last Speaker of the Stars, but its power drained the she-elf tremendously after each use, making the dream world a far superior option. Though the life stone had been a reward for her service to the elves following the final Battle of Forestedge, it was meant to benefit all of Celes'tia but Rosabela was as yet unable to master its power.

The night began no differently than the countless other nights that Jael'Kutter had come to her. He traveled astral to her location from his post at Forestedge and projected his essence into her mind. The warrior always appeared to her dressed in his finest attire, with his handsome, angular features beaming with sincere happiness. His smile was warm and comforting to her and they embraced like long lost lovers rejoicing in the time they had to spend each night.

Jael'Kutter held Rosabela at arm's length and said, "I thought you might never fall asleep tonight. Have you grown tired of me already, my love?"

Rosabela responded with a long and passionate kiss.

When they paused he said, "Perhaps not, but still, what keeps you from our world of dreams?"

She said, "There is much to tell, but know that if I linger awake, it is not by choice but for duty."

"Tell me everything; we have all night to spend," the spirit said.

The she-elf began, "As you know, we have been asked to fight alongside the humans of Griffon's Peak to prevent the alliance of a human assassin's guild and the lycan pack descended from the first pack leader of Celes'tia."

"Yes, I know of your mission and what it will mean to all when you are successful," he replied with endless confidence.

She continued, "Da'Shar thinks this might be an impossible task. He fears that we will fail to find the pack leader and he believes the leader of the assassin's guild to be cunning and power hungry beyond our imagination. The worst part is that our failure could bring about an organization with limitless resources able to conquer the Eastern and Western Kingdoms."

Jael'Kutter considered the situation carefully

and said, "You have the key to success in your own determination backed by the abilities of your companions. I have faith in you and that faith is well placed."

Rosabela smiled. She knew her spirit companion was right, of course. It was Da'Shar's nature to worry and here's to find a way. It was also the nature of her companions to overcome obstacles that would otherwise be insurmountable. She smiled again and looked into Jael'Kutter eyes. He was looking away as if distracted. She suddenly felt uneasy.

"Jael'Kutter...what is it?" she asked.

"You must wake," he said urgently.

"Is our time over? Is it morning?" she asked.

"No, morning has not come, but someone has entered your room. You are in danger! Now go!" he exclaimed.

Rosabela woke with a start. The darkness enveloped her, feeling like an oppressive, malignant presence. Unsure of whom or what had invaded her privacy, she rolled quickly to her left, off the bed, and onto the cold floor. A shadow pounced silently where she had been lying; its blade diving precisely where her throat had been barely a second ago. She called to the elements in the tongue of nature for star fire, engulfing her bed in white light and igniting the sheets and blankets immediately. The shadow sprang away just in time to avoid being engulfed in the arcane flames. The burning linen produced more than enough light for the druid to see her enemy. The attacker was dressed in dark clothing and held a vicious-looking dagger that would have silenced her forever had it not been for Jael'Kutter warning.

The lithe she-elf sprang forward like a cat. She

was unarmed and wore only her night clothes, which were far less substantial than the leather armor her adversary wore. The assassin grinned under his mask thinking his prey had panicked and would soon be impaled on his blade. When the she-elf transformed in mid-air, he had to throw himself backward to avoid being mauled by the slashing claws of the now fully enraged, massive, black bear that landed where he had been standing.

***

Sleep had taken Gaedron quickly, having imbibed more than a dozen stout ales. He never heard the whisper of the wind as his appointed assassin slipped into his room and moved silently to his bedside. The killer uncorked a thin vial then slowly and cautiously poured a sticky poison, drop by drop, down a slender silken thread and into the hunter's mouth. After several seconds, the assassin resealed the deadly toxin and crept out of the room. Gaedron's heartbeat slowed from the powerful thump, thump, thump, to a weak, almost imperceptible flutter.

***

One of the three strangulation specialists moved carefully to the end room where Maejis was sleeping. He was careful to check the door for traps of a magical nature having been taught long ago that wizards were a paranoid lot. When he was certain the door was safe, he inserted his lock pick and turned the mechanism with a soft click. The assassin placed several drops of oil on the hinges to ensure the door wouldn't creak when he entered. As he gently eased the door open and peeked inside, he noticed the mage was sleeping soundly. He crept over and slid one end of his deadly cord under the base of the mage's neck. In one quick motion he drew the thin wire across the wizard's throat, crossing his hands and pulling mightily.

Maejis opened his eyes and spoke one word in a long-forgotten language. The assassin felt his body heat up in a split second but before he could scream in agony he simply fell into a pile of dust and ash.

Maejis sat up and spoke to the dead assassin, "Stoneskin for defense and disintegration for offense…two most useful spells wouldn't you agree?" He brushed himself off and casually walked outside to check on the others.

***

The Plague wanted to kill his mark quickly, but doing so without alerting the other guests of the inn was the real challenge. The Plague was a most unusual assassin in that he could use a dagger, poison, a crossbow, or any number of other traditional methods to kill a man but he preferred to strike his victim empty handed, leaving only a purplish bruise as evidence of his attack. Most thought it was a strange plague that had killed his victims, giving him his pseudonym, but upon closer inspection the truth could be discerned. This was, after all, his calling card and understanding the nature of it had built his reputation with endless infamy. No one knew that his specialty had come from secret fighting techniques found in a faraway monastery where he had once studied. It was the unknown that strengthened the fear of him.

Vlaad did not hear the murderer enter nor did he sense the villain's movement across the room, but the defender did not sleep unprepared. He had learned over the years that The Legion worked best at night when their victims were most vulnerable. This lesson was burned into his memory when Andar was attacked and slain by Gorka Darkstorm so many years ago, and it was continually driven deeper and deeper into his mind as assassin after assassin had come against him in his quest to destroy The Legion.

The Plague concentrated for a moment drawing his internal energy into focus and then he slammed his open palm downward. The resulting sound was not one of breaking ribs or bursting organs. Instead it was one of flesh on steel. The magnificent Aegis Shield of Griffon's Peak had taken the deadly strike's impact. Vlaad rolled off the bed holding the fine shield just under eye level with his body balanced perfectly behind it. His sword was across the room making the defender an enticing target, but Vlaad was ready.

He said, "Your move, assassin…"

***

The cunning assassin tasked with killing Theila came through the window instead of using the door as the other assassins had. Upon entering the room, the assassin noticed a number of demonic sigils scribed on the floor. Had he chosen to enter by way of the door, he would have triggered some magical trap that would have likely been both agonizing and deadly. He smiled under his mask knowing that caution had probably saved his life. He moved over to the warlock's bedside and noticed that she was uncovered and sleeping completely naked. Even in the dark he could see the voluptuous curves that promised endless ecstasy stirring his inner most passions. He thought for a moment that surely there must be some way to complete his task and indulge in the pleasures of the flesh. As he considered the possibilities, the shapely form stirred.

A sweet and sultry voice purred to him, "Come to bed, lover. I want you so badly."

The assassin found he moving before he knew what was happening. His thoughts were muddled and though he tried, he couldn't find the will power to resist the temptation. As he climbed in bed with the luscious form, he noticed for the first time something terrifying; he saw blood red eyes.

***

Landermihl had been dreaming of the days when Griffon's Peak might once again be a city of peace and prosperity as his deity would want it. His dreams reflected his inner most desires, the desire of all goodly paladins—to serve righteously among peaceful, godly folk. He awoke suddenly to searing pain as a wickedly keen blade opened his neck, spilling warm blood down his chest. He gurgled, gagged, and tried to stem the flow of blood with his mighty hands, but try as he might; the wound was too deep having severed both the wind pipe and the adjacent carotid artery. The holy warrior knew no spell or healing magic would save him. He grew weak quickly and fell to the floor. His last moment was spent watching his killer escape.

Ice blue eyes popped opened as the paladin sat bolt upright. Landermihl realized that he had been dreaming. It was a vision from his god. His death was shown to him in precognition. The warrior noticed that his breath was coming in gasps and he was covered in sweat. Subconsciously he brought his hands to his throat feeling for the wound which had not been inflicted yet.

At that moment, the doorknob turned slowly and quietly. The door opened so slowly without a sound and so carefully that Landermihl knew his killer had come. He silently called to his deity and prepared his most powerful spell, the hammer of justice!

***

Yet another member of The Legion made his way up the stairs and down the long hallway toward his mark. He knew his target was in the middle room on the right, having read the slain innkeeper's log as his fellow assassins had previously done. This hit was a simple one. The plan was to move into position in sync with his brothers, pick one lock, open the door a crack, and fire a few poisoned darts into the elven hunter, Wavren. Nothing could be easier for the experienced rogue.

When he arrived at the middle door, he noticed a sign on the door that read *Do Not Disturb!* The assassin smiled at the thought of *disturbing* the elven hunter with a few darts from his blowgun. He picked the lock easily and opened the door a crack. The room was pitch black, making the shot impossible without firing blindly so he widened the door just enough to slide inside for a clean shot. As he eased his foot down inside the dark quarters, he felt tiny filament under his soft-soled boot. It was a trip wire for certain and he had almost set it off.

Ever so gently, the killer braced his weight on the doorknob to withdraw his foot but froze in place when he heard a click, felt a sharp pain in his side, and then he fell completely immobilized. It was at that point he realized the trip wire was a secondary trap and that the door had been set to release a paralyzing dart. The hunter, now standing above, had outsmarted him.

Fighting erupted throughout the inn. Wavren grabbed his long, curved, elven dagger and went to the door. He saw a rogue slip out of Gaedron's room and bound toward the stairs silently. Although concerned for the lives of his friends, he trusted in their abilities just as he knew they would be trusting in him to do what he was trained for. As silently as the infiltrators had come, he grabbed his blunderbuss and vaulted out the window to the street below. If any tried to escape, he would be waiting. The elven hunter whistled once and Stonetalon appeared. The hunt was on and the trail was fresh.

***

Younger elves sleep as humans, dwarves, and other races, but ancient elves, like Da'Shar, practice a deep meditation called *reverie*. Da'Shar had mastered this altered state of consciousness and was immersed in his nightly meditations when the last cut throat came for him. Unlike many of the other assassins, this killer was a savage and ruthless murderer who reveled in the killing more so than the hunt. His ability to approach unseen and unheard were well developed, but he elected to simply walk right in and attack with his mighty falchion, more of a heavy hacking blade like an ax than a sword. Da'Shar heard him coming, but it didn't matter. The assassin came in so hard and fast that the elf found he scrambling in the tight quarters, narrowly evading being cut in half several times before he finally managed to dive out the window to the open ground below.

***

The last of the pre-dawn attacks came barely a second after the first. The timing was so precise that at one moment there was only the sound of wind in the hearth and the next moment there was utter chaos.

Don had been sleeping deeply when his killer pounced on top of him. Unaware of the surprise attack, Don found himself tangled up in his sheets with a thin wire wrapped around his neck. Luckily, the assassin had been too eager for the kill and part of Don's pillow was caught in the garrote. The bard was still in trouble as the assailant tightened the cord. He found it more and more difficult to draw breath. Don had no weapon in reach and no leverage to break free. His only chance was to thrash about and try to roll himself and his attacker off the bed. If he was lucky, someone might hear the ruckus and come to his aid or the assassin might let go to escape for fear of being discovered. As his strength drained away, Don kicked out with both feet and arched his back. He and the killer flipped backwards, head first, to the floor.

***

Rosabela shape shifted into her bear form and had nearly crushed the man who had dared attack her while she slept, but the dark figure dodged at the last minute and rolled out of her reach. She turned and lashed out with a deadly paw, but the assassin dove out of the window, choosing to flee rather than deal with an enraged bear. Rosabela transformed back into her elven form and called to nature as her enemy hit the ground. Vines and roots sprang up from the soil and entangled the rogue's feet. He thrashed and hacked with his blade, but the she-elf was already casting her next spell—star fire. The black-clad human screamed as the brilliant pillar of light flashed down from the heavens and set his flesh ablaze. His writhing and kicking freed his feet from the entanglement spell, allowing him to run off into the night but he would be easily identified by the massive burns he suffered tonight.

The druid dashed out of her quarters in response to hearing a great cacophony of fighting from every other room. The door directly across from hers was ajar and a crashing sound came from it. She threw the door open and saw Don being strangled from behind by another black-clad figure. She had no spells accurate enough to hit the attacker without also hitting the bard so she did the only thing she could think to do. She dove in among them landing perfectly on Don's chest. She heard him gurgle out a groan as her knees caught him in the sternum. When the bard went limp from a lack of air, the assassin turned his attention to the she-elf.

Rosabela hoped Don was alive, but she was too busy fighting the assailant to check. Being small in stature meant that she was unable to produce the required power to seriously injure the stout assassin, but she rained blow after blow into his face with her tiny fists. When the murderer finally managed to

disengage himself from Don's limp form and after
several painful strikes from the she-elf, he kicked
the druid back and regained his feet. In the time it
took to stand, the tiny she-elf had once again
transformed into a huge, black bear. The first
sledgehammer-like blow from the bear caught him
in torso on his left side, blasting the air from his
lungs and tearing through his flesh. Desperate to
escape, the assassin tried to run for the door, but the
druid snapped out with her powerful jaws and
caught the man's leg, ripping flesh and crushing
bone. He screamed once and then Rosabela tore him
apart with both forepaws.

***

Maejis walked from his room just in time to see
a dark figure run out from Gaedron's room. The
wizard drew on his elemental magic and fired a
cone of pure blue cold, dropping the assassin to the
ground. He circled his hands for a second building
blue energy with each cycle of his hands. The
assassin tried to stand but his muscles would never
respond in time. Finally, Maejis murmured the key
word, releasing a blast of ice that exploded on
impact leaving frost in every direction for several
feet. The assassin lay very still.

Maejis brushed his hands off on his robes and
said, "Probably should have saved the cone of cold
for a larger group, but the ice blast worked nicely. I
guess winter came early for you." He chuckled to
himself as he moved to check on the others.

***

The assassin found the red eyes of the naked

woman strangely inviting as he approached. He noticed in the dim light from the moon that she also had tiny horns and then dark, leathery wings unfurled behind her. As terrifying as it should have been, the assassin found himself drawing closer and closer to the woman. As his lips touched hers he finally realized the truth. The warlock had left a succubus to guard her bed. The seductive demon wrapped her impossibly powerful arms around him and began draining his life force. The last thing he remembered was being enveloped in the dark bat-like wings of the demon and then there was nothing.

Theila materialized from the shadows a few moments later. She had been hidden safely in an inter-dimensional pocket between the abyss and the prime material plane.

She called to her demon, "Hallanya."

The succubus replied, "Yes mistress."

She continued, "I certainly hope that wasn't one of my friends you just devoured."

The demon said, "No mistress, he was bad...which made his soul solo well."

Theila frowned at the dried up corpse. She realized she had been too vague with her order to guard her room against intruders. Next time she would specify the requirement for the succubus to detain any intruders for questioning, but that was always the problem with demons; they always obeyed to the letter of the law, never considering the actual intent of the order given.

Theila stepped out of her room just in time to see a massive black bear shred another assassin outside her father's room. The bear had to be one of the druids; how else could a bear get inside the inn? She ran past the bear and saw her father lying unconscious on the floor. She checked his pulse. He was alive, but hurt badly.

Turning to the bear she said, "You are a healer; please help my father."

The bear twisted and compressed becoming a lovely she-elf. When the transformation was complete, Rosabela nodded and began to work on Don. Not knowing what else to do, Theila turned back down the hall and went looking for more enemies. She noticed a body lying in the doorway to Wavren's room. He wasn't moving so she moved to the next room where she heard a deep voice and saw a bright light followed by an explosion of energy that sent another assassin flying through the door, taking out part of the doorframe and wall. A very angry paladin, dressed in a long nightshirt and shorts came stomping out with a glowing hammer in his hand.

Theila raised both hands and said, "Don't attack…its Theila."

The paladin said, "Gather the others; we need to regroup."

Theila nodded and continued her search.

***

The Plague heard all of the commotion and knew his time was limited. He had failed in his task, having underestimated his prey, and since there wasn't enough time to finish the job, he saluted the defender and made his escape through the window. Vlaad dove for his sword and followed the killer with great haste. As he cleared the window sill and landed on the first-story roof, he saw his attacker running down the street at an incredible speed. At that moment, he also saw one of the elves dive through another window and land hard on the roof with a roll and then dive off that roof only to shape shift into a powerful windwraith on the way down. It had to be Da'Shar, but the darkness made it difficult to see. The great black cat landed on its feet and circled around in anticipation of being followed by his attacker. Right on cue, a rogue with a huge, curved blade jumped through the window and hit the roof running. He made the ten-foot jump straight down to the road without slowing. When his feet hit the ground below, he rolled once and came in fast with a powerful two-handed swing from right to left. The druid leapt forward clearing the horizontal attack and buried the man in over eight hundred pounds of teeth and claws. The two rolled over once and Da'Shar landed on the bottom with all four paws raking upward. The assassin tried to swing his heavy blade downward, but the weapon required more room to be effective. He managed to slice into the cat's shoulder, but was disemboweled in trade. The fight ended in a bloody mess of torn flesh and blood-soaked clothing.

Vlaad called to the druid, "You all right?"

Da'Shar transformed and nodded. His shoulder was bleeding, but not too badly. He spoke the word of healing and the gash closed completely with an eerie green glow. Without hesitation, he transformed into his travel form and dashed off after the fleeing assassin.

Vlaad jumped down and circled back around to the main entrance. He sprinted back up the stairs and found Theila at the end of the hall.

"Are you all right?" he asked.

"I am, but my father is hurt and we are missing the two hunters."

Maejis came to them and said, "I found the dwarf. He has been poisoned, but he lives.

Landermihl is with him now."

Don and Rosabela came out of the bard's room. The blood vessels in Don's eyes had erupted under the strain of strangulation, leaving his normally handsome features haggard and bruised. He smiled weakly when he saw his daughter. She did not return his smile. Anger filled her like a boiling volcano about to erupt.

She asked her father, "Are you okay?"

The bard swallowed hard and tried to speak but an unintelligible croak was all he could muster.

Rosabela spoke for him saying, "Thank the fates he will live, but his vocal cords have been damaged. He shouldn't try to talk and will require more healing with lots of rest."

Knowing her father had lived was little consolation given the damage to his handsome face and beautiful voice. Theila gritted her teeth and stormed out of the inn dismissing Hallanya, her succubus, with a wave of her hand and a simple word of power. She needed the resources of her most cunning fiend. The warlock spoke the guttural incantations of the abyss and gestured upward for a few seconds. As the spell surged with eldritch energy, she called the name of her crafty imp, *Trig'zstder*.

The ground buckled and cracked open with a gout of flame and brimstone spewing dirt, ash, and a nasty diminutive beast. The imp had sharp talons on his hands and feet, bat-like wings, tiny horns, red, pock-marked skin with jagged spines down its back, a mouth filled with razor-sharp teeth that looked like those of a shark, and a huge, bulbous nose. There could be no doubting that this was a being of pure evil.

"Trig'zstder!" she commanded.

"Yes mistress," it sneered wickedly.

"Scout the area, remain unseen, and report anyone or anything that appears to be spying on us. Do not attack, even to defend your own life on this plane. Be thorough and be quick. Am I clear?"

"Yes mistress," it whined.

The imp cursed at the thought of being relegated to scouting, but went on its way. Imps are deviously vile creatures that thrive on making any living creature suffer. As such they prefer to attack, kill, and destroy. Of course, it would never directly disobey the warlock who summoned it for fear of being banished for one hundred years, or worse, being spirit wracked by the summoner who knows its true name.

Theila waited impatiently as the tiny demon flew in ever-widening circles around the town. It was invisible to all but its summoner who had no intention of letting the little beast out of her sight for long. After a few minutes, the imp returned and reported.

"Mistress," it wheezed, "there are no other enemies about, but I have found the tracks of a windwraith, an elf, and a bear heading out of town toward Shadowshire."

Theila turned on her heel and dashed back inside the inn where she saw Vlaad talking with the others.

She said, "Da'Shar and Wavren have gone out in pursuit of the fleeing attackers. Should we follow?"

A very unsteady dwarven hunter stumbled out of his room and said, "Durned fool elves gone ta get a li'l payback wit' out me!" He vomited and wiped his mouth weakly.

Landermihl moved in behind Gaedron and

grabbed the back of his tunic just as the sick dwarf pitched forward and passed out.

"This one should be dead and will be if we can't keep him still long enough for his body to recover. I have purged the poison, but its effects have already taken a toll. He should not travel," the paladin said resolutely.

Vlaad considered the situation for a minute and said, "Don and Gaedron require more time to heal. Rosabela and Landermihl should stay with them and tend to their injuries. There are also enemies in need of questioning. Bind their hands and find out what you can. Theila, Maejis, and I will go out to back up the others. Do not let your guard down; if I know The Legion, they are monitoring our movements and might come again to finish their work."

Landermihl and Rosabela went back to their healing duties after tying up the prisoners. It took no time at all for the other three to dress and arm themselves, but following the elusive tracks of a hunter and a druid was a difficult task. Theila sent Trig'zstder ahead to keep them going in the right direction, but the druid and hunter were already miles away. The trio mounted their horses and sped off in pursuit.

CHAPTER 12
PURSUIT

Da'Shar could not believe how fast the assassin was moving. There was some sort of enchantment or magic item carrying the human faster than any horse could gallop, but no creature, even one magically enhanced, could out run a druid. He followed the assassin's trail to an abandoned mine several miles away from Bladeshire where he finally regained visual contact with the killer. The druid watched him go inside and waited in the shadows of the forest for a few moments to ensure the situation was reasonably safe to proceed. Just as he was about to move into the mine shaft, another assassin dashed across the clearing toward the entrance. He was in a full sprint with a massive bear rumbling toward him and closing the distance quickly. Barely ten strides from the entrance, the assassin fell forward as if shoved by an invisible hand. The telltale report of a hunter's blunderbuss ripped through the night air a second later. The assassin had been shot through the head at well over two hundred yards! The bear sniffed the dead human and turned back toward the edge of the forest.

The druid assumed his elven form and silently walked in the direction the bear had gone. He froze in place when he heard the metallic click of Wavren's blunderbuss which was now undoubtedly pointed in his direction.

"Wavren," the druid called in the elvish tongue, "don't shoot."

"You move too quietly for your own good," the hunter replied. "I thought you were one of them."

The hunter released the hammer on his weapon and raised the barrel skyward. As Da'Shar moved closer, he noticed Stonetalon crouched motionless between himself and the hunter. Da'Shar realized it would have been better to be shot in the head than mauled by the bear if Wavren hadn't recognized him. As an afterthought, he realized the assassin lying dead outside the mine had been granted the more merciful of the two deaths.

"I tracked one assassin to the mine. He is likely the leader and one with many resources," the druid said referring to the killer's incredible speed. "We must proceed with caution."

"I can guard the entrance from here with my ally. You should get the others and lead them here," Wavren offered.

Da'Shar shook his head. "It will take too long. I will scout the mine. You can follow me or go back for the others. The choice is yours."

Wavren said nothing but motioned the druid forward. Da'Shar shape shifted into his windwraith form and moved toward the mine. Wavren covered the rear. The elves and Stonetalon paused beside the slain assassin. By the look of his burned clothing and charred flesh, this assailant had attacked Rosabela earlier. Da'Shar thought the bullet had indeed been a merciful death for this one, *But some do not deserve such mercy*, he thought. Justice would have been met if the bear had ripped him apart in payment for the countless lives he had likely taken over the course of his career.

The mine shaft was dark and smelled of sulfur, but the trio moved deeper into the blackness until even their keen elven eyesight was of little use. Wavren concentrated on the connection with his ally and drew upon the bear's innate senses. The bear's eye sight was poor by comparison, but Stonetalon had a keen sense of smell and a sharp sense of hearing. As Wavren sorted out the myriad of stronger smells and sounds, he came to realize that there were several humans ahead, far too many for his small team.

"Da'Shar," Wavren whispered, "we are outnumbered and should not proceed."

The druid, in windwraith form, stopped and changed back into his elven form. He was about to ask how Wavren knew what his feline senses had already told him when a grating sound to their rear echoed through the shaft. Light spilled from the opening of a secret passageway followed by more than a dozen assassins and one appeared to be casting a spell. Realizing they had fallen into a trap and were now surrounded, adrenaline triggered immediate reactions from the heroes.

Wavren fired his blunderbuss but hit an invisible wall. The bullet bounced back and lodged into the ground at his feet. Da'Shar started to cast a spell but quickly reconsidered when he realized it would be futile and likely quite dangerous. Wavren turned in the opposite direction and ran with Stonetalon at his side, grabbing Da'Shar by the arm, but another invisible barrier had already been placed ahead of them. The second invisible barrier stopped them in their tracks with painful results.

From the other side of the barrier one of the assassins called to them, "It looks like you have pursued your quarry well, right into the lion's den. Now what will you do?"

Several of the other rogues were laughing as the leader taunted the trapped elves.

The leader answered the rhetorical question saying, "You will die, of course, just as all who oppose The Legion."

As the assassins turned to leave, the wizard cast a spell of silence on the trapped elves.

He said, "That should keep things quiet just in case you want to call for help or use magic to escape."

***

Vlaad, Theila, and Maejis rode hard in pursuit of the imp. The little demon was able to fly swiftly over stumps and around thick underbrush that the horses were forced to circumnavigate. Theila was mentally attuned to Trig'zstder so finding him wasn't a problem, but keeping him in view was. Needless to say, the companions pushed their steed to their limits for several miles until they came to the edge of the forest. The imp was waiting out of sight when they arrived.

"Mistress, they went inside, but I do not think it is wise to follow them. There is evidence of great numbers inside and as you can see, one was slain at the doorway. They know we are here," he said.

Theila said, "We must go inside, but you have served your purpose and you may return to the abyss now."

The imp howled in anger having made the trip to the prime material plane without getting to kill anything or wreak any havoc. It took a mere snap of Theila's fingers, a single word of power, and the imp faded from sight in a puff of smoke and brimstone.

"I think we will need Zaashik's assistance. He is much tougher and less prone to cause problems than the imp," Theila said as she began the intricate summoning process.

Maejis watched with great interest while Vlaad frowned at the thought of sharing the front line with her demon, but he had seen the voidwalker in action and could not deny the utility of having a disposable warrior if things went bad. He remembered back to several missions when Theila had sent Zaashik into battle against ten to one odds so they could escape. It usually gave them several minutes' head start as well as cutting the enemy numbers down before the demon's corporeal form was destroyed, sending it back to the abyss.

Zaashik slowly materialized, unlike the imp who literally crawled from the depth of the abyss through a dimensional rift. The creature was best described as a floating torso with powerful arms and wickedly hooked claws. It was a shadow being that was nearly impossible to hurt with normal weapons, but magic or enchanted weapons could destroy it over time. As such, it made an excellent bodyguard and front-line fighter.

Unlike the imp, who always had vile things to say, the protector demon was usually silent and followed it's summoner by mental commands. Theila willed it to move forward in search of Da'Shar and Wavren with a secondary objective to attack all others on sight. It floated on a stream of spewing shadow into the mine without fear and was prepared to kill without hesitation.

The trio had only moved a short distance into the shaft when they saw Da'Shar, Wavren, and Stonetalon. The trapped elves motioned the humans away and even yelled, but the sound wouldn't carry. Vlaad was immediately aware that something was wrong. He held up his hand and the two casters stopped and drew their wands. The defender readied his shield and lifted his fine blade in the high guard position. Zaashik glided forward and hit the invisible barrier. Theila urged him on but no matter how the demon pushed or raked at the transparent wall, he simply could not break through its magic.

Maejis cautiously moved forward and said, "I believe they are held within a wall of force. It is a wizard's spell and one far too difficult for a novice mage. Stay alert; there are powerful spell wielders working for the enemy."

The mage continued to inspect the wall of force with his bare hands as if loving admiring a work of art. As he neared the rock wall where the magic barrier met the roughhewn stone, he felt a light whisper of air pass over his palm.

Stepping back he said, "The wall of force cannot be dispelled, but air passes through so it is not a sealed prison. We should be able to hear them, but since we cannot, I have to assume the prison was magically silenced. Let us deal with that matter first."

The wizard stepped back and began casting the counter-spell. When he spoke the final words, he clapped his hands together and threw them out wide, breaking the magical silence.

Da'Shar quickly called out, "The enemy has a secret door behind you and to the left."

No sooner had the druid spoken than a troupe of assassins came through the secret passageway. Several black-clad killers cornered the human trio. Zasshik sailed into the group with reckless abandon pushing the rogues back and taking a dozen minor hits in the process. The demon wouldn't hold the numerous villains for long, but it bought a little time.

Vlaad charged forward and shield bashed one assassin sending him to the floor. The others came in with swords and daggers slashing. None found an opening in the warrior's perfect defense but the ring of steel on steel echoed throughout the mine in rapid succession like a drummer's cadence.

After the initial attack, the assassins backed off to encircle the warrior and the warlock's demon. Vlaad knew Zaashik would fight to the death if commanded to do so, but without an avenue of escape, Theila would never sacrifice her bodyguard. He was more useful alive. Having fought alongside the warlock and her minions countless times before, Vlaad knew that he would need to hold the attackers at bay while Theila and the others dispatched their foes one at a time.

Maejis saw the assassins moving in sync to strike at different angles simultaneously. He was doubtful that Vlaad would survive the coming attack if he didn't do something quickly. Just as Vlaad settled in his stance and prepared for the first of more than a dozen strikes, Maejis dashed forward. The enemy changed targets quickly as the wizard came in, but with a single word, blue energy enveloped the caster. The hacking and stabbing blades hit the blue field and bounced off, leaving the attacking rouges reeling backward with frost-covered weapons and chattering teeth. The frost shield gave him time to maneuver. He spoke another word of magic and vanished momentarily only to reappear two dozen feet ahead. The group of killers was surprised for barely a second, but it was all the time needed to cast his next spell.

Maejis spun in a tight circle throwing his arms out wide saying, "*Novum Arcturi Arcanum!*"

The spell sent an explosion of ice and frost in all directions that did some minor damage to each of the attackers, but momentarily immobilized them and left their limbs unresponsive. He turned, called the mystic word for his *blink* spell once more, and teleported the short distance back behind Vlaad. When he turned again to face the enemy, Vlaad and Zaashik were tearing into the frost-covered band of assassins.

Theila called upon the power of shadow and poured bolt after bolt of numbing darkness at the villains. As the killers suffered the abyssal barrage, she drew her wand and fired off a few bolts of arcane energy for good measure, but confidently held her most powerful, offensive spells in reserve while her minion wreaked havoc. Unlike Maejis, Theila had learned to trust Vlaad implicitly when it came to the defense of the team and she had no intention of putting herself or the team at risk when things were under control. She knew the day would come when her most deadly spells would be required, but it would not be today. She scowled at the effectiveness of the wizard's frost magic, feeling a little jealous, but she was sure nothing could compare to the hellfire and demonic minions she had at her command.

Vlaad and Zaashik took turns cutting down one foe after another until all were dead or dying. It had been an efficient battle, but luck was with them. Vlaad thrust his fine elven blade through the last man and wondered where the spell wielder and their leader had gone.

"We must hurry, there will be more and these tight, dark quarters do not favor us," the defender said as he wiped his fine blade clean and shouldered his mighty shield.

Maejis went back to the wall of force and said, "I cannot break the magic that constructed this barrier, but I think we can pry it from the rough walls and ceiling. We will need a length of rope and a device to drill through the stone."

Da'Shar could barely make out their words through the invisible wall, but he caught enough of the plan to understand what was going on.

He said, "Rope and augers will take too long to find, but I can substitute with something better."

The druid closed his eyes and stretched out his hands to the ground. He summoned the roots from the trees far above and magically enhanced them. Slowly, long tendrils grew in between the corridor and the wall. In several places, the outer walls and ceiling buckled as dirt and stone shifted. He continued to speak to the roots and they grew and moved about until finally the elf's magic grew weak and the roots retracted.

"That will have to do," Da'Shar whispered to Wavren with obvious fatigue. "Perhaps your ally can do the rest."

Wavren and Stonetalon came forward without hesitation. The thin elf pushed against the wall and his bear dug in its claws and pressed its two thousand pounds of raw power against it. Although the wall seemed to shift a little it simply would not fall. Theila motioned for Zaashik to help. The demon had nothing to grasp in order to help pull so it began hacking at the wall itself. The long claws raked stone and dirt away nearly as efficiently as a dwarven pickax and after several swipes, the wall shifted again. Wavren and Stonetalon heaved mightily but the wall was barely moving and the opening was miniscule.

A voice came from behind startling the humans as they watched the slow progress, "Ye ain't ne'er gonna get anywhere workin' like dat."

As the group turned quickly with their hands on

their weapons ready for a fight, Gaedron, Rosabela, Landermihl, and Don moved closer.

Although ghostly white and weak looking, the dwarf walked confidently forward and ran his hands along the stone corridor feeling the outline of the invisible wall of force.

"Eh boyo, ya might wanna move ta da far side. I'm gonna make a hole fer ya fellas," the dwarf said weakly as he drew a long, red stick with a short fuse. His hands were shaking from the remaining effects of being poisoned, but managed to wedge the dynamite into one of the root holes Da'Shar had made.

Da'Shar and Wavren quickly took cover knowing what the dwarf had in mind. The humans watched with curiosity but didn't move until Rosabela ran out. Gaedron lit the fuse and hustled past them heading outside mumbling what sounded like counting numbers in reverse.

The dwarf made it outside and continued counting aloud, "Ten, nine, eight, seven...I hope this works...five, four, three, two, one..."

The massive explosion shook the entire cavern and blew dust and debris throughout the entire corridor to the entrance. The seven heroes came back inside to see the damage. Amazingly, the wall of force was intact, but a hole in the stone cavern, large enough for the demon's hands, was now available. Zaashik grasped the edge of the invisible wall and pulled while Stonetalon and Wavren pushed. The barrier shifted slightly and then finally broke free and turned far enough for the prisoners to squeeze through.

"I think we should move," Vlaad said as the two previously trapped elves rejoined the group.

"I must agree," Da'Shar concurred.

The group moved hastily through the mine toward the surface. The bears were in the lead with Vlaad on point followed by the hunters, the spell wielders, and then Landermihl. Zaashik lingered behind to cover the rear as ordered by its mistress. The evacuation was quick and unhindered but not unnoticed.

"We have learned much about our enemies tonight," The Plague said to one of the few remaining assassins as they watched the heroes escape into the night. "I must report this to the guild master. Send for Allister the mage. Have him meet me in my chambers. We will need him to relay our communications and then we will discuss our next move."

The underling bowed quickly and disappeared into the shadows. There was a nagging doubt that continually ran through his mind as he padded silently through the tunnels to the secret headquarters in the depths of the mine. He had no love for the dead assassins, who had been killed by the heroes, but he knew the day would come when his life would end and that seemed very near after the night's events. He hoped his death would be for a better reason than that which The Legion had sacrificed his brethren tonight. Perhaps his doubt was in the fact that his entire existence had been as a guild member of The Legion, which had always provided him security and opportunities for coin. Now that lifestyle was in jeopardy. These adventurers were powerful, maybe even unstoppable. It was a concern that he could not escape. The mage was sitting at a desk reviewing his spell book when the underling arrived.

"The Plague has need of your services," the assassin reported.

"So soon? Very well, I am coming," Allister replied. "I assume he is ready to kill the fools we trapped earlier."

The underling said, "The fools have escaped your cage."

"Truly?" the wizard replied unimpressed. "Perhaps these heroes of Griffon's Peak will provide some sport after all. Well, how did they fare against the cut throats we left to watch them?"

The assassin didn't answer.

"By your silence I gather our men were slain. That is unfortunate," Allister said nonchalantly.

The assassin wanted to bury his dagger in the wizard's back out of pure spite, but he knew that would accomplish little and the mage was a powerful ally needed by the guild. He picked up the pace and remained silent until their arrival at The Plague's office.

"Do you have anything else for me tonight?" the underling asked.

The thin assassin responded dismissively, "You may go; we have business here that does not concern you."

After the lesser assassin departed, Allister asked, "He obeys well, not unlike a dog."

The master assassin shrugged apathetically and replied, "I was once like him, a servant of one who was by far more powerful than I. Now I run the daily operations of the most powerful guild in the Eastern Kingdom. Perhaps you would be wise not to taunt those who could find themselves in positions of power in the near future."

The wizard paid no mind to the veiled threat. He was certain that those who might pose a real threat to him were always in need of his services. It was a game of strategy that he had played his entire life and he was without peer in it.

"I want you to contact the master and inform him of our progress," The Plague mentioned offhandedly. "He is expecting an update and we should not keep him waiting. Unlike the simple assassin you compared to a dog, The Shade is my superior and will be given his due respect."

Allister noticed a single bead of sweat on the gaunt killer's brow and a nearly undetectable waver in his voice as he spoke of his leader. It was the first time he had ever seen concern, or in this case fear, from The Plague. This revelation inspired the mage to make haste; after all, there was no need to anger powerful allies, much less give them cause to become an enemy.

The mage kneeled down and placed a single lump of coal on the ground, drew arcane runes around it, and spoke a throaty whispering language invoking a spell that set the black anthracite aflame. He spoke another invocation and the small flame wavered for a moment and shifted into the form of a tiny fire elemental. The otherworldly creature hissed and crackled, like a wet pine log thrown into a furnace. Allister stood and motioned for The Plague to come close.

"The elemental will take your words to The Shade through the plane of fire, his home world. Give him your message and your master will have it in seconds," the mage instructed.

"Very well," the thin assassin replied.

He leaned down and quietly whispered his message in a very guttural language that was undoubtedly orcish. Allister had never met the one known as The Shade, but he was certain an orc could never command The Legion. This meant the message was meant for a human who was bilingual, but why would any human waste the time learning such a barbaric language? He wondered how The Plague had learned the tongue of orcs as well. These questions led him to the only possible conclusion. The Legion was in league with the Bloodcrest Forces. Allister had a dark past, one that would be considered evil by many, but there were limits even he would never go beyond. Genocide was one such limit and given the destructive nature of orcs he could never allow himself to be associated with the enemy of humanity.

Stepping backward to the far side of the room and summoning a shield of protection, the wizard prepared himself for combat. If the assassin noticed, he made no indication of it. He continued sending his message through the elemental as if his own death would be a small price to pay to avoid interrupting the transmission.

The wizard circled his hands in an ever-growing pattern that rapidly formed a ball of fire, crackling with energy. After only a few seconds, the flame was white hot and nearly a foot in diameter. The wizard called the triggering word, "*Infernus Magus!*" sending the fireball roaring in, but the assassin dodged to the side at the last minute and rolled across his shoulders, back into a standing position.

"That was foolish," the assassin said.

"You are a traitor to your own race!" the wizard screamed as he prepared another spell. This one unleashed a long gout of fire with a single word, "*Incindarian!*"

The Plague dashed left toward the wall. As the line of flame followed him, he simply ran up the wall and flipped backward over the deadly spewing fire. His acrobatic skills saved him but the wizard was already casting another spell.

"You are a fool to think the orcs will spare you when they come to these lands. They are a horde of savage brutes that know nothing of civilization and will never tolerate our kind unless we live in bondage as their slaves. You will die for your part in this!" the powerful spell wielder promised as he summoned his final spell.

Moving with inhuman speed, The Plague darted across the room just before the wizard could complete his spell. He hit the protective energy field with an open palm strike that sent the wizard flying backward and sent rippling fractures through the shield. Although uninjured, Allister lost his concentration and the spell fizzled. He drew his wand and fired a bolt of white hot fire, but the killer dropped flat to the floor as the blast shot past him. He was up in an instant and sprinting forward. His fists rained several blows in rapid succession on the weakened shield and finally broke through. Allister tried to cast a spell to escape, but the assassin's left hand shot forward and clamped down on his throat with the speed of a striking viper. His words came out as a garbled, choking gasp.

The Plague had death in his eyes, but was otherwise calm and expressionless. The completely blank visage revealed his true nature. He was indeed a cold and merciless killer devoid of emotion. It was the last thing Allister saw before the master assassin drew his thin, almost frail looking right hand back and then struck the final blow. The pain was excruciating as the assassin's internal energy passed through the wizard's abdomen into his internal organs. The assassin dropped the now unconscious and fatally wounded mage, leaving him to die with a ruptured spleen. It was this signature move that had earned him his alias, The Plague.

CHAPTER 13
NOW IT'S PERSONAL

The nine adventurers made it safely back to the inn well after sunrise. Gaedron was still feeling the effects of being poisoned but thanks to the healing prayers of Landermihl and some herbal remedies Rosabela concocted to help flush out his system, the dwarf was faring well. Don was still unable to speak but his eyes were not as swollen from the attempted strangulation he suffered. The well-coordinated attack would have been successful if not for a good deal of luck and foresight. The heroes began discussing the early morning events over breakfast.

Gaedron summed up his feelings saying, "Well, I'm s'pposin' it was me own darned fault fer drinkin' more ale 'n I shoulda, but da whole lot o' sneaks be on me list now. If'n I can't sleep fer fear o' being poisoned den ain't none of dem a'sasins 'r gonna sleep neither. I say we track 'em down and gut 'em fer tryin' ta kill us, not ta mention dey upset me digestion so."

Wavren smiled and remarked, "I am personally surprised anything could upset your digestion," as the dwarf gobbled down his third helping of spicy sausage covered in hot spice.

The dwarf had no retort but grunted once as he shoved another sausage link in his mouth.

Theila cast a sad look at her father who was barely able to sip warm tea given his injuries. She was afraid that his amazing voice would be ruined forever as well as being furious that the assassins had been audacious enough to attack them in the first place.

She said, "I think it is time for payback! I would like to know how they knew everything they needed to set up their ambush. They only broke into our rooms and only we were attacked. The other patrons in the inn were left unscathed. Someone else is involved."

Maejis spoke, "I have been trying to piece that together as well. Do you think it was an inside job? Could the innkeeper or someone on the staff be involved? For all we know, the entire town could be working for The Legion."

Vlaad jumped into the conversation, "I know many of the people here and I am certain the whole town is not working for The Legion; however, their network is vast and my guess is that even if we catch a few spies, we will not likely find their leader or anyone of great importance."

"I agree," Da'Shar interjected. "We should forget about the few spies here and focus on the mission at hand. We must locate the lycan pack, destroy the pack leader, and end the assassin's plans to become like these abominations."

Vlaad spoke again, "Let us prepare for the road and set out within the hour. Though we have suffered injuries from the first attack, I believe all are able to make the ride to Shadowshire, and waiting will only invite another attack. We should take the fight to the enemy instead."

Landermihl nodded his head in agreement along with the others but every move had to be made with caution to avoid leaving exposed weaknesses for their enemies to exploit.

Theila was still less than satisfied. She casually got up and walked out of the inn, heading past the stables. She headed for the local jail, which was not far down the main road. It was where the surviving assassin was being held. She took a moment to compose her thoughts and walked into the front office of the small but stout building.

"Good day, can I help you?" the jailer asked politely.

"Yes, I am here to question the man who attacked my team earlier this morning," she replied.

"I do not think that is a good idea, milady. This man is a dangerous killer and will be tried for attempted murder by the royal court. You should return to your companions and thank the gods that you survived," the jailer kindly advised.

Theila was in no mood for diplomacy. Her life and the lives of her friends and father had been threatened and nearly extinguished. Her father was grievously wounded and might never speak properly again. She tried to remain calm but her anger boiled inside like an active volcano. The jailer noticed not only Theila's clenched fists and furrowed brow, but the seething rage in her eyes that gave the beautiful maiden a dark and vicious appearance.

She tried to speak calmly but the words came out harsh through her gritted teeth when she spoke. "I must see the prisoner," she growled.

Normally the jailer would have escorted an angry visitor out of his jail, but he felt compassion for the young woman given that she had been through so much. He looked at her and decided that she seemed harmless enough. She wore simple traveling clothes and carried no weapons that he could see. He decided that there would be no real harm in letting her go back and spit on the man who had been a one of the attackers.

The jailer said, "I will let you go back, but don't get near the bars for your own safety and don't be surprised if the man you want to question remains silent. He is a trained assassin, a member of The Legion, and will not readily betray his own kind."

Theila didn't like being told these things, particularly in the tone the jailer used. She wasn't a child or some local kid off the street after all, but he didn't know that. She managed a semi-appreciative smile and even said thank you, but she wanted to show the foolish jailer her power by burning the entire building down around him. Restraint won out and she moved through the short corridor toward the captured assassin after the heavy steel door was unlocked and forcibly opened by the guards.

The warlock found the rogue sitting on a simple wooden bench in the last cell to the right. There was a tiny window with bars that let in fresh air and daylight, but it was well out of reach. The prisoner would never escape by himself. Theila looked over her shoulder and made sure the guards and the jailer were out of sight. She turned toward the prisoner who had his head in his hands as if thinking intently. She assumed he was trying to figure out how to get away, but it didn't matter. He was occupied and that made her work easier.

Using the demonic tongue of the abyss, Theila began whispering the words to summon one of her minions. The warlock ensured the actual summoning spot was just on the opposite side of the bars so that her minion and the prisoner could *interact.* As the dark mist of the abyss swirled, a body began to form inside the cell. The assassin was immediately on his feet and looking for a place to run, but there was nowhere to go in the tiny cell. He watched the demon take shape and shook with fear when he realized it was a succubus, perhaps the most sadistic of all demons, known for taking sensual pleasure in the torture and punishment of men. This particular succubus was more than a voluptuous seductress; she was the epitome of beauty from mid-thigh up, having perfectly round hips, a tiny waist, ample breasts, full lips, and smooth skin. It was more than enough to entice men into her grasp and overlook the cloven feet, leathery bat wings, blood red eyes, and vestigial horns on her head. The assassin was immediately entranced and fully under the alluring power of the demon.

"Mistress," Hallanya purred, "shall I kill him for you?"

Theila responded resolutely, "No, I want answers from him."

The succubus frowned in a devilish pout, but said, "What do you want to know?"

The warlock said, "Who are the co-conspirators from last night's raid? I want to know the name and location of every spy, informant, and assassin in the area."

Hallanya winked and said, "It will be my pleasure."

As the succubus summoned her abyssian cat-o'-nine-tails, Theila whispered, "Do it quietly."

The demon looked over her shoulder, smiled, revealing a pair of wicked fangs, and went to work. Theila normally preferred to look away while her minions did their duty, particularly agonizing forms of torture to get information, but this low-life had tried to kill her friends and family. He deserved everything that was coming to him.

Using a long, thin cord, Hallanya tied the man's hands together, flew up to the window, looped the cord around the bars and hauled the assassin an inch off the ground. She took a moment to whisper something into the man's ear. She removed his shirt in one mighty pull, tied one sleeve in a knot, and placed it in his mouth. He bit down on it hard just as the demon unleashed her fury on his flesh. The first lash left red welts and the assassin groaned as he arched his back in pain. The second lash broke the skin and left blood trailing down his back. The third lash sent blood across the room in nine perfect lines. The man was breathing heavily and moaning from the beating.

"Hallanya," Theila called out as quiet as she could. "He can't answer questions if he is dead."

The demon came to the bars and said, "His mind is strong and my charms were insufficient to cajole the information you wanted so I have to break his will. I think a few more applications of my whip will do the trick."

Theila was having second thoughts. The man was evil and deserved to be punished, but she was neither the judge nor the executioner and if the man died, his murder would be on her hands.

The warlock nodded for her minion to continue but said, "If he dies, I will spirit wrack your demonic soul until you beg me to banish you for 100 years!"

The succubus glared menacingly at its mistress and said, "I will use caution but you must trust me. I have nearly 3,000 years of practice and I have mastered my art."

Without another word, the demon went back to work. She alternated whispering into the killer's ear and then flaying the hide from his bones until finally his body went limp. The last strike had been too much for his body to take, leaving him unconscious. The demon drew a small flask from her belt and poured a dark, viscous liquid over the wounds. The smell of sulfur mixed with the metallic scent of blood and nearly made the warlock vomit, but the wounds slowly closed up and the man began to stir. Still nearly out of his mind with pain, but conscious, the assassin moaned.

Hallanya spoke, "Tell me about your accomplices," she purred.

The assassin named several names, most of which were indecipherable to Theila.

Hallanya spoke again, "Tell me about the network of informants and spies," she cooed.

Again, the assassin mumbled almost incoherently, but Theila understood a few words.

Hallanya spoke one last time, "Who orchestrated the attack this morning?"

The assassin shook his head as if trying to clear his thoughts after spending the night drinking ale. Finally he said, "Just kill me...please."

Hallanya looked to Theila in hope of getting the go ahead to kill the miserable wretch. Theila shook her head denying that possibility. Instead, she felt compassion though it angered her to give in to it.

She said, "Heal his wounds...we must go."

The sadistic succubus looked indifferent but did as she was commanded. It mattered little to her whether the man lived or died given that she took pleasure in his suffering; that was all that mattered. When the man's wounds were fully healed, Theila snapped her fingers and the demon vanished in a cloud of smoke. She couldn't leave the man hanging from the bars of the window so she drew her wand and fired a single blast of fire just above his hands, cutting the thin cord. The assassin fell to the ground moaning from the torment he had lived through. Theila left as if nothing had happened.

The jailer said, "Well, did you find some satisfaction?"

The warlock said, "Not exactly, but I had to come. Thank you for your help."

The jailer said, "Anytime."

Theila quickly headed to the stables to prepare her mount. She saw Vlaad and the others upon arrival.

"Where have you been?" the defender asked.

"I had to do some research," she replied innocently.

"So what did you find out?" he asked as if he knew where she had gone and what she had done.

"Not much," she began. "I found out that the bakery was the operations center for the informant network. There were well over twenty spies watching us; all on The Legion's payroll, and the second in command is a man known as The Plague."

Vlaad thought in silence for a few moments while everyone else looked amazed at the incredible insight the warlock seemed to have.

After some murmuring among the adventurers Vlaad said, "I think we have time to raid the bakery if anyone wants fresh bread."

Gaedron said, "Aye."

Don tried to whisper but ended up clutching his throat and using his other hand to motion in the direction of the bakery.

Wavren, Da'Shar, Rosabela, Landermihl, and Maejis spoke in unison saying, "I'm in."

The bakery was barely a block away and across the road from the inn. It was a small brick building with a smoking chimney that emitted the aroma of freshly baked goods. Of course the adventurers were interested in who was doing the baking, so to speak, more so than what was being baked. Don, Wavren, Gaedron, and the bears remained outside ready to give chase to anyone who might try to escape. Rosabela, Da'Shar, Maejis, and Theila followed the two warriors inside but remained near the door where they had room to cast spells if need be. This allowed Vlaad and Landermihl to work unimpeded in the small shop.

Landermihl took the lead. He approached the merchant behind a long counter and said, "I need to speak to the owner of this establishment."

The merchant said, "I am Gheran the baker and owner. Is there a problem?"

Landermihl replied, "We heard you have new employees who have been working without washing their hands. In the name of the king, we insist that you allow us to investigate this matter."

Vlaad smirked at the absurd request but thought it was appropriate given that assassins were always considered dirty, underhanded criminals.

Gheran looked nervous. He motioned to the cellar where all of the baking took place. Vlaad drew his weapon and readied his shield. Landermihl followed suit. Gheran stepped aside as the warriors moved forward.

The narrow stone steps leading down enabled the heavy warriors to move quietly but in single file. The casters remained upstairs, not wanting to give The Legion the opportunity to trap everyone below. Vlaad took the lead and kept the Aegis Shield of Griffon's Peak positioned low just in case the enemy was alerted to their presence. Step by step the cellar came into view. He saw half a dozen gnomes furiously rolling dough and throwing flour everywhere, but there was no sign of The Legion.

Vlaad looked back at Landermihl and said, "Do

you think we came too late?"

Landermihl shook his head in uncertainty saying, "Perhaps our information was inaccurate."

Vlaad gave the paladin a disapproving scowl. He replied, "Theila has…a very convincing method of interrogation. She has never been given misinformation before. Let's look around."

The paladin said, "I have a better idea. Let's let evil simply be revealed." The holy warrior called to his deity in prayer for a moment and then announced in a loud voice, "May the wicked and deceitful shine like midday's sun!"

The gnomes dropped their rolling pins and flour sifters and ducked under the tables as several assassins hiding in closets, behind barrels, and under stacks of wheat began to glow in holy light. The rogues drew weapons and stood ready to fight having been magically revealed.

Landermihl called out to the group, "In the name of the king you are all under arrest for conspiracy, attempted murder, and treason. Surrender now and you will live to face the king's justice. Resist and you will be slain."

Five assassins slowly fanned out in a semicircle around the two warriors with their weapons at the ready.

Vlaad whispered to the paladin, "Does it help you sleep better at night to give an evil man one final warning before you kill him or is it just your way of saying prepare to die?"

Landermihl smiled but did not reply with words. He lifted his weapon hand upward and pointed his shield hand at one of the assassins. A bolt of pure light shot into the man, knocking him backward through a wall of shelves. The assassin grunted in pain but recovered quickly as the others charged in.

Vlaad sprang into action. He had foreseen the coming attack even without the gift of combat precognition given by Andar's spirit. Three of the cut throats came for Landermihl but found their initial attacks were deflected by Vlaad's shield and flashing blade as he dove left to right sidelong in front of the paladin. He rolled once and came up in a perfectly balanced stance with shield ready and weapon in the high ready position.

Landermihl used the opportunity call to his god for protection. A split second later both he and the defender were surrounded by golden fields of mystic energy. He began casting another *hammer of justice* spell as Vlaad inched forward.

The assassins knew they would never get past the defender in time to disrupt the paladin's spell. Instead, they dodged or rolled away hoping to avoid being hit by the powerful holy magic. The bolt was guided by divine magic and could not miss, however. It slammed into a cartwheeling rogue sending him into the hard brick wall like a leaf blown by a mighty wind. He slid motionless down the wall when the spell expired.

Taunting the four remaining killers Vlaad said, "Landermihl, you are making this too easy. Perhaps you should take a break."

The four came in one after the other. The first cut low and passed by when his sword bounced off the defender's mighty shield. The second came in with a heavy downward cut from his blade. The two-handed attack was easily deflected with a sweeping sword parry from the defender's curved blade. The third attack came across from the assassin's right to left as he meant to cut through the warrior's neck. The blade would have been met by the crosspiece of Vlaad's weapon, but was repelled by the golden field of energy before it made contact. The fourth charged in against the Aegis Shield hoping to push the defender back and gain an advantage. Vlaad dropped low, scooped up the assassin, and pitched him head over heels. He landed on his back and looked up just in time to see Landermihl's mighty war hammer come down. His skull gave way to the force like an overripe melon.

Vlaad said, "Five was fun but now we are down to three."

The assassins were in a panic. They slashed and hacked at the defender with reckless abandon. Manipulation of anger, fear, and desperation are all tools that enable a defender to control the battle and Vlaad had learned long ago how to use these manipulations to control his enemies. As the last three began to tire from slamming their weapons into his shield, Vlaad blocked, parried, and dodged effortlessly. Landermihl watched in amazement as each man was systematically shield slammed, disarmed, and dispatched. One rogue tried to recover his weapon. Vlaad ran him through; another lay unconscious from having taken the full force of Vlaad's shield bashing. The last was clutching a bleeding stump that had once been his sword arm.

Landermihl stood over the one-handed rogue and said, "I will save your life and heal your wounds if you will give me information."

The rogue answered by swallowing poison. The arsenic pill worked quickly. Landermihl sighed with disgust at the waste of life.

Vlaad shook the blood from his sword and returned it to its sheath. He shouldered his shield and put a friendly hand on the paladin's shoulder. "Betraying the assassin's guild is a guarantee of death through torment and agony. None give information willfully. Only Theila has ever managed to successfully interrogate a member of The Legion."

Landermihl did not want to know how the warlock managed to accomplish such a feat, but he was certain it was a process requiring the use of her demonic minions. Such techniques were not only unjustifiable but they were barbaric. He checked the bodies of the other assassins. Of the five, Landermihl had slain two: one with his hammer and one with magic. Vlaad had killed one and one had opted for suicide. The other was unconscious but alive. The paladin bound his hands. Vlaad watched in awe as Landermihl hefted the limp body. He was amazed at the holy warrior's strength as the paladin carried the prisoner up the stairs like a sack of potatoes.

The gnomes came out of hiding soon after and began cleaning up the mess as if nothing unusual had happened. Gnomes were a hardy and resolute race, caring for little outside of their focused profession. These wanted nothing more than to get back to work baking.

Once outside, the heroes gathered to discuss the action.

"This one will go to the town guards for transportation back to Griffon's Peak. He will stand trial for his crimes and if I know King Xorren Kael, he will suffer the hangman's noose," Landermihl said.

"Why wait? I can find a bit o' rope or give 'im a quick end wit' me ax," the dwarf said, indicating common dwarven justice.

Maejis interjected, "We might all like a hand in revenge but justice requires a trial."

Vlaad mumbled something that no one heard clearly as he walked toward the stables. Several of the companions looked at each other in confusion.

Theila started to follow the defender but stopped and said, "We should go."

"But what did he say?" the wizard asked.

Theila looked back over her shoulder and repeated the defender's indecipherable words, "Duty is second to justice. Now that justice is done; we have work to do."

CHAPTER 14
SHADOWSHIRE

The road to Shadowshire was pleasant for several hours as the adventurers passed out of Bladeshire and into the unpopulated forest of Duskwood. It was so named for the thickness of trees spreading into massive canopy of leaves above that made midday seem like dusk and at night was an impenetrable darkness. The woods were a dangerous place, particularly at night, but as long as travelers stayed on the roadways, they remained relatively safe.

The hunters and druids scouted forward and to both sides along the trip to prevent anyone or anything from surprising them. The increased security measures were tiresome but necessary given the nature of their enemies. Periodically, the scouts returned to the warriors to report. There had been human traffic all around the road, which was not unusual given the supply caravans and merchants that traveled this route to and from Shadowshire; but otherwise, the way was clear.

"We be nearin' da town limits," Gaedron reported to Vlaad and the others.

"The road has been too quiet. It will be good to sit near a warm fire within the security of locked doors," Maejis said.

Vlaad feared neither man nor beast but even he had to agree that the creepy, dark road through Duskwood was unnerving. He merely smiled and said, "It won't be long; let's pick up the pace."

Everyone felt comforted by his warm disposition, but Theila knew better. She relied on her intuition more so than outward expressions of confidence that could so easily mask the true concerns her soul mate had. She unconsciously ran her thin fingers over the wand concealed in her billowy sleeve. She noticed that Vlaad inconspicuously removed the great shield from its carrying strap on his back and rode with it readied on his arm.

From a distance, the lights from the small hamlet of Shadowshire twinkled as a beacon drawing them near. It was barely thirty minutes away at the pace the horses walked and considerably less as the horses were spurred into a canter. The fine steeds were more than happy to pick up the pace given the spooky nature of the dark road.

A lonely howl, deep and eerie, split the night air adding to the imposing dread of the ride. It was answered by several feral growls and howls that made the horses whinny and neigh in fear.

The hunters and druids appeared from the wood line in a full sprint toward their mounted comrades. The group spurred their horses forward into a full gallop as the scouts closed the gap with all haste.

Huffing and rumbling along at an incredible pace with short yet powerful strides, Gaedron yelled, "We ain't alone no more. Git to da town!"

Not far behind the dwarf, the elven hunter paused, took a knee, and fired his blunderbuss. The crack of exploding gunpowder and the flash of light was not unlike lightning in effect as it illuminated the background. Vlaad looked back and saw the dark forms loping along from every direction and knew the hunter would never out run the lupine demons now closing in. The werewolves had found them. His sense of duty took over as he pulled hard on the reins stopping his fine horse. He pulled hard and leaned in the leather saddled making a quick turn and then spurred his mount toward Wavren.

The rest of the group followed suit as chaos ensued.

The hunters knelt shoulder to shoulder and fired their weapons in rapid succession as their massive allies prepared to hold off the lycans claw for claw. The druids took up positions behind the hunters, preparing spells of healing that would be sorely needed soon. Vlaad and Landermihl were pushing their heavy warhorses toward the front line but would never make it before the enemy struck. Maejis, Theila, and Don prepared their own longer-ranged attacks and began casting long before they were able to join their friends. Bolts of frost and fire exploded in front of the hunters as the first werewolves sprang, followed by spinning blades from the bard. Although effectively halting the first few attackers, the initial blasts couldn't slow the black tide of fur and teeth that came in fast and hard.

Each werewolf was twice as large as Vlaad with infinitely greater strength. Two of the lycans hit Ol' Blackmaw simultaneously. The massive arctic bear was swept away in a flurry of raking claws and snapping maws.

Gaedron screamed out, "NOOO!" as he fired his blunderbuss again and again.

Two more werewolves tore into Stonetalon with savage fury. The ruddy mountain bear swatted one away but two more took its place.

Wavren fired a fine mithril bullet through the head of one and it fell dead. Stonetalon was in trouble but fighting with increasing rage.

The druids were fully engaged casting spells of

healing that kept the bears from being slain outright, but more werewolves were joining the battle.

The steel barding the two warhorses wore not only protected them from injury, but served as a battering ram as the paladin and the defender crashed through the front line. The lycans were scattered for a moment and some were dazed from the powerful charge, but they quickly returned to the fray. Landermihl swung his mighty hammer in powerful upward circles lifting many enemies off the ground and sending them backward with each stroke. His hammer was very effective against the unholy beasts given the nature of his deity-imbued weapon. Vlaad's sweeping sword was less effective, but he managed to buy the hunters much needed time as he plowed through the were-beasts.

The second wave of attackers came in just as the heroes secured their defensive position. Theila sent her voidwalker into battle adding to the frontline strength of the bears, but it was Vlaad who made the difference. Having lost the momentum of his initial charge, the defender leapt from his mount and secured the point of the battle line. To his right the bears stood roaring, slashing, and bleeding but still in the fight. To his left was the summoned demon, Zaashik. The hunters fired behind him facing outward completing the wedge formation. Theila and Maejis were in the safety of the wedge's pocket with the druids in the rear. All were casting furiously as the enemy approached. Landermihl was still mounted, alternating between casting spells of healing and blasting lycans with holy bolts of energy.

"We cannot hold them off indefinitely," the paladin called in his deep baritone voice. "We have to get to the safety of the village!"

The lycans struck again before anyone could respond.

The first beast slashed at Vlaad but could not penetrate the protection of the defender's shield. It was shield bashed once for every two hits it landed on the magnificent heater. Vlaad lifted his elbow up and pivoted his body changing the angle, causing the lycan to slide right into the tearing jaws of Stonetalon. As the bear latched on to its torso, the defender swung his curved blade down on the back of its neck. The severed head rolled out of sight.

Theila set her voidwalker loose from direct commands and blasted away with her hellfire magic. She couldn't waste the time or mental energy directing it at this point. Each werewolf hit by the abyssal flames suffered both damage from fire as well as a more sinister burning of the soul. Such was the nature of a warlock's wicked power. She was effective in her attacks but more and more werewolves appeared. She knew it was only a matter of time before the foul creatures overwhelmed them. Theila looked for a moment to her right and saw Don draw and throw the last of his fine blades. The bard had a look of concern for his daughter, but the canny spy winked at her and drew his cloak around himself and disappeared from sight. She had no idea he had such powerful items at his disposal but at least he might escape.

Maejis stood impassive as he loosed a jet of frost followed by a massive blast of ice that laid several foes low. He was meticulous and calculating in his casting, never once appearing concerned for his own life or those in his party. His spells seemed endless and his focus was no less. To say he was the embodiment of magic might be an exaggeration, but he was a perfect conduit for it if nothing else.

Landermihl crushed the skull of one werewolf with a great overhand strike as another raked long lines in his fine, golden armor. His mount was furiously kicking the enemies away as the masterful paladin controlled every attack from his saddle. There was no doubt why Landermihl, a paladin, had been given command of the king's knights.

In spite of the cacophony of the battle, a long howl broke through the night air. As if a trumpet had sounded the retreat, the attackers disengaged and fell back to the wood line giving the weary warriors a much-needed break.

"Now...break for the village!" Landermihl called out.

No one hesitated for long but several looks of uncertainty remained on the faces of the heroes.

Wavren motioned the others forward and said, "We will cover the rear; move quickly and do not look back."

Rosabela and Da'Shar nodded and quickly headed toward Shadowshire with Landermihl and Vlaad in the lead. Maejis and Theila followed closely on their fine palominos.

"Ye thinkin' what I be thinkin' boyo?" the surly dwarf asked as he drew out several red sticks of dynamite.

"I am indeed," he replied. The hunters set the explosives along the sides of the road, daisy-chained end to end with a small tripwire that would ignite the trap. Just as they were about to leave, Don appeared out of nowhere.

"What are ye about?" the dwarf asked suspiciously.

"No time for questions, my good dwarf, the lycans are right behind me," he replied as he sprinted past having lost his horse.

Wavren and Gaedron shrugged and easily caught up to the bard. They drew upon their hunter skills lending the bard speed and endurance. The technique known as *aspect of the pack* was not a true spell, though it had magical effects and before long the threesome had reached the others on horseback. Moments later, there was a huge explosion that illuminated the night and sent a shockwave through the ground. The hunters smiled broadly.

Wavren winked at his mentor who said, "That'll teach 'em."

***

A single human walked out of the forest not far from the site of the battle. He noticed that more than two dozen of his werewolves had fallen but to the credit of the species, more than half of these would soon regenerate. He took the time to inspect each body. One had been decapitated; one shot through the head with a dwarven weapon, and several had been burned beyond recognition. Some were dismembered, but arms and legs would grow back over a short time.

The band of adventurers was powerful indeed and they had the capability required to kill his pack. The cunning pack leader took full measure of these things and transformed into his beastly form. He howled and several werewolves came to collect the bodies. Lord Carnage would never leave evidence of his presence. Better to remain an enigma.

***

The Foaming Tankard was the largest inn

found in Shadowshire and its thick oaken door was locked and barred when the heroes arrived.

Maejis knocked several times but no one came to invite them in.

"Perhaps we should seek shelter elsewhere," the wizard said coolly.

Gaedron shoved the thin man aside and drew out a long, red stick of dynamite and said, "Inn keep…if'n ye don' open dis door, I'll blow it off'n its hinges!"

A small window on the second floor opened up and the innkeeper squeezed his round head through. He called down to the group, "It is late and we are closed until dawn. You should not be here at this hour. Go away!"

The dwarf was fuming. He stomped around and cursed in dwarvish. Wavren caught the meaning in spite of being less than fluent in the language. Apparently, the dwarf intended to shove the stick of dynamite up the innkeeper's rear end if he didn't open the door soon.

Don came forward. Though his voice was still suffering the effects of his injuries, he said, "Nate, you old goat, it is Don of Westrun. We are goodly folk in need of shelter and you would be well advised to let us in before my party burns your inn to the ground."

Nate the innkeeper said, "By the light…Don of Westrun! I did not know it was you. I'll be down immediately."

Landermihl managed a smile and said, "Is there anyone you don't know?"

The bard replied, "Sure, but they all live in Dek'Thal and speak orcish."

It never ceased to amaze the paladin how popular the bard was and how far his network reached. It was rumored that Don the Bard knew every man, woman, and child in the Eastern Kingdom over the age of three, given that it took about three years to visit each city, town, and village along his common route of travel.

The sound of a heavy brace being removed from the door told the adventurers that the innkeeper had finally come. When the door creaked open, the dwarf had to be restrained by his apprentice to keep the fiery hunter from making good his earlier threat. The others quickly entered, closed the door, and helped replace the brace. The inn was huge, virtually a fortress and even had a stable within its massive walls to protect the horses from things that roamed at night.

"My stable boy will care for your beasts and I will escort you to the central tavern for a drink and a bite. Please follow me," Nate asked humbly.

The stable boy seemed experienced with both horses and even the bears. He led them to their straw beds and brought water for each of them.

Da'Shar spoke sarcastically, "Are you always so hospitable to your guests at this hour?"

The innkeeper apologized, "I am so sorry, but the threat of death looms heavily in Shadowshire and we have endured the worst of it by being cautious. For all I knew you were one of them pack runners."

Rosabela jumped into the conversation, "You mean werewolves?"

The innkeeper flinched as if even saying the words would call the demons into his place of business. He said, "Milady, the night has far worse things than were-beasts but yes, I was referring to them."

Wavren and Gaedron sat at the bar and helped themselves to a pint of dark ale while Vlaad, Landermihl, Maejis, and Don sat at a table. Rosabela, Da'Shar, and Theila sat near the hearth on a long, soft couch.

"What can you tell us about the nights here in Shadowshire?" Don asked with a charming smile and sparkling eyes.

Nate began, "Shadowshire has always had its problems being so far from Griffon's Peak, but things have gotten worse as of late. By the looks of your party, I can tell you are no stranger to combat and I assume you had a run in with some of the *locals*.

Everyone nodded at the obvious comment.

Nate continued, "Well, then you can imagine what we must do to survive. Part of living in these god-forsaken lands means being prepared, cautious, and even suspicious. A man brought the plague of lycanthrope to Shadowshire and those infected become hideous creatures of the night. The howling beasts roam the Duskwood forest looking for easy prey but from time to time they come into town seeking new members to join their pack. It is during those times that our hyper-vigilance pays big dividends."

"Do you know this pack leader?" Rosabela asked.

"I do not, but he is known as Lord Carnage by the locals here. I pray I never meet him for that will surely be the end of my days," Nate returned with obvious fear in his eyes.

"How many minions does Lord Carnage command?" Da'Shar asked.

The inn keep looked down at his boots and said, "Too many."

The elf persisted, "But how many…can you estimate?"

Nate looked up and said, "No one knows how many came with him when he arrived, but well over fifty men and women have been reported missing. We have found fewer than ten corpses of those who refused to join his pack or rebelled after joining."

"I would estimate nearly a score of werewolves fell in our battle," Vlaad reported.

"But most of those will return to the pack after regenerating," Da'Shar added.

Landermihl sighed. He said, "We have a tough road ahead. We should retire and rise early tomorrow."

Nate looked curiously at the heroes and asked, "How is it that you survived a battle having slain so few? These beasts attack in large numbers and should have easily overwhelmed your small party."

Theila looked at her father who only smiled and winked again. She said, "A bard can do many things with his voice well beyond singing and telling tales. His ability to mimic the howls of the pack leader probably saved us."

Gaedron and Wavren realized that was the reason Don had been left behind when everyone else ran for the inn. He had slipped away and called to the lycans. The bard was crafty indeed.

Don said humbly, "It was a small thing really. I am glad it worked, particularly since I was out of throwing blades but I doubt that it will work again. We should consider ourselves lucky and prepare for the next encounter."

The small band of heroes agreed in silence with a few nods and several well-deserved pats on the back. Theila and Vlaad watched the others depart for their rooms. They shared the same nagging thought as they remained seated in the common room. If The Legion joined with the lycan pack, there would be no stopping the flood of evil in the lands. The last engagement had been enough to convince the two that their greatest battle was yet to be fought.

Morning came with the smell of sizzling bacon and eggs on the air. The heroes made their way eagerly to the breakfast table where they found Nate and his wife, Kalaa, preparing places for the nine adventurers.

"Good morning friends, I hope your appetites are hardy. My wife Kalaa and I have prepared a grand feast for you this day. Fresh eggs and bacon with griddle cakes and cream will make you think you have died and gone to heaven," Nate said with pride.

Gaedron smiled broadly and rubbed his ample belly. He said, "I'm hopin' ye made a' plenty. Me belly's been growlin' like Ol' Blackmaw an' a dwarf canna be fightin' wit' out a full stomach. Wavren smiled and sat beside his dwarven mentor. The druids nodded in silence and took seats across from the hunters. The humans came in last.

"Hail all," Maejis said with cheer. He never seemed overly concerned with matters. "I pray all slept well. We have quite a day ahead of us, so eat well."

Theila, Don, and Landermihl entered together.

Don greeted the others with a simple, "Morning…"

Theila and Landermihl remained silent, being in a somber mood.

Nate asked, "Where is the one you call Vlaad? Will he join us for breakfast this morning?"

Theila answered saying, "He is exercising as he

does every morning. He will come soon, but neither food nor glory comes before his ritual practice."

Nate looked stunned. He said, "What manner of man chooses exercise over good food? I think he is a strange fellow indeed if such are his priorities."

The eight adventurers continued to eat, electing not to remark on the subject. This gave the innkeeper the feeling that none disagreed, but also that none questioned Vlaad on the matter either. Nate paused from his duties and walked to the window where he saw Vlaad.

The defender was stripped of his armor and tunic. He held a magnificent sword and shield as if hell itself had opened up and spewed forth an army of demons and devils for him to fight. Nate watched for a moment. What he saw made a lasting impression that somehow proved Vlaad was indeed different, though perhaps strange was an unfitting term.

The warrior stood motionless; every muscle in his body was relaxed though perfectly honed and glistening with sweat in the morning sun. As if the call to war had been sounded, he sprang into action. Leading with his shield, the defender drove forward a dozen feet, hopped back, and spun his curved blade overhead in a parrying maneuver. He ducked low and Nate could imagine one of the imaginary demons flying over as the warrior lifted and tossed it head over heels behind him. Without looking, he thrust his leg backward in a move that would have surely crushed the throat of the fallen enemy behind him. He angled his body as if dodging a spear thrust or perhaps the ripping claws of some beast, followed by a downward slicing strike that would have certainly sheered the spearhead off, as well as any hand or claw. The defender coiled like a serpent and darted forward in what must have been a shield-slamming maneuver, followed by a series of spinning circles that might have been those of a dancing girl but seemed an unlikely move for a warrior. When the spinning ended, the warrior was back in his original position, body relaxed, shield in front, and sword held high. Nate was intrigued and returned to the group.

"What manner of fighter is Vlaad?" Nate asked with sincere curiosity, "I have heard of frenzied berserkers, dazzling swashbucklers, militant soldiers, and even holy warriors yet he seems unlike any of these."

Don looked up from his meal and said, "He is the last of his kind. He is known by many in Griffon's Peak as the King's Champion, some know him as the Wandering Hero, and others know him as a Defender, but I believe he has become something more. He is a shield warrior of the line of Vlorin, though he would deny such a title."

Nate was perplexed. "But what does that mean? Are you saying he is some sort of shield specialist? If you ask me, being good with a shield might buy you some time in a fight, but being a great swordsman is far better."

Don smiled and said, "He is perhaps the finest swordsman in the realm."

The others around the table nodded in agreement.

Nate paused in confusion and then said, "But you said he was a shield warrior."

The bard nodded in agreement and said, "His sword craft is without peer but is nothing compared to his shield work. He has surpassed the need to merely cut a man down. He lives to protect his team and none have ever been his equal in this duty. By sword, ax, club, or spear he will not allow his fellows to fall. Neither fangs nor claws will molest his comrades. He is the ultimate expression of selfless service and dedication to duty in combat."

Vlaad entered the dining hall having completed his shield drills, cleaned up, and dressed while the others ate. He was virtually radiating energy from his workout and commanded everyone's attention as he approached.

The defender said, "Well met friends. I have had a revelation this good morning that requires sharing with you all."

Even Gaedron stopped eating for a moment to listen.

"In a moment of clarity while I was exercising, I realized what we must do to end the threat that lies before us," he began. "We cannot fight the entire lycan pack and somehow I doubt their leader will face us alone on our own terms. Likewise, we cannot fight The Legion with their countless minions, particularly since fifteen years of hunting has never delivered their guild master, Gorka Darkstorm."

"Aye boyo," Gaedron interrupted, "but git to da point afore me eggs go cold."

Da'Shar cast the dwarf and agitated look and said, "Please continue, Vlaad. You have our interest peaked."

The defender took a deep breath and declared, "I will assume control of the lycan pack."

Da'Shar and Rosabela scowled and crossed their arms in utter disagreement. The elder druid spoke, "The only way to do that is to join the pack, challenge the pack leader, and kill him but that impossibility is not enough by itself. You must drink of the dying pack leader's blood to absorb his essence and become Lord Carnage. Doing so would make you the enemy of every goodly race in Dae'gon. You would become that which we now hunt. You would become my enemy."

Maejis spoke up, "What Da'Shar says is true, but if this were possible, Vlaad would be able to deny The Legion from joining the lycans. He could end the lives of the werewolves under his command and the threat we fear would be no more."

Theila could barely contain her emotions. She was both shocked and heartbroken at the same time. The warlock stood up and pointed to Vlaad saying, "You would sacrifice yourself on this quest after all that we have been through. Are you insane or maybe you have lost yourself to that sentient blade at your side. I will never allow you to do this to yourself or to us. Don't you know how this affects us? How this affects me?"

Vlaad bowed his head low and said, "This is a war we cannot win. We were nearly overwhelmed by a few werewolves last night. The next engagement will be worse. The enemy knows our limitations now and threatens all we hold dear and I cannot allow the destruction that will follow if The Legion pairs with the lycan pack."

Landermihl walked up to Vlaad and put his thick hand on the defender's shoulder. He said, "My friend, there has to be another way. Your life has always been centered on your duty but there must be an alternative to sacrifice. Let's not be rash. At least allow us to explore other courses of action."

Theila stormed out of the hall and headed to her room. Da'Shar motioned for Rosabela to follow her. Rosabela was already heading after her when he did. Wavren, Gaedron, Landermihl, Maejis, Don, and Da'Shar stared blankly at Vlaad. The silence was thick and oppressive like summer heat in the desert, yet no one spoke. After many minutes had passed, Vlaad walked out. He knew what he had to do.

Maejis spoke to the remaining heroes, "If we fight the lycans and the assassins we will face hundreds or more and even if we slew them in the next battle, they will regroup and bring more until we are taken. The direct approach is not the way."

Landermihl said, "I have been thinking the same thing all night. Even if I gathered the King's Knights, we would only find ourselves outnumbered again or the enemy would hide and wait. This is the nature of assassins and were-creatures. They will only attack when they have the advantage and their strength lies in great numbers, but Vlaad's sacrifice cannot be the only option."

Wavren asked, "Da'Shar, how should we proceed? You and Gaedron fought Lord Carnage before. How can we win?"

Before Da'Shar could answer the dwarf shook his head. "Some five hunnerd years ago we tracked the first pack leader. When we thought we had 'im he slipped away. This was a cycle lasting for several years. We caught 'im a'gin and he passed his soul to 'nother who's been in hidin' e'er since. These lycan types have a knack fer survivin'."

Da'Shar sighed. He said, "Gaedron is, of course, correct, but there is another way to end this all. We kill the leader of The Legion. This will negate the need for Vlaad to sacrifice himself if the guild falls apart. We divide and conquer."

Now Don was shaking his head side to side. He said, "My daughter Theila and Vlaad have been hunting Gorka Darkstorm for well over a decade and just as your people have been unable to capture or kill the pack leader, my people have been unable to do so to the guild master. Even if we could, there is nothing stopping an able lieutenant from stepping up and taking over as the new guild master. I am afraid we are in between the proverbial rock and a hard place."

Finally Landermihl said, "We must never give up hope. The way will appear before us if we remain focused on the goal, which is to deny the joining of these two vile groups. We must have faith."

Chapter 15
Sacrifices

"Lord Carnage, you have a visitor," a werewolf in human form said to the pack leader.

A lone human walked in. The man was skinny, almost frail looking, but walked with the same confidence of a man twice his size and strength. He wore simple black clothing marking him as an assassin of The Legion. In a formal manner, the thin rogue bowed. When the pack leader acknowledged his presence, the assassin stood straight and addressed Lord Carnage.

"My lord," he began, "I am known as The Plague, second in command of the assassin's guild of Griffon's Peak. I have been sent by the guild master of The Legion to discuss business with you. Would you hear my offer of alliance at this time?"

Carnage replied calmly and civilly, "Your respect is greatly appreciated though I am not currently seeking an alliance with your assassin's guild or anyone else for that matter. I am curious to hear the message you have come so far to deliver."

"The guild master of The Legion, and commander of the Bloodcrest Forces, Lord Gorka Darkstorm sends his regards and gratitude for your time. He wishes to join forces under mutually beneficial terms to strengthen his house and yours. It is his desire to gain the strength of your lycan heritage while offering you the choice of any city and its surrounding lands once the realms have been conquered by our combined efforts. This will enable you to operate in the open just as we wish to end our days as an underground organization."

Lord Carnage smiled to one of his lieutenants showing prominent, oversized fangs and replied, "It is good to hear that our strength is prized and even coveted by others, in particular The Legion, who has a notoriously powerful reputation, but I cannot agree to your terms as I have my own plans for the realm."

The Plague nodded and made his second offer. "My master has empowered me with the authority to negotiate on his behalf. Can we discuss terms that could be advantageous to both sides or would you prefer to add the most powerful assassin's guild to your list of enemies?"

The smile left the pack leader's face. He leaned forward and issued a low growl as his eyes went from a peaceful sky-blue to a deep blood-red. He spoke in a voice that was devoid of fear and filled with malice, "You are a fool with a death wish to have come here into my den alone. Even as a minister of The Legion, you have no guarantee that I will allow you to live under the best of circumstances and you dare to threaten me here, among my kindred? It is sheer morbid curiosity that prevents me from tearing you apart where you stand. Tell me, insolent whelp, what could you ever offer that I could not simply take?"

The Plague smiled darkly and replied, "In spite of your distaste for this discussion, I believe we are now engaged in negotiations. This is a good thing, for I have something that you have long desired and can never obtain by force. You see, The Legion is not merely an assassin's guild. It is a network of informants who traffic every detail of information imaginable. We know where every merchant spends his coin and who he deals with. We have records of every family member in the king's court and every noble family member abroad. Last but not least, we have a detailed historical account of Dae'run going back thousands of years. This is the true source of power for The Legion and something you can neither build nor take from us."

The Lord of Lycans laughed mightily. "I care not at all for the dealings of merchants, kin of kings, or historical musings no matter how far it may go back. You have still offered nothing of value, which should be the crux of any negotiation. Since you have nothing to offer, I see no reason to allow you to live."

It was The Plague's turn to laugh, though it was neither mighty nor even hardy in nature. It was a wheezing sinister laugh and it gave pause to the pack leader.

Lord Carnage was perplexed and said, "You laugh at the coming of your death?"

The Plague stopped laughing and said, "No, I laugh because you have failed to see the value of what I offer. You see, in controlling information and understanding history we have discovered your weakness as well as a way to grant you true immortality."

Lord Carnage paused and thought back to his only defeat some five hundred years ago. He had been defeated by his own brother Da'Shar, who had tracked him down to turn him over to the druidic council for crimes against nature, but an overzealous dwarven companion had accidentally enabled his escape. The cost had been his beloved elven form, but a price paid willingly to live on as a lycan. He knew that if the foolish dwarf hadn't tried to kill him, he would have been delivered to the druids and utterly destroyed after his trial, but instead, he left his mortally injured elven body, taking over the body of a pathetic human. This transformation had weakened him greatly and his recuperation required the better part of five centuries but now he was strong, though even this body would fail one day. He needed the body an elven druid to regain his true power. No druid had ever given in to his offers of power or methods of torture. It was the darkest path a druid could take. Death had always been an easy choice for the few that Carnage had captured.

"I see that now you have found value in the offer of joining The Legion," the assassin stated more than he asked.

"Your promise is a hollow one. You may know what I desire, but you have nothing in your grasp to offer," Carnage replied, though he secretly assumed otherwise.

"Our alliance will hinge on our ability to bring you a worthy elven specimen for your eternal needs. If we fail to deliver, our contract will be void," the assassin offered.

"Very well, we have an arrangement, but when you bring me the host I need, how will you be sure that I will keep my word?" the lycan master asked.

The gaunt killer smiled a knowing grin. "You will have only a few minutes to do your part before the host we bring succumbs to a lethal dose of poison. We will have the antidote. If you decide not to pass on your gift of immortality to our leaders, we will destroy the elf. I am sure you can imagine how this will play out if we are crossed."

"Indeed…" was his reply.

"Then our negotiations are complete. We will see you again soon. Farewell," the assassin said confidently.

Lord Carnage waved him away with antipathy

though a small glimmer of hope could not be denied by the pack leader.

The Plague casually walked out of the lycan's den. All was in order. Now, all he had to do was capture a certain pair of elves, which was not going to be easy, but Gorka had set the stage for this. Soon The Legion would be unstoppable.

***

Time had passed from morning to well past midday and Theila had been thinking a lot about her last words to Vlaad. She did not want him to sacrifice himself even if it was for the greater good. She loved him and had been dedicated to him from the beginning. If he did this, then everything else was for naught. She knew he loved her, but his foolhardiness was only surpassed by his stubbornness. If he would just forget his obsession with destroying The Legion for a few minutes they would have been married a long time ago. With a tear in her eye, Theila laughed at the irony. She loved Vlaad for his dedication and the man he had become. How could she ever ask him to be something he was not? It was all pointless anyway. She was destined to love a man she could never fully have until the damnable assassin's guild was crushed and that had already taken up the better part of her life. It was all so utterly hopeless that she could do nothing but weep. She wept and wished The Legion would just go to the abyss.

Theila thought, *If only…they would go to the abyss*. She said out loud, "The abyss…" as an idea formed piece by piece in her mind.

Wiping the tears from her face, Theila closed the door to her room and magically locked the door.

She went to her pack and retrieved the items needed for summoning. She took rare, white chalk made from the bones of fallen warriors and drew the summoner's protection circle on the floor. It had to be perfect as her life depended on it. With equally rare, red chalk made from the blood of fallen wizards, she inscribed the mystic sigils at the four corners of the room. These wards would ensure the demon she called would be powerless and compelled to answer her questions. As she completed each, the sigils burned with an eerie light. Finally, with a bronze censure and the grey-black anthracite from the deepest dwarven mines, she started a small fire. As smoke filled the room and the flames jumped from the coals, the warlock began her work.

She called first to her imp, Trig'zstder who appeared quickly and asked, "What is your bidding, my mistress?"

Theila ordered the imp to the northern corner of the room. He complied and sat hunched over, twitching nervously as she started the process again. He watched intently knowing that his mistress was planning to summon something powerful indeed. The second demon took shape. Hellanya, the succubus, appeared whip in hand and looking ready to cause mayhem.

"How may I serve you, mistress," the demonic seductress asked evilly.

Theila ordered her to the southernmost corner of the room. She took her place and cracked the wicked cat-o'-nine-tails, impatiently wondering what was going on. The warlock began again; this time the voidwalker appeared. It said nothing but was mentally commanded to move to the eastern corner of the room where it billowed black smoke and hovered menacingly.

Theila took her place at the western corner, took a deep breath, and wiped the accumulation of sweat from her brow. The room was already unbelievably hot and maintaining control of all three demons at once was a terrible strain. She had never even attempted to call them all at once, but she needed them now. Although her plan was a long shot, she believed she might be able to end this never-ending game of chase with The Legion, but she needed information and her minions were not powerful enough to help this time. She needed a greater demon for this task. She paused for less than a moment and considered the consequences. She could be charged with reckless summoning by her Warlock Order if things got out of control, or worse, the demon would destroy her and wreak havoc on this plane. She had to risk it!

In a low voice, almost a guttural growl Theila called to the abyss saying, "From the ninth gate of fire and chaos, I call balrog the tormentor by name. Hear me *Ja'Zaru!*"

Of the many major demons known to wizards and warlocks, the balrog-type is the eldest and most powerful. As such, they are also by far the most dangerous. Each has a name, which can be invoked to bend it to a summoner's will, though doing so is often the last word they ever speak, as the hellish demons seek any weakness or flaw in the protective wards allowing it to destroy the pompous mage who called it. In the past, the ensuing rampage of destruction of a freed greater demon has spanned entire cities before the summoning spell expired and the demon returned to its own plane of existence.

Theila was no mere novice. She knew the price to pay for failure and her preparation was perfect.

Her sigils were geometrically precise and the protective circle was flawless. Upon arrival, Ja'Zaru checked each with a careful eye as hate seethed like a wave of molten lava across the room. The succubus whimpered and the imp cowered; only the voidwalker seemed unafraid. Ja'Zaru recognized the mastery of the warlock's craft and accepted its short tenure as a servant, but would never forget the humiliation by the summoner. Her face, her body, and even an imprint of her soul would be taken for future reference. It would gladly wait a thousand years to repay Theila for her insolence if need be. The scene was vivid.

The demon is far too large for the small censure and is bound by magic to appear as a miniature version of itself, limiting it power on the material plane, but it is fearsome nonetheless. Theila steadies herself and calls to it, commanding it.

"Ja'Zaru!" she yells.

The creature howls in torment as she calls his true name.

Again, she steadies herself in the face of such a powerful being and says, "Ja'Zaru, I summoned thee to do my bidding."

The miniature version of the demon flaps its powerful bat-like wings and flexes its powerful chest and arms as if trying to free itself from invisible bonds. It creates a sword of living fire in its left hand and a writhing whip of liquid flame in its right. The sword slashes and the whip cracks but it cannot escape…it must obey.

Theila calls to the demon, "Foul beast of the abyss, if I call your name a third time, you will be banished for one thousand years, during which time the tortures you have wrought on others will be reflected back upon yourself tenfold. Now I command thee...answer me!"

The demon hisses evilly, but slowly bows down on one knee. It says in a voice that echoes in Theila's head like a thunderbolt, "Ask what you will, witch, but know that your repayment in torture will last ten thousand years when my turn comes."

Theila shudders from exertion and nearly vomits from the strain. She sacrifices her imp to add to her own strength, grits her teeth, and says, "Gather unto me mine enemies that we might end this war between good and evil. We will decide once and for all who should prevail."

The balrog bellows thunderously inside the warlock's head, "Name them and I will do thy bidding."

Theila screams from the pain. She feels blood running freely from her ears and nose. She wipes it away and sacrifices her succubus to heal her fatigue and injuries. The female demon vanishes in a puff of smoke and her wounds are healed, but time is short as she feels her control of the powerful demon slipping. Somewhat revived, she calls to the demon, "Gather the ten senior leaders of The Legion. Gorka Darkstorm, the guild master, will know his chief lieutenants."

The demon knows it has a chance to further weaken the warlock through its connection to her. Being a devious and foul creature of the abyss, it suffers its servitude for a few moments longer in exchange for the chance to kill its master.

Again the balrog booms, "Name the location that I may do thy bidding."

Theila feels her heart pounding in her chest and her breath comes in labored gasps as she fights the mental battle for control of the demon at the risk of her eternal torment. She summons her strength, sacrifices her most powerful demon, Zaashik, the voidwalker, and says, "You will not have me, foul demon! I am your mistress! You will serve or I will destroy you!" The glowing sigils flare white hot, as the warlock sends a mystic surge of energy into the demon, wracking its unholy spirit. The balrog thrashes as if being lashed with a barbed whip. It howls and roars but succumbs to Theila's power.

Theila commands the demon, "Transport them in two days to Pirate's Cove off the coast of Bladerun Bay....now be gone."

The balrog snarls having failed to overcome the warlock, but is compelled to obey. It vanishes in a massive gout of flame and ash that causes Theila to cover her eyes and turn away. Her exposed skin reddens and blisters from the blast, but she barely notices as fatigue from the mental battle takes its toll. Turning to the door, she unbinds the magical wards and turns the knob to find Rosabela standing in the doorway swung wide.

"You shall not stand alone, summoner. Though my place is with Da'Shar and Wavren in the fight against the lycans, I will not allow you to fall in the fight against the assassins to save your love from death," the she elf promised as she moved forward with glowing hands to heal the warlock.

Theila, still exhausted, accepted the druidic magic to relieve her burns and the pain in her head. She said, "Thank you for understanding and for your help."

Rosabela smiled. "We must stick together as the only girls on the team. Besides, I know what you must be going through with Vlaad."

Theila was taken aback by the last statement. "What exactly do you mean?" she asked.

"I can see the connection you have with the defender. He is everything a woman could want: charming, strong, honorable, and handsome. He is so much like my own soul mate, Jael'Kutter," the elf empathized sadly.

This time it was Theila who detected sadness and shared her feelings. "It is tough to love someone, know they love you, and yet remain unable to be with them. Vlaad told me about the sacrifice Jael'Kutter made in the battle at Forestedge. I know your heart must be broken and I am sorry for your loss."

Rosabela looked as if she might weep, but somehow managed to lift her chin and hide her sorrow. She said, "I share my dreams with him now, though we cannot be together often in a physical manner, I can reunite his body and soul with an enchanted stone from time to time, though it is taxing on my own life force. You at least have Vlaad here, even if he protects you by remaining distant. It is the way of men to sacrifice for others in order to protect the ones they love."

Theila laughed at the irony. "It is true. They are so blinded by their duty that they often miss the joy of living…but you mentioned an enchanted stone. May I see it?"

Rosabela produced the magnificent gem from a small pouch. It throbbed with a life of its own. She closed her eyes and sensed the spirit within. This was not a simple soul stone common to warlocks. It was a key, powered by magic. It was made to unlock an elemental gateway. The spells a warlock uses for summoning demons was very similar to the invocation required to access the power of this particular stone.

Theila handed the stone back to the druid and said, "Rosabela, I think I understand the reason why you are so drained when you call to your soul mate with this gem. It is actually a port-key, but it has no source of energy to power the magic required to use it....so the stone draws on your life force. I have been trained to make healing stones, not unlike your own healing magic, but they are of little use to me as I am able to draw life from the beings I summon in times of great need. I can make some for you which could serve as an energy source for this spirit stone."

The she-elf smiled with a look of eager anticipation and said, "It would be literally, a dream come true if you are able."

Theila bowed slightly and smiled. She said, "Though I am too weary to try today, I will create one for you tomorrow. After all, we girls must stick together right?"

She smiled back and said, "So true, now let's see if we can resolve this quest so that we can be with the men we love."

Theila agreed and said, "We certainly can't leave it to the men; we will be old maids by the time they get around to wrapping things up."

The two females came down the stairs together with renewed hope to a group of serious looking males.

"Well then," Theila began, "have you gentlemen worked out a solution to matters at hand?"

Gaedron grumbled something to Wavren who only nodded. Don, Maejis, and Landermihl shook their heads and Da'Shar eyed Rosabela suspiciously.

Rosabela spoke, "Since you all have been unable to formulate a plan, I think we should listen to Theila, who has a workable option for us."

Gaedron scoffed and Wavren elbowed him for it.

Landermihl frowned but remained silent.

Da'Shar looked at Maejis who shrugged indifferently.

Don, in his most diplomatic tone said, "Yes, of course we would gladly hear Theila's ideas."

Theila felt nervous, being the center of attention, but drew confidence from being a powerful warlock. After all, she had tamed three demons from the abyss to serve her and had survived an encounter with a greater demon just moments ago. How hard could it possibly be to convince her friends to simply meet the assassins and kill them on a remote island in two days?

She began with the end in mind, "We must deny The Legion their desire to unite with the lycans. We must capture or kill the leaders in order to do this."

Gaedron spoke, "Aye lass, that be what we came all da way from across da sea ta do. Pinnin' da sneaky buggers down ain't been easy though."

Theila drew courage from the dwarf's admission. She said, "What would you say if I told you that I know the leaders of the assassin's guild were going to meet at a specific place at a specific time in two days?"

Da'Shar looked less than interested. He was concerned with the lycans more so than the assassins, but Landermihl and Maejis showed great interest.

The paladin said, "Truly child? Tell us everything."

Theila again felt empowered with the growing interest of the group. She continued, "The ten senior leaders of the assassin's guild will be at Pirate's Cove off the coast of Bladerun Bay in two days."

Wavren, being a hunter and curious by nature asked, "How exactly do you know this? Is the source reliable?"

Theila's courage crumbled. She would be hard pressed to convince the group to trust the promise of a demon, particularly a demon that she did not control and who had been compelled into servitude, but there was no choice. Just as she was about to explain, Rosabela stepped forward.

Rosabela pointed a thin finger at her brother and said, "Her sources are beyond your comprehension, just as your skills as a hunter cannot be explained to those of us who are not trackers. We do not question your methods, why question hers when we have nothing better to work with anyway?"

Wavren sank down into his chair and Gaedron rose to defend his pupil. He said, "Aye, ye are quick to follow a set o' track when we spot 'em, but da tracks ain't comin' from da pits o' hell when we be pointin' 'em out. So speak true an' be forthright. Did da plan come from workin' wit' demon kind or not?"

Rosabela was forced to concede but Theila took her place and nodded to affirm they had come from demonic means.

Maejis, ever the devil's advocate, rose and said, "So then do we take advantage of this once-in-a-lifetime chance to defeat our adversaries and accept the risk that perhaps the source has misled us, or do we decide not to act out of doubt?"

Landermihl looked past the others and stared

into the warlock's eyes. "I do not fear death or demons, but this plan is risky and could divert us from the true goal, which is to prevent the joining of forces by our enemies. Theila, can you be certain that we are not walking into a trap or being misdirected which will give the enemy time to complete their plans?"

All eyes turned to Theila who paused for a moment. She considered that Ja'Zaru, the balrog, could be planning a trap, but likely it did not know about the connection between The Legion and the lycans. She felt certain that even if the demon wanted to betray her, it would be doing so at the cost of banishment for a millennium. That was a heavy price to pay and one she would exact with her dying breath if need be. No…the demon would deliver. That much she was certain, particularly since she had made the task easily attainable instead of requiring the demon to slay the individual leaders, which could have taken years, even for a demon.

Theila finally responded, "Our enemies will be there. I bet my life on it."

The paladin hammered his fist on the table in finality and said, "So be it. I will fight with Theila against the assassins at Pirate's Cove."

Maejis nodded in agreement.

Don said, "You can count on me."

Da'Shar, Wavren, and Gaedron remained silent. It was obvious that their focus was the lycans, not the assassins, but abstaining from the vote was consent to go along with the group. They would fight alongside their friends.

Vlaad walked in and said, "I was outside preparing my mount for travel, but I heard most of the discussion. Is it true that we plan to meet the assassin's on fair ground to end this once and for all?"

Theila said confidently, "It is."

The defender had his own reservations, but like the elves and Gaedron, he held his opinions for the time being. He said, "My own plans will wait until such time that there is no other option. We will go to Pirate's Cove as a unified team."

Gaedron said, "It be nearly two days ride by horse an' ship from 'ere. We best be movin' if'n we plan to catch da vermin at Pirate's Cove."

CHAPTER 16
THE LEGION

The spy network kept a close eye on the adventurers and reported immediately when, for some unknown reason, the group packed up and headed out of town with great haste. It was as if they had completely abandoned their mission to stop The Legion. Gorka was not pleased when the information arrived.

"The heroes must have had urgent business to simply abandon their quest," The Plague said to his master.

"Indeed," the guild master replied. One might suspect treachery if no other reasonable answer could be suggested."

In all the realms, The Plague feared neither man nor beast. He had slain countless marks, many of whom were experienced warriors or wizards, but none had inspired fear in him. Not one, but the master assassin, known as The Shade, was neither man nor beast…he was something else. To describe him as the epitome of killing perfection would be accurate, but there was more to him than his skill as an assassin. He radiated fear unnaturally. The only comparable example would be the innate ability great wyrms had to create panic. It was called dragon fear, but Gorka was no dragon and he inspired fear with his eyes, not magic. It was a feral, impending doom of sorts. The Plague knew he would die if Gorka turned on him. He knew this with such certainty that crossing the killer had never been an option in the many years he had worked with him.

The Plague said, "My lord, I assure you that if treachery is afoot, I will find the culprit and handle his death personally, but I believe there is something we have not considered yet."

Gorka nodded. He had never trusted any assassin, but he knew where he stood with this one. The Plague was no fool and had too much to lose to cross him.

"Engage the network. Have the heroes followed by no less than a dozen men. I want answers be they a whisper, rumor, or solid truth. Our plans now hinge on the two elves you promised to the lycans," The Shade said.

"Consider it done," the second in command replied as he turned and left silently.

Gorka tapped his finger on one of the enlarged canines that marked his true heritage as a half-orc. The tic...tic...tic sound made him think of time, but he hadn't become the most powerful underworld boss and the commander of Dek'Thal without having to rework plans that took a bad turn. It was the nature of leadership to assess, prepare, execute, and revise as things changed.

Less than two hours had passed when The Plague returned with urgent news. He said, "Master, the innkeeper, a man known as Nate to the locals, overheard the heroes talking about going to Pirate's Cove for a meeting of some sort. He did not know the details, but our men easily extracted this information before he expired."

Gorka nodded, "I assume by the term 'expired' the subject did not die of natural causes."

The underling said, "Actually it is quite natural to die from a loss of blood, which is common when you remove both hands and then both eyes during questioning."

The half-orc smiled wickedly as he imagined the pain the man must have suffered before he was allowed to die. His men were thorough if nothing else. He said, "You have done well. Pay the men double their salaries for their successes and gather up a dozen agents near Bladerun Bay. We will have a welcoming party for the heroes when the reach Pirate's Cove."

"Consider it done, master," the gaunt assassin replied. It was the anticipated answer of course.

The Shade rubbed his hands together in anticipation of the culmination of his plans. He was soon to be more powerful than any other being in history with his current network of informants, the orcish army of Dek'Thal, an elite company of merciless assassins, and soon he would command the lycan pack. It would be a long campaign of conquest, but with his unstoppable army, the Alliance would fall. His vision was like a rare steak roasted over open flames. It made his mouth water.

***

Having pushed through the night, the nine arrived at Bladerun Bay near dawn. The dock master was still asleep so the heroes set up camp near the docks to catch some much needed rest before the last leg of their journey to Pirate's Cove.

Vlaad sat beside Theila. She was already sleeping soundly having endured much over the past few days. He watched her sleep just as he had done countless times before. She was beautiful beyond belief, an angel sent from heaven to accompany him on endless missions through every imaginable hardship and yet her devotion had never wavered. She was everything he could ever want in a wife, yet he had never given in to those dreams. As he watched her sleep, he wondered why. Perhaps he had been afraid that their lives would change in some way that would force him to leave his oaths unfulfilled to his father, siblings, O'ma, and Andar. So much seemed to be riding on his persistence, that he could never simply give up, but the sacrifice was great for both he and Theila.

The wind blew and a single strand of brown hair fluttered over the sleeping angel's eyes. Vlaad reached down and brushed it aside. It was a simple gesture, but somehow it pulled his heartstrings and he felt overwhelmed with sadness. Men were not supposed to cry, at least not hardened warriors, but though no tear fell, Vlaad sobbed inside.

A soft hand, delicate and warm, found his. Eyes closed and perhaps still mostly asleep, Theila moved close and squeezed his thick, rough, palm in hers. Somehow she always knew how to comfort him. Even sleeping she seemed to be his source of strength.

Vlaad leaned down and whispered into her ear, "Soon my love. Soon…."

The defender took a few minutes to rest. He closed his eyes and when they opened again, several hours had passed. He woke with a start. His companions were all sleeping, except Da'Shar, who never seemed to sleep, but merely sat in meditation unmoving. The sun had crested the mountains to the east and people were beginning to stir. Among them, Vlaad saw the dock master.

Carefully, he extracted himself from Theila and walked over to the man. He greeted him warmly, "Hail old friend, and how are you this fine day?"

The dock master smiled a toothy grin and said, "I am fine, Vlaad. What brings you to Bladerun Bay?"

"My companions and I are heading offshore to Pirate's Cove. Is there anything sailing today?" he asked.

The dock master returned, "I don't recall anything heading there, but perhaps one of the local vessels will take you. I am expecting some naval ships in today."

The defender was hopeful. "Do you think the commodore is coming? He is a fine commander and I believe he will lend a hand as we have a long-standing friendship."

"I believe Commodore Bailey knows every adventurer in the realm and has ferried most of them to war on the *Crusader*, at some point, but I cannot say if he will make port today or not. I will tell him you are in town if I see him though," he replied.

"My thanks…my party will be at the tavern eating and resting if a ship comes available," Vlaad said as he shook the dock master's hand.

Vlaad walked over and roused the others. They shook the weariness form their bones, gathered their gear, and headed to the stables. Once the horses were taken care of, the group took a short respite.

Gaedron and Wavren made a quick stop by the docks to buy fresh fish for their allies, who had been foraging in the woods lately and were in need of a treat. It always drew a crowd to have the massive bears in town. Dozens of children came to watch as the hunters fed them. It was hard to imagine the almost docile, playful bears being ferocious frontline fighters in combat as they rolled around, ate fish, and wrestled with the hunters. The children cheered as they did.

Rosabela and Da'Shar stopped by the local herb shop and purchased a few much needed roots and plants for their alchemical needs, after which they joined with the others at the tavern for breakfast. Maejis ate lightly and reviewed a travel-sized spell book. He seemed somewhat self-absorbed, but no one minded given his profession. Most mages were solitary and individualistic in their free time. Don was talking with everyone as usual and Landermihl took the opportunity to pray at the small chapel in town. Theila ate in silence beside Vlaad who had many things on his mind and also remained silent. Everyone seemed content with relaxing during the short wait before the dock master came with news of a ship heading to Pirate's Cove.

The hours passed quickly and shortly after noon, the dock master came to the tavern. He was in a hurry with many tasks demanding his attention, but he handed Vlaad a slip of paper that indicated, Commodore Samuel Bailey had arrived and was already preparing to make way for Pirate's Cove as a favor to the famous defender and his group of heroes. Vlaad gathered up his companions and headed to the docks. He saw frenzied sailors off-loading goods and gathering supplies for the immediate departure. Vlaad saw the commodore barking orders near the ramp to his vessel. He walked over to greet him.

"Hail to you Commodore Bailey, how are you my friend?" Vlaad called to the sailor.

"Ah, Vlaad…so good to see you in good health and in such fine company!" he returned as he saw the famous group with the defender.

"Can we help you prepare for the trip?" Vlaad asked.

"No, my men are very capable, but please make yourselves at home on board," he answered.

Vlaad and Theila boarded the massive naval vessel. Wavren remembered Samuel Bailey and shook his hand as he passed. Gaedron also remembered the famous naval officer, but he grumbled as he passed him, having had a bad experience on a similar ship that nearly cost him his life.

The commodore laughed heartily and said, "Good to see you alive and well, master dwarf."

Gaedron walked past without so much as a handshake and muttered under his breath, "Durned fool human tried ta drown me not so long ago…" The dwarf stroked his white bear that had saved him from the watery grave on that ill-fated day.

Landermihl had been with Vlaad on the last voyage to the Western Kingdom to serve in the Battle of Forestedge. He was well known to the commodore. They clasped hands and shared greetings but only briefly. Maejis knew the famous sailor by reputation only, but greeted him formally in passing. Of course, Don knew everyone and shared pleasantries as he passed. The others came on board and in no time the ship was prepped and ready to debark.

The massive naval vessel pulled away from the docks at dusk and raised sails for Pirate's Cove. Commodore Bailey had pushed his men to make the departure with great haste and as always, his crew proved to be both motivated and well trained. The adventurers recognized these things and made a point to praise the men and their commander, but no one knew if Samuel Bailey had made the extra effort as a favor or if he simply wanted to hurry to get back to sea where he was most at home. Most likely it was the latter. Whatever the reason, the heroes were glad to have the famous sailor as their friend.

Once the *Crusader* had cleared the harbor of Bladerun Bay and was fully underway, Commodore Bailey gathered the special guests together for dinner. The commodore's private galley was small but well stocked with food and drink. As the adventurers sat at a huge mahogany table, a youthful cabin boy served them. Gaedron and Wavren drank stout ale as dwarves preferred, though Wavren was an elf, he tended to emulate his mentor. The other elves drank a light-colored wine that had come from Celes'tia. The humans preferred mead as was typically found in the Griffon's Peak region.

"So pray tell me what mission you fine heroes have undertaken that requires travel to a wretched place like Pirate's Cove?" the naval officer asked.

Though it was no secret, none of the adventurers wanted to say that ill-gotten information had pointed them in the direction of the rouge island. In truth, only Theila knew that it had been her idea to meet the leaders of the infamous assassin's guild far away from civilized folk. She had a feeling that if things got out of hand, it would be better to have their private war contained than to have it spill over into the poor farmers or city folk of other towns.

When no one else spoke, the commodore nodded and said, "I see, then it is a matter of great peril that you have placed yourselves in. Well, I shan't pry, but if you need my men, this ship, or my life, we are at your disposal."

Don spoke as he was prone to do, "Good sir, know that our mission is a matter of business commissioned by the King of Griffon's Peak himself and though you certainly have our trust, we simply have no good way to explain all the details, but rest assured that our enemy is none other than Gorka Darkstorm. We anticipate his presence tomorrow at Pirate's Cove and hope to capture or slay the vile guild master."

Samuel paused for a long time before stroking his short, dark beard, indicating he was at a decision point. He had considering many things in the time he remained silent but finally he said, "I have fought for over twenty years with every manner of cut throat on the open waters from raiders to pirates to orcs and everything in between. During that time, I have had many opportunities to interrogate prisoners who never revealed any singular entity responsible for the crimes on the high seas, but I have long believed that Gorka Darkstorm was that individual. He has known ties to every criminal underworld rouge in the human lands as well more insidious ties with the Bloodcrest Forces. It only makes sense that he is behind the piracy I have long sought to end. If you have somehow come upon the luck required to pin that one down, I would surely like to throw in a hand in his apprehension."

The nine could hardly say no to their host who had every reason to want the guild master dead or in custody, not to mention the fact that he was in command of their ship and he made the rules out on the water. The resulting smiles, handshakes, and nods of approval were nearly unanimous. Only Gaedron sat with his burly arms crossed over his thick chest. He was still fuming about his near-death experience on a previous voyage and being in the same room with the commodore was difficult to bear for the grudge-carrying dwarf. It mattered little in the end, as the others welcomed the sailor's help.

"It is settled then," the commodore said. "I will bring a security detachment of my ten best swashbucklers and we will do our part."

Gaedron muttered something about being happier once they were on dry land, but no one paid him any mind. Even Wavren seemed glad to have Samuel along for the trip.

Hours passed and the night became dawn quickly. Time always seemed to pass far too quickly when the adventurers were weary, but the few hours of sleep were taken in comfort as the ship gently rocked with the moving tides and waves. The soft down beds in the guest quarters, usually reserved for diplomats and dignitaries, made sleeping in particularly tempting, but the call from the crow's nest brought the heroes to the deck quickly.

A bare-chested sailor called, "Twin ships off the bow just short of Pirate's Cove."

Samuel was already on deck with his spyglass when the others came from below. He said the one word already known by the crew, "Pirates!"

The ship exploded in a mass of dashing sailors. They readied huge deck-mounted ballistae and a row of cannons in record time. The sails were fully opened and filled with a westerly wind making the ship move like a knife through the waves. The anticipation was exciting but the heroes, who were unaccustomed to naval combat, felt somewhat left out.

Right on cue, the commodore announced, "We will have them in thirty minutes if they flee around the island and ten if they come toward us. Your talents would be most appreciated if we are boarded!" he said to the nine.

Gaedron rolled his eyes and said, "Aye, but if'n ye try ta sink me 'gain, me last shot'll be in yer arse!"

The commodore laughed heartily and said, "You have my word, master dwarf. The rest of you should do what you do best. Don't wait on my orders to attack but use caution with fire spells."

Theila looked at Maejis and said, "What the heck is that supposed to mean?"

Maejis replied, "Not sure but since the boat is made of wood and we need it to get home, I plan to stick with frost spells."

Theila was incensed, but she considered sticking to shadow spells and summoning just in case.

Commodore Bailey shouted, "They are coming this way. Five minutes to impact!"

Vlaad asked Gaedron, "What does he mean by impact?"

The hunter winked and said, "Brace yerself boyo; durned fool plans ta ram one."

The heroes had fought on land countless times, but suddenly they felt considerably unprepared for the coming naval battle. The armored warriors grabbed onto the rigging, not wanting to be thrown overboard in full mail. The hunters were surefooted and began firing their weapons at long range while their bear allies roared at their sides. The casters were still out of range, but they began preparations for the initial barrage of spells. The druids waited resolutely; only Don seemed perfectly at home. He had traveled countless time by ship and had even taken part in a few skirmishes.

As the vessels closed, the man at arms in

charge of the cannons called, "FIRE!" The resulting explosions were deafening and the acrid smoke both blinded and choked the crew, but the impact on the far ship was incredible. Of the five *long nines* which fired, two hit above the water line and two skipped across the deck taking out one mast and one cannon. The other fell short. The cannoneers made adjustments and repacked to fire again.

The ballistae crews were now in range and the massive harpoons launched in succession carrying half a dozen skewered enemies overboard. Only one of the harpoons lodged in the side of the enemy vessel causing no damage at all.

Theila and Maejis were now casting spell after spell at the uninjured ship. Maejis had greater range with his frost spells, but the shadow spells were able to have a greater effect on the pirates who fell to the deck vomiting as their life force slowly drained away, leaving them momentarily incapacitated.

Samuel called to the helmsman at the rudder, "Hard to port, hit the one on the left!"

The helmsman quickly responded with a powerful spin of the nearly five-foot wheel. The ship was heavy and responded slowly at first, but the iron ram on the ship punched through the right-front quarter of the hull, lifting the enemy ship several feet upward, throwing many pirates to the deck and one overboard. The heroes and sailors had done well keeping their footing, but now the two ships were deadlocked.

Commodore Bailey drew his thick cutlass and called to his men, "Take 'em down boys, no quarter!"

Vlaad, Landermihl, Stonetalon, and Ol' Blackmaw moved on cue, taking the fight to the pirates. As the defender vaulted over the side and onto the pirate vessel he led with the Aegis Shield, diving into more than a dozen waiting sabers and cutlasses. The rapid staccato of blades on his shield could not slow his momentum and enabled the defender to crash through the waiting enemies like a human cannonball. He hit the ground hard, rolled to his feet, and immediately took up his fighting stance with the far side rail to his back and far too many angry pirates between him and his own ship. It was the perfect distraction for the two ferocious bears that followed and the powerful paladin who drove his mighty hammer down on one pirate from behind. For once, Vlaad found himself with no one to fight as the three tore through the pirates effortlessly. Many ran or climbed into the rigging to escape the terrible assault.

The sailors and Samuel soon swarmed over the few remaining pirates on the rammed ship, but the other had repositioned and was preparing to fire on the *Crusader*. Wavren noticed the pirate ship move to close range and line up for the kill. He turned his blunderbuss and fired all at once. One enemy cannoneer fell dead. Gaedron quickly turned to help and fired his weapon, dropping a second gunner. The enemy ship had a bank of six guns. The remaining four cannon crewmen fired their deadly weapons at close range. Two of the cannons were loaded with chains to destroy the sails and rigging. They did their work efficiently. The other two fired solid shots into the side of the *Crusader*. The explosion rocked the ship and sent the casters, druids, and hunters overboard. Don was left alone on deck as the enemy prepared to board.

The helmsman yelled, "Souls overboard!" but no one could help.

Maejis tried to swim to the safety of floating debris but was having great difficult in his thick wizard's robes. The two hunters, who were wearing a combination of chain mail and beast hide armor, immediately sank to the bottom. Rosabela shifted into her bear form, which was adept at swimming, but Da'Shar transformed into something quite different. He had long flippers and a pointed snout with dark leathery hide. Rosabela had never seen such a beast, but had heard of a water form that skilled druids from the coastal areas had mastered. Whatever the case, Da'Shar moved with amazing speed and grace toward the bottom where he hoped to find the hunters.

Theila had been able to call on a skill warlocks used around demonic portals called *endless breath*. This spell enabled summoners to breathe the harsh, poisonous vapor of the abyss. In this case, it enabled her to breathe underwater. She saw Maejis floundering and immediately swam over to him. Her spell would last considerably shorter on others, but it helped the mage to keep from drowning. They couldn't get back into the fight, but at least they weren't dead.

Vlaad and Landermihl turned at the sound of the four cannons firing. They felt the impact through the *Crusader* and into the enemy pirate ship. Turning back to the *Crusader*, the warrior noticed that other than the helmsman, only Don remained on deck to fight off the enemy boarding party from the opposite ship. Nearly twenty pirates swung by rope or vaulted the gap between the two ships. Don drew out two throwing knives and stopped one massive rogue with twin swords. The blades sank in deeply but the wounds were not mortal. Four more replaced the first. Don ran toward the bow and flew up the rigging. He was followed by the four who now had him trapped. Don held on with one hand and whipped a third blade into the shoulder of one pursuer who lost his grip and fell unmoving to the deck. The other three made haste but found their prey swinging from the rigging in a wide arc toward the mizzen mast. As he flew out of range, he loosed two more blades and another pirate fell to his death. Upon landing atop the mizzen mast, he threw blade after blade keeping the pirates at bay.

Vlaad dashed across the deck and dove headlong into a roll, coming up scant inches from the massing pirates from the second ship. A cutlass came down on his gleaming shoulder pauldron before he could ready his shield, but the armor held. The upward driving edge of his heater caught the rogue under the chin and lifted him off of his feet. The sword of Vlorin sang out blindly parrying a saber from his right. The gift of Vlorin had saved him as he had *seen* the attack in his mind before it came. The counter strike sliced the pirate from shoulder to hip diagonally.

Landermihl took up the position beside the defender and used his own paladin's shield, known as a *targe* from the ancient days, to hold off an ax-wielding fighter. His hammer came in low, crushing the ax wielder's knee. The resulting crunch and howl indicated that the man was out of the fight. Just as he thought the bears would come rumbling in to help, Landermihl heard a loud splash followed by a second splash. The bears were now in the water.

Da'Shar had managed to swim fast enough to help Gaedron make it to the surface where Theila was waiting to cast her spell. Once the spell was activated, Da'Shar let the sputtering and cursing dwarf sink again. He wasn't sure if the spell enabled the recipient to speak underwater, but all the way down Gaedron fumed and spat foul language until he hit the bottom. Da'Shar tried to help Wavren but unlike the dwarf, he had been knocked unconscious by the blast and was on the bottom unmoving. As Da'Shar tried in vain to lift the heavy hunter, three bears arrived. Rosabela and Stonetalon gently clamped onto each of the unmoving elf's arms and swam to the surface. Ol' Blackmaw went to the bottom to retrieve his dwarven companion. They swam for the shore having no way to return to the *Crusader*.

Don was again running out of throwing blades but he was safe atop the mizzen mast. As the remaining pirates from the rammed ship were finally cut down by Commodore Bailey and his sailors, the bard could see that the enemy would soon be outnumbered. He swung down from the mast and slid down to the deck where he scavenged a saber and joined his friends in the rout. With the return of the *Crusader's* sailors, the pirates retreated to their own vessel and then quickly surrendered.

The men cheered with upraised weapons, "Hoorah, hoorah, hoorah!"

Commodore was pleased that most of the blood on the deck had come from the enemy, but he noticed his crew was short by several veteran sailors as well as many of the heroes. He noticed Don running from port to starboard looking overboard for his companions and in particular, his daughter Theila. The worry on his face spread like the blood in the water to Vlaad and then Landermihl. As the commander of the ship and a veteran of many such battles, Commodore Bailey knew exactly what had to be done.

"Secure the prisoners in the hold, treat the wounded, and search the water for survivors. You know what to do with the dead," Samuel said grimly.

CHAPTER 17
PIRATE'S COVE

Pirate's Cove was a small isle formed of volcanic rock off the coast of Bladerun Bay where the most notorious thieves and bandits stopped to trade their stolen goods far outside the reach of any sovereign authority. As such, it had become a haven for the vilest strain of criminals humanity had to offer. To say it was a hell-hole was an understatement, though a more fitting term could not be found.

There was a small stretch of beach on the eastern side, closest to Bladerun Bay, though it was surrounded by high cliffs on three sides and inaccessible except by boat or in the case of the waterlogged heroes, by swimming. The bears had made the waterborne trek quickly at the urging of Rosabela who feared the worst for her brother. Da'Shar had been first to the shore and was already gathering *stranglekelp* from the edge of the water, required to revive the unconscious hunter. Theila and Maejis were the last swimmers to arrive, not including Gaedron who was actually walking on the sea floor in the direction of his bear who swam above as his guide.

"Da'Shar," the she-elf said desperately, "he isn't breathing."

"He has water in his lungs; pray that we aren't too late," the elder druid said as he placed the seaweed in the hunter's mouth, rolled the hunter face down in the sand, and began working the water from his body. A considerable quantity poured from his mouth though he still failed to breathe. Da'Shar tried to use spells of healing, but even with the stranglekelp as a medium for the magic, he remained unresponsive.

Da'Shar rolled Wavren onto his back. His head lolled lifelessly with the motion. Rosabela felt utter hopelessness and dread. He was gone. Her brother was dead. She sat in disbelief in complete shock, shaking her head back and forth in denial.

Theila tried to comfort her friend, but the druid was inconsolable. She had lost her love Jael'Kutter and nearly lost her mentor Da'Shar on more than one occasion, now her twin brother. So many good people had suffered and died. It was more than the she-elf could bear.

Rosabela screamed though it was not the wail of loss; it was an expression of fury, even feral rage. She pushed Theila away and tore at armor covering her brother. Da'Shar put his hand on the elf-maid's arm, but she angrily motioned him away. Having stripped the hunter of his armor and shirt, Rosabela placed her hands on his chest and called to nature for healing. Her hands glowed brightly but nothing happened. She doubled her effort, pouring her own life force into her twin but his body simply could not accept the healing without some semblance of life remaining.

A kind voice came to Rosabela from behind saying, "Lass, it canna work wit' out a beatin' heart. It be over dear," Gaedron whispered.

Maejis leaned in and said, "Perhaps not. What if we got his heart beating again? Move aside."

When no one even acknowledged the wizard, he did what casters do best; he moved them with magic. The four friends flew back several feet as leaves in the wind might be blown in the autumn breeze. What happened next appalled the others. Maejis drew magic into himself swelling with crackling energy and then released it into the hunter. The smell of lightning-burned flesh became thick in the air. Maejis went to the hunter and placed his ear on his chest.

He lifted his head, stepped back, and said, "Not enough…"

The mage drew in more energy and prepared to unleash another blast into the elf. The others cried for him to stop, but the caster was already crackling with electricity. His second blast sent the hunter's body spinning through the air and left a dark scorch mark across his chest.

Da'Shar sprang forward, grabbed the wizard by his throat, and said, "That is enough! Desecrate his flesh again and I will tear your throat out!" He made his point clear by half transforming his hand into the feline paw of a great cat.

Gaedron moved to his pupil who had been more an adopted son than a mere student. He gently cradled the boy's head in his thick arms. With a most undwarf-like gesture, he gently brushed the hair and sand from the elf's face. Wavren's eyes fluttered for a moment and then closed. Had it been a trick of his mind? Had he wanted the boy to live so badly that he had imagined it? The dwarf pressed his ear to the elf's chest. The boy's heart was beating, though barely.

"He lives!" Gaedron shouted. "Hurry ye long-eared fools, now's da time fer yer healing skills!"

Rosabela and Da'Shar came quickly leaving the wizard behind with Theila nearby.

Maejis said, "Should I hit him with lighting again just to be sure?"

Gaedron motioned to Ol' Blackmaw. The bear knocked the wizard to the ground with a less than gentle swat and laid down on top of him for good measure, indicating a definite *NO*.

The druids took turns healing the drowned and lightning-struck hunter who was now breathing but still unconscious. His flesh healed quickly with the druidic spells, but there were now ghastly scars across his chest and abdomen where the mage had blasted him. His color slowly returned as the healers exhausted their magic. Time and rest were now required, along with a bit of luck.

Maejis gasped for breath under the incredible girth of the arctic bear, but could not escape. He managed to watch the scene unfold from his sandy, fur-obscured perspective. After some time, the healers backed off and slumped down to the sandy beach from fatigue. The dwarf still cradled the hunter's head hoping the elf would recover. Maejis felt a measure of accomplishment in his ingenious use of combat spells to restart Wavren's heart, but he was most interested in the strong connection the druids and the dwarf had with the injured elf. He understood that Rosabela was Wavren's twin and inexorably tied to him, but the dwarf seemed equally distraught and the elder druid, Da'Shar, was also greatly concerned. Even Theila shared comforting words and caring embraces as if she was somehow related to the elves. He wondered why. For a mage who had been dedicated solely to the study of ancient tomes and his spell-wielding art, these friendships were foreign to him. To say Maejis was a loner among eight companions was oddly accurate. Even now, he lay beneath a ton of fur and flesh separated from the others. With a sigh, he chalked it up to his lot in life.

An hour later the *Crusader* came around the cliff side of the island where a lookout spotted the heroes on the beach. A rowboat was lowered into the water and a landing party stoked slowly to shore.

Vlaad came quickly with Landermihl and Don close behind.

"What happened?" the defender asked when he saw the unconscious and dreadfully scarred elf.

Rosabela couldn't speak. Her words were too easily choked by raw emotions.

Gaedron looked up from his sorrowful vigil and stammered, "He...he...fell in combat, fightin' to da last."

Da'Shar remained silent. Theila took Vlaad by the hand and led the others away from the elves leaving Maejis behind. She said, "We recovered Wavren's body from the sea after the pirates fired into the *Crusader*. Maejis somehow brought him back to life after the druids had failed to revive him. Though it may have saved his life, it was horrible. Even now he has little care for our injured friend. The man is an empty shell, devoid of a soul. I am not sure we can trust him."

Vlaad looked at his dear companion, measuring her words and expressions. In the end, he closed his eyes and said, "I will speak with him." He turned from the warlock and approached the mage, still under Ol' Blackmaw. He called to Gaedron, "Recall your ally please."

The hunter whistled once. The white bear came to rest beside its master. Maejis sucked in his first deep breath since the bear had immobilized him. It was a much-needed relief. He stood slowly and brushed the sand from his clothes.

The mage saw the concern in Vlaad's eyes. He had seen that sort of look before, usually when his instructors in the Northern Mage Tower of Griffon's Peak were about to scold him. He said,

"What is it? Have you something to say?"

The defender removed his mail gauntlet and extended his bare hand in friendship. When the mage reached out to shake it, Vlaad said, "You have been part of this group from the beginning, but so far you have been an outsider among friends. I am compelled to thank you for your help but we need a team player, not a callous loner. You have a choice to make."

The wizard felt the warmth and strength in the warrior's grip. He saw the concern in his eyes and heard the ring of truth in his words. He thought for a moment that perhaps he should return to Griffon's Peak, but something small inside stopped him. He remembered how the others had fought with valor and fraternity, not selfish glory-seeking conceit. He finally realized what was being offered as he stared into the deep brown eyes of the King's Champion. Friendship had eluded him all these long years studying scrolls and spell books.

Maejis said, "I will stay if you will have me." It was as humble and sincere a statement as the mage had ever made. He was surprised that it had come from his lips.

Vlaad nodded, shook his hand and said, "Welcome to brotherhood."

The two were interrupted by a sudden raising of voices crying HUZZAH!! PRAISE THE LIGHT!!! and NATURE BE PRAISED! Vlaad and Maejis rushed over to see that Wavren had his eyes open. Tears of joy fell from the druids, Gaedron, and Theila. Landermihl, Don, and Vlaad clapped the hunter on his shoulders and nodded thankfully.

Wavren tenderly touched the deep scars on his bare chest and said, "What happened to me?"

Gaedron said with sobs covered with ire,

"Damnable pirates tried ta kill ye."

Vlaad said, "Maejis brought you back from the dead."

Maejis knelt beside the hunter and said, "Forgive me for this injury; I was a bit careless."

Wavren smiled weakly and said, "Feels like I was speared by a giant, but if you saved my life, an apology is not required though my thanks are."

The others nodded with approval.

The hunter asked, "Did we win?"

The dwarf replied, "Aye lad; that we did."

Wavren closed his eyes and whispered, "Good, I need a vacation."

Rosabela brought her brother a potion she had been saving for minor injuries. "Drink this; it will help until I can heal you properly."

The potion went down smoothly leaving the hunter feeling warm all over. He fell into a deep slumber for a few hours, allowing the others to discuss plans to continue the mission. Da'Shar transformed into his sea lion form and swam out to the battle sight. When he returned, he carried two dwarven blunderbusses.

Throwing them to Gaedron he said, "I think you hunters will be need these."

The dwarf nodded and said, "Aye brother, me thanks."

The normally stoic elf smiled. It had been over five hundred years since the dwarf had called him brother. He began to think it was time to let bygones be bygones, particularly since he and Gaedron had now come full circle and would soon face his brother Lord Carnage again. He said, "Broderi mon asti," ancient elven words meaning, "you are my brother always."

The dwarf inspected his weapon. Though it

needed a good cleaning and some oil, he was certain it would fire when the time came. Sadly, the powder was soaked, but the *Crusader* had kegs of powder in its hold for the cannons it carried. Gaedron would need to row back to the infernal ship to retrieve it though. He thought to himself, *Oh how I hate sailin'.*

***

Ja'Zaru had been lashing lesser demons and torturing prisoners non-stop since his meeting with Theila of Westrun. Her image was forever imprinted on his psyche and the mere thought of her commanding him—a greater demon of the abyss—drove him into a frenzy of hate and malice. Time was against him however as he felt continually compelled to complete the work she had assigned him. It was the nature of the spell of binding which had summoned him. If he failed to complete the task at hand, he would be banished from the material plane for one thousand years and would be spirit wracked endlessly during his incarceration. That would ensure a lifetime reprieve for the warlock who would doubtlessly be long dead and forgotten before he could return.

Revenge was a fine motivation pushing the demon to leave his anger behind for the time being so that he could devise a strategy to fulfill the warlock's mission and cause her great suffering simultaneously. Demons were particularly adept at achieving their goals through the pathetic summoners who needed their services.

He knew that at a minimum, he had to transport ten assassins to a specific location by nightfall on this day. The task was a simple one. The demon did not know why the warlock wanted these men, but she had mentioned that these were her enemies and that she planned to end a long-standing confrontation. The balrog would at least get some pleasure out of watching the assassins fight the warlock. He was limited by mandate as to who he should transport so bringing every assassin in the guild would violate his parameters. He imagined for a moment the look on the warlock's face if an army of assassins appeared instead of ten. There were other ways to spoil the plans of the warlock though.

Ja'Zaru smiled evilly as countless ideas came to him. He finally settled on the simplest of them all. The truth was a powerful weapon. After all, the enemy of my enemy is my friend. Who better to help than a friend? The demon vanished from the abyss in a blast wave of heat and smoke, reappearing in Dek'Thal moments later. Gorka was eating when the demon appeared. The great hall was easily large enough for the demon to appear in its true form, but Ja'Zaru thought a common shell would be more appropriate. He elected to appear as human.

The demon appeared in a plume of fire wearing the fine attire of a nobleman with silken garments and tall, black boots. His eyes were pits of black smoke, but he was otherwise very handsome with long, black hair pulled back and braided as was common among the desert people of Dek'Thal. The demon expected his magical entrance to shock or amaze Gorka, but the master assassin seemed less than interested as he ate a platter of nearly raw meat, dripping with fresh juices.

"You, assassin," the demon began by pointing at Gorka, "you will be pleased to hear that I have a bargain for you."

Gorka stopped eating for a moment and said, "I know why you are here foul beast of the abyss. Your arrival has been anticipated for some time now and no bargain will be struck."

The demon wanted to slay the half-breed for his insolence, but instead he smiled, showing a mouth full of fangs. The balrog said, "Then you are resourceful indeed. But do you know what I have to offer before we depart?"

"I cannot know the mind of a demon, but you will likely seek to entice me to kill the one who summoned you. Your offer of wealth or power would be insignificant given my position and station," The Shade said dismissively.

Ja'Zaru was taken aback by the directness of this arrogant fool. Still, it was in the demon's best interest to empower the killer. He said, "Then I will not bargain with you, but know that the one who awaits you at Pirate's Cove is not alone. She has powerful friends and great power."

"Power great enough to summon and bind you to her purpose? Demon, I hold all of the cards here. You can offer me nothing I do not already know. I am intimately familiar with your summoning mistress, her warrior allies, and even the foreigners from Celes'tia. I have put these events in motion. I am the architect of these things. Even your presence, though desperate, was an anticipated move."

"Very well," Ja'Zaru replied angrily with a bow, "then we are ready to proceed?"

The assassin snapped his fingers. A massive orc opened the steel-bound oak doors leading to the main entryway to the castle. In walked nine assassins. Gorka said, "My men are ready as am I but before we depart you should know that I will never kill the one who summoned you. Her soul will never be yours. She will become my plaything as final punishment to her foolish ally who has been an insufferable thorn in my side for more than a decade."

The demon glared wickedly at the half-orc. It was one thing to taunt a balrog but to deny a greater demon his desires was a guarantee of death. The demon wanted nothing more than to eviscerate Gorka and destroy all of Dek'Thal, but time was short and the price was too high to pay for failure. The demon said, "Your day will come, Gorka Darkstorm. I am eternal and you will see me before it is all over."

The Shade smiled and said, "I am counting on it!"

The demon realized the crafty half-orc had been pulling his strings the entire time. He wanted the demon to see him as an enemy, but the reason was inconceivable…or perhaps the assassin was insane. Whatever the case, the demon had run out of time. With a gesture, he opened a flaming portal to Pirate's Cove and whisked the ten killers away.

The portal opened on a short stretch of beach at Pirate's Cove. Gorka stepped onto the sand and surveyed the area. Without a word, he motioned to his henchmen to spread out and seek cover. In mere seconds, his assassins were gone from sight. The master assassin smiled at the skill of his lieutenants. Any one of them would be a fine commander in his absence though he had no intention of retiring. This was particularly true since his plans were developing perfectly. Now all he had to do was wait; something assassins were very good at.

Curtiss Robinson

CHAPTER 18
MISTRESS OF THE ABYSS

Ja'Zaru paced back and forth in his foul den of smoke and fire. Having completed his assignment, he was no longer bound to Theila, but he had failed to profit in the least from the encounter with the warlock. The mere thought of her made the fiend howl in rage. Even the assassin had refused to participate in his plans. The human had gone so far as to taunt and enrage the greater demon! It was unthinkable. The balrog fumed with hatred. There had to be a way that he could repay the two for their insolence.

The connection to Theila was still open to Ja'Zaru but his power was limited if he chose to return to the surface world. He would be voluntarily bound to the summoner if he returned and even if he did what purpose would it serve? The balrog thrashed about causing dozens of lesser fiends to run and hide.

"It matters not," Ja'Zaru said to himself, "an opportunity will present itself."

The greater demon called to Theila, "Mistress, your servant calls to you! Ja'Zaru requests an audience." The words were like a thousand swords in his gut. He hated serving mortals.

***

The heroes had recovered their wounded and returned to the *Crusader* to resupply for the coming fight when Theila received the trans-dimensional call from Ja'Zaru. Though the message was faint, the warlock nearly swooned from the unexpected surge of energy.

Don was the only one nearby when she grabbed the rail to steady herself. He immediately asked, "Theila, are you okay?"

Theila responded, "Yes, Father, but I need a moment."

Theila drew her dark powers about her and sent a reply to the demon in the form of a titan-sized image of herself. The image was furious and dreadful with eldritch energy crackling all around that nearly blew the balrog backward.

The demon had suspected such a response. It was the nature of calling to the material plane and why few demons did so willingly. It opened a nearly limitless power source to the warlock who could then wreak havoc on the demon if they so desired. Fortunately, few mortals understood exactly how the reverse summoning worked and rarely chose to take advantage of it.

Ja'Zaru said, "Mistress, my work is complete as you have directed."

Theila's eyes shot fire as she exclaimed, "That is not why you contacted me. Speak quickly lest I destroy you where you stand!"

The advantage was clearly in the woman's favor, but Ja'Zaru was a clever demon with thousands of years of experience. He said, "Mistress, your foe is in position on the southern side of the island. He is well aware of your plans and has likely prepared an ambush for you."

The warlock paused for a moment. If the demon was speaking the truth, then she had to proceed carefully, but what could he want in return for this warning? She spoke with renewed anger. "Why should I trust you, deceitful beast?" The words came out like a hellish sandstorm blinding the demon and scouring his leathery flesh.

The balrog threw his thick arm up to block the painful onslaught. When her fury subsided, the demon said the last thing Theila expected to hear, "The assassin fears nothing. He laughed at your power. His disrespect must be addressed. I wish to kill him in your name."

Theila laughed a terrible and thunderous laugh that made the demon shudder having seen through the lie. Most likely, Gorka had offended the demon with insults and taunts meant to illicit this very response, but why would he do so? It made no sense. This empowered Theila to use the full fury of a greater demon to destroy him. Even the master of assassins had limits. Whatever the reason, Theila knew better than to release the demon on the material plane. It was just asking for trouble.

The warlock leaned forward, dwarfing the demon by three times its size. She said in a calm voice, "If you truly wish to serve me, then I will call on you but your service will be limited to Pirate's Cove and only as long as it takes to deal with the assassin. Wait until I call for you. Do not call to me again."

The demon smiled wickedly bowing before the warlock in subservience. "As you wish…mistress of the abyss."

Theila felt both concerned and powerful given the latest development. She was certain the demon would double cross her if it got the chance, but everything she had ever learned about demonology assured her that she now had complete control of the balrog. It was a rare thing indeed to have such power. She reflected back on lessons from her master instructor. He always said, "Self-assurance always precludes the destruction of the overconfident summoner."

Don waited patiently as Theila resolved the dialog with the demon. When she was able to look her father in the eye again he said, "Is everything okay?"

Theila smiled and replied, "Yes, I have concluded my business with demons for the day."

It was a reassuring proclamation for the bard who put his arm around his daughter and said, "That is good news indeed. I always wished you had chosen a different profession. Dealing with fiends is too unpredictable for my liking."

The warlock laughed lightly and said, "You can't even begin to imagine."

Theila and Don moved across the bow of the great ship and met with her friends moments later.

"I have news, but ill-gotten," the warlock said with a look of concern.

Gaedron spoke up quickly, "Aye lass, den let's 'ave it. We got work ta be done."

The others nodded in agreement giving Theila the opportunity to explain the latest revelation with the demon Ja'Zaru. She was careful to explain the rarity and danger of the situation. Although it presented an excellent opportunity to outright destroy the assassin's guild leadership, all agreed that releasing a greater demon on the material plane was out of the question. It would be a last resort and even then the good attained would likely be overwhelmed by the destruction the beast caused.

When all was said and done, Landermihl stood up and said, "We must proceed with caution. Are we ready to face the devils of The Legion?"

All stood at once and shouted, "Aye!"

Vlaad and Theila remained behind for a moment as the party began tightening armor, sharpening blades, and reviewing spell books. Vlaad had the stern look of grim determination on his face. Theila knew at once what he was thinking. She knew he was concerned for their heroic friends but he was mentally repeating the mantra his dear O'ma had taught him. Duty is second only to justice and it was a long time coming for both.

Jaw clenched and lips as thin as a razorblade, Vlaad said, "It is time."

Theila reached out, grabbed his thick hand, and gave it a reassuring squeeze. They joined the others in preparation for the coming battle that was sure to be the fight of their lives. Whatever happened she would stand by Vlaad until the end. She knew of no place she would rather be.

Commodore Bailey had the crew of the *Crusader* scurrying about as the mighty vessel skirted the eastern edge of Pirate's Cove. The southern shores were not far off but the waters were treacherous. The brilliant naval officer was more than able to navigate the reefs and jutting rocks that could rip his ship to pieces, but he was equally concerned with ensuring their approach was under cover of the massive trees and cliffs that obscured the enemy line of sight. Amphibious landings could be a quick death if the attacking ship was spotted too early. The last thing Samuel wanted was to witness the death of his friends before they hit the beach.

Time passed quickly and after barely an hour of sailing, the sailor on watch in the crow's nest called down to the commodore. Orders relayed quickly and in moments the sails dropped along with the massive anchor, bringing the *Crusader* to a halt. The heroes jumped into landing boats and were lowered to the clear blue waters. A few rugged sailors manned the oars with great skill, enabling the small craft to avoid the rocks and land safely at the easternmost edge of the southern shores. All was quiet and the beaches were empty when the warriors and casters hit the sand but each held their weapons at the ready as if surrounded by an army.

Vlaad took the front with Landermihl while Gaedron and Wavren flanked either side with their bear allies. Theila was a few steps behind the defender with Maejis to her right. The druids were close behind ready to either support the team with healing magic, starfire, or melee as shape shifters.

Keeping to the wood line, the group made careful progress westward. It was a painstaking process moving through the thick underbrush, but moving out in the open was a far riskier alternative. The hunters were excellent scouts and trackers and should be able to detect the enemy before being spotted by the assassins, but the advantage of surprise was an evasive thing. A cunning enemy might set traps, use spotters, or skirmishers that could bait invaders into an ambush site. Fortunately, Vlaad and Theila had extensive experience fighting The Legion, but there was no denying the nervous energy, sweaty palms, and shallow breathing brought on by their combined hyper-vigilance.

***

Wavren was moving quietly to the left of the party when he noticed something out of the corner of his eye. It was barely a flicker of movement but to the hunter, it stood out as an obvious sign gaining his full attention. He sent Stonetalon forward with a click of his tongue and a quick nod of his head. The bear rumbled ahead, tearing through the underbrush with reckless abandon as Wavren quietly skirted to the side attempting to flank a possible enemy position. The bear disappeared from sight without a trace. Wavren pushed forward until he saw his companion lying very still ahead. He raised his blunderbuss and scanned the area but no one could be found. As he crept carefully toward the bear, he noticed several darts embedded in the thick, ruddy fur. Although alive, his ally was paralyzed. Not wanting to abandon his comrade, he did the only thing he could do; he fired his weapon, signaling contact with the enemy. He took up a prone position and waited for his friends.

***

Gaedron heard the report of Wavren's weapon and immediately headed in the direction of the shot with Ol' Blackmaw leading the way. He realized that the hunt was over as he stomped heavily through the jungle. Stealth might still be on the side of the assassins, but his presence was now obvious to anyone within a hundred meters. He didn't like it, but a single shot could mean only one of two things. It could indicate Wavren scored the first kill of the day and was in pursuit of the fleeing enemy or it meant he got off a single shot before falling to that same enemy. He hoped it was the former.

***

Landermihl, Don, and Maejis heard the shot but were unaccustomed to pinpointing the origin of the sound. They turned to see Rosabela and Da'Shar shape shift into the somewhat less substantial travel forms and dart off in the direction Wavren had gone. Vlaad held up his hand just as they started after the druids.

Vlaad lowered his hand and spoke calmly, "We must trust in our scouts who have traveled and fought in the forest for years and years. Our part in this requires trust and patience. The Legion has us divided whether they know it now or not. Until will reunite with our fellows we must not act rashly. Chaos is the world in which The Legion thrives."

Theila added, "Trust Vlaad in this. We have spent our lives fighting these villains. They have a system of fighting based on surgically isolating weakness and hitting when they have the advantage. As long as we move wisely, we will avoid ambush and treachery alike."

Don, Maejis, and Landermihl accepted their words and took up their weapons with renewed determination. The team headed in the direction the druids had gone, but with measured steps and remarkable caution as if every inch taken could be their last.

***

Wavren heard his dwarven mentor and Ol' Blackmaw crashing through thick undergrowth. It was a familiar and comforting sound but he was still unsure of where the bad guys were at this point. In many ways, he was thankful to be alive along with his ally, but deep down he knew he was in trouble. Intuitively he felt certain the assassins were watching him, just waiting to for the right moment to attack.

When Gaedron arrived, the elf motioned for him. The dwarf dove into the small defensive position beside his pupil and began scanning the landscape.

He asked in hushed tones, "Wha' d'rection boyo?"

Wavren couldn't answer. He said, "They got Stonetalon and slipped away."

Gaedron made a sour face and said, "Filthy sneeks an' hard ta track."

The elf shook his head and continued his vigil. The dwarf followed suit knowing the others would arrive soon enabling them to regroup and possibly revive the fallen bear. They had to wait, which was not a hunter's strong suit.

The hunters heard heavy footsteps approaching. It was not likely a light-footed assassin but not wanting to take chances, Gaedron poised his bear to rush the enemy if need be while he oriented his weapon in the direction of the approaching footsteps. As he looked down the sights of his long barrel, he made out the glimmering Aegis Shield of Griffon's Peak. Vlaad and the others had arrived. Not wanting to give up his defensive position he waited until the humans were in plain sight before he called out. The adventurers came over quickly, took up defensible positions, and started assessing the situation.

"What happened?" Vlaad asked the hunters.

"I saw one of the assassins for a split second but lost him. When Stonetalon pursued, he was taken out by a few poisoned darts. He is alive but unable to move. I need Rosie. Where are the druids?" Wavren replied.

Vlaad's face darkened. He said, "They left before we did and should have been here already. We have been reacting to the whims of The Legion and it has cost us Stonetalon and now possibly our healers. We must take the battle to enemy. They have the advantage of stealth and cunning but we have battle prowess they cannot match. We must change tactics."

"What do you have in mind?" Don voiced what the others were thinking.

Vlaad thought for a moment and returned, "The enemy knew we would likely scout with the hunters and has used that to his advantage. By taking out Stonetalon they have given us a liability. We must now care for him. They have also likely assumed we would rush to Wavren's aid when he fired his weapon. They have abandoned this area, not wanting to fight our group head on. Now that the druids are unaccounted for, they will likely be tracking them. We must find the druids and regroup if they have not been taken. If they have been taken, we are at a distinct disadvantage."

"What about Stonetalon?" Wavren asked. "I'll not leave him."

Vlaad put his hand on the hunter's shoulder and said, "Unless you can carry him, we must move on without him. I do not think he will die in his current condition. He was darted for a reason and we must not act as The Legion would predict."

Wavren pulled away from the defender with a scowl.

Gaedron spoke, "I say we make our stand 'ere. We canna leave da boy's ally an' he'd sooner stay behind ta guard him alone den abandon him. We'd be short yet one more o' our team."

Theila interjected, "Rosabela and Da'Shar are still out there. It seems to me we are choosing between abandoning the bear and abandoning the druids. We must move on."

Don nodded in consent to his daughter's line of thinking.

Wavren was truly torn. He loved his ally, but Rosabela was his sister. He had to go or entrust the smaller group to succeed without him. Even if he stayed, he had no way to heal the bear's paralysis and he would be quickly overwhelmed if the assassins returned. Just as he was about to give in, Maejis came forward.

"About how much does that furry beast weigh?" the mage asked.

"Nearly two thousand pounds," Wavren responded, "why do you ask?"

"I can carry him for short time, well magically that is, but will have little time as my spell is not meant to carry such a heavy load," he added.

"What is the most you have carried before?" Don asked.

"I moved my books from the north tower to my office when I was hired by the king," he mentioned.

Gaedron scoffed, "Books and bears be more 'an a li'l different in weight."

Maejis winked and said, "Master dwarf, you have never seen my collection of books."

The wizard rolled up his sleeves and summoned a blue disk of cold vapor that slid beneath the massive bear with ease. As Maejis concentrated and pulled his arms upward, the bear began to rise but the veins in the wizard's thin arms, neck, and face bulged with the strain. As if grabbing a heavy sack of grain, he hefted an invisible load onto his shoulder. His knees buckled a little and his back bent under the weight, but he managed to hold the spell together and the bear hovered on the blue vapor in front of the wizard.

"Well let's go," he said. "I can't hold this thing forever."

Landermihl came forward and asked, "Can I

help you bear the burden?"

"Nope, it doesn't work like that. Besides, we will need you on the front lines when the fighting starts. I can't cast another spell until this one ends and I can't recast this one again today so let's move," the thin human replied.

Gaedron and Wavren set out looking for a trail. After scant seconds, they found what was likely the mark of an assassin's passing. Though barely perceptible, but obvious to the hunters, disturbed twigs and leaves marked the way. The hunt was once again on.

CHAPTER 19
TAKEN

After hearing the report of the blunderbuss, Da'Shar and Rosabela had dashed off in search of the hunter who they assumed was Wavren. Given the shot was far off and was only a single shot; they could only head in a general direction. After a few minutes, the druids realized they had somehow missed the hunter. Quickly doubling back and then circling in an ever-widening pattern might serve to find the hunter, but would take time. It was time they both knew was not available. They stopped and shifted back into their elven forms. Though not as skilled at tracking as hunters, druids are quite resourceful even in an unfamiliar area. Da'Shar took a moment, oriented himself from where they had started, and sat on the ground. Rosabela kept watch. The elder druid began communing with nature. His spirit drew power from the living plants and animals around him and then detached from his body. In a sheer force of will, Da'Shar sent his spirit forward as an astral projection to speak with the spirit of the forest. In a few seconds, he learned the location of the hunters, the main body of their group, and the location of his enemies. Though costly in terms of magical energies, Da'Shar had gambled that they were close enough to Wavren to find him using this limited method. He had no idea he and Rosabela were quickly being surrounded by nearly a dozen assassins. He quickly returned his astral projection to his body but not before the assassin struck.

Rosabela was lying on the ground unmoving. He was also unable to move and felt searing pain where several darts had struck his exposed flesh just below his jaw-line. He was aware that several black-clad rogues were moving in. He and Rosabela were defenseless. It was over.

One gaunt, sickly looking assassin spoke to another considerably heavier one, "Lord Gorka, we have the prize, should we contact the pack leader?"

"Yes, send word for him to meet us in Dek'Thal," Gorka replied. "Things are moving along as I have planned."

Da'Shar knew immediately what was unfolding. He and Rosabela were part of a deal between The Legion and the pack leader. He was certain Lord Carnage wanted to be returned to an elven body more than anything and Gorka wanted the power of lycanthrope just as bad. An exchange had been brokered with his life and that of his pupil at the center of the bargain. He cursed himself a fool for falling so easily to the evil plan.

The assassins scooped up the two elves and moved with great speed to the southern beach where several pirate warships were converging on the *Crusader* and Commodore Samuel Bailey. The sound of cannon fire broke the island air like claps of thunder and the impact of their massive parrot shot echoed hollowly through the ships' hulls. Da'Shar hoped the fine sailors and officers of the *Crusader* would escape death somehow, but he knew the fight would be short considering the overwhelming odds. From his paralyzed vantage point, he managed to see the entire naval battle play out in minutes and the ultimate demise of the *Crusader* as it sank fully engulfed in flames to the bottom of the sea.

Lifeboats from the pirate vessels dropped from their rigging into the water and came quickly to shore. The leaders of The Legion and their elven cargo were loaded and rowed back to the ships. With amazing timing, coordination, and seemingly endless resources the assassins of The Legion had countered every move the heroes had made. Now Da'Shar and Rosabela were prisoners of Gorka and his band of assassins while Vlaad and the rest of the group were stranded on the island. For once in his long years, Da'Shar felt hopeless as the rogues tied him and Rosabela securely to the mast for the journey to the orc lands and their capitol, Dek'Thal.

Time crept by and after several hours the toxin wore off allowing the druids to move but only as far as their bonds allowed. As they shifted uncomfortably, the pirates and assassins began to notice. One of the scalawags kicked Da'Shar as he passed by, just for spite. Several of them eyed Rosabela grotesquely. It was obvious what they had on their minds, but none were brave enough to cut her restraints for fear of facing the shape shifter as an angry bear. It occurred to the druids that the assassins may have made it clear they were needed alive and were not to be harmed. Regardless of why they were still alive, both knew they would face death soon…or worse.

***

Gaedron and Wavren had followed the tracks of the assassin who had darted Stonetalon for a mile when they heard the massive cannon fire battle through the trees. Not knowing what was happening with Commodore Bailey and the *Crusader* was torturous but Vlaad insisted they continue on the trail. They could not afford to split up again. The only option was to make haste.

As the tracks moved through the forest for about a mile, the hunters noticed new signs of other passersby.

"I fer thinkin' da druids came dis way," Gaedron said as he knelt beside the new assassin tracks.

Wavren agreed, "The enemy was in the area set up for an ambush. Several of our foes took to the trees, likely hidden well among the thick leaves."

The hunters moved around in widening circles until they had a full understanding of the scenario. The others watched in confusion, being incapable of reconstructing the past events with such minimal traces of the assassin's passing.

Suddenly the dwarf called, "Ho, come quickly. Dem 'ssassins were set in a wide arc from 'ere ta 'dere."

Wavren saw something peculiar as the dwarf began. It was the impression of elven footprints.

He spoke slowly as he reconstructed the scene. "Da'Shar and Rosie changed from their travel forms into their elven forms here. See how the tracks just appear? We would never have known they passed if they had remained in their stealthy travel forms."

"Aye lad," the dwarf hunter began, "an' dis be where our friends fell."

Gaedron pointed to a spot near a thick tree. Two outlines framed where Rosabela and Da'Shar lay motionless on the soft ground.

Don spoke up saying, "There's no blood. They must have been taken by the same blowgun that incapacitated Stonetalon. They are alive!"

Landermihl sighed, "Perhaps, but we still have to find them and their captors. It will not be an easy thing to free them without putting their lives in jeopardy."

Maejis jumped in saying, "I don't think so. The assassins must need them alive or they would have simply killed them on the spot. Think about it. Why hold them captive? Ransom would be pointless to the assassins. Their resources are endless."

"The assassins will trade Da'Shar to the lycans and likely kill Rosabela. The feud between Da'Shar and Lord Carnage is reason enough, not to mention the value of killing two druids on a mission to destroy the pack leader," Wavren said as the motive finally made sense.

Gaedron nodded, "Aye an' if'n ye be right, we can easily track da 'ssassin's carryin' da extra bodyweight."

Without another word, the hunters went back to work tracking. It was indeed easier to see and thus faster to track the deeper footprints. Within a few minutes, the trail's destination became apparent. The enemy was heading for shore. Realizing the cannon fire they heard earlier was likely the *Crusader* engaging pirates sent to retrieve the assassins, the group moved from a quick pace to a flat out sprint, but each knew it was too late. Their fears were realized as they hit the sandy beach and saw the pirates sailing away. The remnants of the *Crusader* had been reduced to a mass of flotsam and jetsam.

The heroes made a quick search of the wreckage but found no one alive. Dozens of crewmen—blasted, burned, and drowned—floated among the wreckage. The sight was gruesome. Sadness hit each of the adventurers as they realized their long-time friend, the noble commander of the *Crusader*, Commodore Samuel Bailey was gone.

Vlaad clenched his fists as he saw the pirate ships, the druids, and likely his nemesis sailing away into the open sea. It was the same story he had faced his entire adult life. The villains always seemed to slip away to live to fight another day, denying him the long dreamed of respite and life with Theila. His hatred filled his body and he shook with rage. Theila noticed the enraged defender's anger building. She wanted to comfort him somehow, but she had known Vlaad long enough to realize the only way to get him back on track was to bring him back to his duty.

Maejis was already summoning a teleportation gate. The magic crackled and energy sparked until the portal appeared. Celes'tia could be seen on the other side.

Don asked, "Why are we going to the land of elves?"

Maejis replied quickly, "Druids are skilled in finding their own. If we find the druidic council, we can find Da'Shar and Rosabela. If we find them, we find their captors."

Without another word, the group disappeared through the portal reappearing in the center of Celes'tia. As usual, the warriors staggered around after the magical trip but were quickly shaking off the effects as Wavren and Gaedron sprinted toward the largest tree in the city. Though the druidic grove was outside the city limits, Celes'tia housed the druidic elders inside its protective walls. It was a short run across the bazaar and up a spiraling staircase that took scant minutes. Upon arrival, the group took a minute to compose themselves before they entered the sacred bough.

An ancient elf, stooped with years, and leaning on a longbow as a staff, greeted them, "Hail friends and well met."

"Master Daenek Torren," Gaedron began but

was interrupted by Wavren who said, "Speaker of the Stars…"

Gaedron corrected himself, "Speaker o' da Stars, we be in need o' yer help an' da druid council."

Daenek smiled and nodded.

The humans were a bit confused at the authority this elf commanded. It was obvious he was meant to be respected, but Gaedron and Wavren seemed to revere him as a king. He wore simple leather armor and seemed more wild than regal. They remained quiet not wanting to appear brash or disrespectful. Customs were quite different among elves and men as well as dwarves for that matter, but Gaedron seemed to fit in somehow. It was all very odd.

In a whisper of a voice the Speaker of the Stars said, "You have come in need of finding your friend Da'Shar and Wavren's sister, Rosabela."

The dwarf replied simply, "Aye."

"The druidic council cannot be disturbed at this time but perhaps I can help you," the elf returned.

With measured steps, the aged elf walked to a glimmering portal and stepped through. Moments later, he returned with a large, golden bowl filled with pure blue water. He set it down on a table and closed his eyes for a moment.

After several seconds he spoke, "There is one who is inexorably connected to Rosabela. He is no longer truly of this world, but he should be able to help you nonetheless. I will show you where your companions are now, but only he can help you beyond that."

The elf motioned for Wavren to stand beside him. Wavren moved as directed, unsure of what else to do. The others stood by patiently and hoped for a miracle.

"The enchanted censure of Celes'tia can see many things, though it cannot see the future. Look into the water and search for your sister. Your connection to her should be enough to locate her," Daenek explained.

Wavren looked into the blue pool of water and saw nothing at first, but then the water seemed to shimmer and focus as if looking through a telescope. He saw the pirate ships and recognized them at once. As his vision closed in on his sister, he saw dozens of pirates and assassins on the deck surrounding two elves. Da'Shar and Rosabela were alive and for the most part unharmed. They were bound and gagged, making spells and shape shifting impossible.

Wavren exclaimed, "They have my sister and Da'Shar on the pirate ship! They are alive, but I can't tell where they are or where they are going."

The ancient elf continued his instruction, "They are alive. That is enough for now. Look into the water again. Together we will contact the Spirit of Vengeance who protects Forestedge."

Wavren, Gaedron, Landermihl, and Vlaad had all known this spirit as Jael'Kutter before he was slain in the first battle at Forestedge not so long ago. He had been resurrected as an embodiment of mystical energy and now serves as an eternal sentinel for the village he failed to protect when he was alive. Incidentally, he and Rosabela had fallen in love before his death and had remained connected ever since.

As the waters swirled, an image came into focus. The face of a handsome elf with eyes that flashed with lightning appeared. The image widened until the spirit took full shape. Jael'Kutter bowed to the speaker and saluted Wavren with his double-bladed polearm. It was clear he considered him both friend and equal.

Wavren returned his salute and said, "Jael'Kutter, Rosabela has been taken captive. We know she is alive but have no idea where her captors are taking her. We will recover her, but we need your help."

The look on the spirit's face was a mixture of concern and fury. There was no doubt he would do everything he could to help.

"I cannot contact her until she sleeps. I will return when I know more," the spirit concluded abruptly.

"Time works against us and I fear we will be too late," Wavren said with impatience.

Theila spoke up, "We know these vermin. They are either taking Rosabela and Da'Shar to Shadowshire to complete the trade with Lord Carnage, or some safe haven where they will wait to meet him to deal on their own terms."

Maejis interjected, "If they are going to Shadowshire, I can get us to Griffon's Peak in a blink and we can ride from there in a day's time."

Daenek patted the younger elf on the shoulder and said, "I will send a runner to prepare our fastest ship in case they do not."

Wavren asked the obvious question, "Where else would they go?"

Vlaad looked very serious and said, "The Legion is headquartered in the vast catacombs beneath Griffon's Peak, but we have an army of soldiers and knights there. It is rumored that the guild master of The Legion, Gorka Darkstorm, is also commander of the Bloodcrest Forces. If he seeks the homeland advantage, he will go to

Dek'Thal, city of orcs and we must follow!"

The blood drained from Maejis's face. He said, "We can't go there, not with ten thousand soldiers. It is suicide; this is insanity."

"Would you prefer to face a hundred werewolves in Shadowshire instead?" Don retorted.

Maejis straightened his robes in an effort to compose himself. He said, "I suppose we will face the specter of death in either case. I will prepare my spells accordingly."

Gaedron stomped off with foul look on his face. Wavren was close behind.

"Where are you two going?" Don asked, fearing the hunters disapproved of Vlaad's decision.

Gaedron stopped, looked over his shoulder, and said, "Gonna need more shot fer me weapon, a pack full o' 'splosives, and more'n a couple healin' draughts."

"Don't forget to leave a little room for food," the bard said as a jab at the dwarf's love of eating.

The burly dwarf replied with a serious tone, "Be it werewolves or orcs, I plan ta be home fer supper. If'n we ain't in an' out in under an hour, I don' reck'n we'll be comin' home at all. Either way, ain't much need ta pack grub."

Don smiled at Landermihl and said, "Well, that's one way to look at it."

Landermihl winked and said, "I like his optimism. Truth be told, I think he is dead right."

The party made good use of the next several hours gathering combat equipment and supplies. As night fell, the group reconvened with the Speaker of the Stars. It might be several hours before Rosabela got the opportunity to sleep, but the adventurers meant to move at a moment's notice.

Jael'Kutter moved in and around Forestedge with the speed of the wind. His non-corporeal form granted him numerous special abilities including passing through solid objects, flight, and a keen awareness of enemies in the city. His connection to Rosabela granted him the ability to communicate through a dream state as well as take a physical form from time to time, though it was draining on the elf-maid to manage the latter. The exception was when Forestedge was threatened. In those circumstances, Jael'Kutter could draw on the forest and the elements to become a powerful guardian in service to the city and its people.

As he completed his routine survey of the buildings, surrounding lands, and people, Jael'Kutter felt the connection to his eternal companion. In an instant, his astral form sped to her. As he hovered above Rosabela, he noticed she and Da'Shar were ingeniously tied together. Not only did their bonds and gags prevent them from casting spells, but they also prevented shape shifting. Da'Shar imagined the horrible death by constriction from the biting ropes as the thin elven bodies thickened and enlarged into their animal forms. As he considered the situation, Jael'Kutter felt truly helpless. He quickly settled over Rosabela and entered her subconscious mind.

"I am here, my love," the spirit said.

"Time is critical," the she-elf said, "you must find a way to bring Wavren and the others to Goblin Port where we will likely dock enroute to Dek'Thal."

"It was Wavren who sent me to find you. He and his companions are preparing your rescue even now," Jael'Kutter explained with hope.

"They cannot hope to save us if we pass the iron gates of Dek'Thal but hope remains if we do not escape. The pack leader has been called to meet with Gorka. That meeting must not take place. Tell them to stop Lord Carnage at all costs," she begged.

"I will, farewell and trust in us," the spirit said as he wrapped his arms around his soul mate.

In the blink of an eye, Jael'Kutter returned to Forestedge and made contact with the speaker. The message and location of the druids was conveyed. Their destination confirmed, the heroes sped to the ship already prepared to depart for the southern region.

Though Goblin Port was a neutral city set up for trade, tolerance of the opposing factions was held in a delicate balance by armed goblins, crossbowmen, and huge ogre guards. These overseers never strayed from their duties, keeping the peace for one reason. The profit they earned from the inter-faction trade was easily twice that found in the major cities of Dek'Thal, Celes'tia, UnDae'run, Griffon's Peak, or Dragonforge. Goblins made keeping order a simple matter of firing a dozen crossbow bolts into a perceived troublemaker, even if he happened to be innocent. Though barbaric, Goblin Port was actually quite peaceful.

CHAPTER 20
INTERDICTION

The elven long ship glided along the water much faster than the heavier naval ships the heroes were accustomed to. Even the *Crusader*, commanded by Commodore Bailey, could never catch this swift, low-riding boat. The drawback was the elven craft had no organic firepower. The elves had never been known for naval prowess, preferred to evade combat on the high seas, and usually elected to cut their enemies down on dry land.

As the night slowly passed and dawn came peaking over the horizon, Goblin Port came into view. The elven boat had made incredible time. As the group pulled up to the docks the dock master appeared with a dozen crossbowmen and two ogre bodyguards.

In a shill voice the dock master said, "States yer business!"

Gaedron wanted to split the vile creature's head open with his glimmering ax, but held his hands up in a calm and passive fashion instead.

The dwarf said, "We 'ave biz'ness in da bad lands."

The dock master sniggered, "Fodder fer the vultures eh? Well, since ye gots nothing to trade ye gots to pay a tax." He looked at his ogre companions and continued, "What sounds fair boys, maybe five gold coins each?"

The ogres stared blankly, gripping their blackwood clubs menacingly. It was obvious the ogres preferred to bash heads and take everything but they waited quietly constrained by the rules of Goblin Port to keep the peace such as it was.

Gaedron nodded, "That'll be fine. We got seven goin' ta shore. Take thirty-five an' somethin' extra fer some private biz'ness."

The goblin never expected the outlandish fee without facing a long haggle from the dwarf. He fumbled for a second with the small sack of coins and quickly waved his entourage away. As the team jumped onto the dock, the goblin and Gaedron took a few steps to the side to discuss other matters privately. Wavren calmly watched his mentor, constantly on guard though appearing less than interested. Gaedron slipped the dock master several additional coins before the business was concluded, but appeared satisfied in the end. The dwarf joined his fellows.

Landermihl asked, "Master dwarf, you have given freely of your own purse no doubt brokering valuable services of some sort, but I must ask, why you think the dock master will honor any bargain you made?"

Gaedron smiled a knowing grin and said, "Dwarves an' goblins be mortal enemies. I'd rather split 'is skull fer 'im an' he'd rather stab me in da back den look at each other, but one thing dwarves and goblins 'ave in common be a love fer gold. In dis case, I paid dat wretch a nice sum ta keep 'is goons off us if'n we get inta a scrape wit' either da lycans or da Legion. Fer a single gold coin, he tol' me no pirates or elves 'ave made port t'day. I also paid 'im a li'l extra ta let me know when anyone comes ta port wit' nothin' ta trade. Lastly, he knows he can squeeze a bit more outa me when time comes fer 'im ta inform me. We'll know when either o' our enemies arrives."

The paladin could not disagree with the logic though it seemed a less than honorable agreement.

He would have done things differently, but magically compelling the truth from a goblin would make an enemy they could little afford to have.

The small band of heroes quickly set about buying horses in case the enemy slipped past them somehow and a few cloaks to help them blend in with the locals. The beasts of burden in these parts were little more than draft horses and mules, but what they lacked in speed they could make up in hardiness. If it came down to chasing the assassins or lycans across the wastelands, these animals would suffice. All hoped for resolution here rather than in Dek'Thal.

***

A few short hours later, the pirate vessels pulled into port. The captain in charge of the ship carrying the assassins and the druids met with the dock master.

"Hail," the captain barked to the goblin dock master.

The dock master immediately recognized the captain as a pirate. He subconsciously fingered the heavy pouch filled with dwarven gold that Gaedron had given him.

"What's yer business?" he called back.

The captain had been to Goblin Port many times and knew he was going be shaken down for a few coins no matter what his response was. He was on special business for The Legion but that was secret. He decided to lie.

"We're transporting prisoners for the Bloodcrest Forces taken in sea combat," he said.

"Indeed, well since ye gots nothing to trade ye gots to pay a tax." He looked at his ogre companions and continued, "What sounds fair boys, maybe five gold coins each?"

Before the haggling could continue, the leader of assassins came forward and said, "We are in a hurry, dock master."

The dock master was about to raise the price until he realized who he was addressing. The goblin knew this killer. It was The Shade, Gorka Darkstorm. This half-orc had taken more lives than small pox. It was futile to stand against him or even impede his way.

"OOH...ooh...of course, my lord, hows may I be of service?" the goblin said in a quivering voice.

"You may not. Move aside," the assassin said with deadly intensity.

The dock master obeyed quickly and never once thought to notify the dwarf who had paid him so well.

The pirate captain had never seen such dread on a creature's face before. The fear was utter and complete terror. Gorka merely stepped past the goblin and his guards as if attacking him was inconceivable or perhaps it was such audacity that the master assassin was secretly hoping the goblins and ogres would attack. Whatever the case, Gorka remained untouched as were the complement of assassins who followed with their elven hostages.

With unmatched efficiency, Gorka commandeered horses, gathered supplies, and headed out of town. His spies were everywhere of course and had passed information detailing the presence of Vlaad and his companions. He smiled inwardly knowing his plans were unfolding accordingly, but his adversaries were indeed resourceful having beaten him to Goblin Port. It was a mere inconvenience, but could prove entertaining. He pushed on casually informing his lieutenant of the new development.

The assassins were leaving town limits when Wavren spotted them. He rushed to alert the others but The Legion had quite the head start. In seconds, the heroes were mounted and in pursuit. The chase was on, though a trail of dust was the only evidence in sight.

"We'll never catch them," Landermihl called above the thunderous hoof beats.

Gaedron yelled back, "Two horses'll tire carryin'de 'xtra weight o' elves ridin' double wit' rogues."

"How far to Dek'Thal?" Theila asked.

Landermihl had been to Dek'Thal escorting diplomats. He replied, "At this rate, maybe an hour, but the horses will die long before then if we don't slow down soon."

Wavren kicked his horse and slapped the reins across its neck as if to make the point that he would never stop, even if his horse fell dead at that very moment.

Gorka and his assassins rode on but as Gaedron predicted, the two horses carrying assassins and the extra weight of the druids began to slow. The assassins whipped the laboring beasts and kicked them, but their pace could not be sustained.

Gorka pulled his mount to a quick stop. The others followed suit.

"You two ride on with the prisoners. You must reach the iron gates of Dek'Thal. Stop just long enough to water your horses at the small oasis just up the road. We will deal with our pursuers," The Shade commanded. "You seven will stand with me. Do not engage decisively. We are only buying time."

The rogues spread out in a line. Most readied bows, crossbows, or thrown weapons. Gorka did not. He sat impassively in his saddle.

Vlaad called to his friends, "We have the advantage in ranged combat but our fight must not allow Da'Shar and Rosabela to be taken into the city. We must hit fast, push through, and stop the fleeing rogues!"

Landermihl added, "I am our only healer, Vlaad can endure the longest, and Maejis has enough firepower to cover our attack. Theila, Don, Wavren, and Gaedron hit once but do not stop. Catch the others. Once the druids are free, double back and join us here."

Vlaad had no time to disagree though he knew splitting up was exactly what Gorka wanted. He raised his shield as the first arrows came in. Two bounced off; the rogues reloaded and fired again. This time they aimed lower, striking the defender's horse in the neck. The sturdy beast didn't die instantly, but slowed and collapsed just as Vlaad broke through their lines. He tucked and rolled coming to his feet with the sword of Vlorin in hand. He looked up just as Landermihl took two arrows in the chest-plate and one in his own fine shield. The paladin called to his deity, yanked the wooden shafts out of his armor, and charged directly into one of the bow-wielding villains. His incredible horsemanship enabled the clumsy draft horse to ram the assassin's horse, throw its rider to the ground, and manage a wild kick that nearly laid another assassin low. Vlaad looked to Maejis who had dismounted and was preparing to cast one of his many spells. Two assassins circled the defender from horseback and took turns firing arrows at him. They were content to keep him busy rather than engage him on equal terms in melee combat.

***

The hunters were unaccustomed to firing their guns from horseback at a full gallop, but Wavren managed to score a hit dropping one killer from his saddle before passing the line. Gaedron held his shot until the last minute, firing one-handed and point blank into another's face. The assassin's head exploded in blood and gore but the dwarf took a heavy hit from his slashing sword. Gaedron was cursing more from the damage to his fine dwarven chain mail than the pain of the sword cut, but was otherwise undaunted. Both hunters rode on.

Don and Theila could not fight from horseback. The galloping made holding on hard enough so they ducked low to avoid enemy attacks and sped past the eight assassins. Several arrows and daggers whizzed by. Luck had miraculously preserved them but two of the killers split off in pursuit. One drew a heavy mace and the other held a longsword at the ready. Theila urged her common mount onward hoping to keep out of reach of their weapons. Don looked back just in time to duck a vicious swing from the mace wielder. The second strike came in smashing through the bard's guitar into his back and knocking him to the ground. Theila and the swordsman raced on. Don came to his feet with surprising agility and drew two throwing blades. His attacker spun around and charged. The bard waited. The assassin drew near. Don waited until the last moment then rolled deftly to the right. The horse reacted naturally as the bard came under its hooves. It jumped and kicked trying not to stumble. The assassin was thrown to the ground. As he

clambered painfully to his feet, Don launched his
blades. Awestruck, the killer looked down as if
confused by the two blades mysteriously protruding
from his abdomen. When he looked up, he saw
hatred in the eyes of the handsome bard and two
more blades flipping end over end toward him.

***

Gorka watched the battle unfold before him. He
saw two hunters, probably Gaedron and Wavren by
all reports, ride past along with the famous bard,
Don of Westrun, and his daughter. They would
have to wait. He saw the paladin, no doubt the
noble Landermihl of Griffon's Peak, take two
arrows, heal himself, and smash into one of his
lieutenants. He saw Vlaad, a man he knew well
from past battles, lose his horse and roll into a
fighting stance ready for battle. The wizard in their
party was likely the advisor to the king of Griffon's
Peak known as Maejis. His intelligence officers had
cautioned him about that one. Gorka decided he was
the most vulnerable and potentially the most
dangerous of the three remaining heroes. With a
grunt, he spurred his horse forward while the others
dealt with Vlaad and Landermihl.

Maejis had barely enough time to dismount and
call for a spell of protection when a particularly
vicious-looking assassin rushed in. The wizard was
unfamiliar with mounted combat but knew enough
to dive out of the way to avoid being trampled by
the powerful hooves of the assassin's horse. As he
did, he drew a thin wand and fired a bolt of fire into
the back of the rider. It had no effect. Maejis made
note. The rider was protected from minor spells. He
stood up and drew on one of his more powerful

spells.

The killer reined his horse in and made a quick turn just in time to see a massive cone of blue energy coming at him. With incredible speed he sprang from his horse, rolled across his shoulders, and came up with his dagger at the ready. He took half of a second to notice the effects of the attack on his mount. The blue energy had covered the horse in a thick sheet of frost, in effect draining the very warmth from the beast's body. It fell over dead, frozen solid from head to tail. Gorka made note. The wizard was powerful indeed.

***

Theila and the hunters were nearing the slowing enemies. They could see the druids draped and tied across their captor's horses. It must have been pure torture enduring the jolting ride from that position. Wavren rode low hoping his poor mount had the stamina to make it a little further. He could feel the labored gasps as the horse struggled to draw the required air needed to sustain the long run. Gaedron was close behind and Theila was beside him. Their horses were faring little better. Don was no longer with them, but Wavren couldn't worry about that right now. He had to get to his kinsmen.

Gaedron noticed his mount tiring. His weight was wearing on it more so than his lighter companions' were. He did not want to give up the chase but he knew his ride was over when a shudder broke the horse's pace. Both the dwarf and the horse went down in a huge cloud of dust. Gaedron came up spitting and cursing but the horse did not. Without a second thought, the hunter whistled loudly and started running after Wavren and Theila

on foot. Moments later, as if by magic Ol'
Blackmaw appeared beside him. Together they
sprinted on as only a hunter and his ally can. If luck
was with them the assassin's mounts would collapse
soon. If not, Wavren and Theila would be facing the
two killers ahead as well as the one trailing without
Gaedron's help.

***

Landermihl was fully engaged fighting the thin
assassin known as The Plague. The smaller
unarmored man moved with amazing speed and hit
the paladin with bare-handed attacks that rattled his
fine armor and knocked him from his horse. The
hits were comparable to those of a hammer-
wielding tauren. As the mighty paladin recovered
from a hard landing, he lifted his shield in
anticipation of his enemy's attacks but they never
came. Looking quickly from left to right and then
turning in a full circle he found himself alone on the
battlefield with Vlaad and Maejis separated as well.

Gorka circled the surprisingly young-looking
wizard. With his ponytail and travel robes, Maejis
looked harmless but when he began drawing power
for his next spell, his demeanor quickly became that
of a deadly spell wielder. The assassin knew he
would never close the gap between himself and the
mage before the spell released so he waited tensely
for the arcane blast to come in. It was a tactic the
caster must have anticipated. He simply continued
to summon more and more power until the
shimmering blue globe of frost grew to massive
proportions. The assassin saw the concentration on
the wizard's face as he struggled to contain the
building energy. The crackling energy flashed

across his features and made his thick, dark hair wave as if blown by a fierce wind.

The assassin called to his enemy, "If you fail to destroy me, I will feast on the pain of your body before I leave you to rot in the hot sun."

Maejis had no intention of letting that happen as he threw the boulder-sized blast of frost magic with the trigger word, "*Zephyrus Arcti!*"

The effect was spectacular. With a thunderous roar, the titanic frost spell enveloped the assassin carrying him dozens of feet backward, flipping and turning to land in a shredded mass. The black-clad assassin did not move. Maejis took no chances. He drew on yet another spell; this one fired arcane bolts of energy into the limp body like daggers of pure white light. Though the body shuddered with each impact of nearly a dozen magic missiles, there was no life remaining. Maejis approached cautiously. He nudged the devastated killer with his boot, but the crunch of frozen flesh under his foot confirmed the villain was dead. He rolled the body over but did not see a dead half-orc lying at his feet. The face was human. The master assassin had tricked him.

A whisper of hot breath came from inches behind the wizard's ear. It said, "I made you a promise and now it is time to deliver!"

Maejis felt a thick and powerful arm encircle his neck; a searing pain shot through his right kidney as the assassin slowly pushed cold steel into his flesh. The mage was helpless in the anaconda-like grip of his enemy. The pain was excruciating. Maejis could neither scream nor even breathe as the sinister assassin slowly turned the blade, carving out a wicked hole in his back. He felt hot blood pour down his leg and pool around his feet. The assassin carefully, almost kindly, eased his prey to the ground. Maejis could barely focus his eyes. It was as if someone slowly closed the blinds in an ever-darkening room.

The assassin wiped his blade on the dying man's robes and said, "Wizards are so egotistically predictable. You see, the art of combat requires true warriors to know their enemy and as such, I was prepared to sacrifice a lieutenant to your ego while I waited unseen for my opportunity to strike. Now I must go. Forgive my haste, but I have business in Dek'Thal."

The assassin ran to Maejis's horse, mounted it, and galloped off toward his homeland. Maejis heard him ride off. He could hear the wind blowing. He could hear the slowing beat of his heart and the rattling of air as he drew his final breaths.

***

Vlaad saw Gorka ride past on Maejis's horse. Landermihl was heading his way on foot. They immediately feared the worst. As the two ran across the barren plain, they saw Gorka's slain horse, no doubt the handiwork of a powerful frost spell. They saw two unmoving forms near a small rock outcropping. One was an assassin dressed in black and the other was their friend and companion. As they approached it became obvious what had transpired. Maejis killed the assassin. Gorka escaped on Maejis's horse after mortally wounding the young wizard. The paladin threw off his helm and gauntlets. He gently checked the wizard's body.

"Can you save him?" the defender asked desperately.

"I will try, but his wound is deep and he's lost

most of the blood in his body," the holy warrior returned. You cannot help here. Go to the others. Take my horse."

The paladin laid his hands on the dark-haired spell caster and began to call to his deity for healing. Vlaad took a deep breath and stood for a moment. He silently added Maejis to the long list of friends he vowed to avenge. Throwing his shield over his shoulder and sheathing his blade, Vlaad sprinted over to the last horse hoping to find his other companions in better shape than Maejis.

The defender had utter turmoil eating away at his guts. He hated The Legion. He hated every one of them and reserved his deepest feeling of anguish and anger for their leader, The Shade, Gorka Darkstorm who had taken so much from him. As he pushed his sturdy mount on, he noticed that the odds were not completely in favor of the enemy. Maejis had slain one assassin; another was shot through the head by one of the hunters. Not far beyond these dead enemies he saw another bearing several of Don's throwing blades. If he figured correctly, the enemy had ten at first and was now down to seven. Maejis was dying and Landermihl was tending his wounds. If his other companions were alive, then it was seven heroes and seven villains. The problem was Da'Shar and Rosabela. He had to find a way to get them back into the fight.

***

The captives bounced along as their captors slowed their horses. Though bruised and battered, they managed to survive the ride. With a vicious tug, the assassins yanked the two druids down to the ground. The assassins led their mounts to the pool of clear water to drink.

One of the killers said, "We can't keep this pace. The horses have had it and I for one don't care to walk all the way to the orc lands when they fall over dead."

The other replied, "Hey, orders are orders. Would you rather face the consequences of failure?"

"Well, of course not," the first said as he considered the slow painful death at the hands of his guild master, Gorka Darkstorm. "I'm just saying we need to take care not to run these old mares into the ground."

Wavren and Theila arrived shortly after the assassins dismounted but they remained hidden among the rocky slabs surrounding the oasis. They watched as another assassin, one of the two who had tried to pursue them, linked up with the others. Gaedron, Ol' Blackmaw, and Don had managed to follow the tracks Wavren and Theila left behind. They came up quietly and joined their friends among the rocks. Within a few minutes, four more assassins arrived at the oasis. There were a total of seven now.

"We can sit by while they rest and let their horses drink. Once they are refreshed, we will not be able to catch up to them again. Our horses are too few to carry us and they are exhausted," Theila said.

Gaedron scratched his beard and said, "Aye lass, ye be right. We be needin' a dis'trac-shin an' 'ere he comes. Looks like da darned fool d'fender di' na see us come dis way."

Wavren whistled sharply and as if by magic his bear Stonetalon appeared off in the distance and ran up to the group.

"They have seven assassins. We have two bears, two hunters, a warlock, a bard, and Vlaad. I say let's go get my sister and her mentor back," the elven hunter proposed.

"I'll get the druids. Keep the assassins busy," Don said as he winked, ran off, and faded from view.

Theila summoned her voidwalker, Zaashik. The nightmarish abyssian creature flexed its huge chest and glided silently toward the oasis followed by the others. If they were lucky, Don would sneak past and free the druids. If not, they would likely have to fight at a disadvantage.

Vlaad charged right up to the group led by Gorka, his nemesis. He hoped his friends were nearby or this would be a painful end to his quest.

"Halt," Gorka called as the defender approached, "you are greatly outnumbered and cannot hope to survive. Surrender now and we will speak. If you attack, I will slay you and torture your elven companions for your impudence."

Vlaad quickly returned, "We have nothing to discuss. Free the druids and forgo this foolish conquest for power with the lycans or be destroyed."

The assassins laughed at the warrior's audacity.

Gorka extended his hand calling for silence. "You have been a worthy adversary all these long years. Do not insult me with threats you cannot exercise."

As if on cue, the heroes converged on their friend and would have attacked but Vlaad held up his heavy mailed hand and said, "Stop!"

Gorka smiled showing his orcish heritage in the twin prominent canine teeth that would be considered tusks had he been a full-blooded orc. He said, "I hold all the cards in this game. If you attack, I will slay the druids who are helpless. Even if your rag tag band of warriors managed to overcome my highly trained rogues, your friends would be dead and it would all be for naught."

Gaedron leveled his blunderbuss and said, "Ne'er liked da elves much anyway. I say we start killin' jus' ta see."

Vlaad knew the dwarf was bluffing but the point was taken. Gaedron either believed the fight was inevitable or perhaps he was buying time for something else. Vlaad noticed Don was not among the others.

"You ordered me to surrender that we might talk. I am no longer alone and would rather die than surrender so it seems your cards in this game do not count for much. Release the druids or my friends and I will cut you down," Vlaad commanded.

Gorka saw the dwarf peering down the long barrel of his weapon. The elven hunter also had him in his sights. The warlock had drawn her wand but even more deadly was the demon at her side and the two bears to its left and right. All were focused on him. Each seemed ready to die if only to score a single attack on him. Within a fraction of a second, the guild master calculated the odds and nodded.

"Very well then, take the druids. I trust you are a man of honor and will not shoot us in the back. We take our leave," the master assassin said as he and his men mounted and quickly rode off.

A sudden shout from Don alerted the group, "It's a trick. They aren't elves. The rogues still have Da'Shar and Rosabela!"

Gaedron and Wavren fired their weapons, two assassins fell dead. The others rode off out of range.

Don ran up and said, "I thought I found the

druids, but when I tried to free them I noticed they were human. We have been on a wild goose chase."

Vlaad clenched his fists gnashed his teeth in frustration. "Da'Shar and Rosabela never got off the boat. We have been decoyed. They were too important to Gorka's plans to risk keeping druids with him. Somehow he knew we would try to catch him at Goblin Port. Somehow he always knows."

Wavren whispered something in elvish. Gaedron nodded and they walked away solemnly accompanied by their massive bears.

Theila looked to her father and asked, "What did he say?"

Don put his arm around his daughter and said, "It is an ancient saying that goes back to a time when the elves were nearly destroyed by the orcs. The last great elven commander turned to his remaining warriors as they prepared their final charge and said, 'Though we go to our deaths we will not go alone.' Some say it has two meanings. The first is a literal meaning indicating that it is better to die among friends than to die alone."

Theila asked, "And the second meaning?"

Don took a deep breath and said, "If we die, then our enemies die first!"

Vlaad announced, "We must return to Landermihl and regroup. Maejis was near death when I left them and will likely need our help returning to Goblin Port."

The others looked surprised but said nothing. They rode double having lost half of their mounts but made haste and found the paladin praying over the fallen wizard. Maejis was near death. His face was pasty white and his robes were covered in blood…too much blood.

"He fights the pull of the abyss," Landermihl said as the heroes closed in. "Though he is strong, I do not think he will survive."

"Well, heal 'im s'more," Gaedron stated flatly.

"I have done all I can. His wound was deep and he lost most of the blood in his body. Though I managed to stop the bleeding he has been poisoned. I drew out the toxin and purged the wound, but his body has been ravaged by the combined trauma, loss of blood, and venom," he returned grimly.

Vlaad added, "I have seen this before. Gorka is the consummate killer. He leaves nothing to chance. It is his signature, his style, his reputation. He is lucky to be alive."

"Let's get him to the inn at Goblin Port," Landermihl suggested.

Wavren knew his sister Rosabela was a powerful healer. If she were here, the mage would be doing fine. He had nothing against the healing arts of humans, but elves were far long lived and had access to a far greater understanding of magic. Gaedron could almost read his apprentice's thoughts. He knew the elves were powerful but he also read the lack of confidence for the humans that Wavren had written in his delicate features. He motioned for the young elf to leave the humans to their work. Now was not the time to dwell on the differences between races.

CHAPTER 21
DEK'THAL

The group of heroes managed to get Maejis back to Goblin Port where they bought more horses, gathered more supplies, and set up quarters at the inn. Though it took a full day of rest and additional healing from the paladin, Maejis recovered quickly from Gorka's attack. In fact, the wizard managed to convince his friends that he planned to face the assassin again before it was all over. All agreed that it was good to have him healthy again and available for the coming fight.

The stalwart team headed off again in search of the druids and the deadly group of assassins. They had a plan to get into the orc city and rescue their friends, but it was a long shot getting out alive. The problem wasn't fooling the stupid orcs into letting them pass. Maejis was sure he could build a convincing illusion for that purpose. The problem wasn't even finding the druids among tens of thousands of orcs. Wavren was certain Jael'Kutter's spirit could help them accomplish that task. The real problem was getting the druids away from Gorka and ultimately out of the city once they were discovered. Theila had a plan to create a distraction that might keep the city guards busy, but Gorka was no fool. He would rally his personal orc guards (elite warriors) and the loyal assassins under his command from The Legion with cruel efficiency, leaving the small band of heroes overwhelmed by sheer numbers. Even if they managed to escape, the lycans and assassins would still be a threat and their quest would end in failure. The group quietly rehearsed their parts mentally and prayed for a fair amount of luck as well.

***

Da'Shar and Rosabela were transported by caravan from a small inlet south of Goblin Port to the city of Dek'Thal. It had all been masterfully planned and executed by Gorka Darkstorm. He had anticipated nearly every move his enemies made and had managed to counter their rescue perfectly. As he stood menacing in the great hall of Dek'Thal, surrounded by his loyal assassins and more than twenty elite orc warriors, the druids were brought before him. Their ride from Pirate's Cove to the orc city had been none too gentle. Both elves were battered and bruised, half starved, and dehydrated. Upon arrival before the Supreme Commander of the Bloodcrest Forces, the orc warriors forced the elves into a kneeling position as a show of respect.

"It is so good to have you here as my guests. I cannot recall a time when such honored elves as yourselves have been present in these halls. Well, alive that is," Gorka said mockingly as he pointed to row after row of disembodied heads along the high walls of the hall.

The orcs fluent in the common tongue laughed and whispered to the less educated orcs what had been said. They in turn chuckled in reference to the countless elven, dwarven, and human heads that had been brought to Dek'Thal, some of which had been perfectly preserved and remained as decoration in the massive fortress. It was rumored that the city Dek'Thal was named in honor of the first great orc chief who had started the practice of mounting decapitated heads of his enemies. His name was Korgus Dek'Thal, which translates into *Vicious*

Head Collector.

The druids remained stoic and undaunted. They maintained silence and accepted the taunts and rough treatment expected from their orc captors. In truth, they considered themselves lucky to be alive. It seemed likely that sooner or later their value alive would dwindle.

As the raucous laughter and taunts continued, the druids noticed a young orc moving swiftly across the great hall toward their leader. He whispered something into the ear of his commander. Gorka nodded and dismissed the messenger. Without a word, the chaotic band of orcs grew silent knowing something had developed.

"We have news of more foreign guests coming to visit our humble lands," Gorka said with a smirk. "Humans from Shadowshire have arrived."

Da'Shar heard his apprentice whisper through her gag, "No, it can't be." She knew, just as he knew that the guests Gorka referred to were the lycans and Lord Carnage their pack leader. Da'Shar knew their time was near an end. He knew Lord Carnage would torture him to break the will of his student. The elder druid mumbled to his student, "Remember what I taught you. You must not give in to his desires. You must endure everything for the good of our people. Failure is an endless hellish life such that you cannot imagine."

Rosabela gritted her teeth and said, "I will not fail if it comes to that, but it isn't over yet!"

Da'Shar managed an inward moment of joy. His dear Rosabela still had hope. She was ever the fighter and stalwart optimist. He was proud of her. She was everything he had dreamed she would be.

At that moment a contingent of unarmored humans, escorted by no less than twenty heavily armed and armored orcs, entered the massive room. They walked casually and confidently as if the battle-hardened elite orc guard could never hope to stop them from doing as they pleased. The master assassin and regional commander noticed their audacity. Either the lycans were far more powerful in combat than he had anticipated, which was unlikely, or they believed they held all of the leverage in the situation. It was foolish pride.

The pack leader looked at Da'Shar and then spoke in a strong yet measured tone, "Commander Darkstorm, I see you have accomplished the impossible. You have captured the wind itself, contained the storm in the palm of your hand, figuratively speaking. Well done!"

Gorka nodded quietly.

"I am bound by my word to reward your efforts as we agreed in Shadowshire," he announced.

The Shade nodded again.

Da'Shar sensed something amiss. His apprentice was also aware.

"I need a private chamber and the prisoners to complete my transformation. Your reward will be forthcoming. Are your men prepared for their conversion?"

The master assassin finally spoke, "You have my leave to conduct your ritual after which my men will be prepared to receive your bite. There is a small but adequate anteroom behind me."

Without another word, Lord Carnage and his attending followers grabbed the elves and headed through a thick, iron-bound oak door. The door closed with an ominous clang. The pack leader bowed his head, took a deep breath, and smoothed his goatee with his hand. The druids could tell he was wrestling with great inner turmoil. When he finally looked up, his eyes were cold and his jaw was set firmly. He motioned to his men with a nod who in turn removed the gags and bonds restraining the druids.

"What are you doing, So'larian?" Da'Shar asked, hoping his half-century feud was over with his brother.

"You know exactly what I am doing, and do not call me that. I am no longer So'larian. I am no longer your brother. I'm not even an elf," he replied angrily.

Rosabela began piecing the puzzle together. She assumed by the tone of the conversation that first and foremost, Lord Carnage was not planning to kill them. What she could not figure out was why he had come to Dek'Thal unless he intended to take Da'Shar as his new host. Surely he knew they would never willingly give in to his desires. Ultimately, she seemed certain that the fallen druid retained some measure of compassion and regret.

Da'Shar put his hand on his brother's shoulder and said, "Perhaps it is time to come home, brother."

"You are a fool to think I can be redeemed!" he replied with venom.

The pack leader pulled away, eyes blazing red and a feral look coming over him as he turned into his lycan form. The transformation was gruesome and obviously painful as bones snapped and reformed under thick skin growing black with dense, coarse fur. His fingers sprouted hideous claws and his once handsome face elongated and became a lupine maw filled with fierce, jagged teeth. Following suit, the other humans became werewolves in a similar fashion.

The elves backed away unsure of what to do. Their initial reaction was to shape shift into their own beastly forms, but they were outnumbered five to one. It would be a slaughter in the tight confines of the tiny alcove.

Finally, the leader said in a hoarse demonic voice, "You know the likes of Gorka Darkstorm. He will never surrender his will to mine. He will never allow his men to come under my direct control in spite of his alleged attempts to ally with the pack. He has some ulterior motive that I cannot understand, but I know he has brought us all here for some purpose that must be in his own best interest."

Da'Shar seemed so small and vulnerable compared to the seven foot killing machine standing before him. As the squad of werewolves flanked Lord Carnage, the pack leader became even more imposing, yet the elder druid held his ground.

He said in a calm tone, "If you know the master of shadows is manipulating us, plotting for his own good and likely our deaths; why do you continue?"

The struggle within the towering half-man, half-wolf was undeniable. It was as if a battle raged within his mind for control of his body. He trembled in rage and gnashed his teeth scant inches from the druid's face.

"The pack must be strong to survive…you are the key," the lycan said.

The elder druid looked sad, almost heartbroken for a moment.

"If you have come to regain your true form, to become eternal, to rampage across Dae'gon and Celes'tia in my body, then you have erred grievously. Kill me now. I cannot fight you all, but I will never consent to prolonging your torment or empowering your wretched path."

The pack of werewolves crouched and salivated as they waited for the order to tear Da'Shar to pieces as they had done to others who denied their master countless times before. The pack leader hesitated, again fighting inner turmoil. In his mind, it was as if his last remaining glimmer of goodliness held off the army of hell itself. Alone, and cornered with the deep ravine of death to its rear and the endless wave of evil before it, the manifestation of good—an avatar of hope—dug in its heels and faced the great black wave of despair. In mere moments, it was over.

Looking at Rosabela like a fresh-cut steak Carnage said, "Survival of the pack is all that matters. It is undeniable. You have chosen your path but you will bear the image of this one's death as a lingering, stabbing pain for all of your long years. The very gift you deny me will be your eternal curse. Look at her. She is young and beautiful. She is brilliant no doubt, everything a master hopes for in his student. Her death will not be quick. I will extract every scream, every ounce of torment and when she is near death, I will leave her to you and you will heal her. It is in your nature. You will be unable to bear her suffering, knowing that I have left her enough blood, enough flesh to live for days."

Da'Shar could not help looking into the doe-like emerald green eyes of the young she-elf who was more a daughter than student. She thrust her chin forward, clenching her jaw and fists tightly. She was willing to accept her fate. Da'Shar had trained her to do so but he was unable to stop the images of her torn body from stirring his own inner turmoil. He pictured her in agony as the pack of were-creatures tore her apart. It was his love for her and his own imagination that drove him to a precipice where cornered, he was forced to choose between Rosabela and a diseased eternity of lycanthropy.

"I can see you struggle against your own beliefs. You know you can save this one by sacrificing yourself to me. We will be stronger together than we are individually. The strength of the pack comes from brotherhood. The irony is we were both druids once and brothers but fate separated us. We can now be brothers again. Join me and live beyond nature."

Da'Shar knew it was all a lie. Lycanthropy has never been about brotherhood; it is a curse. It is an existence devoid of free will—a sentence of slavery. There is no choice; there is only survival, the pack mentality, and the endless hunger for flesh. The elder druid felt his blood boiling, his heart pounding in his chest and his legs tense at the moment before he sprang unexpectedly forward, changing into his windwraith form. The panther-like great cat hit the were-beast full on. Their combined weight of over one thousand pounds splintered the door frame and brought down part of the wall as they crashed into the great hall.

Orcs and assassins drew blades immediately but Gorka smiled and calmly said, "Ah, entertainment."

***

Landermihl, who was disguised as a heavy orc warrior, leaned over to Maejis, disguised as a troll shaman, and whispered, "How long will your enchantment last?"

Maejis whispered back, "The enchantment will last for several hours but you have to play the part well to be convincing. If we fall under suspicion, the spell will fail."

Vlaad also disguised as an orc warrior, added, "Just look angry and pretend you want to kill everyone."

Wavren, appearing as a troll scout, nodded toward his mentor and said, "Sounds like a certain dwarf we know."

Gaedron, who was too short to pull off being an orc or a troll, was hog tied and gagged, pretending to be a prisoner and doing a realistic job of it. His curses and struggles were quite convincing.

Theila was playing the part of an undead priestess while Don looked like an orc rogue.

The undercover heroes approached the checkpoint just outside the massive black gates of Dek'Thal with all hope that their illusion would hold and grant them entrance in the orc city. If not, they would be quickly surrounded by the city guard and summarily torn to pieces.

A large and particularly vicious-looking orc stopped the group and asked something in orcish. Don had anticipated this language problem and spoke up quickly in broken orcish.

"Speak common or the trolls and zombie-witch will think we are plotting against them. They are a suspicious lot," he said in a droning common dialect.

The guard looked at the trolls and the undead priestess suspiciously. Maejis thought they were doomed for sure and kicked Gaedron in the ribs as a distraction. When the dwarf went to cursing and flailing about, the guard smiled and waved them past.

He said, "Never had a problem with trolls; we see eye to eye on dealing with smelly dwarves." He punched Gaedron in the eye for good measure.

Wavren had to resist the urge to cut the fuming hunter loose and let Gaedron show the orc how dwarves deal with smelly orcs.

Once inside the main gates, the disguised adventurers began scouting the bazaar and business section of the city for official-looking buildings where prisoners might be kept. This was a tough thing to accomplish given every structure was made of indistinguishable stone or animal hide. The signs were hand painted and in orcish. Luck was with them however, when they saw their stolen ponies tied up to the crude post outside a stone hall in the central square. It was their only lead until night time when Jael'Kutter and Rosabela connected.

As the team approached the massive double doors, they could hear the cheering of orcs and the sounds of wild animals. The noise had obviously drawn the door guards inside and away from their posts. It made undetected and unquestioned entry possible. As they pulled Gaedron down from his horse and moved into the building, they saw a huge gathering of orcs outlining a makeshift ring where two beasts had apparently gone wild. All at once the group recognized one of the beasts as Da'Shar in his windwraith form. The other was no doubt a were-creature and most likely Lord Carnage judging by its size. Not wanting to spoil their illusion, the seven were forced to watch in awe as the two feral shape shifters battled.

Da'Shar was lightning quick with his raking claws but Lord Carnage had an advantage of sheer strength displayed as he easily pitched the heavy cat into the wall. The druid hit hard but returned to his feet and began circling his prey. Almost instantly, the wounds inflicted by Da'Shar began to mend. The pack leader growled but did not attack.

"Don't be a fool," he said, "I cannot be destroyed."

The druid was unable to speak in his beastly form but his doubts were conveyed as he launched into another series of clawing attacks. His right paw hit followed by his left. The claws dug in deeply and the corded muscles of the jungle cat drew the lycan into bite position as the two fell backward. The were-creature thrashed about violently, painting the floor with red strokes of fur. His howls of pain were maddening to the crowd of orcs who passed currency back and forth betting on the outcome.

It was obvious to Rosabela that the werewolf followers had no intention of letting their master fall in combat. As they fanned out using their pack-like tactics, Rosabela cast a charm of healing on Da'Shar. It was unlike the potent quick-healing spells she preferred to use in combat. Instead, it was designed to greatly increase the recipient's ability to heal. It evened the odds given the lycan's own regenerative skills but nothing would prevent his death if the lesser werewolves joined the fight. She had to intervene.

Wavren saw his sister appear from a side room, cast a spell, and dive into the brawl just as a group of smaller lycans joined the fray. At first, the massive black bear Rosabela had become easily swatted the lesser werewolves away, but they quickly regrouped. Wavren whistled loudly and out of nowhere his ally, the mighty Stonetalon appeared.

A second whistle summoned the polar bear, Blackmaw, but before Wavren could raise his weapon, Gaedron grabbed his arm and said, "Not yet boyo. Give 'em a second."

Wavren, still disguised as a troll, realized their illusion was intact and would be better off if it remained so for a while longer. It would be a quick death to appear as an elf in the main hall of the orc city Dek'Thal.

The two bears and Rosabela held back the attackers allowing Da'Shar another few seconds to deal with his nemesis one on one but time was not the true problem. The heroes would draw more suspicion the longer they were in plain view of the orcs and that would surely unravel the illusion that camouflaged them from a city of more than two hundred thousand orcs and trolls.

Vlaad saw a patrol of armed orcs coming up the road to investigate the growing crowd. The fight between Da'Shar and Carnage was raging and unlikely to end soon enough. The hall was a mass of chaos as orcs passed money, cheered, and screamed curses back and forth. It was at that moment he saw Gorka across the room staring at him. The half-orc seemed oblivious to the fighting and the gambling that had dominated everyone's attention. Vlaad knew their time was up as his lifelong enemy gestured to him. The master assassin drew his dagger and slowly pantomimed slicing his throat as if to say, "Time to die."

The defender turned to his companion and said, "Theila, we need a distraction and fast!"

The warlock nodded and ran outside where she passed the orcish troupe on her way out. The soldiers disregarded her as she appeared to be a decaying priestess but that illusion would crumble soon. Theila ran behind the central hall and tried to find a place to work undetected, but orcs were everywhere. When the coast was clear, so to speak, she called upon one of her most powerful spells and one she had never dared attempt. She called it *helstorm* for obvious reasons.

As she summoned the powers of the abyss she noticed her scabrous, rotting flesh faded away leaving pure, tanned skin. Her tattered priestess robes became traveling clothes. Last but not least, the grey, matted, dirty hair became beautifully thick auburn locks with the telltale rebellious wisps that dangled across her cheeks. Her disguise was gone. In the guttural, thick abyssian dialect she spoke drawing forth a black smoky mist-like energy. Sweat collected on her brow as she strained to absorb the requisite power and all at once she released it with the invocation, *typhus-pyro-cirrus.*

The clouds became dark and the wind gusted ominously, stirring up all manner of dust and debris. Local shopkeepers scurried about uncertainly trying to keep their goods from blowing away and then it began. Massive gouts of flame and ash rained down in a howling torrent of death. The hide-covered shops were quickly enveloped in fire followed by the wooden and even mud-thatched huts. Theila was unaffected by her spell's fiery power and even reveled in its destructive nature. This was what it meant to be a warlock, to be a spell caster of the darkest magic.

The screams of burning and dying orcs quickly overcame the spectacle inside between Da'Shar and Carnage. The elite guards as well as the city patrol ran out of the great hall which began to shake and crumble under the terrible effects of the warlock's spell. The lycans and heroes paused long enough to notice that the building was coming down around them. They made haste in their attempts to flee the now burning and disintegrating great hall. Last to escape was Vlaad. He watched his hated enemy slip through a secret door and evade him once again.

The illusion had faltered under Gorka's keen eyes leaving the humans and elves vulnerable, but the destruction in the city was more than distracting enough for the orcs to care at the moment. They fought to save their city from a rampaging fire that was consuming everything they held dear. In that moment, Landermihl looked to Vlaad with shock. His crystal blue eyes showed regret. Innocent lives were lost for their escape. Property was utterly destroyed. These people would suffer greatly for the price of being orcs. Vlaad could not hold his gaze. He looked away thinking of Theila, his dear companion, as the others gathered nearby.

Gaedron smiled and said, "Smells like roast pork ta me."

Landermihl cast an angry look his way, but said nothing.

Wavren said, "It's not over yet. We have to clear the city before they come for us. We can't win against an army."

Rosabela and Da'Shar nodded.

Don asked, "Where is Theila?"

The group looked around and saw the warlock as they had never seen before. Her clothes were the same and her physical features were unchanged, but she was different. She seemed to radiate a morbid joy at the destruction she had caused. To say she was evil was less than accurate, but there was no doubt that remorse was the last emotion she was capable of feeling.

She calmly strolled up to the group and said, "I

suppose mankind and orcs have one thing in common; fire is their oldest enemy."

The group stood aghast. It wasn't what she said, but how she said it that made her teammates shudder. It was as if she could picture this destruction consuming all lands and all of its creatures without discrimination but more was at stake than the warlock's sanity so the group moved toward the gates.

Curtiss Robinson

CHAPTER 22
ESCAPE

The assassins, lycans, and Gorka managed to escape and gather several blocks away from the inferno that had destroyed the great hall and most of the central bazaar. Though dozens of Dek'Thal citizens were killed and hundreds were injured, Gorka and Lord Carnage seemed content to find the lost prisoners and their friends who had orchestrated their escape.

Lord Carnage began, "My men will find them, and your men must contain them."

The Shade was a blank slate of emotion. He replied, "They will likely move toward the main gates to the south of our position. It is the closest exit. I will see to it that my troops do their part to secure the city in case I am wrong."

The pack leader nodded and said, "The hunt begins. We will meet back here with our quarry."

As the lycans assumed their lupine forms running off in every direction, Gorka turned to the few remaining assassins. He paused in thought before issuing orders. It occurred to him that he had lost many allies in this venture, but it mattered not at all. They were tools in his arsenal and nothing more. He considered the companies and even battalions of orcs and trolls he had sacrificed in battle, particularly in the contested regions, to rise in power. He had promised the tauren people land for their services and the souls of traitors and enemies were promised to the zombie-like undead as payment for their allegiance. All were weighed and measured against profit and personal gain. As he lingered a moment longer over the throats he had slit and the deals had he made to achieve his status and authority, a thin smile appeared on his face. He knew it was all worth it.

"Plague, you are my senior officer. I place you in command absentia of The Legion. Go back to Griffon's Peak, lay low, and conduct business from the shadows until I return. Your work here is done," the guild master commanded.

Without a single word, the thin assassin bowed and slipped out of sight having no idea why the plans were changing. He was thankful for his commission as ad hoc guild master but was somewhat disappointed that the deal with the lycans appeared to be delayed, if not broken.

Gorka summoned his elite guards and spoke to the commander of the local patrols. He said, "We have saboteurs and traitors in our midst. Spread the word that elves and humans have attacked Dek'Thal and desecrated the great hall. It is an act of war and we must capture or kill the offenders."

He intentionally left the orders vague, knowing the lycans would fall into the category of traitor unless he specified otherwise and of course, the brutish orcs were easily rallied at the mention of war. They spread the word quickly and in no time the entire city was mobilized and hunting the traitors.

Though he was remiss for failing to unite the lycans with The Legion, a new opportunity had presented itself. Instead of gaining an uncontrollable ally in Lord Carnage, he would rally his current allies politically. As an afterthought, he dismissed the entire lycan alliance plan as unattainable given the resistance Da'Shar had shown to being turned. It was clear that he would never willingly allow his body to host the spirit and disease that was the mantle of lycanthrope and if it wasn't good for an elf, then it certainly wasn't good enough for his loyal assassins. It was easier to simply kill them all.

The first of the werewolves spotted by the mob of orcs was loping along to the west of the now burned out great hall. His name was Orem and he had been with Lord Carnage from the beginning. He had been a loyal follower by choice, more so than by the coercion of his master. He had reveled in the power of being a member of the lycan pack with hundreds of lives taken by his terrible power. Needless to say, he was not caught unaware as the group of orcs came around the corner of the marketplace screaming curses and war cries.

The first orc to attack was a mere soldier with crude armor and an old rusty mace. In a most predictable fashion, the orc swung his weapon from right to left horizontally. Orem caught the massive incoming swing at the wrist and wrenched the thick green arm a half turn beyond its limit. The resounding crack and howl that followed made the other orcs pause for a moment. It was long enough for Orem to dash away through the crowded streets.

As he sped through the alleyways and shops, Orem noticed the mounting forces converging on his position. He made one last turn and found himself in a cul-de-sac. He was trapped and by the look of hatred in the bloodshot eyes of more than twenty armed orcs, the werewolf knew his time had come. He let out a deep howl that carried throughout most of the market and was echoed by several of his feral brethren. As the mob came in all at once, Orem disappeared under a flood of clubbing, stabbing, and hacking weapons.

Lord Carnage had heard the death-wail of his

top lieutenant and assumed the worst. Gorka, the half-orc leader, had finally seen the truth of the situation. He had come to realize that without Da'Shar as a host, the lycan pack leader would not have the strength and will to dominate. As such, he would never transfer his gift of immortality to the orcs. The façade had faded and now the lycans were marked for extermination. This turning point had been anticipated but Lord Carnage had hoped to escape Dek'Thal with the druids before it came to pass.

The pack leader was an experienced survivor. He knew what to do and with a howl of his own he called to his remaining forces. The howls were repeated through the city walls making the desolate and dreary stone buildings come alive with an eerie echo. It was terrifying to even the stoutest orcs and trolls for a moment, as it seemed the entire city was overrun with werewolves. The tactic lasted for several seconds enabling the pack time to unite and form up on their leader near the southern gate where they saw a small group of orcs blocking the escape of Da'Shar and his companions.

"The enemy of my enemy is my friend," Lord Carnage announced to his pack as he pointed toward the elves and humans. "We must fight to escape this place and they will breech the gate. Kill anyone who stands in their way."

***

Vlaad had taken the point with the two bears on either side. Landermihl and Maejis followed him, ready to cast spells while the druids, hunters, Don, and Theila guarded the rear. Vlaad was set to dash into the orc guards at the gate when he heard a warning from behind.

Wavren called out, "Lycans coming up fast!"

Da'Shar transformed into his panther-like windwraith form as Rosabela became the massive black bear to hold off the werewolves. The hunters leveled their fine weapons and prepared to fire when to their astonishment, the pack leader motioned for his feral warriors to attack the orcs. It took all of their willpower not to engage the beasts but with orcs now coming from every direction, they quickly chose to support the unusual allies.

Gaedron called out to his friends, "Orcs die first! Give 'em hell!"

Wavren turned and fired his blunderbuss into a charging gate guard. The shot hit him in the shoulder spinning him around but he came forward with a huge club. Vlaad intercepted the hit with his shield, spun around left, deflecting the momentum to his right, and slashed the orc's meaty legs leaving him incapacitated. A werewolf shot into the air over the defender's head and landed among several more guards with teeth tearing and wicked claws slashing. The guards drove their swords and axes into its hide but the beast kept fighting. Its ability to heal kept it alive but would never outlast the onslaught of wounds it incurred. Suddenly, its fur started to glow with bright gold hue as magic from the great paladin protected it. The werewolf doubled its efforts and tore out the throat of the closest enemy.

Vlaad dashed in among the werewolves with Stonetalon and Ol' Blackmaw to his right and left. The orcs were pushed back easily allowing the team to maneuver through the gate but there were trolls, tauren, undead, and of course orcs gathering outside the city gates. Escape seemed impossible and the entire orc militia was gathering to their rear.

The lycan pack was taking a beating on all sides. They had formed a protective ring around the less armored humans who were dishing out spells of every sort. Theila was calling down great gouts of flame while her protective voidwalker fought back enemies trying to get to her. Maejis was alternating between frigid bolts of frost and arcane volleys of energy. He fared quite well holding back the soldiers who tried to end his casting with immobilizing waves of cold. Don held his few throwing blades in reserve but managed to dodge in and out of the wizardly combat with swift efficiency finishing off stragglers.

The druids served as the rear defense holding back the mass of armored orcs which were growing in number by the second. Lord Carnage had taken his place beside his brother Da'Shar and was dealing death blows with the speed of Da'Shar's windwraith form and the power of Rosabela's bear form. Few chose to stand toe to toe with the pack leader and those who did, found the flesh-rending claws and a cruel maw more than they could handle. It was an impressive display for the druids who finally realized the power and lure of lycanthrope. It was an unholy power yet one with great benefits. The druids fought on in spite of being drawn to Carnage, but both felt the pull more and more as they witnessed his power.

Wavren had fired his weapon from every possible angle to keep their flank clear but the enemy was getting closer and closer with every shot. Finally, he shouldered his weapon and drew out two red sticks of dynamite. He lit the fuses and tossed them quickly. Gaedron saw the move and covered his pupil with an amazing cycle of fire. The shots were so fast that aiming became futile but the enemy was so close, every shot hit someone. It was simply not enough. The orcs overwhelmed the hunters with sheer numbers. Barely a second later, the dynamite blasted a path through the horde of bad guys.

The defender was moving with amazing speed. He blocked a dozen hits and absorbed damage from a dozen more. His armor was damaged and his fine shield was battered but he never slowed. His training under Andar had prepared him for this moment. His mind was focused and his body was attuned to its commands. It was a stalemate of never-ending attacks against shield blocks, parries, dodges, and counter strikes; at least as long as the two mighty bears held their positions. Vlaad spared a glance to see the ursine allies fully enraged and still bashing through the growing number of tauren, trolls, and undead coming to Dek'Thal from abroad.

As the paladin, Landermihl, called to his deity for healing and rained thunderous blows from his war hammer, he realized the hunters were down and his party would never hold off the hundreds upon hundreds of vicious orcs.

In his powerful booming voice he yelled, "To the last, for the glory of Griffon's Peak!"

His magically enhanced voice gave strength to his team, bolstering their will to fight. The bears roared with strength, Maejis called down a blizzard of ice shards, the druids growled with determination, Don sang out a battle hymn, and Vlaad transcended battle focus and became a blur of movement.

In the midst of Landermihl's call to arms, only one understood that there was no hope of survival, no chance of escape. Theila saw the world around her in slow motion. She saw her companions fighting valiantly and in a state of premonition she saw them slowly fall to the endless sea of blades. The hunters had already fallen while protecting the flank. The elves fell next, cut to ribbons with the lycans quick to follow. Don the Bard, her dear father, was crushed under the tauren hooves and orcish boots as the army surged forward. Maejis was cleaved in half by a massive ax-wielding troll. The goodly paladin, Landermihl, fought to the last healing the defender and the bears, but was targeted by lightning bolts from the Bloodcrest shamen. Her heart sank and grief took her when the bears fell and her love, Vlaad, was left alone. He held on in vain and withstood more damage than imaginable. She felt every sword, spear, and ax in her heart when he could take no more. Time stopped and Theila found herself standing before Ja'Zaru in the abyss. He was kneeling before her awaiting her commands. She did not understand how she came to be in the abyss and why the powerful demon was kneeling before her. All she could remember was the vision of death.

The mighty balrog spoke, "Mistress, I await your command as we agreed at out last meeting."

Theila recalled the greater demon indenturing itself to her. She remembered that Gorka had taunted and disgraced the demon and that it had wanted revenge but this was not Pirate's Cove and she never summoned the beast for fear of releasing it on her world.

The demon whispered compassionately, "I can save your companions. Release me on the orcs of Dek'Thal and my wrath will fall upon your enemies."

Theila looked over her shoulder and saw a tiny window leading back to her world where time stood still. She could see her friends, her father, and her love, Vlaad, alive. Her premonition had revealed their gruesome deaths, but this alternative was uncertain. It was always that way with chaos. Deep down inside something felt wrong, but her grief, her hatred, and her desire for revenge washed it away like a rushing river.

Theila looked back to the subservient demon. Its wings were furled and its head downcast. One knee was down and its mighty fists rested at its sides. The balrog seemed fully under her control and was ready to do her bidding.

She drew in a deep breath and said, "What is the price for your service?"

The demon looked up and said, "Destruction is my payment."

Theila noticed Ja'Zaru's flaming tail switching back and forth like a cat anxiously awaiting an opportunity to pounce. She said, "I am no fool; our agreement was for Pirate's Cove. I will not release you to run amok from Pirate's Cove to Dek'Thal."

The cunning demon looked up with an evil grin and said, "Then we need a new agreement, mistress."

Theila closed her eyes. She pictured her friends in her mind. *Their lives could be spared*, she thought. She considered her father, Don. His death in her vision had been horrible. Finally, she pictured Vlaad. She could never allow him to die. She loved him with every fiber of her being. It was this love that gave her pause. She knew what the demon wanted and giving in to him would mean never having what she wanted. The choice seemed to take an eternity to make as she weighed the lives of her companions against her soul.

"Speak your terms," the warlock commanded.

Ja'Zaru knew he had won. The greater demon stood to its full height. Its wings spread and he threw his head back laughing with uninhibited evil. As the massive balrog returned his gaze to Theila he said, "You will serve me in life and for one hundred years after."

The warlock took a knee in subservience. The balrog laughed maniacally. Its patience and cunning had paid off. He would have revenge against Theila and now had a willing conduit to gain revenge on Gorka.

***

The fight was raging as the few heroes and lycans struggled to hold off the army of Dek'Thal and hundreds of its citizens. The sight was both heroic and hopeless. Though dozens of troops from the Bloodcrest Forces were dead or dying at the hands of the small band of elves, humans, and Gaedron the dwarf, the end was close at hand.

Landermihl was the first to notice Theila speaking the guttural incantations required in summoning. He could not understand demon-speak but his goodly nature cried out to him. He felt the presence of a malevolent force and cried out to the warlock, "NO!"

Don was quick to link the paladin's reaction to Theila's casting but he had always trusted his daughter. What he saw next was both horrifying and awe inspiring. The ground shook and erupted in flames consuming Theila. The arrival of the most terrifying of all greater demons sent the world into chaos around them. Many orcs and trolls fled, often crushing anyone caught underfoot. The undead backed away cautiously and the tauren shook with fear.

As the blood-red winged demon rose to its full height of nearly twenty feet, the heroes found themselves suddenly backing away from Theila and her summoned ally. The warlock pointed toward the heart of the city. The balrog bent low and then sprang into the air with a great buffet of wind from its massive leathery wings. It flew over the cowering army and landed beside the great hall where the orcish king, Ba'Grash Bloodletter, ran the city's affairs. In one mighty stroke, the great hall was reduced to rubble. Ja'Zaru continued to unleash his fury on Dek'Thal with hellish glee.

Theila glided along behind the demon on a cloud of ash and fume. She summoned a cyclone of flame that set the city ablaze. A few bold orcs raised the weapons and came to defend their homes. She cast flaming spheres and jets of liquid magma incinerating them in seconds but her spells were nothing compared the damage Ja'Zaru was wreaking. In his right hand, he snapped a whip of pure abyssian flame that ignited all manner of flammable material. In his left hand, he wielded an ax of magical fire that was able to rend stone and iron fortifications effortlessly.

Still awestruck by the unbelievable display of power, the heroes watched in horror. Lord Carnage rounded up his few remaining lycans and quickly left Dek'Thal. The orcs were scattered like sheep. The scene was surreal with fire, smoke, and endless destruction making Dek'Thal seem like the abyss remade. Amid the razed city, a single being came forth to challenge the demon. Gorka, High Commander of the Bloodcrest Forces, and Master of Assassins appeared a top the last standing two-story edifice, the Temple of Shamen.

"Beast of the abyss, it is me you want. I alone can quench your thirst for revenge. Come and be done with it!" The Shade dared announce.

The effect of the half-orc's words rippled outward like a shockwave. The Temple of Shamen had long been a holy place for Dek'Thal's magic and its occupants were undoubtedly responsible for empowering Gorka's words. The demon turned, fully intending to meet the puny half-orc in combat, but before it could attack a dozen orcs surrounded it, hacking with zeal. The demon killed two with a mighty stomp; three were incinerated with the fiery whip and the others were swept away with the blazing ax, but two dozen replaced the first group. Theila called down fire and blasted the orcs without remorse. Many died, few remained, but none fled. The orcs redoubled their numbers in defense of their city and their inspired leader.

Maejis gathered his wits and tried to snap the others out of their stupor. Don and the druids came around quickly, but Landermihl and Vlaad remained awestruck for some time. The hunters were healed by Rosabela and Da'Shar and regained consciousness soon after.

"Wha' in da name of Moradin's beard 'appened?" Gaedron asked in shock.

Rosabela half answered, "Theila…"

Da'Shar continued for her, "The warlock has saved us all and doomed the realm."

Vlaad glared at the druid and said, "She saved us, now we must save her."

Maejis quickly interjected, "She sacrificed herself for us. If we do not leave now, her sacrifice will be in vain."

"I'll not leave my daughter," the bard said weakly.

"She is no longer of this world," Landermihl began, "she has become demon-kin and must be destroyed."

The defender wanted to deny it, to scream that they had all gone mad, but he knew it to be true. He put his head in hands and tried to focus on his duty. He thought to himself, *Duty is second only to justice*, but somehow it all seemed meaningless without Theila beside him. He loved her. He had always loved her, but now that she was gone his heart ached for her like never before. His mind raced with indecision.

Wavren looked around suspiciously. He noticed the tracks left behind by Lord Carnage and his minions. He grabbed Gaedron's attention to quietly point out his discovery. The dwarf nodded.

"Da orcs be getting' wha's been comin' to dem fer a long time now. Our work 'ere be done. I say we be off ta finish our mission. We got a lycan pack hurt an' on da run," the dwarf said gruffly. "We gotta be goin'," he said emphatically.

The druids moved toward the hunters. Maejis joined them. Don stood beside Vlaad and Landermihl stood alone.

"Aye," the dwarf began, "we will finish Carnage an' his lycan boys, Vlaad an' Don choose death an' honor. So be it. That leaves one."

Landermihl spoke saying, "I believe our mission to end the joining of The Legion with the lycan pack is complete. I have been called by my god to fight the demon but I cannot allow the warlock to live as a pawn of demon-kind. She is now an infection upon the land."

Maejis sighed as he realized the paladin was

correct. He moved back with the humans.

Vlaad was grief stricken by the truth of the paladin's words. He knew Theila was not evil but he also knew she had to be stopped. Instead of condemning Theila or going against Landermihl, Vlaad did the only thing he could think of. He focused his rage on the one person responsible for all of the pain in his life, the one being responsible for taking everyone dear to him.

Vlaad said, "We stop the demon, then we focus on the true fiend responsible. Gorka Darkstorm must die."

Don liked the compromise and nodded emphatically knowing when it came down to deciding between his daughter's life and letting evil reign on Dae'gon or killing The Shade, he would gladly take option two.

The paladin scowled but consented for the time being. In his righteous edict with his deity, demons were always a priority followed by their evil summoners, but in this case, The Shade was a reasonable target. Besides, he needed Maejis, Don, and Vlaad. Going alone would be suicide.

Without another word, the team split. The humans moved quickly toward the path of destruction Theila and the demon created. The elves and Gaedron headed south in pursuit of the lycans.

CHAPTER 23
DESPERATION

Theila and Ja'Zaru had killed dozens of orcs trying to get to Gorka, but the sturdy soldiers of Dek'Thal had heard the call of their general and had come en masse. It wasn't simple courage and it wasn't a matter of being magically compelled that sent so many orcs to their death. It was something else. Gorka had inspired the chaotic race. With the aid of the shamen, the very real destruction of their city, and a singular being willing to stand up to a greater demon, the orcs had come from every inch of Dek'Thal to stand beside their leader.

Gorka watched his followers join the fight by the score. It was fanaticism at its best, such that even trolls and tauren had joined in the fight and were coming to see Gorka in his finest moment (who was taking full advantage of the situation). He stepped back from the edge of the temple's balcony to get a running start. After a deep breath, Gorka dashed toward the edge. His human heritage gave him a lanky build suitable for running and his orcish heritage gave him powerful muscles. He utilized both aspects to propel himself across the gap between the balrog and the temple. As he flew through the air, he howled, "For blood and glory!"

The mass of Dek'Thal citizens paused with awe. The twenty-foot-tall balrog looked up from his rampage just in time to catch the flying half-orc square in the chest. Its surprise was complete when Gorka slid down its sternum leaving a deep gash from neck to gut. The pain was exquisite and how the monster bellowed in agony. Ja'Zaru dropped both weapons instantly and began flailing about as if swatting a swarm of bees.

Having completed his initial attack, Gorka threw himself backward fully arching his back into a backward flip that brought his feet into position to absorb his fall. When he hit the ground, he rolled with the landing and came up into a fighting position. The effect was incredible.

His followers roared, "Protect the commander!"

The citizens responded, "To the death!"

The balrog was swarmed by hundreds of flailing, slashing, and hacking soldiers. The crowd of citizen began firing arrows, crossbow bolts, and hurling spears. It was more than the greater demon could withstand. Its greatest asset, fear, was gone. Theila noticed none of it. She felt nothing and cared not at all. She was dead inside, unfeeling and emotionless. All she had left on this plane was death and she dealt it in spades.

Shielded by the massive balrog, Theila was able to fire every manner of attack known to warlocks. She cast corruption spells that weakened her enemies, life-draining spells that numbed their limbs, and an inferno of fire spells that burned everything. Orcs, trolls, tauren, and even a fair number of their undead allies fell to her wrath. It was as if Theila had become the avatar of hell itself unleashing a judgment of damnation on all living things, yet the inhabitants of Dek'Thal came on anyway. They came as a massive and unstoppable tide of fury.

Vlaad and his few remaining companions had maneuvered from the south through the burning wreckage of the city to a point where they could see the flood of orcs pouring through the northern, eastern, and western streets. Theila and her demon had slain every living soul behind leaving charred and burning desolation in their wake. The scene was both terrifying and amazing. Vlaad could hardly believe his dear sweet Theila was responsible for this catastrophe. He looked back to his companions for some sign of hope. They offered none.

Maejis said, "This is beyond our abilities. She has sacrificed herself for us. We cannot save her now, as there are too many."

Landermihl offered no comfort saying, "She begat this evil and now it will consume her. May the light of goodness have mercy on her soul."

Don was there beside the mighty defender. He placed his hand on Vlaad's shoulder with resignation. He said, "Though she is my daughter and I would give my life for hers, I do not see a way out of this alive. What can we do?"

Vlaad had spent his life in pursuit of his duty and justice. It had been his mantra since his dear O'ma had taught him what it meant to be a man of honor. He had put it before his own needs, even before the love for Theila who meant everything to him. His mind raced with fear, the one emotion he had always been able to conquer. It was not a fear of death or of pain. It was the fear of living without his true love. It was a fear he simply could not overcome. In that moment, he realized there was only one choice. He had to save her. It was insane but it was all he had to work with.

Vlaad grabbed Maejis by the collar and yanked him in close. He looked at the thin wizard sternly and said, "Prepare a portal. There won't be time later. The demon is a dam holding back a rushing river of orcs. When he falls, the flood will destroy everything in its path. Be ready!"

Landermihl screamed at the defender, "This is

insanity. You can't get close enough to even make a difference. She'll burn you alive if you get in her deadly range and if you wait until the demon falls it will be too late. This is suicide!"

Vlaad had tears welling up in his eyes. He had no words to help the paladin understand but he had to go. Landermihl saw it in his clenched jaw and pursed lips. The holy warrior nodded and called to his god for a blessing on the defender. It was the only thing he could do.

Without another word Vlaad drew his sword, pulled his magnificent shield off his back, and set it into place. He dashed off to do his duty and save the woman he loved.

Don yelled to Vlaad, "Duty is second only to justice! You can save her, I know you can!"

Landermihl looked accusingly at the bard. He asked, "Why do you give him false hope?"

Don replied with a quavering voice, "Theila is my daughter, my only family left in this world. I gotta believe he can save her. He is her only hope."

Maejis set the rune stone in place and prepared his spell to summon a portal that would take them back to Griffon's Peak. The spell would only stay active for a short time so he would have to time the invocation carefully. If he was too early, Theila and Vlaad would be stranded in Dek'Thal. If he was too late, they would all die before it opened. Portal magic was best used far from combat for these very reasons.

Vlaad felt the temperature rising as he neared the balrog. He could see Theila's tiny form behind the demon. She was showering the orcs with a hailstorm of fire and death magic. He pushed on through the heat. When he got within range of her magic, she turned on him just as Landermihl had predicted. Her first salvo was a massive fireball spell that hit his shield with such force he flew back a dozen feet. The heat was intense, but his flesh did not burn. Vlaad remembered the last time he saw his O'ma so long ago. She had given him two healing potions and a special ring that had belonged to his father. The potions had been consumed early in his career, but the ring had always been on his finger and was imbued with a variety of protections, particularly against fire. Vlaad was certain it had just saved his life.

The defender moved quickly back to his feet and set his defenses for the next attack. He carefully shuffled forward, keeping his shield positioned for the incoming blast. The second attack was a continuous gout of flame that pushed against his shield like a gale force wind. Vlaad dug his toes in to brace against it but the spell pushed him back. He could feel the searing heat through the shield and his heavy war gauntlets. The ring on his finger was likely being pushed to its limits.

When the attack ended, Vlaad glanced up to assess the situation. Hundreds of orc and orc allies were dead in front of the demon but thousands were still coming. Among the embattled orcs was the assassin, Gorka Darkstorm. He was commanding the battle personally. Vlaad had to resist the urge to go after him. Even though seeing him dead would be worth his life, he could not so easily forfeit Theila's.

He refocused his efforts and made a third attempt to reach her. This time, Vlaad found Theila distracted by the surge of orcs. As she poured hellfire across the battlefield, the opportunity came for the defender to make his move. Like a striking cobra, Vlaad coiled his thick legs and sprang forward, shield bashing the warlock. Though her ability to cause destruction was great, Theila's primary defense was a thin layer of robes which did little to absorb the powerful blow. She went down immediately and lay very still.

The demon sensed the loss of its summoner and turned on Vlaad. It drew back its gargantuan ax and drove it down hard. The sheer power of the attack would have sundered any other shield and killed any other human, but Vlaad carried the Aegis Shield of Griffon's Peak and he was no mere human. He was a defender, a shield warrior, and trained in defense. Instead, the blow was deflected into the ground and Vlaad immediately reset his position.

The orcs rallied against the distracted demon, hacking with reckless abandon at its unprotected backside. Axes chopped, swords sliced, and spears stabbed into its legs and feet. Arrows, crossbow bolts, and a countless magic bolts blasted into its broad shoulders and lower torso. The demon could not afford to fight on two fronts. Sensing its own demise, Ja'Zaru sprang into the air, flapping his mighty wings, and wind buffeted everyone below. The move took the orcs by surprise buying the balrog much needed respite, but when the demon circled around its mistress and the human were gone.

***

Though the lycan pack moved with great haste, the hunters drew on their own talents to increase their endurance and speed. The druids were even better equipped to move across the open plain and desert regions than the hunters, which tipped the scales in their favor even more.

Wavren and Gaedron tracked the lycans easily from Dek'Thal. It was obvious that Carnage had no intention of staying in the Western Kingdom. His pack was reduced to less than a handful of werewolves and they were all seriously wounded from the battle. He was looking for escape and time to rebuild. It was a matter of survival instincts and the protectors knew it.

With the orc city miles behind, the heroes finally caught up to the lycans. Lord Carnage sensed the approach of his brother, Da'Shar. It was futile to continue the exodus when he knew a confrontation was imminent. It was better to end it now rather than find himself surrounded by a town of goblins and ogres who would never tolerate fighting in their port or anything that might interrupt trade. He stopped and spoke to his three followers.

"Brethren," he began, "we must survive and through cunning or ferocity we shall. Be ready, but do not attack unless attacked. There is much to lose here."

The lycans were bound by the bond of blood to agree, but they did so willfully as well.

As the druids and hunters approached, the lycans returned to their human forms and remained passive. They trusted their leader who had always watched over them and somehow always understood what was best for the pack.

The elves and Gaedron slowed their approach when they saw their quarry stopped and waiting for them.

"Hail and well met, brother. I see you too have escaped the city of orcs though your number is diminished," Lord Carnage stated.

Da'Shar transformed into his elven form and spoke as Rosabela and the hunters remained combat ready with the bears ready to charge in at a moment's notice.

He said, "Indeed brother, we have fared well, but it is your number which has diminished. We parted company with the others by choice."

The pack leader took the insult casually. He replied, "It is true, many of our men were destroyed in the defense of your team. We willingly fought by your side and were glad to have you as allies with us against the orcs. It is as it always should have been."

Da'Shar saw through the lie Carnage was weaving. The pack leader wanted to have Da'Shar's group join his pack. He could sense the lure of power and the offer to become were-creatures coming. He allowed the pack leader to continue with a nod.

Carnage continued, "So you feel it then? You can sense the power we have to offer. I know you have been taught by the druidic council to fight these urges. They claim it is an unnatural disease but I know it to be a symbiotic relationship where the pack thrives on the strength of its members. You can have it all you see. You can wield the power of a druid and surpass its boundaries."

Da'Shar broke in saying, "You have sacrificed balance and nature to increase your power as a shape shifter. You have lost what it means to be a druid."

The lycan returned, "In what way? You can shape shift as can I. You can heal, as can I. You can cast elemental spells, as can I. So how are druids so different than lycans other than being inferior in might?"

"A druid's mission is to heal others; a lycan can only heal itself. A druid can call upon the power of nature and the elements to serve others, a lycan can only destroy the land with these powers. Most importantly, a druid shares a bond with its animal partner while lycans are a diseased abomination enslaved to its parasitic base instincts."

Carnage turned to his followers and said, "I fear we are at an impasse. Perhaps we should test who is the fittest to survive."

The lycans raised the fists and rooted, "Challenge, chall-enge, chall-enge!"

Carnage returned his gaze to Da'Shar and asked politely, "What do you say brother? Shall we decide this in combat with the highest stakes?"

Rosabela saw the challenge coming and feared for her mentor. She had witnessed the raw power of the pack leader and was doubtful that any single druid could best him in combat, but she could never disgrace her mentor by saying so. Instead, she transformed into her elven form and joined the debate.

She said, "It would be dishonorable to have the two senior members fight this out when there are younger members who are available to settle this matter in their stead. That is, if one of your underlings has the courage to face me."

The group was silent for several moments. Wavren and Gaedron had their weapons at the ready and were prepared to set their bear allies loose if the lycans made any hostile moves. The pack leader knew he had been outmaneuvered. He was a greater werewolf, a true lycan, and by far more powerful than his minions. In single combat he was the best choice, but the crafty she-elf had eliminated that option. He now had to agree to pit one of his followers against the younger druid or simply attack the group. As he weighed the likelihood of victory, he thought back to the battle he fought centuries ago with Da'Shar and the very nasty dwarf who stood across from him. He knew they would defeat him again. The odds seemed unfavorable given the two bears, two druids, and two hunters facing his three men and himself. The odds were in the favor of the druid winning if she was crafty, but the reward would be an elven host if she lost. It was too tempting to pass up.

"Very well then, I will assign one of my men to fight in my stead but the stakes must be agreed upon," he said.

Da'Shar took a moment to consider his student. Rosabela was fearless, confident, well trained, and ready to do her duty, but was she willing to sacrifice her body to the pestilence of Lord Carnage if she lost? He looked into those deep green eyes that were an endless sea and saw love for her brother, for her mentor, and for Jael'Kutter but most of all, he saw the steeled will of a veteran druid.

Da'Shar said, "The stakes are simple. Our disciples will fight for our very existence. If Rosabela loses, you have your elven host in me. If your student loses, your essence returns to the druidic council for judgment."

"Does everyone agree?" the lycan asked his minions.

All nodded.

"What of your companions, Da'Shar?" the lycan asked.

Wavren said nothing. Gaedron was silent. They wanted to fight and destroy the lot of them.

Da'Shar spoke in their stead, "They are bound in honor and their silences are their consent, but know that if you fail to keep your end of the deal, the first shots they fire will be in your head."

Gaedron and Wavren spoke as one saying, "Aye!"

Carnage did not need to consult with his followers to know who he would choose to represent the lycan pack. Among his many years as a lycan, only one had been with him since the beginning, a thickly built human named Sunder. When Carnage snapped his fingers, Sunder stepped forward and eyed Rosabela intently. He had the look of a devious and calculating villain with a high, straight forehead and a low, thick brow ridge. Though his intention was to intimidate the she-elf, Sunder found himself looking in the most penetrating green eyes he had ever seen. Though they belonged to a lovely and frail looking elf-maid, Rosabela's eyes were more akin to predator than prey.

Sunder reassured his master saying, "This won't take long, boss."

"Go for the throat," was his only reply.

The other two werewolves were on edge, eager to jump into the fight.

If Da'Shar was concerned for his pupil, he showed none of it. He never took his eyes off of Carnage. He fully expected the lycan pack leader to fight to the end and was prepared to intercede if need be.

Wavren was of course concerned for his sister, but his focus was down the length of his blunderbuss where Lord Carnage remained in his sights. Gaedron was likewise trained on the leader of the werewolves.

Lord Carnage nodded and Sunder transformed. Rosabela called to nature for enhanced strength and speed. Her body teemed with energy as the lycan came in without hesitation. Rosabela anticipated Sunder's attack, given his cocky nature, and just as he leaped the agile she-elf rolled to her left and lashed out with her staff, catching the lycan across its forelegs. Sunder crashed to the ground in a heap but was up and snarling almost instantly. Rosabela spun her staff overhead and to one side ending with one end under her arm in the low ready position. Sunder was surprised that the druid had elected to fight in her elven form. He was certain she was considerably less vulnerable as a bear, but he was no fool. If she chose to fight as an elf, it was for a purpose.

Sunder circled for a moment then came in with a quick snap meant to serve as a feint. Rosabela dashed out of range easily. He circled again and then came in with a vicious swipe from his claws but Rosabela blocked with her staff, leaving his hand numb from the wrist down. It seemed that Rosabela was toying with him. She remained entirely defensive and not only refrained from using her shape-shifting skills, but she hadn't employed her offensive spells.

Carnage noticed the unusual tactics as well. He watched closely to see what she was up to but nothing seemed out of place. It was then that he noticed a small handful of leaves in her left hand. In all of his long years as a lycan, he had fought thousands of times and had only been defeated once. That defeat was at the hands of this druid's mentor. He knew Rosabela had been well trained but he couldn't believe she hoped to defeat his best werewolf with a staff and a handful of stupid leaves.

Sunder grew tired of the games his adversary was playing. He had orders from his leader to end this fight quickly after all, and there was nothing the she-elf could do to him that his regenerative powers could not handle. With that thought, he came in fiercely hoping to overwhelm the tiny druid. He jumped high into the air and came down with claws raking and fangs tearing. The nimble druid threw up her staff with one hand to intercept the claws but the lycan snapped it like a twig. He came down fully on top of her and saw his target, the soft flesh of her delicate neck. He snapped once but she squirmed to the side. He missed by an inch. He pinned her right arm down with his left hand and grabbed her hair with his right. Sunder yanked hard revealing a perfect target in her exposed jugular, but as he came in to tear her throat out, the cunning druid shoved her left hand into his mouth and deep into his throat. Though he tried to bite down, he found that his gag reflex wouldn't allow it. Suddenly, he realized that he couldn't breathe. He pulled away and rolled off of the druid to dislodge her hand but he still found it difficult to breathe. He was choking on something. Sunder tried to cough and then to vomit. Finally, he swallowed hard and the blockage cleared. He took a deep breath of air and regained his senses long enough to see his adversary casting a spell.

Rosabela drew great roots and vines from the ground to hold her enemy in place. Once fully rooted, she called for starfire. The gleaming pillar of light shot down from the heavens and burned the lycan's back. Sunder howled in agony and tore at his restraints. When he was finally free, he turned to attack the druid but he stopped when he realized she was smiling.

She said, "I had hoped the wolvesbane I shoved down your gullet would kill you outright, but by the looks of your wound I have to assume it merely shut down your healing ability. It was a gamble but one that seems to have changed the game greatly. Now we will see how well you fight!"

Rosabela shape shifted in her massive bear form and stood up on her hind legs. The deep and powerful roar that followed, promised death in no uncertain terms. The lycan came in fearlessly. The first strikes were predictable. Sunder was faster as he slashed a rapid one-two hit on the bear, but Rosabela was stronger as her counter sent the smaller were-beast to the ground. Though protected by dense fur and thick hide beneath, the druid bled from eight lines which crossed her massive chest. The lycan was gouged from Rosabela's claws, but suffered from bone-crushing blunt force trauma as well.

Sunder came in slashing again but this time evaded the deadly counter using hit and run tactics instead of the direct approach. The she-elf accepted those hits with growing rage. As the werewolf shot in again, Rosabela changed tactics. She pulled back at the last moment and stood up. Sunder ducked low narrowly avoiding a skull-crushing blow, but was unable to back out in time to avoid the bite that followed. Rosabela sank her teeth into the werewolf's shoulder and held on tight. Sunder struggled but the bear was too powerful. He raked at the bear's flanks but was in too tight to do much damage. Rosabela used her mighty paws to pull him in closer and then dropped her full weight down, pinning him to the ground. Having immobilized her foe, she changed her bite location from Sunder's shoulder to his neck. The loud crack that followed was a clear indication that she snapped his spine. Sunder moved no more.

"Well done," Carnage said with sincere admiration, "you would have made a fine lycan. Sunder was my oldest living associate and a deadly warrior."

Rosabela shape shifted into her elven form and fell into the arms of her mentor. Da'Shar gently eased her to the ground and began healing the deep gouges across her chest and sides, but never took his eyes off his nemesis.

Gaedron asked, "What now? Ye plannin' on runnin' a'gin?"

Lord Carnage replied, "I am a man of my word."

"Aye," the dwarf returned, "an' I be mayor o' Dek'Thal. Yer kind ain't ne'er been known fer honor or truth tellin'."

"Well, then perhaps a display of good faith is in order," he added.

The lycan master turned to face his men. He closed his eyes and concentrated for a moment. At first, the werewolves were confused but confusion became understanding when pain shot through their bodies. The werewolves crumbled to the ground and shook with agony as their blood boiled under the mental command of their master. They were dead in less than a minute leaving Carnage the last of his kind.

"I have kept my word; you are honor bound to do no less. I shall return to the Druidic Grove to be judged."

Da'Shar stood up and said, "We will honor the agreement, but you will not return unbound."

While the hunters held a steady aim on the pack leader, Da'Shar bound his wrists with an enchanted cord of shimmering silk. It was unbreakable and would resist even the razor-keen edge of Gaedron's glimmering blue axes. Da'Shar then placed a most unusual collar around Lord Carnage's neck. It was lined with mithril spikes on the inside and bound with more of the silken cord on the outside. It was a device designed centuries ago to prevent a shape shifter from assuming a larger form, which would quickly fill the collar beyond capacity, thus strangling and impaling the wearer. Carnage accepted the bindings with stoic calm.

"We headin' ta da grove?" Gaedron asked, fully expecting Da'Shar to make haste back to Celes'tia.

Da'Shar looked back toward Dek'Thal and said, "That would be best."

Rosabela was still lying in the sand. Wavren went to her side and helped her to her feet. He remained silent but his sister spoke saying, "We started together, perhaps we should finish together."

Gaedron smiled and said, "Me thinks da lass got a bit o' fight left in 'er."

Rosabela grimaced as she finally made it to her feet. She managed a wink and replied, "The mission isn't over just because we took the pack leader. The Legion is still out there."

CHAPTER 24
JA'ZARU

Vlaad ran in full plate armor, sword and shield in hand, with Theila thrown over his broad shoulder. To say that he was encumbered would be a ridiculous understatement. Sweat ran freely down his clean, shaven head and into his eyes. The defender was overburdened beyond belief, yet he ran. It was of no consequence that his muscles burned and his back ached. He could not slow his pace. Through the gasping of air, which could never be drawn fast enough to quench his need for it, Vlaad ran. When he came to the edge of the city, where his companions should have been, he found no one waiting and even worse, no portal. He looked left and right, but saw only the vast wasteland that spread out before him. A dozen thoughts and every doubt imaginable raced through his mind as he dropped his sword and shield, falling to his knees in exhaustion.

Vlaad lowered his love to the ground as gently as possible. She was still unconscious from his attack. He heard the yelling chaos of a thousand orcs not far behind but it didn't matter. Without the portal, there was no hope. This was the end.

He lovingly brushed the notorious tendril of hair from Theila's eyes and whispered, "I am sorry for nothing in my life save it be this moment. Death comes for us now and I wish I had made you my wife long ago."

Theila's eyes fluttered open. They were different now; black as soot from pupil to iris and somehow vacant as if she were a soulless thing, not the woman Vlaad had known and loved for so long.

Vlaad stared deeply, hoping she would respond in kind, but the warlock was a shell of her former self, a pitiful tool of the abyss. His heart sank. She sat up slowly then moved into a standing position. Vlaad stared frozen in horror at the woman who was no longer his dear Theila. With a casual demeanor, the warlock began casting a summoning spell. The ground opened up with an eerie shadow-like flame leaping upwards. The smell of brimstone and sulfur filled the air. The heat made Vlaad shield his face. From the flames of the abyss, an equine form took shape but it was an unnatural thing with a fiery mane, tail, and hooves. Its eyes were blood red and smoke poured from its nostrils. Legend named the beast as a Nightmare, but Vlaad knew it as the demonic *Felsteed*. As Theila climbed on its back, the orcs drew near. Vlaad knelt motionless as his dear companion rode away leaving him alone. Deserted by his allies, abandoned by his true love, the defender fell to the hacking death of a thousand orcs.

***

Vlaad found himself running again. He was still in Dek'Thal and Theila was slung unceremoniously over his shoulder. He shook his head in disbelief trying to muddle through what had just happened. He had died, Theila had escaped on her Felsteed, and his companions had abandoned him…or had it all been a dream? It was then that he saw the balrog circling overhead. The vile demon had used one of its most powerful weapons against the orc city to make its escape…*hell's-fear*. It was a potent spell that brought out the deepest and often most terrifying fears imaginable. As Vlaad looked back, he noticed that he was not the only one affected. Every orc and orc ally in the city was cowering in fear or running with reckless abandon as if insanity had overcome them. Only the commander, Gorka Darkstorm, was unaffected and he watched impassively as the defender scrambled toward the city's edge.

Vlaad had seen in the fear-borne delusion what could happen, what one possible future might be. It was the nature of the demon's spell to draw on deep-seated subconscious thoughts. In this case, Vlaad had seen his own worst-case scenario and he decided it must never come to pass. His gut tightened as he neared the edge of the city and the residual fear nearly overcame him until he saw his companions.

Maejis began casting the portal spell that would surely transport them all to Griffon's Peak but safe passage from Dek'Thal would never release his beloved Theila from the pact she had made with the demon to save the group.

"We make our stand here!" the defender ordered as the mage completed his spell.

"This is folly," the paladin said. "We cannot fight the entire city!"

"No we cannot, but we can destroy the demon before we leave," he returned as he lowered Theila gently to the ground.

Don was there holding his daughter's hand, unwilling to accept that she had become a vessel of evil. He said, "I will stay."

Maejis took a deep breath and sighed, allowing the portal to fade into nothingness. He dug a small strip of leather from one of his many pockets, put it between his teeth, and pulled his long, black hair back into a ponytail. Using the leather, he tied it back and then said, "I will buy us some time."

He took a few steps and *blinked* twenty meters ahead, just outside the main gate to the orc city. Drawing a smooth block of black granite from his many pockets, he began casting a spell. The words were barely audible but the gestures seemed to resemble that of a great music conductor calling for his orchestra to bring forth a grand crescendo. His hands went up, then scooped low again and when his hand came up the second time, a giant wall grew out of the small reagent. It filled the gateway completely, sealing off the entrance. Maejis trotted back to his companions.

"That will buy us some time. The orcs will have to go around or scale the wall. Either way, we must hurry," the wizard insisted.

Landermihl turned to the defender and warned, "A balrog is like nothing you have ever faced. Its strength is greater than any giant and its hide is tougher than dwarven steel. I cannot heal and attack at the same time so you must decide our strategy."

"Landermihl, keep me alive; I will control the beast's attention. Maejis and Don, hit it with everything you have. We must bring the balrog down before the orcs get around Maejis's blockade," he replied with determination and a full understanding of what failure meant.

The group nodded and set their sights on the dreaded demon, circling above. Landermihl called to his deity and cast both protective magic and damage-enhancing spells on his team. Vlaad was granted a protective aura that would provide some resistance to the heat and fear that the demon would radiate. His sword was not enchanted with holy magic but his shield now glowed an icy blue. Maejis had his own protective magic, so the paladin bestowed a blessing of nearly endless energy for spell casting. His *mana* now flowed directly from a divine well-spring from within. Don had neither great wizardry nor magnificent arms to enchant, but the paladin understood demonology and how to fight evil. He placed his hands on the bard and called for a blessing of discernment that would enable Don to strike unerringly. Knowing that his work would require an uninterrupted flow of healing spells, Landermihl prayed for holy empowerment, becoming a living conduit of divine magic. His faith emboldened him in spite of the insurmountable odds the small group would soon face. His last words as the demon began his descent were, "For the good of the realm and may the light favor us."

Ja'Zaru was thousands of years old, some say he was timeless. However old, he had been around long enough to know that surviving combat required more than simply being bigger or stronger. The balrog knew his edge would forever be in controlling the fear of lesser beings. He took his time circling the foursome below. He could sense their apprehension as he drew nearer. Even the greatest heroes of all time suffered his demonic fear…they had much to lose, after all, being mortal. This was not a limitation Ja'Zaru had. He could not be killed, banished yes, but being utterly destroyed was not possible on this plane. It gave the demon great confidence.

Vlaad thought back to his training under Andar. He calmed his mind and watched the incoming attack. Being ready was always the key. His enchanted blade whispered simple instructions, more reminders of things he knew.

"Dodge first, deflect or parry second, and

absorb the blow on your shield last. Demons are powerful but slow. Movement will keep you alive," the blade of Andar insinuated telepathically.

The balrog flew in low trying to scatter and stun the group.

Vlaad dove into a roll as the demon passed by. He came to his feet and watched the others scramble away.

Ja'Zaru pulled up and stretched his tremendous wings outward. His massive cloven feet touched down lightly. He turned to face the adventurers just as a charging warrior drove his full weight behind a glowing blue shield. The attack was insignificant to the mighty demon, but the audacity of the attack infuriated him. It was surprising if nothing else and that was enough to warrant an overhead chop with its flaming ax. The warrior angled perfectly and the weapon sank deeply into the ground.

Maejis was working his hands in tight circles by his side. Each hand movement made his ponytail bounce left and right. The spectacle would have been amusing but the look of intense concentration on the wizard's face was enough to inspire dread had there been onlookers. As the mystic power coalesced into a growing mass of shimmering frost, the mage raised his voice invoking the spell trigger saying, *ARCTOS INCANTUM!* The icy missile raced unerringly toward the target. It ripped into the demon's shoulder blade causing the beast to arch its back and turn away from the defender at its feet. Maejis saw his death at that moment as the balrog inhaled deeply and breathed out a long, gout of fire and ash. The flames lasted mere seconds but when the smoke cleared, only a black scorch remained.

Vlaad took the initiative and hacked with his sword from right to left, spun around and drove the point of his shield into the balrog's leg. Again, the damage was insignificant but it drew the monster's attention back to the defender. The reflexive stomp that followed shook the ground but missed Vlaad altogether. A second attack followed as the defender crouched at the ready. The long, fiery whip reared back for a massive strike but it struck Vlaad's shield with no effect. Landermihl's enchantment was paying off.

As the demon drew its whip back for another strike, Don flew into action. He was seeing the fight in slow motion, allowing him to fire off two daggers in the blink of an eye. The blessing of discernment directed his tiny blades perfectly into the demon's armpit. The damage was magnified by the lack of thick hide, causing a blood-curdling roar from the balrog. Don wasted no time diving behind the cover of a large boulder as Ja'Zaru slammed his ax where the bard had been standing.

Vlaad drove his shield into the demon again just as a bolt of frost sank into the creature's back. Apparently, the crafty mage had blinked out of harm's way. Two more daggers appeared in the monster's neck followed by another icy blast. The ranged attacks were coming from every direction at once causing great confusion for Ja'Zaru and enabling every manner of hacking and shield-slamming attacks from Vlaad. This strategy went on for several minutes until the balrog fell back on its innate spell powers. With a single word, it pulsed wave after wave of intense heat. Don screamed and backed out of range. Maejis cast *fire-ward* and then *frost-shield*, but the heat was too intense. When his fire-resistant magic robes began to glow, he quickly disengaged leaving Vlaad alone with Landermihl, healing from afar.

The holy warrior called for healing from his deity just in time to save Don from an agonizing death. Miraculously, the bard's wounds mended instantly. Black-charred flesh fell to the ground and healthy pink skin appeared. The paladin sensed that Vlaad was in trouble and called for healing again. He directed the holy power toward the defender who was standing his ground under a hellish onslaught.

Vlaad's shield glowed bright blue as the demon's radiating heat washed over him. His own ring, given to him by his dear O'ma, tingled under his mailed gauntlet. His armor was made of the finest thorium mesh with dragonscale plates. It was designed to resist this particular type of attack, yet each pulse weakened him and threatened to destroy him utterly. He was in trouble, but if he turned his shield to flee he would surely burst into flames. He had no choice, he had to hold out. Suddenly he felt stronger, somehow refreshed. Landermihl was near. The great veteran of Griffon's Peak was streaming divine healing directly into him.

Ja'Zaru was certain this fight would end soon. No human could endure a balrog's *abyssian wrath* spell, yet this human remained. It was inconceivable, but he had another spell to fall back on. The demon cast hell's-fear. It came as a blanket of utter despair that spread like a rolling fog. Vlaad was hit first but held his ground. When the spell surged over Don, Landermihl, and Maejis, the effect was undeniable.

The wizard tried to return to the fight, but as the intense fear took hold, he found that he was unable to speak. Maejis watched helplessly as the demon raised its massive hoof and stomped down on Vlaad. The defender went down under the crushing weight. Before he could attempt to stand, the balrog raised its ax high into the air and heaved it downward. The resulting crunch could be nothing less than a death blow. Wide-eyed, the mage starred helplessly. If only he could cast his spells he might have been able to save poor Vlaad. Don was next. The demon lashed outward with its flaming whip. As it wrapped around the bard's torso, Maejis witnessed his burning, screaming death. Landermihl tried to call to his god for aid, but the demon reached down and picked up the holy warrior with one hand. Landermihl struggled for a moment until Ja'Zaru devoured him, armor and all. Maejis tried to run, but found he was unable. He stood immobilized and incapacitated as the demon approached.

Don's experience was no less gruesome but his hallucination included the dismemberment of his daughter before his very eyes. He was helpless and overcome with grief when the demon came for him.

Landermihl was the avatar of goodness, however. His connection to his deity and his experience with demons was enough to fend off the nightmarish hallucinations, but he was still paralyzed and unable to help his companions. For the great warrior, this was no less torturous knowing that without healing, his team would fall.

Vlaad had faced his greatest fear earlier and with the protective spell Landermihl placed on him before the battle, he was impervious to its effects now. He stood balanced on the balls of his feet, shield up, and sword in the low ready position. His look of determination was such that Ja'Zaru was taken aback.

"Human," the demon began, "how is it that you remain?"

Vlaad never relaxed his guard. He replied with seething defiance, "Because I must!"

The demon responded with respect saturated in eternal hatred, "Then we will finish this, mortal, but know that your determination cannot stand up to my power. I am eternal, a force of destruction beyond your comprehension."

Vlaad nodded as if to say, *So be it!*

***

Wavren could see the sprawling fortress city of Dek'Thal in the distance as he dashed across the open plain. He paused and drew on his hunter abilities granting him *long-sight*.

"There is Theila's demon, and ..." Wavren trailed off in disbelief.

"What boyo? Whadaya see?" Gaedron asked as he drew on his own hunter skills to look into the distance.

Da'Shar and Rosabela had Carnage in tow but were more interested in the hunters than their prisoner.

"What is it?" Rosabela asked.

"Well," Gaedron began, "unless I be seein' things, looks ta me like Vlaad done picked a fight wit' Theila's balrog, an I canna see anyone else standin'."

Wavren added, "The others are down. We must hurry!"

"We can't drag Carnage along," Rosabela said.

"And we certainly can't leave him behind," Da'Shar added, having pursued his adversary for centuries.

Carnage moved forward and joined the discussion saying, "I will fight."

Gaedron scoffed.

The lycan reiterated, "I will help you. Release me."

Wavren leveled his weapon at the pack leader and said, "Shut your mouth, beast, you can't be trusted."

Gaedron smiled broadly and said, "I done taught dis' un too good," referring to Wavren's dwarf-like approach to the problem. "I say we gut 'im."

Da'Shar had to make a decision and time was against him. He knew his brother well. He knew that Carnage could only be trusted to do what was in his own best interest. If he got the chance he would run, or worse, turn on the group and kill them all.

Carnage stepped up to Da'Shar and looked him in the eye. He proclaimed, "I do not want to face the druidic council. My end is certain if I do. Let me prove that I am not an evil being, only a fool who chose an evil path."

"Redemption?" Da'Shar asked with the smallest hope hidden behind a mountain of doubt.

"He be playin' ye fer a fool ye long-eared tree hugger," the dwarf accused.

"Perhaps," the elder druid returned, "but what else can we do? We have no time and little choice. Vlaad needs us."

Even Rosabela, who held her mentor in the highest esteem, shook her head no.

Carnage called on long-neglected druidic skills and sent his mental avatar into Da'Shar's mind. Within the powerful druid's psyche, Carnage was vulnerable, stripped of his lycan powers, and appeared as an elven youth. It was a memory Da'Shar preferred when thinking of his brother.

"You risk much coming here...entering my mind. I am the master of this domain," Da'Shar mentioned as his own mental projection towered over his brother's.

"It is the only way I can be sure that you will accept my words as truth," he began. "I destroyed trust long ago. Fear not, I will show you my intentions instantly as we are short on time."

The plan Carnage revealed was simple but would likely consume them both. Carnage would serve as a healing source while Da'Shar would serve as a direct conduit to heal the group. In an instant, the deal was struck and the mental connection was broken. Da'Shar touched the enchanted collar and the silken bonds with a simple oak branch and said, "Do not disappoint me." The bonds fell away.

The lycan dove forward and became a wolf in the flash of an eye. Gaedron sighed deeply but took off after him with Wavren by his side and the bears lumbering along as well. Rosabela paused a moment and put her hand on her mentor's arm. She said nothing but her thoughts were conveyed in her empathetic touch, indicating that she was with him...always.

CHAPTER 25
THE RECKONING

Ja'Zaru came in with his mighty ax. The powerful over-handed chop was unstoppable but Vlaad anticipated it. The spirit of his mentor was with him. He dove sidelong, evaded the attack, and came up at the ready. The ax sank deeply into the sandy ground. With corded muscles, the demon yanked his weapon back and simultaneously lashed out with his dreaded whip. Again, the combat precognition granted by the sword of Andar prompted Vlaad's motion. With a deft feint forward, the defender tricked his adversary into shortening his strike. Skipping backward a step caused the now misdirected whip to snap scant inches away from Vlaad's shield. The shield warrior dashed forward, smashing his heater into the demon's leg. The effect was minimal but Ja'Zaru howled as if skewered on a spit. Vlaad spun around and hacked at the balrog's calf. Reflexively, the demon kicked backward. Vlaad absorbed the blow on his shield but flew back as if stuck by a charging bull. The sheer power would have killed a lesser man and though his wind was blasted from his lungs, he continued.

The defender hit the ground and rolled backward into his stance and called, "Pitiful beast, I am but one and mortal, yet for all of your eternal power, you cannot finish me."

Ja'Zaru spun to face his enemy with hatred burning in his eyes like the very flames of the abyss. He inhaled deeply and exhaled fiery ash that was no less deadly than dragon's breath. He snaked his massive head right and left to ensure the deadly cone's effect. Several seconds passed leaving a blackened patch of obsidian where sand had once been, but when the hellish blast subsided, a smoldering red, glowing warrior emerged.

Vlaad gasped for air and strode forward. The defender had lost his cloak, leather jerkin, tabard, and sword sheath. Every combustible item had been devoured by flame. Even his neatly trimmed goatee, mustache, and eyebrows were gone, yet somehow he lived. The ring of O'ma was no mere trinket, but even that should not have saved him.

The balrog was stunned. It was impossible. Nothing could have survived the blast, not elven steel, or even dwarven mithril. It defied all reason. Ja'Zaru could not understand what had happened and suddenly felt something he had not felt for centuries. He felt doubt. The same doubt that causes hesitation. The same doubt that is immediately followed by the fear of impending doom. It spurred the warrior into action.

Vlaad advanced. His determined walk had more than purpose; it had a singular focus—the destruction of Ja'Zaru. He picked up his pace into a trot as he closed the gap. Ja'Zaru threw his massive ax. Vlaad casually ducked as it passed overhead. He broke into a sprint. The demon drew its whip back to attack as the defender came into range but found Vlaad was getting larger with every step. His body, armor, and weapons flashed in intervals as he doubled in size, then tripled, and finally quadrupled. By the time he was in melee range, the defender and the demon stood eye to eye. Vlaad hit the balrog at full speed; his shield leading the way. The resulting *clang* could only be compared to a gargantuan gong used for warning an entire city of invaders. Ja'Zaru flew backward and landed hard among the rocks.

Vlaad looked past the demon and saw his friends assembling around the lycan, Lord Carnage. Da'Shar had one hand on the half-man, half-beast and the other was channeling energy directly at him. The others prepared spells and readied weapons.

The demon rose to his feet, growled, and recalled his flaming ax. In a most undemon-like manner, Ja'Zaru began to circle defensively. The battle had turned in favor of his mortal enemies and the balrog was not about to risk one thousand years of banishment without reassessing the situation. He could see and even feel the powerful flow of magic being channeled by the druid. This was the link he had to break in order to achieve victory. The greater demon lashed out with his whip, fully expecting an instant kill, but somehow the defender intercepted the attack with his shield.

Vlaad rolled to his feet after diving in front of Da'Shar. He took up his stance, shield forward, sword in the high ready position. The demon tried to circle again, but the defender angled to cut him off. Ja'Zaru's eyes narrowed as he thought through his options. Twin reports from the hunter's weapons shattered the air. Tiny bullets pierced his thick hide causing minor pain and endless frustration. The flash of magic followed as a massive harpoon of solid ice cut into his shoulder. When the golden hammer of justice thumped heavily into his chest, the demon realized he could not outlast the team of casters behind the enlarged warrior. He charged forward with the full power of the abyss.

As the balrog's whip cracked across Vlaad's shield, followed by a rapid forehand-backhand ax attack, the magic sustaining the defender's gargantuan size weakened. Vlaad felt it, Da'Shar felt it, but most of all, Carnage felt it. The magic flowing from him through Da'Shar and into Vlaad felt like ghostly claws ripping at his internal organs. Blood flowed freely from his lupine muzzle as if he had swallowed a dozen razorblades. The lycan's response was to call on his innate powers of regeneration. It was enough for now, but even that had its limits.

"Finish the balrog!" Rosabela called as she bolstered her mentor's magic with her own.

Landermihl wanted to help the lycan with his own healing, but such blasphemy would never be tolerated by his god. Trying would be wasted effort. He turned his healing toward Da'Shar and Vlaad instead.

Don knelt beside his daughter and whispered, "We need you Theila. Only you understand this creature you have summoned. Only you can end this."

The warlock did not stir.

Maejis fired off another salvo of frost magic, this time calling on his most powerful evocation. The air cooled instantly around the demon and hundreds of dagger-like shards of ice and snow pelted the balrog for several seconds. In return, the demon curled its massive wings around itself forming a barrier against the attack. Vlaad came in with a powerful diagonal swipe from his sword followed by a spinning shield bash, knocking the demon back several steps and cutting cleanly through the right wing.

Ja'Zaru regained his balance, dug in his massive hoofs, and sprang forward. He allowed his whip to dissipate and came in with a two-handed grip on his ax. The left to right circling blow had every ounce of power and hatred the demon could muster. Vlaad could not dodge without endangering his companions. He did the only thing he could. He braced his shield and took the blow full on. As the hell-spawned ax met with the gleaming shield it yielded a thunderous explosion of flame and steel that threw Vlaad back a hundred feet.

The demon was now unarmed having destroyed his weapon in the attack, but Vlaad's famous shield, the symbol of the Champion of Griffon's Peak, once carried by the mighty Andar, was sundered in two. The defender's shield arm was obviously broken, hanging disfigured and limp at his side as he rose to his feet. The demon had gambled and won. Ja'Zaru smiled.

The hunters began firing their weapons at a furious pace and even sent their dear allies, Stonetalon and Blackmaw, into the fray. They had to buy some time. Landermihl followed them having expended his magic reserves. Maejis had narrowly escaped death from the balrog's attack but was once again calling spell after spell. His robes flapped in tatters, and his ponytail bounced with every move. Da'Shar had been thrown backwards from the blast and lay face down, unconscious. Rosabela stepped forward taking his place as the conduit between Carnage and Vlaad, but the pack leader was near death. His breathing was labored and life blood ran from his nose and ears. For a moment, she thought it was over.

The she-elf placed her hands on the lycan and called for healing. Nothing happened. She concentrated and tried again, but again nothing happened. With determination, she begged nature to respond to her calls, yet the lycan remained unaffected.

Carnage coughed up foaming blood, crawled to a kneeling position, and managed to gasp, "Nature will not heed your call, young one. I am an affront to all that is good."

Rosabela nodded and said, "You have endured for us all so I must try."

The pack leader shook his head and said, "It matters not at all."

"What will you do?" the druid asked.

The lycan replied with sadness in his eyes that reminded her of Da'Shar, "You cannot help me, so I will die fighting as I have lived...on my own."

The bleeding and battered were-creature pulled himself into a standing position and closed his eyes. He concentrated and his wounds began to mend before her. Though weakened, he took Rosabela's hand and placed it on his scorched shoulder and motioned for her to continue her mentor's work. She felt a moment of pity and then drew on his essence to invigorate Vlaad, an act of sacrifice that would claim his life. For a moment, she thought she saw the glimmer of hope in his feral eyes and then it was gone, replaced by the life-draining pain he willingly endured.

Ja'Zaru's confidence returned as the burned and broken warrior staggered forward. The shield was gone and the source of power to heal the warrior was all but depleted as the life energy waned within the lycan. The demon knew it was over. He reveled in the moment.

"Can you sense your end...mortal?" the demon taunted.

Vlaad said nothing. He merely took up his fighting stance and prepared for battle. As he waited, he noticed Theila was standing by her father. She began casting a spell...

The hunters fired but the demon took the hits in stride. The bears swatted mightily at his feet; he ignored them. Even the frigid blasts from the wizard and the powerful blows from Landermihl meant nothing at that moment.

"You are beaten, defeated...and now you will die," Ja'Zaru promised.

As the balrog inhaled deeply to breathe abyssian fire, his chest expanded fully and his eyes were ablaze with yellow flame. Vlaad held his position, jaw clenched, and weapon at the ready. Time slowed for that moment as the sword of Vlorin imparted its knowledge, but the defender did not move. The paladin's enchantments would never protect him. Flesh charred and fell away. The process of healing such continual damage was maddening. Time resumed its natural course as the wicked jet of black and red washed over the resolute warrior. An eternity passed in those moments as Ja'Zaru's attack blacked out both sight and sound when suddenly, a flash of steel pierced the demon's maw and passed through the back of its head. Ja'Zaru threw himself backward trying to dislodge the blade, but the damage was done. Thrashing about madly and spraying black ichor in all directions, he finally collapsed into a pile of ash. The demon's physical form was destroyed and his essence banished back into the abyss.

"It is over," Vlaad whispered as he shrank down to his normal size and fell to his knees.

"Heavens be praised," Landermihl said with gratitude.

"Indeed," the defender replied as he turned back to his beloved Theila.

The warlock was standing, hands smoldering with black energy. Don was smiling proudly beside her.

"It was you?" the defender asked. "You saved

me?"

"I convinced him to focus all of his energy into his attack, allowing you a small breech in his defenses," she returned.

"That is not all," he insisted, "you shielded me."

Theila shook her head and said, "I could not, as I was bound by the pact with Ja'Zaru."

"Then how...?" Vlaad asked with confusion. He looked back to his other companions.

Gaedron and Wavren had taken a knee to the right and left of the bears. Both had their heads bowed solemnly. Landermihl and Maejis looked on with respect as well. Rosabela and Da'Shar were cradling the bloody remains of an elf none of them had ever seen before. He had a younger appearance than Da'Shar with delicate features and a look of peace. Don, Vlaad, and Theila approached.

"This is my brother, So'larian. He has been returned to his elven form," the elder druid began solemnly as tears flowed down his sharp, elven features. "He has been...absolved... of his crimes against nature."

Rosabela added, "He gave all that he had to empower Vlaad and in the end suffered full retribution for a lifetime of evil. Before he died, he said, 'I am free.'"

Landermihl nodded and remarked, "No greater gift hath any man, than he lay down his life for his friends—a sacrifice worthy of redemption."

Gaedron and Wavren responded in unison saying, "Aye."

Vlaad held Theila tightly with his good arm and for that moment, all was right in the world. He smiled and said, "I love you."

Theila replied with a kiss and a loving

embrace.

"Eh boyo, I don' mean ta in'erupt, but we need ta be movin' on," Gaedron reminded.

"Of course," Vlaad replied. "Maejis, can you get us home?"

The mage responded with a series of hand gestures and the invocation required. A shimmering portal opened up with Griffon's Peak on the other side. The hunters and druids stepped through with Carnage's remains. Landermihl, Don, and Maejis followed. Just as Theila entered the portal, Vlaad noticed a lone orc watching from the gated parapets of Dek'Thal. It was Gorka. There could be no doubt.

The orc commander called to his rival, "Your battle was inspiring. To defeat a greater demon is no small feat. Even I was unable to do so with ten thousand orcs and trolls. Perhaps the gods have blessed you this day, but that will not always be so. You have a lifetime of days ahead of you and the gods are fickle. Perhaps my day will come when next we meet."

Vlaad was bloody, broken, and exhausted. He was in no shape to fight or even debate with his nemesis. Though he had hate in his eyes and venom in his veins, it was time to leave. He scooped up the pieces of his once mighty shield and stepped toward the portal. His final words as he entered were, "Duty is second only to justice…but both can wait, for now."

Curtiss Robinson

CHAPTER 26
GRIFFON'S PEAK

The heroes appeared in the northern mage tower of Griffon's Peak after the typical gut-wrenching portal experience. A host of caregivers and healers were made available to quickly provide food, medical attention, and equipment repairs but the mission required more before they were allowed to truly rest. Da'Shar's brother was taken for burial preparation. Great care and reverence was shown for his body, in spite of being an enemy of the lands; such was the respect for the heroes.

The city's priests assessed the heroes and found the group both battered and exhausted, but Vlaad's injuries were extensive. His flesh was burned and one arm hung limply at his side. He showed evidence of numerous other injuries but none were life threatening. The healers set his arm and bandaged his wounds but remarked that his body had been inundated with magic and would not be receptive to their spells. Incidentally, he was still healing on his own to some small degree. Perhaps the druidic magic was sustaining him.

Minimal time was taken to clean up and make ready to meet with the king and his advisors for the debriefing, but the stalwart group made the best of it. After shedding armor, changing clothes, and washing the filth of combat from their bodies, Don the Bard led his friends down the countless winding stairwells and out into the courtyard. It was a long walk through the city proper, down streets thick with merchants and citizens, and across lush gardens filled with children. It was a surreal journey for the battle-weary adventurers but one met with appreciative nods and salutes. Seeing the casual lives of so many people who could never fathom the dangers outside the high stone walls was disconcerting but such was the way of things. A small measure of pride filled each of the nine as they realized the comfort and security these folks enjoyed was paid for with their blood. These thoughts made the twenty-minute walk pass quickly, bringing them to the inner sanctum of the king's palace in no time.

A burly guard in magnificent plate armor met them saying, "Hail Defenders of Griffon's Peak and welcome home. The king has been expecting you."

Don nodded and replied, "It is good to be home. We have news."

The guard beckoned them inside and closed the massive steel-bound oak doors behind.

King Xorren Kael sat majestically on his throne with his council of advisors to his left and an equal number of ministers to the right in a broad semi-circle. Each was adorned with the finest clothing and jewelry the kingdom had to offer. Each held a finely crafted gold goblet filled with elven wine or dwarven mead from faraway lands. Directly behind the king a small contingent of body guards stood ready with crossbows and armed with matching swords. The picture was impressive if not awe inspiring.

"My friends," the king began, "I have heard of your actions abroad and have waited in eager anticipation to learn the details. Please sit and bring us up to date."

Don bowed and motioned to his companions to take their place across from the king and his advisors. Vlaad and Da'Shar sat in the center with Theila, Don, Maejis, and Landermihl to Vlaad's left while Rosabela, Wavren, and Gaedron sat to the right of Da'Shar.

With a simple gesture, King Xorren Kael signaled for Don to begin. The bard spoke on cue, "Sire, our mission to stop the union of The Legion and the lycans was successful. The leader of the werewolves was slain and his pack was destroyed."

Da'Shar shifted uneasily in his chair. Though he knew the realm was a safer place with his brother's evil pack eliminated, he felt something should be said in honor of So'larian's sacrifice. He knew that now was not the time and the humans would not likely understand.

The king leaned over to one of his advisors and whispered a few words. The man simply nodded in return.

"What is your report on the assassin's guild?"

"Sire," Don began, "they have lost many agents during this campaign but I fear they are still a considerable threat to the city."

"Indeed," was his only reply. A second advisor leaned in and whispered. The king nodded and said, "What is the relationship between The Legion of Griffon's Peak and the orcs of Dek'Thal?"

The bard stood up, looked to his companions for a moment, placed his hands on the conference table, and bowed his head in frustration. After a brief moment he said, "The Shade, who was once the Guild Master of The Legion, is in league with the orcs. We believe he is one of the top commanders of the Bloodcrest Forces."

Murmuring began as the advisors and even the stoic personal guard realized the implications of having the single most powerful criminal organization in the realm operating within Griffon's Peak, while their enemies abroad now had unfettered access to the information needed to mount a direct assault.

"Your news is not unanticipated," the king began. "We must root out the evil within our city walls in order to deny the orcs their advantage, but for now we have other pressing matters. Tell us what you learned while in Dek'Thal. Surely there is more to the story."

Don was the most famous of all bards and a cunning agent of Griffon's Peak. He was well prepared to make a perfect account of the events the band of heroes had been through from the moment they left the human city. Maejis, also an advisor to the king, added in many details that Don glossed over. Together they were able to sum up the overall situation in Dek'Thal. It became apparent that the orc city, quite far from Alliance-held lands, would be difficult to approach from the standpoint of a direct assault. Even if the armies of the Dae'gon Alliance marched on Dek'Thal, they would likely encounter a long and grueling siege against the high stone walls complete with iron-bound gates, parapets, and ballistae crews. Logistically speaking, the siege would require tens of thousands of soldiers and even more logisticians to supply the war efforts. The most difficult part of such a campaign was the war-like inhabitants of the city itself. Every man, woman, and child would join the fighting once the walls were breached. Most of those inhabitants were well trained in either the sword or spear and most could be classified as experts with an ax or club. It was the very nature of the orc and troll society. As the debriefing concluded, King Xorren Kael leaned back in his throne and took several moments to digest the dreadful information.

"A direct assault would be folly," Xorren remarked, "but perhaps there are other means we might employ in the future to weaken our enemies. I will speak privately with my advisors when time allows. For now, we must assume The Legion is feeding our weaknesses and most precious secrets to the enemies. If I were the leader of the orcs, I would be developing a plan to destroy Griffon's Peak while the intelligence is fresh. I know the beasts to be aggressive and cunning but I do not believe they can attack before the winter sets in. We have until the first of spring to prepare. Until then, we will hunt down and eliminate every spy, assassin, and saboteur in league with The Legion."

Vlaad rose to his feet slowly, still recovering from his injuries. He announced, "My lord, I will take up this fight within the city, but first, I have personal matters that require my immediate attention."

"Very well," he replied. "When will you begin your search and what resources will you require?"

"One week to rest and one week to prepare my affairs should suffice. I will need access to your intelligence network, your wizards, and the entire city guard," the defender replied.

"Done," the king agreed. "I will have the minister of security prepare the proper authority and you will have the full backing of the royal seal. I have one last question for you. It appears as though your last battle destroyed the symbol of the city's champion. Should I commission the royal enchanters to design a new shield for you?"

Vlaad bowed his head in humility and said, "I would be honored for their assistance, but I will personally craft a new shield. There is much I have learned from our enemies and the symbol of

Griffon's Peak must never fail again."

There was great symbolism in the words Vlaad spoke. It was clear that he felt personally responsible for the failure to stop Gorka Darkstorm and The Legion over the years. It was also clear that he fully intended to make amends to the king and the citizens he represented in the coming days.

The king mentally noted that more so than the shield, Vlaad was the symbol of Griffon's Peak. He also wondered that just as the shield needed to be replaced after a lifetime of battle; perhaps Vlaad was nearing the end of his career. It was a hard life full of demanding responsibilities. Though noted, Xorren said nothing.

Before the meeting could be adjourned, a messenger appeared from a side door. He was ushered in to deliver a small note to one of the king's ministers. It must have been of great importance to interrupt the meeting. The note was read quickly and the minister stood up, walked over to the king, and whispered its message.

King Xorren Kael turned quickly and faced the minister as he finished. The king did not look happy. He said, "By whose authority?"

The minister looked pale. He said, "Sire, it comes from The Black Order...the guild of warlocks...the grandmistress signed the decree herself."

"Then I pardon all such crimes," he replied.

"Very well, sire. I will send word. The Order will not be pleased and may I remind you that they are entrusted with these matters based on their extensive knowledge and experience. They regulate their own affairs by your order. It might be prudent to allow these matters to unfold before we act. She is entitled to a trial after all," the minister added.

The king alternated between scratching his chin and rubbing his forehead. He was clearly in conflict. Finally he said, "So be it. Guards!" he called.

In seconds, a squad of well-armed guards formed up in a line behind the adventurers. Vlaad and the others looked around suspiciously, but none made any move against the king or his men. To do so was treason and punishable by death.

Vlaad looked to Theila and asked, "What is happening?"

"I can only assume that I will be tried and punished for crimes against the kingdom," she said sadly, knowing that her role in summoning Ja'Zaru must surely be the cause.

The elves and Gaedron felt compelled to stand up for Theila, but this was a local matter. Elves and dwarves would never permit humans to interfere in their affairs aside from bearing witness on her behalf.

Maejis spoke up saying, "Your Majesty, Theila is one of us. She fought for you and her actions seem justified by my account. As a wizard, I often find myself challenged with decisions that could be questionable, but in the heat of battle, such decisions must be made quickly."

Xorren raised his thick hand and said, "We have laws to protect the kingdom. We must abide by them and allow the system of justice to prevail. If what you say is true, then Theila will be absolved of guilt and released in due time." Maejis nodded and stepped backward signifying his compliance.

Justice...the very word on which Vlaad had based his entire existence now sent him reeling. His mind seemed unable to comprehend how things had come to this. Duty is second only to justice. He could hear his dear O'ma saying it over and over, yet now it seemed hollow...pointless...grotesque.

Landermihl was also an advisor to the king, but when Vlaad looked to him for support, the holy warrior frowned and crossed his arms across his broad chest. It was apparent that he agreed with the king and undoubtedly had his own reasons for condemning Theila's work with demons. Even Don, Theila's father, was unable to act. He knew the law as well as any and consorting with demon-kind was frowned upon in all cases, though tolerated as a necessary means. His voice would be heard soon enough, but the look of betrayal in Vlaad's eyes was condemning. It was the look of a man who had suffered too much, who was at his breaking point.

King Kael read the missive, "Theila of Westrun, Warlock of the Black Gate, you have been accused of consorting with demons beyond the limits of your rank and station. Your actions have been deemed reckless and detrimental to the safety and order of Dae'run. You are hereby stripped of your soul stones, wand, reagents, and magical devices until such time that a hearing can determine cause to proceed to trial. As king of this land and by recommendation of the Grandmistress of the Black Order, I place you under arrest. Guards, please escort the accused to the Warlock's Guild where she will be placed in confinement until further notice."

Vlaad was infuriated! Though he was in no shape to stop the guards, he moved between them and his dear companion. He was unarmed and had no armor but his defiant visage warned a vicious death if the guards moved to take her.

It was neither the order of the king nor the drawing of swords which gave the defender pause.

It was the gentle touch of the woman he sought to protect that calmed him. Somehow it drained him of his anger and as he turned to face her, he saw only compassion.

Theila whispered, "This is not the end. Together we have faced every manner of beastly creature and evil being that this realm can conjure. Together we will endure and overcome. Do not lose yourself or what you stand for to stop what I have caused. Patience and temperance will see us through."

She kissed him and walked past toward the guards who stripped her of every weapon and enchanted item she possessed. Before they were done, Theila stood all but naked. Even her shoes and robes were taken, leaving a thin undergarment to protect her from the cool air. The warlock maintained her composure and never took her eyes off of Vlaad. As the guards encircled her and left, Vlaad turned to his king seething with hatred.

Xorren was first and foremost a king, but he was not without humanity and compassion. He knew no words would comfort Vlaad but he said, "You have my word that she will be well cared for."

Don approached the defender to comfort him. Vlaad's hateful glare stopped him cold.

Landermihl and Maejis moved to either side of the king half expecting Vlaad to attack him on the spot. Vlaad didn't seem to notice or care.

Finally Vlaad spoke. He said, "I have given the better portion of my life for this kingdom as my father did before me. I have fought in every province under your rule from the stinking swamps in the south to the rugged mountains in the north. I have done so out of loyalty and love to the people of Griffon's Peak. I have bled for you and sacrificed for you. I never asked for riches or land or power, but now I ask of you one thing. Release my beloved and end this madness or on my oath, I will hold you responsible."

The council chambers went deadly silent. All eyes turned to the king who was unaccustomed to being threatened and unwilling to have his authority subverted. After a moment required to fully compose himself, the king replied evenly, "Vlaad, you already have my word that Theila will be well cared for but be warned that you are walking a treacherous path here and now. I cannot tolerate the breaking of our laws by Theila nor will I tolerate disregard for the decisions made to enforce them. Be strong and consider the words she spoke. Patience and temperance will win the day. You are dismissed."

Landermihl, Don, and Maejis moved quickly before Vlaad could say more. They whisked him away with great urgency and much bowing as they left the chamber. The elves and Gaedron remained for a moment.

"What else remains unsaid?" the king asked.

Gaedron bowed slightly and spoke, "Yer hi'ness, I know it be no bus'ness o' mine, but if'n ye are willin' ta hear me, I'd like to say that boy ye jest dis'mis'ed be one hell o' a fine lad and his lady ye done sent to da dungeon did more fer findin' our enemies than the lot o' us coulda done wit' out 'er. I know laws be laws and no dwarf would e'er deny their place, but she ain't no criminal and she sure ain't no threat to da realm, at least dat be one opinion."

As Gaedron snapped another quick bow and stepped back, Wavren stepped forward. He said, "I concur," obviously showing his mentor had said all that needed to be said.

Da'Shar moved forward and said, "My apprentice and I healed the defender during the campaign. His willingness to protect us given the risk to his own life sets him apart as the embodiment of self-sacrifice but that isn't all. In the last battle, Vlaad suffered more than any living being known to me by legend, history, or personal account. I fear it has changed him somehow. I request he be given great latitude in the days and weeks to come until he comes to terms with all he has been through. I pray this incident today was merely the straw that broke the proverbial camel's back and not a precursor to something worse."

The king nodded and asked, "Lady Rosabela, would you like to add to the discussion?"

Rosabela spoke with barely contained contempt, "You know Vlaad and Theila better than all of us. Use your heart, as it is all that separates a noble king from a tyrant."

Cold water could not have surprised the King of Griffon's Peak more had it been thrown directly in his face. Da'Shar frowned deeply. Gaedron couldn't help but smile. Wavren bowed and escorted his sister out of the chambers with reddened cheeks spreading all the way up his considerably long ears. The elves and Gaedron departed with a curt bow and set off for their homeland. The king rubbed his temples and called to his attendant for a tonic of willow tree bark as the group left. He had much to contend with and his head was already pounding.

Curtiss Robinson

CHAPTER 27
AFTERMATH

Dek'Thal was busy with laborers cleaning up the city. The demon had damaged nearly every building beyond repair and slain hundreds of orcs including the orc king, Ba'Grash Bloodletter. Scores of trolls, dozens of visiting tauren, and several undead were also carried off. Most were burned beyond recognition but many were crushed from the demon's rampage. The loss of so many caused such instability that many of the weaker goblin-kin races left the city to live in the caves and hills. Dek'Thal was no longer a safe haven for them.

Since the attack, the city guard was ordered to continually march along the high walls to ensure a follow on attack could not catch them by surprise. The infantry sent out scouting parties and the archers stared across the dusty wastelands hour after hour. The wizards and shamen spent their time casting every manner of divination spell known trying to detect spies, saboteurs, and anyone who might be a threat to their city. This drained the already strained city resources and required many of the old men, women, and children to forage for food, scavenge for building materials, and provide basic services. Even the war chiefs and city officials found themselves engaged in every manner of toil.

It was indeed a time of hardship for the citizens of Dek'Thal who continually grumbled about demons, humans, dwarves, and elves. Any orc or troll, who previously considered themselves neutral toward their ancestral enemies, now had a first-hand hatred for them. The battle had obviously weakened the city, but it had strengthened and unified the people against the Dae'gon Alliance. When it came time to enlist new recruits, the Bloodcrest Forces would find more than enough willing volunteers who wanted revenge and through it all, Gorka Darkstorm had come out on top.

The half-orc never planned for the demon to attack Dek'Thal directly, but he had intentionally antagonized Ja'Zaru, knowing the demon would seek vengeance and thus access to this plane. Any summoner foolish enough to trust a demon was just as likely to suffer its wrath as she would be to direct the demon to kill her enemies. It was a gamble, but it had paid off in an unexpected way. When the demon brought all of Dek'Thal together, Gorka was able to assume the full mantle of leadership. He was already the supreme commander of the Bloodcrest Forces; now all he had to do was play his final card. With the king among the dead, Gorka used his network of spies to spread the word that he should be chosen to reign as king. Given his personal assault on the demon, it was an easy message to sell.

Gorka predicted it would take less than a month to ascend to the throne and from there he would command the Kingdom of Dek'Thal, in addition to the Bloodcrest Forces and The Legion of Assassins. If he had acquired the lycan's power, he would be unstoppable, but in many ways the political power of the Throne of Dek'Thal was far better. He considered it all as he stood high above the city atop the Shamen's Temple and watched as his minions worked. His mind raced with visions of conquest and at that moment, nothing seemed beyond his grasp.

Celes'tia had heard the news long before the four Protectors of the Vale returned from the human lands, which had pre-empted the cheering reception the heroes found upon arrival. Wavren and Gaedron were immediately surrounded by their fellow hunters who shook their hands warmly and patted them on the back in congratulations. All Gaedron wanted to do was get some much-needed rest and a fine meal, but Wavren reminded him that the duty of a protector was more than fighting enemies. The people needed to hear of their exploits and experience their success vicariously. It was a source of hope for the less adventurous, who could never truly understand the sacrifices a protector endures or the dangers beyond the elven nations and its guarded borders. Gaedron gave in but only after securing a few pints of Dwarven Dark, his favorite ale.

Rosabela and Da'Shar had more important business that could not wait. They gathered their packs and the wrapped body of So'larian from the transport ship. An escort of Windwraith officers cleared the way for them to proceed to the druidic enclave. Upon arrival, a dozen withered elves, no doubt hundreds of years older than Da'Shar, took their places among the ancient meeting place.

A particularly wrinkled elven woman sitting in the center position spoke first, "You have the body of the lycan known to us as Lord Carnage?"

Da'Shar winced noticeably and replied, "We have the body of my brother, So'larian, who became the lycan, Lord Carnage."

The druidic council murmured among themselves for a moment and finally the High

Mistress of the Druidic Enclave asked, "How is it that you have the elven body of So'larian? His body was destroyed and his essence was transferred to the human, Lord Carnage, when last you met."

Da'Shar took the hidden insult in stride. He was, after all, responsible for the failure to first prepare So'larian as a druid leading to his turning from nature. He and Gaedron were responsible for failing to return him to the druidic enclave some five centuries ago. It was obvious that his ability to end this menace was in doubt.

Rosabela uncovered the corpse and spoke confidently, "Here is the proof. His body was returned to its elven form when he sacrificed himself to save us."

"Dear child," the ancient druid began, "you are far too young and idealistic to understand the true nature of this situation. Da'Shar, on the other hand, knows all too well that we have convened to ascertain the truth."

"What does that mean?" she asked her mentor.

He replied, "Though we believe this body confirms Lord Carnage found absolution in his final moments, only the council can set his spirit to rest."

"Tell her the rest," one of the ancient males added.

"Rosabela," he began, "…I fear…"

"What Da'Shar? What is it?" she asked with mounting concern.

The high mistress replied, "He suspects that you unknowingly helped Lord Carnage escape. We have seen this in his mind."

"How can that be?" Rosabela pleaded.

"Never mind," Da'Shar returned with finality. "Let us be sure before we cast dispersions."

Rosabela stepped back with a look of horror as

the council invoked a spell of necromancy, not unlike her own incantation before the Battle of Forestedge when she spoke with the spirit of Borik. The group pulled mightily, but the spirit would not appear. The body floated up and circled the enclave. As the mighty druids continued, Rosabela saw the doubt in her mentor's face turn to anguish, but it made no sense. She was there when the lycan fell. Just as suddenly as the spell began, it was ended. The body returned to the ground.

A somewhat less wrinkled female addressed Da'Shar, "You have failed to bring the true form of the lycan to us. We cannot return the spirit to nature as long as it lingers and as long as it remains it will grow, feed, and spread. Lycanthrope is a living disease and one you have been charged to end."

Another druid spoke saying, "Da'Shar, we have put our faith in you thrice and each time you have failed us. You will be compelled to do the will of this council now. You will be given a *geas* that will bind your fate to your success."

Da'Shar replied, "I understand. I vow to accept your punishment should I fail."

"Do you know where the spirit of the lycan resides?" the high mistress inquired knowingly.

"I do," he replied.

"The spirit of Lord Carnage must be brought to justice at all costs. The carrier will be weak for many days. Now is the time to strike. Your own life depends on it," she commanded.

The venerable druids came together in spell casting again, but this time it was Da'Shar who was lifted up. Mystic energy passed through his body like ghostly winds. As each of the twelve bound him with their power, Da'Shar screamed. When the rite was over, he collapsed in a smoking heap.

Rosabela ran to him and helped him to his feet. The druidic council dispersed without another word.

"Master, what did that mean? What is a geas and what must we do?" Rosabela asked with as much fear of the answer as she had for the consequences of their failure.

Da'Shar shuddered, fell to his knees, and had a vision. His body jerked violently for a few moments and then he lay very still. Rosabela immediately noticed his brow was covered in thick sweat. She wiped it away only to find his skin was cold and clammy. Da'Shar moaned for a moment and then sat up. He looked haunted and sickly. His pupils were dilated wide open.

Not knowing what else to do Rosabela focused her thoughts and entered his mind. The landscape was not what she expected. Da'Shar was having a vision of the final battle with Ja'Zaru. Rosabela watched as the scene unfolded. She saw the balrog punish Vlaad unmercifully as Da'Shar healed him over and over. The others attacked and were repelled by the demon. When the demon struck Vlaad, shattering his shield, Rosabela saw Da'Shar and Carnage fall. Her memory took over at this point. She had taken Da'Shar's place as the conduit to pull life force from the lycan to sustain Vlaad. She noticed the look of horror in Da'Shar's face when he regained consciousness and saw Carnage give his last breath to save Vlaad. This was the moment Vlaad had slain the demon. The moment of victory overwhelmed them. The team rejoiced and then mourned the loss of Da'Shar's brother. The scene flashes forward and Rosabela watches as the human priests try in vain to heal Vlaad. The scene flashes forward again to the meeting with King Xorren Kael. Theila is arrested for crimes against the kingdom and Vlaad becomes enraged. The vision fades, leaving Da'Shar and Rosabela stunned.

"Master, please tell me it isn't true," the she-elf said, holding back a flood of tears.

"A geas is a spirit vow and in many ways a curse. For my previous failures, I have been commanded to bring back the spirit of the lycan or I will...expire," he replied.

"But the vision...how could I have known...I didn't know," she sobbed.

Smiling weakly Da'Shar placed his arm around his pupil and said, "When I fell, Carnage used you. He projected his essence through you and into Vlaad. Though it saved us from the demon and likely spared hundreds of lives, it damned us all to this fate."

"What will we do...what can we do?" she asked hopelessly.

"I will do my duty. For the good of all and by order of the Druidic Enclave, I will slay Vlaad...our dear friend and ally," Da'Shar said with great remorse and stoic determination.

Curtiss Robinson

ABOUT THE AUTHOR

Curtiss Robinson is a full-time soldier, lifelong martial artist, science fiction/fantasy enthusiast, and RPG gamer. It is from this unique perspective that he constructs worlds of fantasy and adventure. Currently, Curtiss lives in Irmo, South Carolina, where he serves on active duty with the National Guard and enjoys spending time with his amazing wife and children.

Website: http://curtissrobinson.com
http://daerun.com
Facebook
https://www.facebook.com/author.CurtissRobinson
Twitter: https://twitter.com/curtissrobinson

For more of Curtiss Robinson's books from Beau Coup Publishing:
Amazon http://amzn.to/1gngz1w

Published by Beau Coup Publishing
http://beaucoupllc.com

Curtiss Robinson

Curtiss Robinson

Curtiss Robinson

Curtiss Robinson

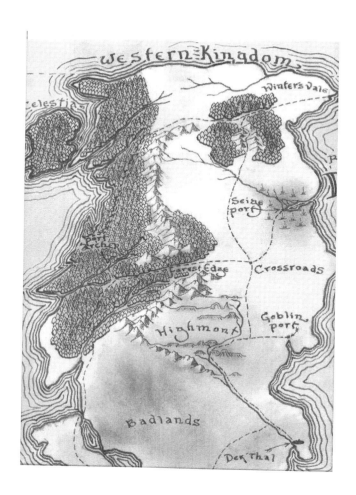

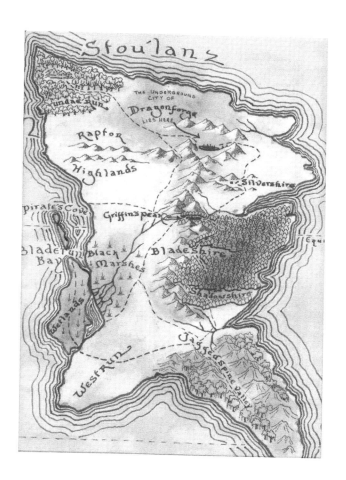

Curtiss Robinson

A Preview to Book 3 - Now Available on Amazon

Guardians of the Mountain

Vlaad was in a foul mood as he paced back and forth in his stateroom.

"How dare the king allow Theila to be imprisoned!" he fumed. "After all of the sacrifices we have made for the kingdom, he should release and exonerate her without a second thought." He slammed his fist on the table for emphasis and felt a shockwave of pain in return.

The defender's shield arm still ached from the battle with Ja'Zaru as a he unconsciously worked the stiffness out. His mind went back to the battle. He recalled every detail vividly: the fire that washed over his body, the sheer power of the demon's ax, and especially the fear spell. Nothing in his entire life had ever been so terrifying than to see his beloved Theila under the power of the balrog. Death was a welcome alternative and when the orcs came, he gladly accepted his end, but it wasn't real. It had all been a fear-induced illusion of some sort.

Coming back to reality he thought, *is this any different? Theila was taken away by the Black Order and might be imprisoned or tortured for her self-sacrifice. No one would ever understand our sacrifices.*

Vlaad knew he would not suffer his dear Theila's torture or imprisonment for long, but he would never be permitted to see her in the dark dungeons of the Black Order. The sect of warlocks was far too secretive and suspicious. Using brute force would end in a painful death for him and even if he had half of the king's guards at his side, there was no certainty in retrieving Theila. She could be in some parallel rift between this world and the abyss. Such things were common for warlocks; in fact, these *safe havens* between worlds had saved Theila not so long ago when The Legion had come for them.

A voice came to him suddenly, "Vlaad we must discuss urgent matters."

It was certainly the sword of Vlorin calling to him, though its call was faint when he wasn't holding the enchanted weapon. He felt compelled to grasp the blade and hear the instructions it had to offer, but something gave him pause. As he reached for the sword, he had a most unusual thought. For a second, his mind flashed back to the battle with Ja'Zaru, the balrog. He recalled his final strike and the last surge of healing from the druid, Rosabela. His life had been spared by the death of Lord Carnage. The thought made him feel something deep in his gut. A great sadness came over him that could only be compared to the feeling he had when Andar was slain. He felt the grief and thankfulness of one who owes his life to another. He felt the stirrings of vengeance for the death of Lord Carnage and at that moment his slowly mending wounds felt considerably better.

***

Upon returning to Celes'tia, Wavren and Gaedron parted company with Rosabela and Da'Shar to check in with Daenek Torren, the Speaker of the Stars. Their unannounced visit was anticipated by the speaker, who saw most events in the enchanted scrying censure just before they occurred.

"Welcome home, heroes," the speaker said.

Wavren knelt beside his mentor out of respect. The speaker was the most revered elf in the kingdom who ruled Celes'tia as its king, though his position was, in truth, more broad in scope.

The elven hunter spoke, "Sire, our lands are safe for the moment; what news do you have?"

Daenek motioned for the hunters to rise and said, "I fear the work you began with the lycan pack is far from finished."

Gaedron swore under his breath and muttered something about Carnage but Wavren couldn't hear enough to make it out.

"Master Gaedron, you know well that such things are to be expected. Evil is not so readily snuffed out, just as good must also find its way in dark times."

"Aye," the dwarf began, "but dis time we had 'im. How in da nine hells did 'e git away?"

Daenek's downturned mouth, closed eyes, and deep sigh showed obvious disgust. After a moment he finally said, "His body was destroyed, but his essence resides in the human, Vlaad."

Wavren gasped and Gaedron stood up and stomped around in a rage. The dwarf cursed, "Dat damnable trickster done sneaked inta his last host! If'n I e'er git me hands 'round his neck, by Moradin, I'll kill 'im barehanded!"

Daenek placed his hand on the dwarf's fur-lined shoulder and said, "I fear your countrymen will need you for other challenges. You will have to leave this business to your disciple."

The dwarf paused in mid-stomp and said, "Me

countrymen? What'd ye mean?"

The ancient elf led the pair to the mystic bowl that showed many things to the Speaker of the Stars. When the hunters looked into the clear, pristine liquid, an image appeared. It was perhaps the largest mobilization of evil the Stou'lanz had ever seen. Thousands upon thousands of undead marched out of UnDae'run, swept across the northlands, and washed over the dwarven villages like a flood. When they reached Dragonforge, the massive capital city of dwarves, an epic battle was fully underway. Gaedron saw himself among his brethren as the two armies tore into each other.

"By the beard of Moradin," the dwarf whispered in disbelief as he made a hundred calculations at once. "When will dis come to pass?"

The speaker shook his head and replied, "It is one possible future. It might never come to pass or it could be tomorrow.

"To'marra? I best be goin' if'n I'm meant ta lead our boys," he said with a curt bow and a warm handshake to his pupil. "Do yer best boyo; I'll canna 'elp ye wit' Carnage but ye know all I have ta teach." Without another word, the dwarf was gone.

"Tell me about Carnage. How do we get him out of Vlaad?" the remaining hunter pleaded.

The venerable old hunter looked at Wavren. He had been young and ambitious like the boy standing before him, but that had been nearly two thousand years before. He saw the look of determination in Wavren's eyes and deadly intensity in his expression. The Speaker of the Stars said, "Vlaad must be slain before the essence of Lord Carnage blooms within him. Once he embraces the change, the cycle will begin anew and the evil within will be difficult to stop."

"Vlaad is an honorable man and my friend. Is there no other way?" Wavren asked with little true hope.

The speaker withdrew something from his pocket and said, "If the essence of the lycan were compared to a mighty oak, then Carnage is like this acorn in my hand. Crush the shell and the tree cannot sprout into a seedling. If the acorn is allowed to sprout, then it can readily be transplanted nearly anywhere and grow into adulthood, dropping countless acorns across the land. Vlaad is merely the shell, the protective casing so to speak. He will be cast aside once the evil within matures. His death is assured in any case."

Wavren sensed there might be something more. He waited patiently, but the withered elf before him said nothing. The two remained impassive for what seemed like an eternity when finally the speaker whistled. A great horned owl flew in and dropped a single arrow at Wavren's feet.

The hunter reached down and picked up the simple shaft. It had a most intriguing design. The fletching was moving as if made of golden fire and the tip was simply sharpened wood. Wavren looked up, fully intending to mention that he preferred his blunderbuss but what he saw next struck him speechless. Daenek Torren was holding his legendary bow out before him. It was perhaps the oldest elven relic in existence. "I cannot take it," he managed to stammer.

The Speaker of the Stars replied, "Before I became the leader of elves and inherited the gift of prophecy, I saw this day. I knew from the moment you began your journey as a hunter that you would wield this weapon in my stead. Take it and use the phoenix arrow to give Vlaad the second chance he deserves, but be warned. If he accepts the mantle of lycan pack leader, you will face a most deadly adversary. Now go. Embrace your elven heritage with the bow, Soul Fury. Your duty awaits, along with your destiny."

Made in the USA
San Bernardino, CA
12 May 2014